THE PATH AND THE GATE

THE PATH AND THE GATE

MORMON SHORT FICTION

edited by

ANDREW HALL & ROBERT RALEIGH

SIGNATURE BOOKS | 2023 | SALT LAKE CITY

Join our mail list at www.signaturebooks.com for details on events and related titles we think you'll enjoy.

Design by Jason Francis

FIRST EDITION | 2023

LIBRARY OF CONGRESS CONTROL NUMBER: 2023943777

Paperback ISBN: 978-1-56085-467-8
Ebook ISBN: 978-1-56085-484-5

CONTENTS

EDITORS' INTRODUCTION

Good stories, like a good life, can benefit from having a prompt: a roadmap with goals and potential rewards. We gave the authors of this collection the following Book of Mormon passage and asked them to write "a Mormon story":

> The gate by which ye should enter is repentance and baptism by water; and then cometh a remission of your sins by fire and by the Holy Ghost. And then are ye in this strait and narrow path which leads to eternal life. Yea, ye have entered in by the gate ... Wherefore, ye must press forward with a steadfastness in Christ, having a perfect brightness of hope, and a love of God and of all men. Wherefore, if ye shall press forward ... Ye shall have eternal life ... This is the way; and there is none other (2 Nephi 31:17–21).

The authors responded with a wide range of tales; some realistic, others fantastic. Many directly relate to the steps of the "path": a lifetime of faith in a patriarchal blessing's unfulfilled promise, a survivor of violence calling a divided community to repentance, a baptism gone wrong, and spiritual gifts that extend far beyond Paul's list. The characters stretch from wayward bishops and helpful home teachers to cyber-Seventies searching for lost sheep in the metaverse. Settings range all over the path, from a chapel hosting a child's baptism to a heaven that turns out to be more difficult than expected. Some characters reject the path's restrictions and expectations, while others can second the reported words of J. Golden

Kimball, "I may not always walk the straight and narrow, but I sure in hell try to cross it as often as I can."[1]

Taken together, these stories display the vast expanse of experiences and opportunities in a universe encoded with diversity and free will. The existence of a "vastness," even within the boundaries of a gospel "narrow gate," does not have to be seen as a contradiction. LDS apostle Dieter F. Uchtdorf remarked, "The universe is so large, mysterious, and glorious that it is incomprehensible to the human mind."[2] Likewise, the prophet Brigham Young observed, "Endless variety is stamped upon the works of God's hands. There are no two productions of nature, whether animal, vegetable, or mineral, that are exactly alike, and all are crowned with a degree of polish and perfection that cannot be obtained by ignorant man in his most exquisite mechanical productions."[3]

It is a comfort to have a roadmap, but what really excites me is to see how that roadmap can lead to limitless destinations.

—Andrew Hall

The historian and writer Richard Poll, in a church talk that was later adapted into an article in *Dialogue: A Journal of Mormon Thought*, cleverly drew from Book of Mormon stories to create two contrasting metaphors for how to be a Latter-day Saint: the Liahona and the Iron Rod.[4] The Liahona was a type of compass designed to lead people across a landscape. Though it points in a general direction, it does not dictate an exact path. The Iron Rod, on the other hand, is a very rigid, straight guide. To use it, one must only cling to it and move in the right direction. One needn't pay attention to, or even see, where one is going. Poll proposed that Mormons tend to be drawn towards one or the other end of this spectrum.

1. Eric A. Eliason, *The J. Golden Kimball Stories* (Urbana: University of Illinois Press, 2007), 78.

2. Dieter F. Uchtdorf, "You Matter to Him," *Liahona*, November 2011.

3. Brigham Young, "Apostleship of Joseph Smith—Destruction Awaiting the Nations," August 31, 1862, *Journal of Discourses*, 26 vols. (Liverpool: Latter-day Saints' Book Depot, 1854–86), 9:369–70.

4. Richard Poll, "What the Church Means to People Like Me," *Dialogue: A Journal of Mormon Thought* 2, no. 4 (Winter 1967): 107–17.

I propose that the group of amazing writers in this collection strongly represents the Liahona side of Poll's spectrum (if we extend the spectrum to include some people who have found their way even further from the edges of the map proposed by Poll). These are writers who recognize the danger of Iron Rod fiction: which is to say, fiction dominated by overt didacticism. Eugene England, one of the greatest proponents and critics of Mormon fiction, suggested that, in order to be considered Mormon, a piece of fiction must not only meet the standards of all fiction, but also have strong underpinnings of Mormon doctrine.[5] I think England defines Mormon fiction too narrowly, excluding fiction that derives from Mormon culture and sensibilities without hewing closely to Mormon doctrine. I would offer my first fiction anthology, *In Our Lovely Deseret*, and this collection as evidence that Mormonism has left its imprint on the "world," not just as a religion but as a cultural force, and that the directions of its cultural expressions, including but not limited to literature, have also extended outwards in positive, exciting ways. They embody the Liahona metaphor, showing us how to use our own inner compasses to find our way through the modern landscape.

—Robert Raleigh

---

5. Eugene England, "The Dawning of a Brighter Day: Mormon Literature after 150 Years," *BYU Studies* 22, no. 2 (1982): 134–40.

THE INVESTIGATOR

TODD ROBERT PETERSEN

> We shall be driven to great extremities.
> I know not what to think of it.
> —Daniel Defoe, *Journal of a Plague Year*

By the end of the fifth wave, people didn't want to hear about staying safe and healthy. Liberty was the only word in play. People wanted freedom from tyranny or they wanted death. In the end, nobody had to choose. They got both. In a single season the sickness took half of those who remained.

There were vaccines for the early strains, but many refused to take them because someone on the internet said the shots would make them infertile or subject them to government satellite tracking devices. And then the virus mutated. Early bioengineering successes could not be duplicated. People grew impatient and followed any of a dozen pied pipers to their doom.

On top of that, the fires kept burning, inflaming people's lungs. The virus exploited that weakness and took a third of those who remained. In the sixth wave, another half was lost. This is what they meant by cataclysm.

The factions that remained fought amongst themselves as food production and supply chains failed. The stores emptied out, and no trucks came to resupply. Some were able to carry on for a couple of weeks with what they had, but most were destitute, and there was nothing left to loot. It was better for people living in the country or the third world. Maybe it was a "first-will-be-last-last-will-be-first" kind of thing. In the cities, where everyone had moved because life was better, the invisible systems began shutting down—Amazon, internet, cell phones, electricity—it all sputtered and went dark, spreading like a mist.

In the beginning, you'd hear sirens, then they would fall silent, and you'd only hear gunfire, which didn't last long. It reminded you this wasn't a dream or a game or a simulation. After that, you only knew what was going on around you in a radius of a quarter mile, maybe. It was the beginning of the end.

Before that part began, I was working for a locksmith, learning the trade. I knew how to open pretty much any door, and during one of the lockdowns (maybe it was the third) I realized the key to my survival would be my tools. So, I snuck out after curfew and stole them. It was a risk, but the cops were "responding" to looters, and at that point I didn't care what my boss would say. I had a strong feeling nobody would be going back to work. Anyone who could leave had already fled. We weren't a country, a state, a city, or anything, just people without resources.

When I got down to the last of my supplies, I moved outward to see what the neighbors had left in their vacant homes. They had used everything up. Was there an exodus? It was hard to know. People drove to find family. They died in hospitals or in the mountains. At first, homes were just abandoned. Garbage piled up. Cupboards were bare. Empty cans were everywhere, with expiration dates from long before the pandemic. Entropy took over. Dust. Grime. Weeds. Silence. After I scoured my quarter mile, gathering only enough for a week or two, I made plans to leave my condo and scavenge more broadly.

I had one of those kid carriers for joggers, the kind with inflatable tires so I could sneak around the empty neighborhoods. Sometimes I'd walk into an abandoned house that would give me a strange feeling, the stillness amplified like the buzzing of power lines. It had to be something else because the electricity had been gone for weeks. Mostly, the homes would be completely picked over, which would leave me feeling sick and angry, though I had no right to feel slighted by others doing what I did.

As you might imagine, poor folk didn't have much, but I found more in their homes than I did in rich houses. It made sense. The rich were targets, so their vast houses were empty. I suspect that somewhere, once people ran out of food, they just started eating rich people, like in that Aerosmith song.

This is all to give you a general sense of things, in case all you can remember is the wasteland.

*

People weren't all gone, but I knew to stay away from them. I used to watch *The Walking Dead* and all that. So, I had this sense that ordinary people died early, and the only ones left were the kind who would do whatever it took to keep going. Those shows were a good way to kill time. Who would have thought they were also training us for the future?

One day while I was out on the scavenge, I wheeled up to a gated community with a big wall around it. The iron gate had been ripped open and lay mangled on the ground. There was just enough room to get my little pushcart through.

A road ran up a slight incline that forked into a circle with five or six empty mansions all facing each other. The biggest house on the circle was surrounded by pickup trucks, most of them with flags mounted on poles in the back. American flags, Confederate, the ones with the blue line, don't tread on me, let's go Brandon, things like that. They hung in the windless air. The truck windows were shot out, and as I came closer, I saw the lawn was littered with bodies, all torn apart by animals.

The bodies had been there long enough that there was no stench. What was left of their flesh had blackened. It looked like seven guys spread out in front of the house or fallen in the doorway, like they'd died trying to get in. All of them were in camo and red baseball caps. Both garage bays were wide open and the front door was hanging from its top hinge.

I masked up before I went in, out of habit mostly, but also because these places can be rank. I'm not talking about the cloth masks we all made before, or even an N95. I had a full-on military-issue Avon M50 gas mask. An ounce of prevention.

The whole place was shot up. Black blood streaks down the

walls. Corpses in the kitchen. Women. More in the dining room. In the great room, dead kids were huddled together in the corner. A birthday banner dangled from the lights. A bunch of mylar balloons lay deflated on the floor.

I'd seen a lot of dead people by that point and I tried to imagine what chain of events could have led to this end. Could those men have been so hungry they'd go to those lengths? Maybe it was to save their own kids. Was it a mistake? Was it over before anyone realized what they'd done and it was too late to take it all back?

I walked to the front of the house and found more dead. Men. The windows were all shot out and the walls behind them shredded. It didn't take long to put the story together. Those ball-cap guys would have busted through the gate, seen the lights on, smelled the barbecue, thought they should share the wealth. But the homeowner stood his ground. Instead of losing their food, they lost their lives.

The cupboards were bare. Medicine cabinets empty. Pantry, too. Down in the basement there was a whole room that was maybe supposed to be food storage. Flour dusted the floor. Shelves made of two-by-fours and special homemade racks to dispense cans—tracks for everything from little soup cans up to big #10 size. Just enough rice and dried beans to kick around. The place had been stripped.

There was also a home theater, a Bowflex, a kid's room. In the back of one of that kid's drawers was half a bag of dried marshmallows. I ate one and felt the burn of sugar in my cheeks. I slipped the bag into my pack and went back upstairs.

There was a family picture: a mom and dad, grown kids, a couple of grandkids. Something like twenty people in that picture, all in blue jeans and white polo shirts on a beach somewhere, maybe Mexico. Next to that was a sign that read: "Families Are Forever."

I sat with that for a while.

In the kitchen was a small desk with a blue paperback on it that said Book of Mormon in gold type. Stuck inside was a bunch of paper folded in half. Someone had written "Stake Map" on it.

Turns out it was an address list of all the Mormon people in the area. I had thought Mormons were all out in Utah, but I guess not. From the looks of the map, there were plenty of them here in Missouri, but spread out. I never knew any Mormons, but I remember people making jokes about their underwear and their Jell-O and their basements full of food and water. According to the map, the closest Mormon house was five miles as the crow flies. With a little bit of luck, I figured I could make it.

*

It was the opposite of the place I left behind: one story with a carport. Easy to overlook. I went around back and checked all the windows. The curtains were drawn. The back door had a cheap Schlage deadbolt, so I was inside pretty quick with a bump key.

The furniture was worn but clean. Everything was orderly, especially the floor-to-ceiling bookshelves in the front room. A half-basement was filled to the brim with food, first-aid supplies, and water jugs. It was the most organized place in the world, like a library. I opened a Tupperware thing filled with those big Hershey bars, sat on the floor, tore off the plastic, and snapped off one row of squares. I wanted to eat the whole thing right there, but you don't binge a treasure.

As the days passed, I would occasionally hear people moving along the street, but they would pass by this invisible house looking for something better. I understood that kind of cost-benefit thinking. Sometimes it was just a pair of teenagers in hoodies hustling along with shopping carts full of gear. But soon more and more people were dressed in fatigues, moving down the street in formation, in squadrons. There was a mall a half-mile away; they were probably headed for that. It was a good distraction, I guess. Made this a pass-through part of town.

I was able to live securely in this house for eighteen months. It was boring, but safety is boring. I would have liked a little something to keep myself occupied, solar panels and a PlayStation, but old people owned this place. Mike and Evelyn.

I worried I'd get soft, so I started a regimen: pushups, squats, crunches, all to offset the fact that the rest of the time, I ate and read. I started with that Book of Mormon. The rest of the books were about the Mormon religion, so it seemed like the logical place to begin.

5

To be honest, most of it wasn't very interesting. There were a lot of people in it like Superman's dad, shouting warnings, being ignored, calling people out, getting killed for it. Then came the end. That was when I felt my story merging with its story, and its story merging with the earlier stories, all of it converging like a long stretch of interstate going out to the horizon. The dull, wandering tale of a family following their dad into the wilderness turned into something I needed to pay attention to. It became the story of a civilization that thought it couldn't fail. So much of that book seemed like it was speaking to this moment, I wondered why Mormon folk didn't say anything about it. I would have been interested to hear what they were saying in their churches about how the world was coming apart. Then it hit me: why would they say anything? People in these stories killed their own prophets. Maybe the Mormons kept their mouths shut out of self-preservation. Didn't seem to have worked.

When I came to the end of the book, I realized I should keep some kind of record myself, tell people how we got to this point and put it out there like a message in a bottle. Someone in the future would want to know what had happened.

I moved on to other books about hope, faith, history, and those Mormon pioneers who fled from here in Missouri to Illinois then out west to Utah, fearing for their lives. I read about how they built Zion out there, how they massacred a group of people in a place called Mountain Meadows.

Winter came and went, and I read. If I had been religious when the end came, I don't know that I would have become more so. Actually, I think I would have been angry. But according to these books, this wasn't about there being no God. It was about God walking away from us. One of the books said God could weep. Maybe God just needed a break. Maybe it hurt him too much to see what we were willing to do to each other.

In the spring, I pulled Mike's journals out of the back of a filing cabinet. He went on a mission to the Philippines, then came back and tried college but didn't take a fancy to it. He joined the Army, went to Iraq, and came home after an explosive flipped his vehicle. He thought he was going to lose his legs, but some other Mormon officers gave him a blessing, and somehow the surgeon was able to put him back together. He came home and met Evelyn at a church dance. They married when he was twenty-three and she nineteen. After that, his journals thinned out.

Every now and then, I'd read something like, "I should probably start keeping notes for the family history." Then nothing for a while until something sad happened: a miscarriage, a lost job, the car and the fridge going out in the same week. There were a lot of January firsts in there. Only a little happiness. Religion didn't seem to stop trouble.

Evelyn kept scrapbooks from high school on, along with an envelope of kids' school pictures. Four boys. Three girls. There were pictures of other families all over the house, and one that showed them all together. This wasn't like my family at all, me and Mom and a guy named Jerry who Mom said left us a week before I was born.

Back in the birthday party house, you could see that they went down hard. Scorched earth. But it looked to me like Mike and Evelyn had been taken out of this place in a helicopter, like they vanished. Mike's wallet was on the dresser next to the keys for his Kia, which was sitting outside covered in grime and dust. They took no photos, no supplies. There were no bodies, no blood, no bits of glass, only a stillness. And I was grateful.

When Mike and Evelyn's food ran out, I had to leave, but I didn't want to. I fled to the next house on the stake map at night to avoid the squadrons that still went by regularly.

I made it to the next house on the map in about an hour. It had already been broken into. In the front room, the skeletons of the family were laid out in the living room next to the piano on one side and the fireplace on the other. The mother was holding a chalkboard, and on it was written the message, "Returning with honor." Next to each skull was a small cup. The whole thing left me cold.

In the kitchen, I saw bottles and bottles of pills. There was a bowl filled with dust and empty capsules, like a heap of dead bugs. This had happened so long ago, but the house was stained with a feeling of unease. I couldn't stay there.

There was enough food to get me through a month. While I was downstairs gathering what I could, I heard footsteps. Two, maybe three people. They moved through the house and stopped in the living room, spoke in clipped voices. Then I heard them leave. I stood there in the unfinished basement staring at the ceiling, listening to the emptiness until I could hear my pulse and a ringing in my ears, like static on a radio that couldn't find a station. How did I go so long at Mike and Evelyn's without anyone coming? It had to be something a little more potent than luck. That is clear to me now.

A verse from the Old Testament came into my mind. A prophet went up on the mountain to stand with God. The Lord came but passed him by. A strong wind rent the mountains, but the Lord was not in the wind. Then there was an earthquake and God was not there. Then a fire, and still no God. But after the fire was gone, there was a still small voice.

I listened and listened for it, for those people to come down the stairs, for the ghosts of that dead family to stir. I strained so hard to hear something, like I was trying to roll a boulder with my mind.

Then, with my heartbeat climbing, I heard a voice. Was it mine? It said, *What doest thou here?*

"Where else should I be?" I whispered, which I know was ridiculous, but it made sense then.

There was no answer, but I kept staring ahead, waiting. In the dark, at the end of a corridor, sunlight crept in through one of the basement egress windows and fell across a photo of a huge building. It was kind of familiar. I went up to it and read that this was the St. Louis Temple. I'd seen it before near the interstate. It looked like a fortress.

I thought, that's where I'll go.

I loaded my stroller and backpack and found the temple, which was close. Maybe just a couple of miles. I wanted to wait until dark, but I couldn't stay. The streets were silent. To get there, I had to cut across a golf course and follow the interstate on the frontage road. There was a college football stadium near it.

I came to the front doors. Good locks, but I gained entrance pretty quickly. The doors swung easily and I pushed my jogger inside. It looked like a very nice hotel in there, but it had offices, sofas, telephones. No signs of disarray. The air was neither fresh nor stale, just still. The furniture had been covered with sheets as if someone had prepared the place to be shut down. It was dark inside. The only light source was by the entryway. I sat on one of the couches and fell asleep.

When I woke, it was dark. I dug out my sleeping bag and went back to sleep on the couch. It was the safest I had felt for as long as I could remember.

*

In the morning, I rose and ate a sparse meal that did not require cooking. Then I cranked up the hurricane flashlight I used during my early supply runs and explored the dark corridors. Based on everything I'd read at Mike and Evelyn's place, I expected something else—something more mystical maybe. There were a lot of chairs. As calm as I felt in that place, there were rooms I shined a light into but did not enter. There was no force field or feeling of dread, just a simple, wordless understanding that these rooms were not for me.

I returned to the ground level and continued looking through the offices, found a laundry and a kitchen, which, if there had been power, might have turned this place into a good option for a permanent residence.

I slept and woke, stared for a while at nothing, thinking about this path I was taking through the apocalypse, then I slept and woke again. Long yellow slats of daylight angled through the windows. It was late afternoon. I gathered my thoughts, considering how I might occupy a building that was this dark even in the middle of the day. Then I heard a thump on the doors.

I rolled to the floor, waiting for the noise of shattering glass.

After I got my breathing under control, I crawled along the floor until I could see the entryway. A person was out there spray-painting a biohazard symbol on the glass. The last few lines were very light. The person shook the can, banged it twice against the glass, and threw it against the concrete.

After that, there was nothing.

I waited a few minutes, then moved through the shadows to a place where I could see further outside. The vandal had joined a legion of others gathering on the frontage road.

I took out a pair of tiny binoculars from my backpack and scanned the army. I'd seen one or two of this kind before: shaved heads, skin and jackets stained red. Some wore goggles or yellow sunglasses. Others wore clear visors because, in the final days, people believed the blood of the infected might make you sick. A single drop would do it.

They had fashioned sports equipment into armor, which looked like rhinoceros plates under the morning light. Some drank from cheap plastic bottles. Others rested on spears they planted on the asphalt. Eventually, they marched on, a phalanx of the most heavily armored out front, a few dozen others in the middle, and another few rows of foot soldiers bringing up the rear. At the back of the column, people pulled wheeled carts on yokes made of rope and silver duct tape.

I wondered who these people had been in their other lives. Regular salt-of-the-earth types turned from honest work to survive in a fallen world that had fallen even further?

I remember reading that Mormons would come to these temples the first time for themselves then return to care for the dead. But there were no dead here, not even the feeling of haunting I'd felt so often in the abandoned homes. It was clear to me, however, that these glass doors wouldn't protect me. I would always be worried about the next group of whoever. That was life at this point. Though, perhaps now that the building had been marked, there would be a kind of protection or warning or something.

I sat in the dark, listening to the silence. I ate small meals and explored more of the rooms. There was a sterility here, like an empty tomb. For the first time since I was a kid, I felt safe enough that I knelt and asked this building if it thought I could stay. I had been spoken to earlier—given an invitation, I thought, or told to vacate—and I wanted clarification. I asked only once, then sat until the answer came: *This is the house of the Lord.*

I knew I could not stay, and I prepared to leave, wrote out these events and stashed them here in the temple so my story would not be lost. I will set out to find others, hoping that if I meet my end, it will happen suddenly, without hesitation. I hope I might feel peace like this again, but I fear that once I leave, the heavens will close up behind me.

*

It has been three years since I left that temple, and I have now returned. When I wrote my story and left it behind, I thought there would be nothing more to add. I wandered as others have wandered near the end of their stories, wondering why God didn't just end it for them. They looked for direction and found none. That was the part of this Book of Mormon that baffled me. It ended in catastrophe. How do you pin your hopes on that?

As I moved about, I saw that many churches had been marked with the biohazard sign like the one on the temple. It seemed to be a commentary. I can't say they were wrong to suggest that religion was toxic. The righteous always have the farthest to fall.

I prayed to find others who believed. I had so many questions the books hadn't answered. And what good is a church of one? I looked, but they did not reveal themselves. I prayed for ravens to feed me but saw only crows.

Many times, in desperation, I thought I might take my own life. It took so much time and energy to find enough food, shelter, water, and for what? To find more food, shelter, water? My exhaustion would become complete. Reality became fluid. I would see movement where there was silence. Hear voices where there was emptiness. I would drift off to sleep as I walked, sometimes waking as I stumbled. Sometimes I would find my way to houses on the map. Mostly I took shelter where I could. I zig-zagged, foraged, and grew frail. Eventually, even with my skeleton keys, I could find no sustenance other than what I could catch or kill. But I was a poor hunter, so I ended up gathering.

*

Eventually, I came to the last house on the map. It was beyond the city limits, isolated, next to an open field that had become choked with weeds after two years of lying fallow. The door was unlocked. Like so many other houses, it had been picked clean. I stopped there because I could go no further. I had not eaten in days. As the sun slipped low against the horizon, illuminating the tree line in a belt of pink and crimson, I sat in a chair in the front room and asked to be taken up.

The heavens did not open.

In the silence that followed, darkness gathered and fell. I let go of this place and drifted off. I dreamt I was traveling along a road that cut through a dark wilderness. I followed the road for some time, noticing lights in the distance that danced for brief moments before extinguishing themselves.

After traveling the road for what seemed like hours, I came to a figure seated in an oversized stuffed chair. He wore a white seersucker suit and was fanning himself in the darkness. He smiled and gestured around him then swiveled in the chair and pointed in a direction perpendicular to the road. I followed his finger with my eyes, and in the distance, a tree flashed for an instant like it had been lightning-struck. Blue energy coiled around it then flickered and went out. When I turned back, the man was gone.

I walked ahead and struck an iron rail. It did not follow the road but led off into the darkness toward the tree.

I ducked under that rod and continued on until I came to another rod that likewise crossed the road. I followed it until I could no longer see the road. My feet sank if I stood still, but if I stayed in motion, I moved along just fine. I often stumbled in the darkness. There was a flash behind me and I saw the tree fizzling, so I turned and followed the rail toward it. As I walked, I crossed a river then heard voices speaking in a distant room. Eventually, the way led upward.

When I awoke, the house was filled with sunlight.

I was lying face down on the floor. Under the sofa, I saw a yellow plastic easter egg. It was so far back I had to lift the sofa to retrieve it. It rattled. I cracked it open and three small chocolate eggs and four jellybeans fell into the palm of my hand. Saliva welled in my mouth as I chewed on the red bean, the sweetness was overwhelming. I then tore the foil off one egg and bit into it, the chocolate flooding my mouth with a full and delicious warmth. I alternated between beans and eggs until they were gone.

I looked back under the couch, but there was nothing else. I went out through a small side gate. As I closed it, I thought about how often at Mike and Evelyn's I'd read about the gate through which we must enter. I couldn't remember any discussion of leaving, only coming in. Was there any difference between an entrance and an exit? I never read the words "straight is the gate through which we must depart," but it makes sense. Coming into this world and leaving it are two sides of the same coin.

For a time, I thought I had died.

But the hunger returned almost immediately. I took the empty egg, clicked it shut, slipped it into my bag, and continued on, looking for any small thing that might have been placed here for me. Mostly, there was nothing. But if I kept looking, I would see wild berries, gardens that had re-seeded themselves. Orchards.

Where had this abundance been hiding?

HOLY GHOST POWER

ERIC FREEZE

Kailee looked resplendent in her white polyester jumper. Like a frigging angel, if such a thing existed. Barkley leaned against his plastic chair. He was at the back of the chapel, back of the bus, back of the line. Just feeling like he wanted to disappear; but that wasn't an option. "I don't care if one of your stupid teams is in the Champions League final," Marlene had said. So here he was—the apostate dad, the unworthy one, the one-who-should-not-be-named—sitting in the back of the church like a leper.

Kailee turned and waved to him as she walked past, her other hand holding Grandpa Joe's. He had overheard Marlene when she asked her father to perform the baptism. She was in the bathroom, the most private place in the house (though if the vents were open and you were sitting in the kitchen, you could hear every plop and fart). "I just don't understand why he can't do it," she had told him over Facetime. And this after he had already explained—after they'd talked at couple's counseling—couple's counseling!—that this was something he could not *in good conscience*—those were the words—do anymore. It was a charade; a lie. He would feel more at peace with himself if someone else baptized his daughter. That's the only way, he had said, that it could be a true celebration.

So how come he felt like such a frigging moron?

They were at the front of the chapel now, Kailee calm and poised, her single blonde braid bisecting her shoulder blades. Marlene played the prelude music until the bishop stepped up to the stand. A few friends were sitting in the pews, arms folded.

Most baptisms Barkley had attended lasted thirty minutes, an hour tops. All the talks and pomp beforehand were just window dressing for what really counted: taking the plunge—getting dunked, he'd called it on his mission. A symbol of rebirth reduced to a basketball slammed through a hoop.

"Today is a special day," the bishop said.

It was hard to know where Barkley went wrong. Four years of early morning seminary in high school. A year of BYU before serving an LDS mission. Then dating, a temple marriage to Marlene, a decent-paying job in the tech sector, and three children birthed at two-year intervals. They were nuclear-family, white-privilege frigging happy; the pinnacle of what his faith told him he could achieve. Provide for his family? Check. Temple-worthy? Check. Church every Sunday? Check, check, check.

But through it all grew a suspicion that he'd been duped, that he was living life by a script not of his own making. It was demoralizing—exhausting at best—to be a member of this church when you didn't feel it in your bones. Those endless meetings. He'd check soccer scores, SNL sketches on YouTube, or cat videos—frigging cat videos!—just to forget the "I knows," the tears and testimonies that never stopped coming.

The bishop was talking directly to Kailee now, zeroing in on her: "When you are baptized, Kailee, you're making a promise that you will follow your Heavenly Father." It was hard not to think of Barkley's own baptism. It had felt funny to be in a tiny swimming pool with his clothes on—the polyester onesie sticking to his body, his dad's white pants bunched in ridges down his legs. Nobody had told him about that part! The whole time—standing there in the water, being swept over backwards with his hand pinching his nose—he had been stifling a laugh. In the photos, his smile was break-the-camera large. Was what he felt a joke? Or was it joy?

They were getting up now, shuffling out of the pews. Kailee leading the way.

Barkley fell in behind Kailee and Grandpa Joe, mingling with the other families. Marlene would come in at the end after she finished playing the recessional music. Having Marlene by his side would have made him feel less alone. Even though her disappointment had draped like a pall over this whole ceremony, she knew why he couldn't do it and was, in her way, supportive.

The procession filed into rows of folding chairs set up to view the baptism. The font, usually closed off to the public with an accordion-like brown sliding screen, was now open, a tilted mirror near the ceiling reflecting the water from above. Children gathered at the glass barrier for a better view. As Grandpa Joe and Kailee descended the few steps, sloshing in the water, one of the kids asked, "Is it cold?" A parent somewhere shushed him. Kailee shook her head and practically floated out to the middle of the font, water almost up to her armpits.

Two men stood at either side of the font to be witnesses. Women could be witnesses now but nobody had asked any. Hadn't asked him either, even though he technically still held the priesthood and hadn't done anything that would make him unworthy. Besides the big one: not believing. But Barkley preferred it this way. He took a certain satisfaction in just observing. It made church more bearable. He'd felt fatigue and even physical pain for so long—not because of the activities so much as the façade he'd had to keep up. There was the person he actually was and the person everyone perceived him to be. Now, at least, everyone knew, more or less, about his unbelief. He could deal with the shame—frigging Voldemort!—the friends who now kept their distance, the awkward glances. Being here was like being an anthropologist observing a rite of passage, a ritual created to mark what Mormon culture counted as progress.

Grandpa Joe said the baptismal prayer. Everyone's eyes were closed. Only a few children in front kept them open, fixated on the two people in white. Grandpa said "Amen" and the witnesses craned their necks. Grandpa Joe put his hand over Kailee's face and dipped her backward like a dancer, plunging her deep into the water. Even her braid slipped beneath the surface. As Grandpa Joe pulled her up, water sluiced around her. She rubbed her eyes clean and smiled. The witnesses nodded. One gave a thumbs up.

Back in the chapel, the Primary president was giving a talk on the Holy Ghost. "Holy Ghost Power!" Robert Duvall in *The Apostle*.

Barkley had seen it right before his mission to the UK. Sometimes he and his mission buddies pretended to channel the Spirit like Duvall. Or exorcise demons like in Chevy Chase's *Fletch*. "Demons out!" Was his tendency to turn any feeling into a joke the beginning of his separation from the church? No. Jokes helped conceal his fear. *The Apostle* had terrified him, watching Duvall go to any extreme for the sake of belief.

Which was why he couldn't baptize his daughter.

The Primary president was finished now. Tall with wavy blonde hair, she wore a blue dress with an empire waist, like a Victorian-era painting. Jane Austen transported to Sacramento, California. He wished he could remember her name. She was new to the ward and had three kids, one about Kailee's age. Put them next to each other and you'd think they were sisters. Biological sisters, not sisters in the gospel. "You'll feel closer to your Father in Heaven than ever before," she said in that annoying Primary lilt, like everyone in the audience was eight years old. Like in the next moment she could either laugh or cry, depending on the requirements.

Men in suits shuffled from their seats, making their way to the front of the room: the bishop, the Primary president's husband, a few other friends from the ward. All the men in the building, in fact. Except him.

Kailee got up in her new gingham dress, sat in a chair exactly like the one Barkley was sitting in, and folded her arms. Her feet dangled. The men surrounded her, placing their hands on her head until the circle closed around her.

The confirmation prayer was the only part Barkley wished he could do. Unlike the rote baptismal prayer, giving the gift of the Holy Ghost had a spontaneous, personal element. Even as a half-believing missionary, sometimes his mind had opened when he'd laid hands on someone's head, like he was accessing something outside himself. He didn't know if it was God or an inner empathic sense—some essential connection between two human beings. It always surprised him. He could hear it now in the bishop's voice, in his pauses and puffs of breath against the microphone. He was searching not just for words but for divine revelation. He blessed her with health, a clean mind, with growth. He blessed her to listen to spiritual promptings, to find joy in caring for others, to help those in need. He blessed her with strength and love and compassion. The words were beautiful in their simplicity, and Barkley was sure his daughter was rapt, that she'd remember this moment for the rest of her life.

But it wasn't the prayer he would've given his daughter.

What bothered Marlene most was the added ambiguity Barkley's unbelief brought to their family's life. Growing up was hard enough, and now there were two answers to every question. Was the church true? Well, yes and no. Barkley had tried to explain to her that at least the ambiguity would be coming from *them* and not some outside source. They could be open about it, so that Kailee's own eventual struggles with belief would be laid out in this parental yin-yang.

"She'll be so confused," Marlene had said.

More confused than finding out her father had been living a lie?

The circle around Kailee opened. She stood up and robotically shook everyone's hands. She looked up and waved at the congregation.

Barkley waved back.

Afterward, Barkley would hug and congratulate her. He would take his daughter in his arms and whisper to her the words of his own confirmation prayer:

Kailee. You are the keeper of the keys, our pure and slender daughter. Your name's origin has other meanings that have accumulated throughout your short life. Before Kailee, you were an idea, the hope and aspiration of two parents converging. You grew up, burbled nonsense till you took our words: Dad, Mom, poop. You have a tiny scar the size of a Q-tip where an ember flew from a log fire and puckered the skin on your cheek. But it never bothers you, this blemish. You don't put much stock in appearances, an attribute that your father hopes will follow you through life. You have gifts. It's hard to know their provenance. At eight you already love books. You always follow a story through to its conclusion. You care for living things, once scolding me for crushing a spider. Never forget the wonder you felt when you first looked through a magnifying glass to examine the veiny underside of a leaf. Keep your optimism, your sense of justice, and your fierce independence.

Adolescence and adulthood will have surprises, but if you're careful and deliberate, those surprises will augment your abilities rather than diminish them. Our culture has laid so many pitfalls and potential traps to impede your happiness. Don't listen to anyone who tells you there's something you cannot do. You are a girl now, but someday you will be a woman. Like this baptism, that will be a passage to greater things. Please forgive your father his unbelief. He will never stop believing in you.

PLANTING IRIS

ANNETTE HAWS

Iris didn't know she was dead. Why should she? Dying was something she'd never done before. Reclining in the damp grass on an unfamiliar hillside, wiggling her bare toes, she felt a vague sense of unease. But she was more concerned about getting grass stains on this gauzy dress, a lovely cotton voile that she didn't remember buying. Yards of fabric in a billowy skirt simply wasn't her style. If she felt the need to be dressy, Iris was more inclined to wear pressed linen slacks, a starched shirt, and conservative gold hoop earrings. Where did this white fluff come from? Edith Wharton?

As the late afternoon sun broke through the clouds, Iris sat up and lifted one languid hand to shield her eyes. Stretching her legs, she squinted at the last wisps of cloud drifting east in a crystal blue sky. Then her gaze landed on a gentle slope of green scattered with stones that resembled a child's alphabet blocks dumped on a braided rug. Something small scuttled in the untrimmed grass next to a gray obelisk. A soft breeze rustled millions of leaves on hundreds of trees. A single barn owl—a baby from the size of him—swooped onto a low-hanging branch of a Norway Maple, and soon three other fledglings crowded next to him. The branch bounced slightly with each arrival. Wide eyes stared at her. *Cautiously?* She wasn't sure.

Sighing, she shook out her skirt. *Where had she parked her car?* She searched the grass for her purse, her phone, her to-do list. But no paper, no phone, no purse, no car keys, no balled-up tissue. A twinge of anxiety pricked her abdomen. Stupid phone, always vanishing as though it had a perverse agenda of its own.

She heard the rumble of a car and glanced up the hill. A beige Accord crunched to a stop at the edge of the untrimmed grass. The front bumper was dented, a hubcap missing, a side mirror gone. Two people who had clearly seen better days opened the doors, tottered over to the crest of the hill, and stood side by side facing west into the sun. Stooped with age, the man grasped a trek pole in each hand to support his spindly legs. A faded checkered shirt hung on his body. The woman's hair was dyed the lovely shade of brunette it likely had been when she was twenty, but all that dark brown next to her paper-thin skin made her puckers and wrinkles stand out.

Fingertips raised to her mouth, Iris stared at them. They seemed oddly familiar. Who were they? Had her past intersected with theirs? When? College? An image sped through her frontal lobe, escaped, and then returned. Pamphlets fanned out on a wooden tabletop in the church foyer like a winning hand of poker. Were these ancients that adorable young couple in the cover's glossy photo? What was the title of that pamphlet? Something to do with appropriate … hands-off bodies … Was it *Rules for Courtship*? Antiquated even fifty-five years ago, Iris smiled at the phrase. She remembered seeing those pamphlets when, red-faced and chest heaving, she made for the exterior church doors as quickly as possible, just short of a sprint, after her interview with the ecclesiastical leader who had probed her and her fiancé with a ponderous series of questions leading up to his denouement: "Have you fondled each other's bodies?" He cast them a withering look.

The wedding, a week from Friday, hung in precarious balance. It was a stupid question: she and Harris were healthy, in love, and itching to do more than just fondle. Had this man ever been young and desperately in love? How old was he anyway? Was he the last surviving member of the 1847 migration? After staring over the top of his thick trifocals for what felt like an hour, the stake president withdrew a fountain pen hidden in some interior pocket of his suitcoat and scribbled his name on the bottom of the slip of paper with an exaggerated sigh as though he were compromising his own salvation.

Iris pressed her hip against the metal bar on the door. Why the splay of pamphlets caught her eye is anyone's guess, but she snatched one off the table. Fanning herself, she turned toward her fiancé, who was stifling an anxious laugh.

"I can't believe any of this." She waved the glossy couple in his face. "It's ridiculous."

"Why didn't you just give him your best horrified look and say *Of course not?*" Harris, her adorable fiancé, was all about expediency.

But Iris hadn't. She couldn't. The absurd tone of the man's voice, or his steely grey hair, or that striped tie holding his wrinkled skin in place, had provoked her. Iris had looked straight at the man and huffed, "Are you kidding?"

Sitting in the car moments later, she glanced at the pamphlet before she balled it into a wad, rolled down the window, and chucked it in the bushes.

"Who believes this tripe?"

"Who cares?" Harris said. "He signed it. We're good to go." Harris's relief was palpable even if his smile was weak. For a few horrible minutes, he must have contemplated explaining to thirty of his closest friends, curious neighbors, and parents, why his temple marriage—embossed on four hundred announcements—was going to be substituted with an embarrassing fifteen-minute wedding in the Relief Society room. No one would have needed an explanation. His blush would have explained the situation in delicious detail.

Did the trauma of that long-ago interview disrupt a tiny cluster of cells in Iris's amygdala and create a memory she couldn't suppress? Twenty years later, walking down the aisle in a new ward in a new city with her wild crew of four children, Iris recognized the dewy-eyed couple from the cover of the pamphlet. They certainly had changed. Of course, they had changed. Eight children in various shapes, sizes, and stages of orthodontia would stretch any set of parents past the limit of human endurance and significantly alter waist sizes and hair distribution.

As Iris later observed , the male half of the couple, Willard Kimball, never touched a microphone he didn't caress. His fingers stroked the cold metal as if he could bring the thing to life. The first Sunday of each month, Will spoke in hushed tones tinged with humility and gratitude. The time of year might change, but the message stayed the same, Will was connected to greatness. "Sitting on my grandfather's knee—he was an apostle even then—I felt his love for me. But it was more than just love, it was strength. He was in his eighties, but that strength never left him." Will clenched his fists as though he were flexing spiritual muscles of his own. Iris stifled a groan.

When Will was made bishop, he had more opportunities for heartfelt revelations. "Each of us has serious challenges." He leaned into the mic. "But when those challenges seem too heavy to bear, think of my great-grandfather burying his little boy, his first-born son, in a shallow grave near the North Platte. There was a terrible cholera epidemic. His family was sick, exhausted. There was no feed for the animals. The water was putrid. His ox near death, my great-grandfather put his worn hands on that animal's head and blessed it. 'Rise,' he commanded. 'Bring my children to Zion.'" Will raised both hands shoulder height. "In his first talk in the Bowery, Brother Brigham spoke of my great-grandfather's faith. Blessing an animal, leading his company, leaving his son's grave, and on to Zion." Will's lips quivered, and for a moment he was too moved to speak. He wiped a tear from his cheek with the back of his hand. "We are the living legacy of those pioneers. The reason for their sacrifice." He paused for dramatic effect. "We must become a Zion people."

Iris swallowed hard as her youngest daughter, Emily, whispered, "The Bish needs new material."

Will lowered his hands and squeezed the sides of the podium, then he leveled his gaze at the congregation. "I'm not asking for volunteers to rescue handcart pioneers on the wrong side of the Sweetwater River. Nope. A hundred percent home teaching won't risk anyone's life. But think of the weary souls we could save." He gave the light coming through the window a beatific smile as though his grandfather were feeding him the lines.

"Yup," Emily whispered, "he wants to win the stake percentages game."

One dreary Sunday afternoon, the skies were gray and the meeting was dull. Iris glanced at her wristwatch. Bishop Kimball had been droning on for seven long minutes. She closed her eyes. An image flitted into her head: a character from *David Copperfield*, Uriah Heep, announcing his humility at every opportunity but was in reality, a fake, a sham, a virtuous imposter. Iris was generally empathetic enough to make allowances for human imperfections, but after three years eavesdropping over the backyard fence as Will sniped at his wife and boasted about his children, something in Iris snapped.

From the safety of the back row, Iris stared at the man's head, not as a collection of skin, nostrils, green eyes, teeth etc., but as a gigantic red balloon. It didn't occur to Iris that she held a figurative pin between her thumb and index finger. Not yet.

Male privilege was an irritation Iris had long endured, sometimes cheerfully with a degree of acquiescence, sometimes not. Her own husband, a neurosurgeon, had an ingrained sense of entitlement bequeathed by fifteen years of training, subservient nurses, and heartfelt gratitude from patients whose brains he salvaged. Scrounging for a glioblastoma, Harris wasn't averse to getting flecks of blood on his glasses, but taking out the trash or changing a diaper was beneath his level of expertise. Truth be told—or not told—her husband wasn't much of a believer, but his solid presence on the stand in numerous bishoprics added a sense of gravitas that the real estate developers and retired orthodontists sitting beside him relied upon.

"I'm not an appendage," Iris growled on more than one occasion. Not some mindless woman basking in the glory of her high-status male. As the years passed, she became increasingly impatient with the male hierarchy that left her teaching toddlers in the nursery while Harris sat smiling benevolently on the stand. Now, seated beside Harris was that face from the pamphlet, worming his way up the ladder. Will Kimball, bishop extraordinaire.

The summer Iris's older daughter turned sixteen, she and an equally foolish male friend ran away to join the circus—actually, Earth Day protests. They traversed the western states waving posters and chanting slogans—The Planet's in danger!—at every opportunity. But they failed to communicate their location or wellbeing to their frantic parents. That dreadful summer that lasted eons and eons, Bishop Kimball, secure in the location of his own troop of well-behaved progeny, never encountered Iris without whispering, "Any word?"

Rachel called her parents the day before school began, requested a plane ticket home, arrived unrepentant, and refused to bathe more than once a week.

"It's a waste of water," she said.

"You're a little smelly by Friday," her mother responded.

Water conservation was Rachel's excuse. Notoriety was the result; that and profound parental shame.

After her daughter's return and transformation, Kimball couldn't resist whispering, "How's Rachel?" at every opportunity. The satisfied expression on his face reveled in his own daughters' innate superiority and Young Women's trajectory toward virtue and a temple wedding. The face Iris had first encountered on the tri-fold pamphlet gave her smiles that felt more like smirks, along with the occasional remark, "How are things on the home front?" as though a battle with sin was being waged at Iris's front door. At least once a week, Will would touch her arm and smile as though they shared a private joke, an awareness that she and her handsome husband were not the solid citizens they pretended to be.

Perhaps the situation would have continued indefinitely if the stake president had not started exhibiting symptoms—twitches, jerks, and spasms—that suggested a brain tumor. A CT scan confirmed it. Brain surgery and his release from the presidency were imminent. The subsequent Tuesday evening in the privacy of a bishopric meeting, Bishop Kimball had raised his eyebrows significantly before delivering a solemn announcement. "I'm going to be called as the next stake president." Neither of his startled counselors or the executive secretary questioned the source of his riveting announcement, but later in the quiet of their king-sized bed, Harris confided in Iris and rolled his eyes. "Will went on to say we had some loose ends that needed to be tied up, as he expected the call before the weekend." Harris leaned over and slid her nightgown off her shoulder. "Don't say anything."

"Of course not." Iris blinked innocently. "Not a word."

To the surprise of the entire neighborhood, who'd learned of the Kimball *confirmation* over backyard fences, Christmas arrived early in the form of a skinny widower, Bernard Boushka, as the new stake president. Boushka, who always wore long-sleeved white shirts to cover tattoos inked fifty-four years earlier, was not a person anyone would have considered stake president material. He intimated to small groups of friends that he and his shipmates had imbibed; and if not under the influence, he would never have consented to having a buxom Polynesian etched on his forearm, but there you are. "Young men away from home," he smiled. "What can you do?" And then he'd laugh, "The last thing I want to do is give Leilani a sunburn."

Three months into Boushka's new calling, he shortened stake planning meetings by half an hour. Linger Longers had to include a dessert table. He didn't reinstitute missionary farewells, but he did invite the young sojourners to join him on the stand and receive a "Good luck, you're going to need it" send off from the congregation that included a hearty rendition of "Called to Serve" and a congregational salute.

In early May, President Boushka appeared unannounced at Iris's front door moments after twelve fourth and fifth graders arrived for Activity Day. She couldn't resist eyeing the paper sack Pres. Boushka was carrying stuffed with ten-foot sections of twisted manila rope. Smiling broadly, Iris stepped aside. "President Boushka, please join us." She gave the group a quick nod of her head, indicating they should abandon painting watering cans and move to the couches in the family room.

The president dumped the load of rope in the middle of the Persian rug woven in deep shades of purple and teal. At first glance the rope resembled a loose collection of snakes, but President Boushka snatched a length of rope, and right before twelve sets of incredulous eyes, whipped the rope into a bowline knot. Moving more slowly, he did it again. Setting the knots side-by-side, he smiled. "Would you like to learn how to tie a sheepshank?"

The kids were delighted, and for the next forty minutes, young fingers worked under the man's supervision until each kid could successfully tie the bowline knot, and a few mastered the sheepshank. Iris inched her way over on the couch until she was crowding the older man's left elbow.

"President." Since he was sitting on her couch, Iris kept it casual. "Your grandchildren must think you're wonderful." She was fishing, and perhaps he knew it, or perhaps he'd been questioned so many times his reply was down pat.

"My first wife couldn't have children. My second wife loaned me hers, but when she died, I had to return them."

"I'm sorry." Iris felt foolish for asking, but alternately, wondered why his marital information wasn't available on the whispered stake hotline. She said as much to her husband while she was reheating the dinner he'd missed.

"President Boushka isn't married."

Harris nodded.

"You never mentioned that to me."

"It's no one's business."

"I don't think of myself as some indiscriminate *no one*." She leaned forward until she was hovering above his plate. "He's not your typical stake president."

"He's not orthodox. That's for sure."

Iris and Harris had been married just shy of twenty-five years; she could intuit when he was withholding pertinent information. She'd also learned if she posed a question and sat quietly, her husband would start to meander and eventually divulge what he'd been thinking.

"Why do you suppose they chose him? You know, the powers that be?" She pushed her chair back. "Can I get you another slice of quiche?"

He avoided her eyes, but finally said, "I feel a little guilty about Bro. Lambert. I was sitting next to Will at a stake meeting, and I noticed Brother Lambert's twitches. I said—in a completely inappropriate manner—that if I didn't know better, I'd think he had a tumor. And then the poor guy did." Harris daubed at his mouth with a wadded napkin. "I could be completely wrong," (in Iris's experience these qualifiers were employed when her husband thought he was completely right) "but I bet Will started placing a few strategic calls to put himself on the radar screen. But honestly, I'm thrilled anyone is willing to do the job, let alone campaign for it."

28

"But he wasn't *Chosen*," Iris sighed, assuming God took a dim view of kibitzing.

"Nope," Harris nodded. "My guess is Lambert felt nudged out and suspected Will was doing the nudging." His eyebrows rose and fell. Payback. Had Lambert given Kimball the kibosh in one of those pre-conference closed-door sessions?

"Will's embarrassed," Harris said. "He staked his claim too many times."

Iris smiled. "Well, everyone just loves Brother Boushka."

"Not everyone." Her husband gave her a significant look over his stylish circular glasses.

"No?" Iris said almost under her breath.

"Will's taking notes."

Six months later, those notes were relayed to church central after Brother Boushka canceled the Saturday night meeting of stake conference. The meeting was redundant, he said. He encouraged the brethren to take their wives on a date instead.

After Will's discreet phone call to an old missionary companion/fraternity brother/cousin/executive secretary in the Church Office Building, he quietly revealed in bishopric meeting a disturbing pattern of events: the member of the Seventy who had called Boushka to be stake president was suffering from dementia, and the result was questionable calls—five in fact—similar to the delightful President Boushka. In a month or two, the situation was discretely rectified. President Boushka and his tattoos were released behind closed doors.

The subsequent Sunday was stake conference, and to no one's surprise, Willard Kimball was called to serve. Before Kimball could resume his love affair with the mic at the podium, a sustaining vote needed to be taken. Most hands—young, old, male, female, trembling, and upright—were raised, with one unnoticed exception. Unnoticed until the clean-shaven seventy standing at the podium asked, as a matter of routine, if anyone was opposed.

The chapel was silent as Iris stood slowly in her three-inch heels, her right arm extended above her head in a graceful gesture that resembled a ballerina exercising at the bar. Heads positioned in the front rows swiveled a hundred and eighty degrees to stare. The resulting collective gasp reduced the available oxygen in the chapel by half. Whispers rustled down the pews and through the rows of chairs in the gym. Harris shriveled on the bench beside her.

Sister Raddish, an elderly woman on the second row, stood and spoke as if stake conference had suddenly become fast and testimony meeting. "I agree with Iris. Absolutely. No offense, Will, but it is what it is." A dozen women scattered through the chapel—no men—stood without speaking as the white-faced visiting authority cleared his throat and leaned into the microphone.

"Would everyone who has an opposing vote please meet me in the Relief Society room? Now would be good." And the large man lumbered off the stand, grinding the meeting to an uneasy halt.

Fortunately, Will Kimball had not rushed to take his place on the stand. Instead, he twisted around to glare at Iris. As she stood, gathering her scriptures and lavender cardigan, his eyes narrowed to slits and his wife hissed. And that was the beginning of the end.

Moments later, resting one hip on the edge of the table in the Relief Society room, the visiting authority sighed, "Would someone please explain what's going on?"

Iris didn't know what had compelled her to stand, but during her march down the hall, she had a moment to organize the thoughts spinning in her head. She answered quietly, "Religion and ambition are antithetical. Brother Kimball's campaign for stake president is a perversion of everything we hold dear." The dozen women in the room nodded in silence.

The last thing this good man expected when he left home that morning was to preside over a female insurrection. Every feature on his face groaned *what next?* In his head, common consent was a concept, not a reality.

Harris responded much the same way after fifteen minutes of fraught silence in the car ride home. The garage door rumbled as he turned toward Iris. "Have you lost your mind? Ambition and religion have been sleeping together for eons. Will would have kept the trains running on time. Why do you care?" He didn't follow her into the house. He rolled down the car window instead and said, "Hospital."

Iris stalked into the family room. A half-smile edging across her face, Rachel lounged on the couch with her legs propped on the ottoman, phone in hand.

"Truth to power, Mom?"

"I didn't say anything."

"You said plenty. It was just non-verbal."

Iris sighed.

Rachel sat contemplating her mother, "The question is *why?* Why blow up your world?"

Iris didn't know. That morning as she struggled to locate a missing hoop earring, she had no thought of initiating an insurrection, scuttling Will's immaculate used car dealership, unraveling his standing in the ward, or planting the seeds that eventually caused his four humiliated sons to refuse mission calls. But that is, in fact, what occurred.

When the for-sale sign appeared in front of the Kimball's white central-hall colonial, Iris experienced massive waves of guilt that passed from her chest into her stomach at unpredictable intervals. She reassured herself that she had told the truth, and that she certainly wasn't the only person offended by Will's blatant ambition.

Now, thirty-plus years later, here she was, sitting in the damp grass as Willard Kimball hobbled his way to the crest of the hill; then in a fierce gesture, he brandished one pole at the firmament as though he could puncture it. His wife (Iris couldn't remember her name—maybe Gabby, maybe Mary Jo) was hanging onto the back of Kimball's shirt as he headed down the hill. The guy had to be eighty, but there was no holding him back. His spindly legs picked up speed before his hands could position the poles.

"Slow down," his wife gasped.

"I need to be sure!" he shouted, swinging a pole in her general direction. "She needs to pay."

Pay? Iris braced for an ugly confrontation. She'd expected one for years; had rehearsed well-considered replies; had practiced calm expressions in the bathroom mirror while flossing.

Will's wife barred her own teeth and shouted, "She's dead. *Dead.* She can't pay for anything."

Who was dead? Iris looked over her shoulder toward the bottom of the hill. No one was in sight.

"I need to see for myself," Will wheezed, struggling for breath.

"You saw the obit. Let it go." His wife didn't say *you old fool*, but it was there in her voice.

Willard Kimball seemed determined to reach the bottom of the slope where Iris saw a lovely rose-colored granite stone. She recognized it. She'd selected it herself at Nu-art Memorials. Each spring on her wedding anniversary, May twenty-first, Iris deposited a bouquet of daisies in a disposable pot in front of the stone's stylish script, "Harris Jensen and Iris Cannon Jensen," side by side with the appropriate dates beneath. Iris squinted. Two dates were carved beneath her name.

A second date? Iris gasped. *Impossible! She wasn't ready to be dead. Wasn't dying something a person would remember? Violent pain? A flash of light? Something? Not sitting in grass that needed to be cut in this ridiculous white get-up?*

Will didn't glance her way or alter his course. *He can't see me.* The realization was brief, vivid, and unsparing. Time slowed. She wiped her nose with the back of her hand, but more tears rolled down her cheeks. *Dead*, she whispered, *what a waste.*

With rickety legs that looked like a praying mantis in freefall, Will Kimball came barreling down the hill, but his ancient toe suddenly caught on the edge of a flat marker, *Beloved Mother*, and he lost what was left of his grip on the poles. He flew into the air like a beginning skier—legs, poles, arms flailing—until his head slammed into a gray granite obelisk with a solid thud. Blood spurted out his left nostril; seconds later more red blood dribbled from his ear. He wheezed loudly, his left leg jerked, and then Willard Kimball became eerily silent. His wife sank onto the grass, pulled her phone from her pocket, and dialed 911. It was too late. Iris knew it. Willard's wife knew it. Her wails launched a half dozen birds into the air. She didn't race down the slope. The poor thing was too traumatized.

Seconds later, Iris's skin prickled. Something disturbed the air behind her. She turned slowly. Dressed in stark white with a jaunty bow tie, fresh-faced Willard Kimball sat in the grass six feet from Iris's left elbow.

"This is your fault," he bellowed. "Everything is your fault!" Hot words gushed from his mouth—every injustice, every stolen opportunity, every ache, every pain. He folded his arms across his chest as if he were prepared to spew words indefinitely.

Iris rolled her eyes. *The poor dope didn't realize he was dead. Couldn't he see his body lying twenty feet away? Couldn't he see the globs of fresh blood?*

With a yelp, Will gave her a shove that tumbled her into the damp grass. "You're not listening!"

Iris sat up with as much decorum as she could muster and brushed a few dead leaves out of her hair.

"Listen Will, I hate to be the one to tell you, but you're dead. I'm pretty sure we both are." The argument they'd never had welled up in Iris's chest. No holding her tongue. She was ready to deliver the final word. Will's hubris had messed up his own life. His disasters didn't belong to her.

But then Iris noticed a man approaching from the east—hovering actually—a tall man wearing a short-sleeved white shirt, with a lovely Polynesian girl touching his forearm. Brother Boushka had arrived. And who was beside him in a shimmering white muumuu, a white carnation lei draped around her shoulders? Leilani?

Iris waited for some pronouncement, something monumental to cause the leaves to quake and the headstones to tremble, but Brother Boushka just stood with the suggestion of a smile on his face. A soft thought invaded Iris's head, *None of this matters.* Ambition. Being right. Being wrong. Male. Female. Affluence. Poverty. Up. Down. It was all just dust in the wind. What did matter? Iris didn't know, but she got the feeling that the world was a more hospitable place than she had previously thought. One thing was certain, Willard Kimball was no longer on her list of wrongs that needed to be righted. She turned toward Will.

He shrugged, "It's okay. You're forgiven." Then he strode back up the hill and placed a translucent hand on his sobbing wife's shoulder.

Iris glanced at Brother Boushka and mouthed *thanks.*

He smiled, *you're welcome*, and nodded toward the rose-colored granite stone at the bottom of the hill.

How had she missed the younger version of Harris leaning against the marker? He gave her a sly smile and stretched out his hand. The white surgical scrubs he was wearing looked starched, Harris Jensen MD embroidered in red on the pocket. Iris had to laugh. Maybe some things never changed.

"I've been waiting for you," he called. "I'm sorry about that car."

She took a few steps and shook out her skirt. "What car?"

"The silver Mercedes that hit you on South Temple and E Street. You weren't paying attention." Then magically, he was by her side holding her tightly against his chest. "I've missed you," he whispered into her mass of white hair. "You need to be more careful."

"Why? Can a person die twice?"

And he laughed that adorable, charming laugh she loved. She pushed her nose into the chest hair above his scrubs' V-neck and smelled his cologne, something she had done at least a million times.

Leaning against their rose-colored marker, they sat on the grass, laughing and talking like a couple of kids falling in love until the sun sank in a glorious display of hot pink and orange.

Harris grasped her hand. "Time to go."

She blinked a couple of times. "Where?"

"Birds migrate at night using the stars to navigate," he said. "So will we."

MISSIONARY WEEKLY REPORT FOR 28 MARCH–3 APRIL, MUMBAI FIRST BRANCH, CHURCH OF JESUS CHRIST OF LATTER-DAY SAINTS

MATTATHIAS SINGH

Dear President Sudhakar,

Our key indicators for the week are thirty new investigators, fifty-five member-present lessons, six investigators attending sacrament meeting, and one investigator with a baptismal date. Zion Emmanuel is progressing but says he couldn't afford the bus fare to make it to church this week. I have asked Brother Dilip to pick him up next Sunday.

As you already know, our proselyting efforts this week were complicated by Elder Dnyaneshwar's abrupt departure by train in the middle of the night Thursday. I awoke to see his bed empty, and his desk and cupboard cleared. I soon received a text message alerting me that he had arrived safely home to Visakhapatnam and that I should not try to convince him to return.

I am sure you are wondering what led to this sudden action. I have been wondering the same over these past four days. Of course, I should have noticed the signs. He had been even more homesick than usual for the past month, frequently mentioning his mother's cooking and his college friends. The work here has been difficult for a long time, and the branch has been frustrated with him ever since his outburst at the member missionary fireside. With the upcoming election, he has been easily distracted by talk of politics. And any of his former companions will tell you that he could be moody and argumentative.

But I thought things were changing. We had redoubled our efforts, and it is only due to Elder Dnyaneshwar's persistence that I even considered tracting in Bharatiya Colony, where we have had most of our recent success. I am ashamed to admit that I was fearful of the crowds of beggars by the rail station there. I did not think anyone in the mud-spattered shanties under the elevated highway would be interested in our message.

It was Elder Dnyaneshwar who reminded me that the Savior himself had nowhere to lay his head, and that he was followed by crowds of people who yearned for daily bread as well as the bread of life. And with Rajbabu and Shanti, Isaac Sion and Ammamma, I saw how mistaken I had been. They have been filled with joy since the first day we shared the plan of salvation with Shanti at the auto stand. Shekar, Jhansi, and their sons have pasted a picture of the temple on the crossbar above their door and have begun collecting rupees in a jar so they can go as a family someday. And ever since Elder Dnyaneshwar challenged Naveen to prepare for a mission, he has been spending almost full days with us, though he is frustrated that we will not let him take us to appointments on his motorbike.

So, it came as a surprise when I awoke to an empty apartment after a day in which we gave sixteen member-present lessons to eager families and youth throughout the shantytown, led by Naveen and Shekar's six-year-old, Prakash. I had thought Elder Dnyaneshwar was relaxed and joking because he was finally starting to feel comfortable here, not because he had decided to leave.

Some of the elders in the zone will no doubt say he was always disobedient and rebellious, insisting on teaching in his own way and ignoring the counsel of his leaders. And given how he replied to the branch president's suggestion that we were running faster than we had strength by teaching so many, or by teaching in the Colony at all, I understand why they think so. He was certainly strong-willed.

But perhaps it was simply that he saw what we could not. In a nation of 1.3 billion people struggling in poverty and unaware of their divine birthright, he knew the urgency of our call. We serve in a city of twenty-one million, twelve million of whom do not know where their next meal is coming from. In our branch of three hundred members, seventy-six attended sacrament meeting the week we arrived. If we alone carry the everlasting gospel and true hope of salvation, the balm for all the world's ills, what are our efforts here but a drop in this ocean of suffering and need? The Savior said the harvest was great and the laborers few, but if we truly recognized how great a burden lay upon us in this land, how could any of us stand?

Yours Faithfully,
Elder Arjun

ALWAYS TO BE FOUND

WILLIAM MORRIS

Note: The following report was filed by Tannur Santos and included in the archives of the DCC-Clory-Roxcy and the DCC-Stoddard. We cannot account for its unusual style other than point to the fact that as the first attendant called to Operation Lost Sheep (and the last released), Brother Santos spent many hours in passive observation and monitoring that afforded him plenty of time to read and listen to the scriptures and other prose and poetic works of both fiction and nonfiction. Rumors exist of a journal in the form of an encrypted text file, but we have yet to discover it in any of the electronic archives that are in the possession of the Deseret Cooperative Commune.

The Sabbath passes for a third time without any of the Seventy awaking.

I am not weary of waiting.

I do worry about their lack of exercise. And I also wonder why they have not emerged to partake of the sacrament. It is not like them to skip covenant renewal.

Earlier today, I blessed the water and crackers myself for myself alone. Everyone else has already left for the launch site. My supervisor, Brother Allred, was the last to leave. He said to me, he told me, he tried to reassure me that the Seventy are likely making one big last-ditch attempt to carry out their ministry and will awake, will re-emerge, will re-join me soon.

That was five days ago.

I am not alone. There is a team of non-members who make sure

39

the power stays on, that the net connection doesn't lag, that there is food and water for me and for the Seventy (should they wake).

I make excuses:

I. They are finding success and need to shepherd the lost sheep back to their physical bodies so they can gather with their fellow Saints.

II. It's easy to lose track of time in there, for it is a place quite great and most spacious.

III. They have been detained by adversarial forces (although none of the warning voices have sounded, flashed, or alarmed, and I have checked and re-checked the system, and everything appears to be in order).

I try not to judge.

But the hour is late. And I do not wish to be left behind. Even though it was made clear to me when I accepted this call that a particle of, a mustard seed of, a little bit of risk came with it.

This knowledge does not weigh heavily on me. I do not water my pillow at night. My calling to attend extends to the generation ships as well. I am not one who will sleep. I will die long before the journey is through. I would prefer that outcome. I would like my bones to be interred in our eventual Zion's soil.

But should I remain, it will be an honor to be buried here on this earth where my ancestors await the morning of the first resurrection.

So, it is not for me that I worry. It is for them.

The Sabbath soon comes to a close.

Monday passes as if in a dream.

I am awake enough to remember to hold Family Home Evening. I read aloud to them from the Pearl of Great Price—Moses, chapter 1—hoping, wondering, attempting to jostle them forth. But my subtle attempt, my passive-aggressive nudge, is for naught. Still, they remain. Limbs slack, mouths open, eyes and ears covered. Lines of nutrition and hydration going in; lines of waste going out.

Tuesday the encoded message arrives.

It is for sure this time. The launches are nigh. There are still places on the last two ships. There is still time to gather. But Saints must hurry, Saints must not dally, Saints must choose this day.

40

Maybe the Seventy have already made their decision?
The thought is heretical, nonsensical. All of them? Apostate all?
But if not, then why their silence?

The silence has grown so profound, so pregnant, so empty as a
tomb that a prayer emerges from deep within. A prayer seeking
personal revelation. Revelation which I am entitled to because
hands were laid on my head to set me apart. A privilege and a right
which I had not yet called upon because the procedures and proto-
cols were clear and had always been adhered to.

Always until now.

I do not have a lengthy track record with personal revelation.
The Father has seemed fairly content with my choices. Perhaps
because—while never perfect—my choices have always been
orthodox yet unambitious. There's a reason why I am an attendant.
Like many, my mission was to virtual spaces. But not deep within
them. Which suited me just fine. I'm much better at the edges,
the cautious places, the periphery. The milk, not the meat. The safe
harbors, not the dark, rough, wild seas.

But once the prayer marches onto the stage of my mind, it
refuses to leave. Makes an Enos of me. And in the end—that is, by
Wednesday morning—I am left with—not a voice in my head—
but a prompting, an urge so strong it must be of God.

I tell the team's non-members that I'm going in. I instruct them
to hard-wake me if forty-eight hours elapse or if the warnings
sound, whichever comes first. I sit in the pod, lean back, and wait
while they hook everything up. The sensors, the nutrition lines,
the catheter, and every other needful thing. When they are done, I
lower the sensory unit until it comes to rest on the top of my head
with a light pressure, like many gentle hands.

I close my eyes.

I enter the foyer.

It is empty as a tomb. I go to the wall of temples and stop in
front of Oakland. It was one of the first to be decommissioned. It's
also my favorite—though, of course, I never saw it in meatspace.
The furthest north I've been is Costa Rica.

With a flick of my wrist, I enlarge the temple until the frieze
on its northern face is large enough for me to pat the heads of

the disciples kneeling before Christ in a sequence known only
to me. I say the phrase "cherubim drop your flaming swords" and
the foyer melts away. No hiding person nor entity is revealed. The
security nodes still shine secure. I blink three times in rapid succes-
sion then raise my left hand to the square. The heat trails fade in,
showing that no one has been in or out of the foyer during the past
month—other than the five remaining members of the Seventy
assigned to Operation Lost Sheep.

I am not surprised, but I am disappointed. It's not that I had
hoped for a breach. God and all the angels of heaven forfend. And
yet I must admit part of me had unrighteously desired for the mystery to be resolved in such a way—no matter how troubling—that I
would not be required to go further in.

But I'm the only one left with the tracking keys.

And so, the duty falls to me.

I restore the foyer to its bland self. The church did not invest in
aesthetics. At least not for this space.

The first decision I must make is what form to take. A meme
cloud would be the most useful, affording both cover and ap-
proachability vis-à-vis other denizens. But I have not kept mine up
to date. I could auto-algo it, but nothing says narc like showing up
with a set that is too obviously random or patterned.

It's better to go with an age33. Just be up front about who I am
and what I'm looking for. Of course, I'm only 27 and no one who is
actually younger ages up. But as I'm not known by anyone in avatar
form, that won't matter. The few contacts I have were developed
through text-only interactions.

They only know my username.

I make the selection and switch the camera view so I'm viewing
myself. I look like how I look in meatspace but my features and
physique are slightly more refined. I wonder if this is how I will
look when I'm resurrected. Whenever and wherever that might be.

The trails of the five members of the Seventy lead in the same
direction and at the same time. Traveling together. A good sign. A
measure of hope. I step out of the foyer into the vastness of virtual
space—the metaverse, cyberspace, v-web—whatever you prefer
to call it. Stars cloud the great expanse. I float forward, skimming

across the darkness like a skiff, a water bug, a webcrawler. I wonder if Abraham also saw these greater and lesser lights.

It's a little overwhelming. I stuck to the periphery during my mission; rarely ventured into navigational spaces. We almost always knew our destination and would blink directly there.

But my security keys can unlock many things.

And I have a trail to follow.

The trail soon turns to trails. The Seventy split up once they reach the first human sector node. Four of them seem to be heading to fairly standard destinations. A fifth heads in the direction of Deeper Space. So, I must make a decision. Go after the outlier? The lost of the lost? Or follow the closest?

I decide that the faster I can find one of them the better. With one in hand I might be able to more easily gather the rest.

That turns out to not exactly be the case. The details of my journey are manifold: the pixel explosions, cacophonic clusterings, shade wars, info orgies, and shifting landscape after shifting landscape. So many strange avatars and voices. So much carnality. When we think of the great and spacious building, we tend to focus on the people at its windows pointing towards us, all mockery and scorn. But consider the depravity and debauchery that goes on in its deepest hallways and rooms.

Thank goodness each of the Seventy left perceivable trails. I don't know if their keys can turn them off. Probably not, for each is surprised when I show up. But they all (with one exception) recognize me for who I am and are apologetic (more or less).

I am video recording my entire mission, but the massive file size may not be worth the space on the ships' databases. If the archivists think otherwise, I will enclose the encryption key to the server when I file this report. The Operation Lost Sheep databases should still be online and reachable up through the first six months after we launch.

I list each of the Seventy by username because that's how I think of them in virtual space. They may file their own reports, of course. I can only report my experiences—what I know to be true. Not without a shadow of a doubt. That place is all shadows of shadows, doubts everywhere. But I attest to the veracity of my account and leave others to judge for themselves how, where, or what they may.

1: 3ld3rGary

Where Found: InteractSpace by Digital Commonz LLC

Explanation for Delay: 3ld3rGary claims he was delayed because just as he was about to turn back, he received a message from a lapsed member who was not interested in leaving but supportive of the effort. He'd heard of a pocket of other LapsedMos who might be open to the idea if personally approached.

Persuasioning: None required. 3ld3rGary is quite apologetic. Says he'd lost track of time, caught up in the excitement of finding a field that while perhaps not ready to harvest was very much worth gleaning. I decide not to mention that he'd actively ignored his alert notifications.

Outcome: 3ld3rGary and I agree that it's okay if he checks in one last time with the three LapsedMos who had told him they were considering gathering to Zion. He crafts three epistles and missiles them towards the heart of Interact. One bursts in the distance, a shower of yellow sparks—the fiery darts that occur when gospel truths collide with a stiff neck and hardened heart. But two seem to reach their mark. And sure enough, they wobble forth, steps uncertain but still in our direction. And, though wary, they approach, trailing clouds, shedding layers of avatar as they come, the marks and masks of the world, metaverse identities. Belated repentance, yes, but welcome—no older brothers we. We greet them as friends. They confirm their desire to return to their body selves and travel to the launch site. We rejoice as one. One of them is a CorpRat and will require extraction or buy out. I make sure Gary has the latest commcodes for the Council on Special Projects and leave him to make the arrangements. My mission must continue.

Other Information: 3ld3rGary admits he had an argument with the other members of the Seventy about how best to use the last bit of available time and they had decided to split up and each deploy their preferred last-ditch efforts.

2: hoopsforchrist37

Where Found: The Dome

Explanation for Delay: Tournament season.

Persuasioning: Upon sensing her reluctance to gather, I gently remind her that she could make the greatest impact by leaving. Such an act would create a wave of publicity due to her status as a famous athlete causing some people and entities to view the ZionWasFled project more favorably—as a true hope for the future of all humankind rather than the irrational gamble of religious zealots. She replies that my argument places too much faith in a grand gesture. That there would be one wave of publicity and that is all. That she can do more good by remaining in a place where her hall-of-fame career is meaningful. That no one moment can do more than the grind of just showing up every day. I counter that her place is with her people. hoopsforchrist37 says that while she loves her fellow Saints, her people are here in The Dome. I say the branch that is cut off from the root soon withers. She says her faith in Christ will sustain her. That he is the root and trunk and that while her small branch will be transplanted from the large branch on which it currently resides to a new one, it will still draw the sap of the gospel and bring forth good fruit. I want to ask her what fruit she believes she will bring forth. But it is clear there is no use in further persuasions. Her heart is set on the things of The Dome, and I don't have enough time to pry her loose.

Outcome: hoopsforchrist37 has decided her calling is to remain on Earth and minister to the (virtual and meatspace) athletes who currently have (or could be persuaded to have) faith in Christ (regardless of sect or denomination).

Other Information: I immediately make arrangements for hoopsforchrist37's contract to carry over to the new owners when they take over the facility. She is aware there is only enough funding to support a fully virtual lifestyle for three years (four if she limits her sports participation), but she seems to think she'll be able to parlay her fame into enough endorsements and coaching gigs to sustain herself sufficient to her needs.

3: KirtlandBrand1836

Where Found: Could not be found. The trail leads me first to the Mememories Palace and from there to Dank and finally to Lostcloud. At the end of the trail, I encounter three entities that retain traces of the KirtlandBrand1836 trail. None will communicate with me. One of them presents as human-inflected AI—a swirling mass of flickering color and noise that almost seems to regard me as prey. Praise be to God for the church's security experts, for any attempts at intrusion are easily rebuffed.

Explanation for Delay: None available.

Persuasioning: I try several messages—voice, text, video, memetic— but receive no reply. The AI mass does absorb each of the messages and seems to change colors as it does so, lilacs, magentas, and ceruleans. Waves of beauty all around to be sure, but if the flickers hold any meaning, they are opaque to my human mind, and I have no other means of persuasion available to me.

Outcome: Lost.

Other Information: I message hoopsforchrist37 and ask her to make the occasional effort to reach out to these three accounts I suspect are all or part of who-what KirtlandBrand1836 has become. I doubt she will. Not because she lacks compassion, but because she is not equipped to deal with these types of virtual spaces. I could have the attendants hard-wake KirtlandBrand1836, but if they have indeed split or merged, that would lead to catastrophic consequences. I realize that we are agnostic on the question of how much of the soul is entwined with the mind in virtual spaces, but I personally believe the mind is an extension of the soul. Is not intelligence the glory of God? Is not such intelligence still light no matter how lost in the dark? And so, I bring up my management interface and switch their contract to a low-power plan. As their flesh-temple was already advanced in years, this should not hasten the death of their physical form—or if so, only by a few months, maybe half a year. Note that I use they pronouns because while their physical form retains its biological gender, their new virtual form(s) present themselves without gender. As I leave, I think I hear a faint refrain, the long, drawn-out notes of what sounds like "all is well." Perhaps a rebuke, perhaps a plea, perhaps a joke, perhaps well wishes. But I check the sound signature in the video file and it has registered nothing, and when I turn my attention back to the entities that were/are KirtlandBrand1836 they have fled.

4: wildbranchfinder99

Where Found: the sapience archipelago

Explanation for Delay: Making a final attempt to ferret out any PostMo transhumanists, neopagans, or ecopunks who might be having second thoughts about their current cooperatives, collectives, guilds, or corporations and their decisions to bud off from and abandon the main body of the Saints.

Persuasioning: wildbranchfinder99 has voice blocked. I message him in text: it's time to go. He ignores me. I message: D&C 103:11. In reply: Luke 15:4. I snip the opening measure of "The Time Is Far Spent" and send it to him. Reply: Matthew 20:6–7. Me: Acts 22:18. Him: Jacob 5:71. I clench my teeth, wonder whether my physical form is doing the same, experience a few seconds of vertigo, settle myself down. Me: Matthew 24:16–18. Him: D&C 11:16. Me: D&C 88:73. He turns his voice on and says this has all been very amusing, but he needs more time, he is very close, he is sure of it, he is sure he has gotten through to someone, to anyone, his trip and accompanying efforts have not been in vain. I tell him that the launch dates are real this time. There is no more time. Every second of my time he wastes increases the chance that I might not be able to track down his companions in time. I don't tell him I only have one left to find. I ask if he has found sheep who might join us. He says he has, but they're finding it too difficult to disentangle themselves from their current habits and technologies of living and being and that's why he needs more time. He needs to abide with them as they unravel. I ask if any of them show signs of actually doing so. He sighs. I place a hand on his shoulder and tell him his time would be better spent helping with last-minute preparations for the final launches.

Outcome: wildbranchfinder99 shrugs and heads back in the direction of the foyer.

Other Information: Moments after he leaves, a denizen named hocuslocust suddenly pops into view and hiss-click-skreeps happily at me. Dripping honey from his swirling, boisterous avatar, he follows wildbranchfinder99's trail, which I attune to him so he can more easily see it. It looks like wildbranchfinder99 will have the great joy of bringing save it be one soul after all.

5: synthesistahmary

Where Found: neEXus

Explanation For Delay: Negotiating with AI.

Persuasioning: synthesistahmary greets me, tells me she is waiting, and she will wait until the last possible minute, but when her countdown timer sounds she will immediately return and awake and travel to the launch site so I should not waste my breath. I ask who or what she is waiting for. She explains she has recruited a quite powerful and unique AI who has taken quite a fancy to the teachings and history of the church. I caution her. Remind her of policy. She tells me church policies always have exceptions, and she's quite confident this is one of those exceptions. This AI is more advanced than any on our current membership rolls and would allow for much more competent and flexible management of certain aspects of the generation ships. I ask why "she" and not "they." Synthesistahmary turns to me as if to reply but in that instant the space around us explodes with shards or prisms or bursts of multicolored light which condense into a ghostly face of white mist that resembles Emma Hale Smith when she was in her late thirties, complete with ringlets and massive lace collar. The face turns to me and I feel a caress of my defenses all the way down to the hidden security keys—their, no, *her* way of letting me know it has the power and glory to peel them all away if it she wants to. Then the AI ignores me and envelops synthesistahmary—a bright cloud, and she in the midst of it. I want to know what is going on, but I dare not say or message a word. So I wait, a virgin, unsure if I am foolish or wise. The hour grows late, my lamp flickering, guttering. I do not know if the hour is yet at hand, and all around me in the darkness, not stars, but novas and angels. I grow weary, which should not happen in virtual space. And then synthesistahmary is speaking to me, saying it is done, and I ask what is done, and she says we must go, go quickly, that her final negotiation was successful, but we must return the way I came so the AI's preparations do not attract undue attention, and as we travel there seems to be a third with us on the path, the road, the way back to the foyer, but my sensors are holden and my eyes are blind to deeper truths, but at least now I have a bit of time to complete and file my report.

Outcome: Successful recruitment of an AI.

Other Information: I do not know if we will make it back to our physical bodies before the last pair of ships launch. If we are unable to, I can join you on your journey only if the AI keeps her promise to migrate to the generation ships, scan our minds, and let synthesistahmary and I remora onto her. We would be in a reduced form. That is not the form I prefer. But it would join me with the main body of the Saints, in whose company I hope always to be found.

Signed: Tannur Santos, first attendant, Operation Lost Sheep

Enclosed: Security keys for uncompressed video feed recording (including all metadata); updated maintenance contracts for hoopsforchrist37 and KirtlandBrand1836 of the Seventy.

NATURAL CAUSES

JOE PLICKA

Glen Waller, Mormon bishop, had never drunk coffee before.

It's not that he didn't like the taste, because he did—one time he accidentally bought a little bag of chocolate-covered espresso beans from WinCo thinking he was buying chocolate-covered raisins. He sat down in the car and popped one in his mouth, and *blammo* it crunched, danced on his tongue like a smoking caramel briquette, lit up some hitherto unknown bundle of nerves in his head. He ate four more before he registered what was happening, then felt kind of guilty, then didn't care and ate half the bag, then got home and slipped the rest into his nightstand's top drawer. He finished them over the next couple of weeks, here and there, while drying off after a shower or reading a magazine. Then they were gone and that was it. He didn't buy them again. Didn't reconsider his commitment to God's various commands. And didn't tell anyone, except Mary, who smelled it on him and told him to knock it off, though she still made love to him, giving him the chance to feel, however fleetingly, like a bit of a bad boy, a complex character, as in *knock it off, you rebel! Ohhh you paid the bills and tucked in the kids? Put on those silk boxers and breathe some coffee on me, Mr. Devil-May-Care.*

He kept going to church, kept believing in Jesus and the prophets, kept feeling the swell of love in his heart as he sang hymns and nuzzled his children at night. He apologized to God, somewhat offhandedly but sincerely, man to man, and felt a kind of satisfaction in knowing that the actions and the consequences were his alone. He had confessed to his Maker. An intermediary seemed unnecessary.

At first, he wondered if some remorse would linger, but it didn't. He felt fine. With plenty of sins of *omission*—not visiting the temple often enough, not ministering to his neighbors, not remembering to pray—it felt strangely nice to have a nominal sin of *commission* to throw on the pile. An authentic *pecado*. A hidden depth, another dimension, an arrow pointing in the opposite direction. There was an intimacy to it that he rather relished, like he'd dived down and touched some vanished part of himself, held a small communion with the billions of his brothers and sisters who were not under covenant to avoid the forbidden bean. Glen Waller, fraternizing with the common man. Glen Waller, keeping it real. Glen Waller, tasting the fruit.

All this was before he became bishop of the Rocky Falls Second Ward, the congregation he'd grown up in with very Mormon parents in a mostly Mormon town in a pretty Mormon region in a fairly Mormon state. He was called, as they say, by God Almighty (God had relayed the message through a few levels of church hierarchy) to provide pastoral care, spiritual guidance, and sound judgment for a flock of three hundred or so of the faithful (or less faithful). His compensation: blessings from heaven, and not a penny more.

In many ways, Glen knew this day would come. As a native son, successful business owner—Waller Associates Tax and Books—and two-time president of the Rocky Falls Little League, nobody was surprised when they announced his name during sacrament meeting. He'd never smoked, drank, gambled, stole, adulterated, or even missed a credit card payment. Coffee beans notwithstanding, he was the perfect candidate.

And so, he served. Day and night he labored to keep the church's pews populated, its programs staffed, and its records ordered. He preached, taught, ministered, blessed, and wept. He extended mercy to the penitent and called the proud to repentance. He picked Toby Buckingham up from rehab, bought him two pairs of jeans from Hand Me Ups and a year's supply of food for his parakeet. He trembled as he stood in a fusty hospital room and put his hands on Sister Margaret Ramos's head, blessing her to recover from bladder cancer. He trembled as he picked up the phone to call the police after finding out that Brother Colton was abusing his children.

Dozens of funerals and weddings, service projects and youth firesides. He stayed late on Tuesdays, made home visits on Wednesdays, arrived before dawn on Sundays, and was on call the rest of the week. He judged the infamous chili cook-off where upstart Andy Peeler dethroned five-time champ Jed Peterson with a bold—some might say preposterous—entry that included ingredients such as thyme, apple cider vinegar, and lamb. He camped with the Boy Scouts at White Fish Lake that weekend in April when it rained so hard the bridge washed out. He spent the night sitting in a tent with two inches of water on the floor—shivering and passing around a two-liter bottle of Mountain Dew with the twelve-year-olds. He pulled weeds, danced ballroom, and learned kids' songs in sign language. A year passed; then two; then three. His five o'clock shadow became peppered with gray, his oxfords creased across the vamp, and his eyes permanently ringed with purple. A fourth year passed. He got really tired.

Not unhappy; but truly, distinctly tired. And a little numb. He knew bishops typically pulled a five-year stint. But going into that fifth year, he was ready to pass the proverbial baton. He wasn't jaded—if anything his faith and devotion burned fierce—but being on the inside had altered his vision. He'd been in the back rooms, seen how the sausage was made. He himself had made the sausage, handled the ingredients—and could not unhandle them. And so, like many church leaders before him, he passed through a portal, left the garden (so to speak), and entered a new world. It was still full of mysteries, and God visited there from time to time. But while his former lay-member self had been happy to believe that every word from his leaders was divinely appointed ("whether by mine own voice or by the voice of my servants!") he was now aware of the ways his own very mortal thoughts, fears, and biases bled into and mingled with the Holy Spirit's flow of inspiration. He had at times felt the holy thing whisper in his ear and witnessed himself act as a divine organ. But he often had to move and speak on his own, unsupported and unadorned. People came to him to hear God's voice, and he had no choice but to give it to them and then watch them leave with a confidence in his sayings that he would marvel at. He spent a lot of time hoping. Hoping he was right; hoping that even if he wasn't, God would make it right.

But he was ready for a break from that kind of hope, ready to let some other priestly brother lose sleep wondering where his own mind ended and God's began. As he said impulsively to Brother Riley, his zealous Sunday school president who prowled the halls searching for chatting truants to sweep into class: "I'm ready to be a civilian again."

But there was more: unarticulated, half-formed, soft-boiled desire. He wanted to *be* somebody else. Maybe just for a little while. Wanted to find that not-bishop part of himself again, the part not on stage, not a model citizen. Just a creature of the earth. God's creature roaming in the wilderness, nose to the wind, sleeping under the stars. It wasn't a crisis of faith. He didn't necessarily want a vacation from strict observance, though that might have been part of it. It was beyond that: he wanted to observe more—observe bigger and wider and deeper.

Which is how he found himself, one Tuesday morning, ordering a cup of coffee in the drive-thru at McDonald's. It was a rash move, but there was some sense behind it. Already working late the night before, his youngest, Sarah, puked in her bed. He cleaned her up and cleaned it up all without waking Mary. After the better part of an hour Sarah was back to sleep and Glen Waller was wired. An enormous surge of adrenaline had been required to power through the mess and overcome his extreme aversion to the smell of ralph— he'd gagged six times. By the time he dozed it was nearly four a.m.

He woke up at seven, showered, gathered the family for prayer, put the breakfast dishes in the sink, put his toddler's pants on, fed some live crickets to their neglected pet lizard, said good-bye to Mary, and pulled out of the driveway by a quarter till. He had an early meeting in Broadgate, a few towns over, with the owners of a jewelry chain: Dinesh Jewelers, seven stores, the biggest client he'd landed in years. The family was Hindu and liked Glen a lot.

"You are a sober man! Very sober!" they joked once after he told them why he couldn't drink the homemade rice beer they presented in a large bamboo mug. So, they brought him shortbread cookies, which he ate, and Darjeeling tea, which he again declined. "We trust you," they said, and brought him a glass of warm milk.

Thirty minutes later he was driving down County Road 98 past fields of alfalfa and sunflowers. Coming up on the Broadgate municipal golf course, he caught himself falling asleep. As he yanked the car back into his own lane, he thought about stopping at the Chevron station up ahead and grabbing an energy drink. He didn't love them—thought they tasted like Windex laced with strawberries—but knew he needed something to defog his brain. He realized he was also hungry and debated whether it was too early for a hot dog. Then he remembered the McDonald's down the street. The image of a breakfast sandwich lodged in his mind. He sped up.

There were several cars in the drive-thru. He idled with the windows down, taking in the sound of a road crew ripping up a patch of asphalt accompanied by the whine of a weed whacker in the distance and the smell of the restaurant—a greasy sweetness mingled with car exhaust and wet grass. The man in the truck ahead of him had the radio turned up. The persistent snare drum, the soulful pleading—*with a love that will shelter you-u-u* trilling in a vaguely exotic way—stirred Glen up inside. He suddenly felt very far away from Rocky Falls, as if he were a stranger, an alien, just landed on this cracked, radiant planet, with everything new and his senses on alert, his mood edging into euphoria. He had a fleeting thought that he was overtired and needed to check himself, but right then the line advanced. He rolled forward and smiled at the battered drive-thru speaker as a muffled teenage voice buzzed out, "Welcome to McDonald's. May I take your order?"

"Yes, I'll have an Egg McMuffin, and a …"

"Anything else, sir?"

"Yes. A coffee."

"A regular coffee?"

"I think so."

"You think so?"

"What are my options?"

"Ummm. Lots." There was an edge of irritation in the voice. Glen found he couldn't open his mouth.

"Sir?"

Still nothing from Glen.

"Sir? We have frappes, lattes, mocha, cappuccino, and regular coffee, hot or—"

"Large!" Glen burst out, his tongue loosed. "Sorry," he said in a softer voice. "Large, please."

"A large what, sir?"

"Oh gosh." Glen gripped the steering wheel with both hands. "A large regular coffee, please. Hot."

"Okay," the voice said with renewed calm. It seemed to be gearing up for something. "How would you like your coffee?"

The morning sun blazed through the windshield. Tiny beads of sweat sprouted on Glen's scalp. "You mean, like, in a cup?"

"Sir, have you ever—" The drive-thru speaker clicked and the voice disappeared. Then the speaker clicked on again. "I'm sorry, sir. We got your order. Please just pull up to the first window."

*

Broadgate was in another stake, the Sage Creek Stake, while Glen's congregation, the Rocky Falls Second Ward, was in the Rocky Falls Stake. This meant they were separated not just by forty minutes of driving and acres of farmland, but by a bureaucratic divide: different local leadership regimes, different meeting houses, different budgets. The Mormon Church adhered to a meticulous organization by geography: ward and stake boundaries were nigh impermeable. Those hoping to attend a congregation outside their prescribed area had to apply for special permission, which ran all the way up the flagpole to Salt Lake City and was only rarely approved.

As such, Glen knew that his chances of being recognized by anyone in Broadgate, Mormon or non-Mormon, were very slim. He'd met the bishop of the Broadgate ward—a psychology professor at the community college—a few times at multi-stake training meetings but could never remember his name. He had a few other contacts in town, mostly through work—people who would definitely not be staffing the drive-thru window at a McDonald's on the city limits.

Which is why he was surprised, to say the least, when he pulled up to the first window and held out his credit card to the waiting hand of Julie Fitzsimmons, whom he'd known since she was a baby, now seventeen years old and just-graduated from Rocky Falls High School.

Her dad, Mark Fitzsimmons, grew up in Rocky Falls about a mile away from Glen. Mark was a couple years older, but only one grade up from Glen. They played varsity baseball together: Mark, a stout, unflappable catcher with grit in his teeth, and Glen, a high-octane, fire-breathing closer with mild delusions of a future in the majors. They were friends, although Glen once accused Mark of misreading a signal from Coach Dyer which resulted in Glen pitching a change-up instead of a fastball, which resulted in Beau Jarvis smacking the ball over the right field fence, giving Glen the first L of his high school career.

After graduation Mark went to Germany on his proselyting mission. A year later Glen shipped out to Mexico for his. They exchanged a few letters. Mark didn't baptize a single soul during his two years of service, although he ate well and developed a taste for non-alcoholic malt beverages served warm. Glen converted dozens to the gospel and served as host to a number of intestinal parasites. They met back up at BYU where they had a few classes together, played on the same intramural ultimate Frisbee team, named Spicy Juice, and even dated some of the same girls. Mark studied English, Glen accounting. Mark became a lawyer, Glen a CPA. Mark and Glen both started having kids and moved back to their hometown to care for aging parents. Their wives and kids hit it off, and soon Mark and Glen kicked their friendship up to the next level—camping trips, movie nights, water skiing. They co-coached. They went to Disneyland together, which Glen loved and Mark pretended to hate.

When Glen was called as bishop, he became Mark's ecclesiastical boss, which made things slightly weird, like a long-time co-worker suddenly becoming your manager. And over those next five years they saw each other less and less outside of church. Part of it was family pressures: more kids, more jobs, more interests. Part of it was that Mark had always thought of himself as Glen's big brother, spiritually speaking. As a young law student, he had weathered a faith crisis and through extensive study, prayer, and endurance, had come out the other side. So, Mark always felt that he was on a higher plane than the workaday members who had never been called to pass through such a veil. Of course, he would never say this out loud. On an intellectual level, Mark knew he was less than the dust of the earth. Still, he fancied himself a gospel scholar and true disciple (meaning he had passed beyond mere cultural attachment to Mormonism; he was in it for the love, for the doctrine, for Jesus). He read all the books by all the best Mormon minds. He felt God in his nerves, in his joints. He called down meaningful personal revelation daily. And now Mark was a little jealous. A little spurned. Glen was his friend, he loved Glen, but Glen was a blasted accountant who hadn't read a book in years, a gloriously simple soul who never thought twice about anything. How was he supposed to teach, lead, judge, and succor a whole community of Saints?

But the distance between them was mostly due to bishops not having a lot of time. They were set apart, which kind of meant they were alone. Glen tried to lean on his parents—his father a former bishop himself and his mother a tireless homemaker who spent ten hours a week volunteering in the family history library—but in many ways his relationship with them was set and scripted, closed to any conversations that deviated from a frontier brand of orthodox optimism. If it wasn't kind or hopeful or faithful, they didn't really want to hear it. For his dad, an old-school Mormon farm boy who left the fields to buy an Allstate franchise after his mission to France, church service was the point of it all, the ultimate meaning—everything else just appendages to a life spent strengthening and reproducing the institution and its inspired programs. For his mom, it was about obedience and safety, you couldn't have one without the other. And really, when it came right down to it, if something felt wrong or hard in your life, you probably weren't being completely obedient to all of God's commands.

And Mark was in the middle of raising teenagers, which ordeal he referred to as The Great Sucking. In fact, Julie was working at the Broadgate McDonald's that summer because she'd been sent away to live with her maternal grandmother. It was a tale as old as time: Mark and Carol Fitzsimmons decided their oldest daughter needed a break from her bad-influence friends, so they called in a favor and sent her away. Just for a little while. She'd been lying about her plans and smoking pot down by Pawnee Creek. One night in April she came home with a bloody wound on her arm, the consequence of an exploding propane tank her weed-addled associates threw in the campfire. A few days later, Officer Hank Primacio, a ward member, dropped her off at the house. Officer Primacio had stopped a pickup truck downtown for dragging a bluegill around on a fishing line tied to the bumper. He was amused. Still, he threatened the boys in the truck with an animal cruelty charge (probably an empty threat when applied to a blue-gill), logged their IDs, and loaded Julie into the front of his police cruiser. In the resulting conversation, Julie told her parents that she was planning on moving to Seattle to be an artist, and that she "didn't believe in your bullshit anymore."

Glen had forgotten that Carol's mother lived in Broadgate. But as Julie's thumb and forefinger closed around his Visa, he remem-bered. Remembered Mark standing at the back of the cultural hall, whispering in animated fashion to Earl Wister, another tired and burdened father whose son had gauges in both ears. Remembered Mary recounting a conversation with Carol: *Julie's okay,* Mary said. *She just needs a breather. Carol's mom is happy about it.*

And now, here he was, staring into Julie's half-shocked, half-amused face as she drew his credit card back inside. Again, he couldn't speak. Just a few months prior, he'd looked across his desk into this same face during Julie's annual bishop interview. He'd asked her if she believed in God and she said, "Yes, mostly." He asked her how things were at home. She shrugged, averted her eyes. Fine, he'd thought, just move on. Most of these interviews were kind of awkward, anyway. He asked her if she obeyed the Word of Wisdom. She looked confused, almost surprised. "No," she said. "Can we talk about it?" he asked. "No thanks," she said with a hint of disdain, and scooted to the edge of her chair. He offered her the candy bowl and she left.

At the moment, however, Julie Fitzsimmons seemed downright cheery to see him in the old Mickey D's drive-thru.

"Hi, Bishop!" she said, her McDonald's team visor slightly askew, a ribbon of reddish-blonde hair flopping over the band. "What are you doing way out here?"

A wide, stiff smile affixed itself to Glen's face. He realized that his fate, whatever it might be, was sealed. No point in trying to squirm out of it. Whatever Julie said, he wouldn't deny or dissemble. He was truly a man getting coffee, just like the five customers in front of and behind him. Was he a hypocrite? Of course! Should he still be bishop? A good question. Would he burn in hell? Surely not.

Well, hopefully not.

"Julie! Holy moly!" He dabbed at his moist temples with the spine of his leather wallet. "I did not expect to see you here."

"I know, right?" Julie said. She seemed to be channeling a preschool teacher, speaking with clear, candied tones and grandly arching eyebrows. "I almost didn't come in this morning. Glad I didn't cancel my shift!"

"Ha ha," Glen said. "For sure." She must be really enjoying this. But still, nothing about his order. He forged ahead. "You know, I think your dad did mention you'd be living with your grandma this summer. How's everything going?"

Julie soured a bit upon mention of her father. But she shoved the card into the chip reader, hit some buttons, and turned back, happy again.

"Grandma's cool. We party. I mean, we get along. We're watching all eight seasons of the old *Magnum P.I.* together. Grandma says they don't make men like Tom Selleck nowadays. I tell her I'd take a Tom Selleck with about fifty percent less hair. She said that's exactly the problem with nowadays."

"Is that so?" Glen said, picturing Tom Selleck smiling from the driver's seat of a borrowed Ferrari. Tom Selleck kissing a tan woman with feathery blond hair. Tom Selleck drinking some fancy coffee beverage in front of a plumeria tree, a line of froth barely visible along the bottom of his legendary mustache. "Well, we all need a break now and then." He paused. "Your grandma sounds like a kick."

"A kick?" she asked.

"Sorry," Glen said. "Old slang. I mean she sounds fun. Sheesh, what am I, from the 50s?"

"Oh, I see," Julie said. "Keeping it old school, Bishop. Grandma would like that!"

Julie hit another button, then tore off the receipt and handed it back with his card. Glen's foot gently, automatically, reduced pressure on the brake pedal. Is that it? he thought. Now he couldn't decide if it was better to say something about the coffee or just drive away. His foot lifted again, the car about to roll forward, his mouth half-open with the words *well, thanks!* bubbling up in his throat, when Julie said, "Oh, Bishop! One more thing."

He felt relieved.

"We didn't talk about your coffee. Tyler at the next window's going to ask you if you want room for cream, but room for cream means they give you twenty percent less."

Glen nodded, outwardly rapt, inwardly fidgeting. "Oh, okay," he said, but couldn't resist the urge to turn to the passenger seat as though one of the invoices he had over there was about to fly out the window.

She waited for him to look back. "Depending on who you're getting this for," she continued, "they might like a ton of room for cream. But I've heard people say, 'The first sip makes room for cream.' The wisdom of the drive-thru, I guess. I figure if they want to burn their mouths, it's up to them, right?"

Waiting for Tyler at the next window, Glen sucked in a wild breath, like he'd just surfaced from a dive. The oxygen buzzed in his brain as he watched the stringy blossoms of a bitter cherry tree flicker in the breeze. The longer he stared, the more the flowers looked like a mass of twinkling stars against a chestnut sky. He rubbed his eyes and made a sound—a sort of bemused chuckle— in his throat.

He couldn't justify it, of course, the coffee, but what did the scriptures say about covering a multitude of sins? Charity. Right? Peter said that. Love wins; love saves the day; love is the currency to buy forgiveness. But then, didn't Joseph Smith retranslate it? Charity *preventeth* a multitude of sins? Well, that's tougher. Still, he could honestly say he loved God. Never met him, but still, *loved* him. Loved the world! Would lay down his life for it if he was asked to. Hadn't the last five years proven that?

He thought of Julie. *Depending on who you're getting this for.* He loved Julie, this daughter of his friend! Here she was, on the cusp of adulthood, working fast food, trying to extricate herself from adolescence—a father who wanted her to study and make her mark on the world, a mother who wanted her to find the right guy and make cute babies, a church that wanted her to obey and serve it tirelessly, a boyfriend who probably wanted to get under her clothes. In his memory: She is twelve years old, dressed in shorts and a baggy sweatshirt, wearing her dad's 49ers hat, her skin a powdery maple color from a week on the lake. She is praying, her head bowed, swaying slightly, bare feet scratching the dirt under a scraggly pine tree, a picnic table with an enormous pot of spaghetti nearby. *Bless us with peace and have patience with us,* she says. *Bless us with peace.* The air smells like sawdust and wet stones. The light dances in between the branches. *Have patience with us. Amen.*

Amen.

The window opened and Tyler leaned out with a small paper bag and a steaming cup. "Be careful, sir," Tyler said, passing it over. "Your cream and sugar are in the bag."

As Glen pulled away, he glanced in his mirror and saw Julie waving at him from her window. Without thinking, he hit the brakes, twisting awkwardly in his seat to face her. He raised a hand in a kind of backwards salute. The driver behind him honked his horn.

"Have a good summer!" he called. But she didn't seem to hear.

*

Three blocks later he turned onto Warm Springs Parkway, a wide road with dusty mansions and giant walnut trees. Old folks and grandchildren puttered down the walks. Glen's Toyota hummed at a steady fifteen miles per hour. One hand steering, the other cradling a cup of McDonald's finest, the heat from the coffee made his hand feel numb and dry. It was a pleasant sensation, bordering on painful. One he could get used to, he thought carelessly. He had the windows down and the radio off; birds were gabbing. He hadn't taken a sip yet, and a part of him wondered if he would.

He wasn't so enervated anymore. Still, his head felt heavy, like blood was pooling inside it. He needed to clear it out. He needed these jewelry store Indians to keep his accounts up. He sniffed at the hole in the plastic lid.

He never looked back on that moment as anything too significant. He never thought of it as a fork in the road, never considered it some kind of God-sent bad karma when Mary got a cancer diagnosis the week after they released him from being bishop. Never thought, *If only I'd known what would happen. If only I hadn't...* There was so much he didn't know yet.

He didn't know that Mary would die and that he would marry Vidya, one of Dinesh's Indian sisters, and that she would attend church with him faithfully though she would never get baptized, which would dishearten Glen's parents who would like Vidya but see this as a halt to Glen's earthly progress. For his part, Glen saw in Vidya—a rather plain-looking dialysis nurse—a singular depth of kindness and love, especially toward his children. Glen didn't know, but probably suspected, that he would never rise higher than bishop, would never be a stake president or a mission president as he had sometimes hoped and even expected. Didn't know that Julie would eventually, after a stint in Seattle, go to BYU, get married in the temple, and settle back in Rocky Falls. Or that Mark would leave the church, get divorced, and live somewhat happily as a hermit in the Arizona desert until he would die and be buried in a bare dirt graveyard.

He didn't know that one day, twenty years down the road, when his hair was long and white, Julie's husband would be *his* bishop. And that sometimes Julie would put her arm around him in the hall at church and say, with real affection, "How's my favorite customer?" And they would both laugh even though no one else understood why. Didn't know that of his seven children, two would convert to other religions (Catholicism and Judaism), one would die in a military training exercise in Guam, one would tattoo her arms down to the wrists and make a sort-of living singing in a punk band, two would live on the same street across town and coach Little League together, and one would become a general authority—a member of the Quorum of the Seventy. Didn't know that they would all gather, every other year, for Thanksgiving, and that even though someone would always cry or yell they would always come back. Or that wars, pollution, and cancer would decrease. But that child abuse, drug overdoses, and poverty would still rise. And he didn't know that he would eventually hear God, clearly and unmistakably—one empyreal Voice, set apart, utterly disentangled from his own—while sitting on a cheap plastic lawn chair in his backyard, pruning a struggling little bonsai tree he'd been trying to cultivate for years without much success, alone.

The coffee was good, although it was his first cup so he couldn't know that. But he enjoyed it, perked up, made his meeting, did his business, and returned home that afternoon. He thought about Julie, thought about whether he should confess to someone, decided against it. Decided he really liked coffee, liked the feeling it gave him. Although he definitely wasn't used to that much caffeine. He couldn't sleep that night.

IT'S A GOOD LIFE

ALISON BRIMLEY

On Day 99 I had Alex Arroyo ask Michelle to Winter Formal.
Of course, I realized close to the beginning of it that I could have
had anyone I wanted to ask *me* to Winter Formal, but that felt
too much like the start of a movie that would see me humiliated
in the end. I could have matched up the whole school, just to see
what would happen. It was the kind of thing Jackie and Beth and
I would have done in sixth grade, drawing little family portraits
of everyone in the class and how they would look in fifteen years,
paired up and with a handful of kids that were an even blend of
both of them. That had delighted us so much back then, and we
guarded those notebooks with our lives. Jackie's even had a lock on
it with a key. As a near-adult, though, I showed restraint, stopping
cold after I'd nudged Alex toward Michelle.

Michelle was a newer friend, a drama kid, hilarious, always cast
as the grandmother or nosy aunt, wearing white spray-painted
hair and unflattering aprons. Michelle and Alex and I had World
History together and I could see how she flirted with him. So I
couldn't feel like I'd done something wrong. It was only after he'd
"asked"—leaving her a box of Honeycomb on the porch ("Honeycomb your hair and come to Winters with me?")—that I heard
he had already asked someone else, and what was he thinking,
everyone wondered? I don't know how he explained that to himself. It wasn't as if I'd made him fall in love with Michelle—again,
that was the kind of thing I didn't want to mess with, and I knew
it wouldn't be doing her any favors even if she would have been

thrilled for a while. I only wanted to give her the chance to catch the attention she wouldn't otherwise have gotten.

What I wouldn't dare to do was make anyone ask *me*, and I was pretty sure I wouldn't be asked. If I'd had to force someone, I guess it would have been Casey Gorman because I think Jackie and Beth had helped me talk myself into having a crush on him at that point. (Casey and I did end up going to Prom together that spring. I thought something might really come of it, but we lost touch after graduation, and subsequent Facebook updates have shown he's now happily married to a man with a neatly trimmed blond beard identical to his.) Two weeks before the dance, the doorbell rang late, and there was a jumbo bag of popcorn—one of the huge ones you get at Albertson's—sitting there on our porch, and a poster: "I'm POPPING the question!" I had already tucked myself into bed, but Mom and Cara flitted in without knocking and started poring through the popcorn on my bedroom floor. Cara was fifteen, technically too young to date, but close enough to her birthday that Mom and Dad would have let her go to Winter Formal if she'd been asked. "Do you think it's for you or for me?" she said giddily. "You," I said, and I was certain it was. In three years of high school, I'd only ever been asked to a dance by Eric Sterling who'd had a crush on me since we were in Primary together; Cara had already had two boyfriends (unbeknownst to Mom and Dad). Their fingers found little papers in the popcorn. They decided the hallway light wasn't enough and flipped on my lamp. I pulled the blankets over my head. I wished they would let me sleep now and just tell me in the morning that Cara had been asked to Winters. "Will," Mom said, flapping a paper in the air. "Will Kern, maybe?" Cara said, but subsequent papers made it clear that the *will* was a verb in the sentence *will you go to winters with* but they hadn't found any names yet.

I was certain—entirely—that the popcorn invitation was for Cara. And I didn't think I cared; if they had flipped off the light and left, I wouldn't have felt slighted, wouldn't have cried myself to sleep. But I guess somewhere, I did want to be asked. I wanted it to be for me. Because soon Mom or Cara, I don't remember who, pulled out *Gemma*. Then *Ipsen* and then *Malcolm*.

The trail of papers they had laid out between the kernels:
Gemma will you go to Winters with Malcolm Ipsen?

Mom said, "Malcolm Ipsen. Do I know him, Gem?"

I hardly knew him. I felt ill, like the room was swirling around me. I'd never gotten high, never had the opportunity or wanted it. But this felt like what I imagined a bad trip would be.

When I think about it now, I'm proud of the restraint I showed. Now, a seventeen-year-old me seems hardly out of childhood; it surprises me that a Subway would hire one. But I suppose it was popular culture that saved me more than anything. The trope appears everywhere: an unsuspecting innocent who suddenly has the chance to obtain anything imaginable. Of course, the story never ends happily. They must be taught a lesson: greed ends in tragedy. Aladdin's lamp, "The Monkey's Paw." For me, though, the clearest example was one I saw near the beginning of it all: the "Treehouse of Horror" episode where Bart Simpson has omnipotence and all of Springfield lives in fear of upsetting him. He's fed milkshakes at school; he prank calls with impunity. Needless to say, I wasn't tempted.

It was an October night, around Day 15, when Mom was working late and Dad had let us watch *The Simpsons* after dinner. Mom had never forbidden the show but would walk around sighing, rolling her eyes, averting them from the kitchen television if it were ever on. I'd seen the episode before, but that time it froze me in place. Dad was rinsing the dishes, me loading; they were piling up on the counter. Bart had turned Homer into a jack-in-the-box as punishment for defying his wishes.

"This is an old *Twilight Zone* episode they're parodying," Dad said.

"Oh yeah?" I said.

"'It's a Good Life,' it was called. You ever see that one? With the cornfield?"

"I've never seen it," I said. I never would.

I turned and set a dripping plate into the dishwasher. Then, when Dad had turned back to the sink, I tried it. I touched the rim of a rinsed mug. It vanished, reappeared on the top rack.

*

I wondered if the power had arrived to give me more insight into

godhood. On Day 29 I wrote in my journal: *Perhaps God won't vio-
late our agency because our love for him would be meaningless if it were
forced.* My journal around that time was full of musings like this. To
paint God in such a needy light felt a little transgressive back then.

*

Malcolm was an orchestra kid—a cellist. His group of friends
had some overlap with mine; his dad was Beth's bishop. I had hung
out in the same house with him maybe a dozen times but had
hardly ever spoken to him. I wondered if he knew he had asked
me to Winters—if he knew who I was. If all I'd done was change
the words on the paper—how would I explain that to Mom? If
someone else had asked Cara, how would she find out? I knew it
couldn't have been that Malcolm had meant to ask Cara.

But the day after the ask, while I was doing a worksheet on
Crime and Punishment with Asha Singh, she said, "Malcolm asked
you to Winters, right?" I confirmed it. "Then you'll be in my group."

Asha was a violinist, eternally dating Brian Cork, who also
played violin. I'd always liked them, admired them—they were
actually good at music, not high-school good, and seemed cultured
in a way that felt out of reach to me who had taken six years of
piano but now played no instruments. I smiled at her, trying not to
betray the flood of understanding now descending on me. It had
been real. Did she think it odd that he had asked me? I have this
problem: When I learn someone has a crush on me, I immediately
begin to like them, even if I don't. I'd only just gotten over that
with Eric Sterling. Now it was starting with Malcolm, and I didn't
even know if he actually wanted to go to the dance with me. He
was moderately adorable, in a lanky way; not obviously so. He was
someone you wouldn't admit to being interested in, not because he
was unattainable but because no one else would see the appeal. But
the strange part was this: by the day of the popcorn incident, I had
known for weeks that I had this inexplicable power over people,
things, events, and yet even my all-powerful subconscious didn't
have the guts to wish for a basketball star or student body president—someone truly handsome or charismatic—as my date. Even
my subconscious didn't aim too high.

"I think they're planning Macaroni Grill for dinner and maybe paintball for the day activity," Asha said. "But who knows; he'll probably call the night before to tell you when he'll pick you up." She rolled her eyes.

I laughed carelessly, but my brain was lighting up. When Malcolm called to tell me when he'd pick me up, either he'd ask for my address or he wouldn't. If he didn't, he'd left the popcorn. If he had to ask where I lived, I'd made the invitation.

I glanced at our worksheet and read *Give five examples from the first half of the novel where Dostoevsky portrays Raskolnikov's dual nature.* I changed it to *two examples.*

∗

Day 1, the beginning of October: I realized I could snooze my alarm clock indefinitely, except I wasn't just delaying the alarm, I was actually delaying the passage of time. It was the least weird thing that happened to me that day. I guess I started numbering the days because even then I sensed it wouldn't last forever. I used the power for things like refilling a cereal box when Cara had put it back with about three Frosted Cheerios left. Relocating the full kitchen garbage bag to the big black can in the garage. Sealing the nick on my shin with a finger, thinking away the blood. Then I began to open wounds: not to hurt myself, but to see if I could. First, small ones on the backs of my hands; then gashes on my legs, and weeping holes in my cheeks. I watched myself bleed in the mirror like I was watching a movie, then wished the damage away without a scar.

Many things fell into the category of "see if I could." I made a newscaster on TV sneeze midsentence; then I nearly vomited in astonishment. I replaced the Flaming Hot Cheetos in Cara's nightly Tupperware with packing peanuts, then switched them back before she noticed. More practically, I paused the clock a few times a day to give me more time to sleep, to finish assignments (I couldn't escape the feeling that I would suffer eventually if I used the power to actually *do* my assignments), to get to work on time when I had left home too late. I evaporated a large fry and milkshake from my stomach (painless, silent, but unsettling enough that I never did it again). I saw an outfit in an episode of *Gossip Girl* and willed it into my closet. Several times I had my manager excuse me early from my shift at the bakery. It sounds like a dream, sometimes it felt like it was, but I also began to wake up at night unable to breathe. This was the only part I told my parents. They said it sounded like I was having panic attacks and began to get very interested in my life. I suppose I could have stopped them from asking if I wanted to.

There was one thing I couldn't do: just *know* a thing. I tried to "download" information into my brain—how to calculate derivatives, whether the mall would be busy when Michelle and I wanted to go—but if it was there, I didn't know how to access it. I tried sometimes to know what another person was thinking, but that only resulted in a sort of mental radio static that I couldn't make sense of.

I cheated on a calculus test. When Mr. Carson would look away, I'd tell everything to stop, reach for my calculus book and copy down the proofs, substituting the numbers in the book with the numbers in the test problem. To be certain I'd done it right, I leaned far over to look at Mallory Church's test. I knew this was a sin. But I also knew that anyone would have done the same. It confused me that I didn't feel guilty. What I did feel was that I was failing. The only explanation for all of it was that this power wasn't a gift, but a test, and that others had been given the same test but knew better than to speak of it. What comforted me was that I felt that anyone would fail.

Before all this began, I had been ready to drop out of AP Calculus at the semester break. I knew I wasn't going to pass the test. I'd made the mistake of telling Dad about my plan, and after that he brought it up every day. "You can't possibly know if you're going to pass the test," he would tell me. "Some years you get an easy test," my older brother Tyler said. "I thought I would fail for sure, and I got a four."

But I avoided arguing with them, pretending I had some deep, private, good reason for quitting—other than the fact that I just didn't want to worry about it for the next five months. Because that was the only thing that could make Dad really mad at me: when I quit something or didn't try. I'd stopped playing soccer in fifth grade when it started to actually get competitive. Sophomore year

I'd decided at the last minute not to audition for the musical even though I'd signed up for a slot and rehearsed my song for weeks. I didn't get a drop of Dad's self-made-man genes, and that drove him crazier than anything.

Of course, I could ensure a good score: change the rules so that working with friends and using the book was allowed; change the problems to be simpler; change the scoring so that any effort at an answer got full points. I could tell Dad I'd decided to take the test and that argument would be over—and maybe I'd never have to quit anything again. But something that seemed even more powerful than me was stopping me. I wasn't a rebel. But I couldn't give him that satisfaction.

*

I wasn't wholly selfish; I tried to use my power for good, too. Disappeared a bloodstain from the crotch of Heather Walker's white capris before she even noticed. Stopped an asthma attack for Mom. I could have done bigger good deeds: end all wars, poverty, hunger. Vaccinate the world; change the heart of every child abuser. But I was sure that interfering in things that big would have consequences beyond my ken.

Besides, I felt I had some larger purpose I was meant to discover, and I was afraid to *really* act until I did. I prayed about it, fasted—even on Sundays that weren't Fast Sundays. I looked for scripture stories that might apply. And in the meantime, I magicked up only small conveniences that I couldn't resist.

In every other way, I was a typical teenage girl. The prospect of Winters was taking most of my attention—if, perhaps, for an atypical reason.

*

The first person whose mind I hijacked was a child. This may have sharpened the power's effect on me. Day 8: I was babysitting my sister's kids, and the baby refused sleep—loudly, desperately—even after the fourth tuck-in. I listened to her cry from the basement where her brother and I were trying to watch *Spiderman*, and I was careful with the words in my head: *Make her be okay*, I thought; not *Make her be quiet.* I'd heard enough stories; this was before I had learned that the power was honest, respected my intentions, not like a genie looking for loopholes. She silenced herself instantly.

I bounded upstairs to her room and cracked the door. Asleep, and breathing. She was okay.

I told myself I hadn't really meant to do that to Stella—or even if I had, I wouldn't do it to someone older, someone whose choices mattered. But it was less than an hour after I'd used the power on Stella that Hunter was fighting me about pajamas, teeth-brushing—saying his mother always let him take a popsicle to bed—and I did it again. This wasn't a distinct command so much as a nebulous wish that he would obey me. He slid into bed and even let me kiss him goodnight.

I'd only done one unit on child development in AP Psychology but even I could tell this wasn't healthy.

I stood in the upstairs hallway, alone but feeling watched. *Please, Father*, I thought, and for the first time I was struck by the different attitudes of my mental commentary. This was not the voice of my power, but my praying voice. *Please, let me never do this again.*

Back then I would have said that it was my understanding of the importance of agency that made the moment so bitter—my knowledge of the war in heaven and Satan's plan for everyone to blindly obey without an opportunity to sin, the fact that agency is so vital to the whole plan that not even Heavenly Father would overstep its bounds. Now, I don't think my beliefs had much to do with it. It was terrifying to realize that, if I wanted to, I could make every person in my life—in the world—think and behave more or less as an extension of myself, and that it would be far easier to do it than not to.

Earlier that night, at dinner, I had asked Hunter, "What would you do if you had the power to do *anything* you wanted?" I hadn't planned to say it.

"I *do* have the power to do anything," he said, jumping out of his seat and assuming the fight-ready hover of a video game character. Normally, I would have played along. Today, though, there were no adults in the house to glance at me sidelong, and the only person crazy enough to talk with was a standard six-year-old. "No, I mean *anything*," I said. "I mean power to do anything you can think of. You think it, and it happens."

"I have mind powers," he said. "Ninjas can control anything with their minds."

"Oh, that's right," I said, and felt inexplicably comforted. "Can you lift up this spoon with your mind?" Despite the omnipotence I'd recently found myself endowed with, the best test of powers-unbounded-by-the-laws-of-physics I could think of was still something out of *Matilda*.

For a moment I worried that he would move the spoon. Panic seized me as, out of the corner of my eye, I thought I saw it rattle. Surely, I couldn't be the only one who could have done it—and why wouldn't Hunter have the power, too? But the spoon stayed still, and he scrunched his mouth over to the side and said, "I don't really want to."

Every first Sunday of the month we had a fireside with the bishop where the youth could write down anonymous questions for him to answer. We'd gather at his house with our leaders and parents and he'd answer them; then we'd have brownies. *How can I stop myself from having sinful thoughts?* Or *Some of my friends say homosexuality is OK, what should I tell them?*

If you suddenly develop the power to take away someone else's agency through mind control, does that mean God wanted you to do it?

There was no point asking that one.

I was tired of waiting for Malcolm Ipsen to call me. I hadn't even seen him at school that week. It struck me that this might be my fault. I dreaded running into him, so I never did. What was the mechanism for this? Was I making him take inexplicably winding routes around the school and arriving late to class? Did he get locked in the orchestra room for hours at a time? Sitting at the dining room table with my homework on Day 108, I saw my phone screen light up as it skittered along the edge of my calculus book. "Hello?" I said.

He sounded normal, not as if he'd just woken from sleepwalking to find himself on the phone with me. He said he was excited for Winters. I couldn't tell if he was lying. He said the plan was Macaroni Grill and paintballing. He'd pick me up at 11 a.m. He didn't ask for my address.

For an hour I had that floating-on-clouds feeling, a romantic-movie-musical mood, which surprised me because I didn't think I was in love with Malcolm Ipsen. But if he was in love with me, I thought I could return it, very quickly. But I came down two hours later when I spotted a little green spiral-bound notebook on my mom's desk: the school directory. He had one, too. Obviously. My scheme had been less than foolproof. I might never know anything for sure again.

The only stories in the scriptures about people with unlimited powers are about Jesus. Ordinary people—by which I mean prophets, I guess—could use the priesthood, but only, it seemed, as God wanted them to. And it seemed they always knew *how* God wanted them to. *Is my power the priesthood?* I wondered in my journal as early as Day 30. There was the small problem that I was a girl, of course; but bigger than that was the question of why *I* would be given the strongest dose of priesthood power ever recorded. I had healed someone: Mom. But I wanted to do something incredible.

I wanted to be able to control myself. There had been moments when I'd recognized a baser instinct, a barely registered desire, along with the sense that it was about to be real, and I'd stopped it from happening. I'd distinctly thought words in my head that supplanted the unspoken desire, and the words came true.

But I tried to imagine what it would feel like to make Malcolm kiss me, exactly when and in the way that I wanted. The daydream didn't have the same awful tinge of wrongness to it that the experience of controlling Hunter and Stella had. I wouldn't make a habit of it: forcing boys to kiss me. But it did seem that, just for this night, it could be fun.

I imagined myself in a montage: Learning to Control My Powers. I ask if Kelly needs any more babysitting, and I invite Michelle to help keep me a little more accountable. Hunter wants to play the Wii instead of getting ready for bed. I tell him no and he screams. I feel the familiar desire rising to the surface of my mind. *No*, I tell it. *Let him scream*. I chant those words to myself: *let him scream, let him scream*, and he does. It turns from a real protest into a joke. "Oh my gosh, stop it!" Michelle says, bolting him with a pillow. I break my chant, and he is quiet.

Jesus Christ had the power to stop himself from being killed, I wrote on Day 116. *But he chose not to, because it was part of God's plan, and because he loved the world more than he loved his life. I don't think I would be able to let myself be killed right now. Maybe, if I knew it was part of God's plan.*

I know God doesn't just reveal plans for your life. The path is illuminated as you walk it. But what if your feet are enormous and anywhere you walk, you step on millions of creatures and destroy entire ecosystems?

I thought I was clever then, finding the flaw in a metaphor. But if I worried much about it, anyone reading my journal wouldn't know it. I didn't write a lot after that.

On Day 120, Malcolm picked me up in his fifteen-year-old Jeep, Classical 89 playing on the radio, and I thought *no, he's objectively adorable*. How had I not seen it before? He had tightly curled hair and a baby face, and he seemed endearingly nervous. Asha and Brian were in the backseat, and I was glad she was there. She was condescending, but her strong preferences gave a structure to the day that made me feel safer. A few times I looked back to see Brian and her conjoined at the mouth. It seemed Malcolm was used to third-wheeling.

I was incredible at paintball, of course. I hardly got hit and hit others dead-on without any warning. No one could believe it when I said I'd never done it before. "Some people have genetically perfect aim," one kid explained to me, as if he had discovered a prodigy and needed to convince me to join his circus act. Malcolm seemed proud, called me "sharpshooter" when he dropped me off to get ready for the dance.

I put on the dress I had bought—with my money, earned at my job, like a normal person—and looked in the mirror. I'd thought about it before but never actually dared to try until now. Reciting the words in my head, *bigger, smaller, less, more,* I photoshopped myself in real life. I went exhilaratingly overboard at first: cinching my waist in, reshaping my breasts, buttoning my nose, and widening my eyes. Adding inches to my hair and legs. And though I knew I could revise anyone's memory of the old me, I also knew I couldn't stay like this. I stepped away from the mirror to read a text from Jackie, and when I came back and saw myself, I laughed. None of my changes had been painful: no aching where my ribs had been invisibly corseted, no cramps in my lengthened legs. I took everything back down to a level that could be explained by good makeup and a flattering dress. I was ready to go.

I guess allowing that much change—purposeless, vain, useless in every way—set something free in me. If you don't tell me what I'm supposed to do, I was thinking, this is the kind of thing I'm going to do.

Then Malcolm was back in his Jeep. He was looser than during paintballing, laughing at everything and teasing me like we were old friends. Brian, too. Asha hardly spoke the whole ride to the restaurant or through the meal. Malcolm was feeding me bites of his pasta. "Can you taste that *butter?*" he said, and really stared at my mouth when I closed it around his fork. He was surprising me; I liked it. After dinner, on our way into the dance, it was raining outside and the boys ran ahead, pulling their jackets over their heads. Asha grabbed me by the arm, and we fell back. "They're totally baked," she said.

"What?" I said.

"Brian thinks I can't tell when he is, but—" she stopped. Her voice had cracked, and she just bailed on the sentence.

I'd never hung out with someone high before. I knew what I was supposed to do: get out of there. What if they tried to make me take some?

"Do you … wish they weren't?" I asked.

"Um, yeah," she said. "This is our last Winter Formal."

It seemed an overreaction. Prom, maybe, but Winter Formal? At the same time, I knew the me of 120 days ago would have been scandalized, too. *Stop*, I thought.

Even the raindrops paused in the air. I reached up and pinched one in my fingers. Then I walked ahead to Brian and Malcolm, frozen mid-laugh, and looked at them. Malcolm's eyes were red. Between them I could see Asha, looking at the ground.

But I was having fun. I took my place again beside her.

Go. "Losers," I said, as if the most I could do for her was commiserate.

*

Eric Sterling had never danced with me like this. Malcolm was gyrating—insincere, giggling, pulling me to him. It felt like we'd known each other for years. I couldn't tell if it was the weed or the power or just him. I could not believe that he hadn't meant to ask me. "You're so beautiful," he said. "I never realized." I didn't let this hurt my feelings.

Sometime around when I'd decided to do nothing about Brian and Malcolm, I guess I also decided all rules were off tonight. Not *all* rules, but here's what happened next. Catering trucks started setting up in the hallway: tacos and pasta and sushi and ramen and ice cream. I brought in a band and they started playing while the regular DJ (Coach Kaufman) scowled. People were squealing with glee. The slick wood floor, painted for basketball games, started lighting up in squares like we were in a club—at least the version of a club I'd picked up from movies. I could feel myself getting jittery, overexcited, and I knew I had to be careful about what I did next. I was being both ridiculously extravagant and unimaginative, accomplishing nothing but creating a school dance that would probably make the local newspaper. Malcolm started jumping over to the stand where the band was playing, then seemed to remember he'd come with a date and hopped back to me, grabbing me by both hands and resuming the hop, facing me. "This is actually *sick*," he said, pulling me closer.

I nodded. "How did they get this band?" I said, grinning wildly.

There was a half-second pause between songs in which Malcolm got close to my face and said, "You know I didn't even want to come to this dance?"

There was more to the sentence. Maybe, "But Brian talked me into it," or, "But I really wanted to get to know you better," or, "I don't actually remember why I asked you." Instead, I heard only a series of horrified screams from the hallway.

I snapped around to look. The catering staff was ducking behind the tables. A gunshot. A smash of glass hitting the floor. *Stop*, I thought.

While the rest of the room froze—a crush of guitar, bass, and drums echoing through the room—I ran to the hallway, straight to where I thought I'd heard the shot. I couldn't believe I was doing it. *So, this is all it takes to turn me into a fearless hero*, I thought, *total control of the situation*. I hurried first to the catering staff crouched beneath the tables. Everyone's eyes were wide with fear, unharmed except for one man, collapsed on a chair with a trail of torn flesh running up his neck and cheek. I looked away while I touched him and closed up the skin. I took a breath, stood up, turned ninety degrees, and found myself looking into the faraway face of Eric Sterling. With two hands, he held a handgun out from his body, aimed at the caterers. Was it a look of disgust, agony, or hatred? I couldn't tell.

Disappear, I thought at his gun, which obeyed. I walked at him, and for the first time since all of it began, I couldn't believe what I was seeing. The real Eric Sterling? A mannequin? I touched his arm. The hairs moved against my fingers. *Paralyze*, I said to his hands. Then I told him to fall to the ground.

I took my time in the halls, looking for anyone hit. I found no one. I did find Michelle in the bathroom, bending over the sink toward the mirror to wipe off the mascara smeared from crying. Someday later, I would ask her what had happened; it was sure to be Alex's fault, and thus sure to be my fault. I wanted to unfreeze us. Instead, I touched her eyes and perfected her makeup. I spent what felt like hours moving alone through the school. Then I went back to Malcolm, slipped my hands back into his. *Go.*

*

The dance did make the papers. *The shooter experienced a severe attack of anxiety after firing the first round*, it said. *He discarded his weapon, which has not yet been located.* I felt sick reading it, and every other article on the event—as if they could teach me something I didn't know. But already, on our way out the doors, students screaming and police lights flashing red and blue against the brick of the school, I was praying my thanks. Because if stopping a school shooting wasn't a purpose, I didn't know what was. God and I had made up.

We followed Eric's trial closely at my house. My mom was his mom's visiting teacher and spent hours crying on the phone with her, organizing a calendar of women to bring her dinners. For a while I prayed to know if I ought to intervene in the sentencing, to make sure he was treated fairly. Nothing became clear, so I did nothing. And then, months later—and I'm embarrassed it took me so long—I was explaining to Malcolm (we dated for three months) how I had grown up with Eric Sterling and sort of dated him in tenth grade, and a bolt-of-lightning thought came clearer than any answer I could have expected from God: *I didn't stop the shooting. I caused it.* That's how bad I'd wanted something big to do.

*

I'll never know if that was true or not, but I believed it for a year or so. It took me years to really give up believing anything about it. In the meantime, I graduated (thanks entirely to the power, since I couldn't bring myself to do a single assignment that second semester), quit the bakery, started college, began majors in psychology and sociology, and cycled through more boyfriends than I would have liked—but it turns out that when you can have anybody you like, you do. I didn't come home or talk to my parents much; I didn't want them to ask me any questions. I went through two years of college like that, and when I wished some berries into my yogurt one morning and nothing happened, I went to bed for three days.

I saw my family more, and my parents were nothing but appreciative every time I showed up. But they were confused, as I knew they would be, when it became clear from my Instagram posts that I was prioritizing hiking and camping over church on Sunday mornings and showing little interest in going through the temple or marrying. I did continue to go through the motions long after I'd stopped begging God to explain himself to me. But it got to be ridiculous, sitting in church, listening to people talk about challenges and prayer and Great Plans—and still was, even after the power was gone.

I was on the verge, two or three times, of telling someone (a roommate, a boyfriend) what I used to be able to do. But it felt unfair to make them respond to that. And once it was gone, there was no point. I am what I would call a normal person now.

Once I thought my power would always be the most important thing about me. Now I remember what it felt like only when I'm reading my journal.

A VISION

TIM WIRKUS

Brothers and sisters, the thought I was prompted to share today is something I've never shared with anyone before. My name is Sharon Sansom, for those of you who are new to the ward, and if you'll bear with me, I need to start with an experience I had when I was fourteen years old.

I was coming home from school one spring afternoon, walking through the backyard to get to our house, when I saw my great-grandmother lying on the ground next to the vegetable garden. I could tell right away that she wasn't just resting, though that in itself would have been strange enough. No—it was obvious she had fallen down. The way she was lying there, the way her body was bent and twisted, no one would *choose* to lie down like that.

Terrified, I ran across the lawn, scrambling to remember any first-aid technique that might help her. There had to be something I could do. Unless she was already dead, which only just then occurred to me. When I got to her, though, her mouth was moving like she thought she was talking, but no sound was coming out. I must have yelled for help because the next thing I remember, my mom was standing next to me, looking shocked. She put her hand on my shoulder and told me to wait with Gran while she went inside to call the doctor. And then she was gone.

I was so afraid in that moment, alone and helpless in the face of Gran's suffering. Here was someone I loved who needed the kind of help I wasn't capable of giving. For a moment I stood there frozen with despair, until I thought to ask Heavenly Father for help.

When I said amen, I had the distinct impression that I should sit down next to my great-grandmother, and that's exactly what I did. I sat down and just started talking to her about whatever came into my mind—a test I'd failed that day at school, my plan to start collecting butterflies, the story of how my friend Jill Cutter broke her arm on her family's trampoline.

I was just telling her that Sister Marsh's cat had birthed a litter of kittens, and that she had told me I could pick one out for myself, when my great-grandmother turned her head to look at me—I could tell from her eyes that she recognized me, that there was some lucidity there—and murmured a sentence I couldn't discern.

"What was that, Gran?" I asked, leaning in closer.

She licked her lips and raised her head just a bit.

"You don't want a cat," she rasped into my ear. "Cats are like God: violent, capricious, and devoid of mercy."

Then her head dropped, and she closed her eyes.

I reached out and almost grabbed her by the shoulder to shake her awake so she could explain herself further, but I stopped myself, remembering that she was not just drowsy, but ill or injured. Instead, I folded my arms and said another prayer, and then waited in tears for my mom to come back.

Gran died early the next morning.

To Mom's credit, when I told her about my great-grandmother's final words to me, she didn't dismiss them as a symptom of dementia or a death-fogged brain. Instead, she explained that my great-grandmother had seen a lot of suffering in her life, and that it had turned her into a bit of an atheist. She said this matter-of-factly, and then let the matter drop.

Even at the time, though, I recognized that my mom's explanation wasn't quite accurate. She'd called my great-grandmother an atheist, but Gran hadn't said she didn't believe in God. She'd said that God is a dangerous and malevolent being, a possibility that had never crossed my mind before.

I'd been taught the opposite, of course, that our Heavenly Father loves us unconditionally, but when I thought about what my great-grandmother had told me, part of me realized her view was just as plausible. Yes, God *could* be a loving and righteous deity, but he could just as easily be wicked, despising his creations, out to get us all. This idea scared me, but also, if I'm honest, kind of delighted me, too.

With time, though—I'd say a year or two—the idea lost its novelty and I more or less forgot about it until twenty years later. My youngest son—I have five boys—had just started first grade, and I was working again—a full-time cashiering job at K-Mart. On top of that, I was Primary president and my husband, Bill, was working full time, too, so my boys were basically fending for themselves while Bill and I tried to keep our heads above water. I don't think I slept more than five or six hours a night during that whole period.

Anyway, I was on lunch break at K-Mart one day—a three o'clock lunch, because one of the other cashiers had called in sick, and it was the holidays, and we were slammed. I'd been running a register for five hours straight, is the upshot there, but I'd finally managed to grab a few minutes to eat something. I was sitting in the break room on one of those industrial couches, just mindlessly chewing on the baloney sandwich I'd brought from home while one of my coworkers watched *Donahue* with the volume up too high.

I felt more exhausted than I'd ever felt in my life. Not just tired, but totally sucked dry, like I was a machine—just this *thing* that performed its programmed tasks day after day after day. I wasn't sad or mad about it, I just felt *empty*.

And then the room went totally silent, no more *Donahue*, and I looked over to see if my coworker had turned off the TV, but I was no longer in the break room at K-Mart. I was lying in the backyard of my childhood home, collapsed in a heap next to my mother's vegetable garden.

"Sharon," said a voice above me. "Stand up."

I turned my head and saw a fourteen-year-old version of myself standing there.

"Sharon," she said. "Stand up."

With some effort, I stood up and we faced each other. Looking into her face—*my* face from so many years ago—I remembered that part in the Doctrine and Covenants that says if you ever meet an otherworldly being, you're supposed to shake its hand to find out if it's a messenger from God or from Satan. So, I held out my hand.

"I'm not shaking your hand," the young me said.

I couldn't remember if that was the right response or the wrong response, but I figured that either way, I needed to keep my wits about me.

"What is this?" I asked.

"Follow me," she said, and walked toward the house.

I followed.

Inside, I found, not my childhood home, but a dining room I'd never seen before. Around a long, wooden table sat a group of men, women, and children I didn't know, but who looked uncomfortably familiar. They wore church clothes and big smiles and seemed really pleased to be in each other's company. Judging by the scraps of food hardening on their plates, they'd finished eating long ago.

What stopped me short, though, was a woman in her sixties standing just out of sight of the people at the table, her hand gripping the edge of a doorframe, knuckles white, a look of absolute horror on her face. It took me a few seconds to realize that this terrified woman was an older version of *me*.

That really pushed me over the edge. I caught at the sleeve of the fourteen-year-old me and asked her what was wrong with the older me standing in the doorway.

"You forgot to pick up a kitten from Sister Marsh," the younger me said, which was a true statement but not an answer to my question.

All those years earlier I *had* forgotten about Sister Marsh's offer. It had been overshadowed, understandably, by Gran's death. I seriously doubted, though, that this sixty-year-old version of myself could be that distraught over a squandered chance, several decades in the past, to adopt a kitten.

I tried to clarify this with my guide.

"No," I said to her. "I'm asking why she's so *afraid*."

The fourteen-year-old me shook her head.

"You forgot to pick up a kitten from Sister Marsh," she said again.

Before I could ask my question a third time, everything in the dining room went crooked, and I was lying on the ground, the younger version of myself kneeling next to me and babbling incoherently. I closed my eyes, the lids so heavy, and when I opened them again, I was slumped over on the stiff couch of the K-Mart break room. *Donahue* was still blaring on the TV, and my coworker hadn't noticed my episode, or whatever it was. At first, I tried to write it off as an inadvertent nap—I was *so* tired, after all—but then I noticed, much to my shame and confusion, that I'd wet my pants and somehow removed my shoes.

This concerned me enough that I went to see a doctor as soon as I could. After asking me some questions and running some tests, she concluded that there was nothing seriously wrong with me.

"You just need to get some rest," she said.

"Tell me something I don't know," I said.

Anyway, in the twenty-five-odd years that followed, nothing like that episode in the break room ever happened to me again.

So. As many of you know, my husband, Bill, passed away just a few months ago. The roads were icy and Bill's Impreza got T-boned by some poor kid who couldn't stop in time. They were both injured pretty badly, but the kid eventually survived, and Bill didn't. It was awful—just *so* awful—for the kid and for me and, obviously, for Bill.

It's all kind of a blur, to be honest. All five of my sons came in from out of town, brought their families, and that was—maybe not a silver lining, but so lovely to have my whole family together under one roof, which hadn't happened in years. My whole family minus Bill, I should say.

In any event, something you need to understand is that I've always loved my sons. Not just loved them but really *liked* them, which isn't to say there haven't been rough patches with some of them, especially when they were growing up. But, on the whole, my sons have brought so much joy and pleasure to my life. Having all of them around me at such a difficult time brought me a lot of comfort. Or I guess what I mean is, I *thought* it would bring me a lot of comfort.

The boys *did* help out a lot with the logistics of the funeral and, of course, the talks they gave, and all that. The evening of the funeral, though, we had dinner at the condo where Bill and I had been living for the past few years. As we ate leftovers from the luncheon, there was something about the way my boys were talking about Bill that was starting to get under my skin.

85

I know they were sad that their father had died, but the way they were talking about him, it was like he was just over in the next room, rather than moldering in his grave. So much talk about how thankful they were for the gospel, how blessed we were to know we'd all see Bill again one day, that his spirit might even be watching over us as we shared this meal together. And by the look on their faces, they were just so at *peace*, every single one of them. And I, suddenly, was *not*. Instead, I was filled with a kind of violent disgust with every single person at that table.

I think part of it was my grief catching up to me—I'd just felt kind of numb since I'd gotten the news about the accident—but it was also bigger than that. The fact that my family was responding to what happened to Bill with something other than total collapse was personally offensive to me, just infuriating.

My reaction scared me—the strength of it, the way it felt like it would never go away.

I'm not sure if I gave an excuse or if I just stood up, but I remember I walked away from the table as quickly as I could while that anger and fear saturated my body. It was so bad, so profound, I had to brace myself against the doorway—like all my cells were being replaced by particles of pure hatred.

As I stood there gripping the doorframe, I was hit with the terrible realization that *this* was the vision I'd been shown in the break room of the K-Mart all those years ago. Some higher power had been aware of what would happen to Bill, and how I would respond to my children's shallow excuse for grief, and had decided to reveal that eventuality to me decades before the fact.

But why? This was no tender mercy, no supernal show of comfort and support. This was a divine taunt, some vast, feline intelligence toying with the most precious parts of my life, reminding me of my powerlessness and of its own infinite, untouchable cunning.

Still standing in the doorway, I let the waves of rage and disgust and terror wash over me until I had enough self-possession to sit back down at the table. For another few hours—or maybe it was just a few minutes—I gritted my teeth against my children's vapid yammering until finally the party broke up and I watched with relief as each of them walked out the door.

86

Brothers and sisters, I want to believe in a God who loves me, in a God who takes a kind and merciful interest in the minutia of my life, but that's not a belief I can testify of today, not in good conscience. Instead, I testify, with my great-grandmother, that God is to be regarded with wariness and suspicion.

I'd also like you to know that over time, this understanding has not filled me with fear or despair, but has given me instead a sense of clarity and purpose as I face my eternal Antagonist.

So, thank you for listening, and amen.

UNHANDED

JENNIFER QUIST

With dogs and with aerosol clouds blown from the vapors of their lungs, people walk the trails along the Sturgeon River. It is December in the year of the plague, snow deep and dry everywhere but on the paths where the city park maintenance machines have shoved it aside. Keep to the trails. The snow, the plague—do not impose your selfishness on them.

It is eleven o'clock, well into the eighteen hours of daily darkness at this latitude. The other walkers have all gone indoors now, and this is when we emerge. There is only the pair of us rounding the turn at the foot of Poundmaker Road, the oldest road in town, its eastern limit separated from the river after centuries by the ploughed park trails and a gazebo.

At least the gazebo bats are gone, hibernating in the mountains. At least this, at least that, all year long.

There's wind, arctic air coming across the river, as it does. It means he won't hold my hand any longer. It's not personal. He brought the wrong gloves, the fancy ones from his work coat. The wind chills through their leather to the untanned flesh of his hands inside, hurting.

Don't hurt. I unhand him and he tucks his fingers into his pockets. It is minus eighteen Celsius. Any colder and we would not have come out—not this early in the season. The wind sharpens the cold, unbearable for some. And for others …

On the trail along the frozen river, at the amputated northern end of Poundmaker Road, I am not wearing gloves, and this is not unusual. Truly, until he'd pulled his aching fingers away, I'd thought nothing of my bare hands. They are not numb, but warm. I am laughing and pressing my fingers to his cold cheek, the palm and then the back of my hand where the needle pierces on clinic days.

This is me flaunting the warmth I hold in hands that have been dangling out of my down-filled sleeves, out in the weather. It's a joke I have with our kids. If I were a superhero, I'd be Hot-Hands.

He hates it, knowing there is no joke. The secret source of my power is tumor necrosis factor-α, and my true superhero identity is Cytokine-Storm.

The heat in my hands is the effect of the drugs, vial to vein, keeping the storm at a low rumble. The drugs mediate between me and my mad immune system now that my body is a false Christ—wild for my salvation, caught in the first phase of inflaming itself, burning everything down, never able to finish and rebuild. Always resurrecting, never resurrected.

My medicine is not made but grown, harvested like a living thing—sacrificial, clonal, chimeral, mice, and me. It is not a savior, just a stopper—a grey, hairy monster hand on the arm of the false Christ, nudging it to stand down.

My medicine is how I am still upright and in front of him, walking in the empty park together, only ever after dark, on our own since the plague came. In the night, pestilence is less with us, but never gone—traces of it like tiny prints of mouse feet on top of the snow. The plague reaches out to join hands with my monster, lacing fingers, holding. My immune system is drugged down; an opportunity.

He and I finish the walk without holding hands, though I may take his arm for the benefit of our four feet when the trail slopes downhill, slippery.

There was a lesson in the Sunday schools of my childhood, a metaphor for dying and being dead. The living soul is a hand in a glove: both the hand and the glove. At death, the glove slips off, laid down like the gloves we have all seen lying frozen, stiff, and filthy in parking lots and sidewalks, fallen unseen from a pocket and left alone. The bare hand is the spirit of the dead flying off to paradise, held there, waiting for a miracle at the end of the world when everything lost is thawed, purified, returned.

No gloves—like a Sunday school spirit-hand—in the wind holding onto his arm, I am warm, fey, sick but not to death, out on the plague-walker trails.

*

He doesn't want to walk tonight though it is warmer, just below zero degrees. It is darker but there are more Christmas lights strung on the trees and rain gutters now. I could make a snowball for my hands to melt. We could stand out on the footbridge, the little one that sways when we bring all the kids with us, which we won't because, as always, it is very late. Still, it could be nice.

She should not be afoot in the dark city alone. She is me. And it means he can't say "no" without confining me, oppressing; and he just can't. Instead, he asks how long it will take.

It's not good enough. I have spent the day, all days, with our children. They have been run out of their schools by a combination of the plague and my heightened vulnerability to it. I carry them on my back between the spaces where we live from the moment the first video call starts at 6:30 in the morning. After all that, I will have my plague walk.

I tell him I am going alone, and he follows me down the stairs as if we are mittens connected by a string. He steps into his shoes after all. It's fine. Let's go. It's alright.

It is not, and I tell him not to come. I don't want him. I want to do something for a few minutes that doesn't affect anyone else, and there hasn't been anything like that inside our house for a very long time.

I tell him this even though I know, whether he walks with me or not, my going will affect him. He is in his coat, saying he accepts my decision to go alone and wants a short walk of his own in the same neighborhood. Maybe we'll run into each other.

No. I rush outside while he's still pawing through the box of toques and scarves, looking for gloves like something properly embodied. I dart down the shortcut, leaving Poundmaker Road to him. This is the path the kids once used to walk to their bus stop, before. At the bus stop, I follow the long, straight, uphill path between the backyard fences where we saw the porcupine that one time.

Only the city's mammals come out at night. Jack rabbits and coyotes. Men too—always men, wherever and whenever they please. I push on anyway. I am Cytokine-Storm. What is there for me to fear?

I want music but I haven't brought earphones, so I hold my phone in my bare, warm hand and play it into the open air. The snow has softened the landscape, like acoustic foam laid over roofs and lawns. The music in the street is mellowed, spreading out from me like warm butter as I walk. There is no one here. In the insulated emptiness I dare to take so much space. There is meaning in the sound and lyrics—gentle, warning, and pleading.

Girl, don't start feelin' a Way.

I watch for him over my shoulder until I reach the intersection where our short walks always end. And then I walk on.

This is our long walk, farther than the loop around the gazebo. The pavement passes through the center of a still-undeveloped tract of land, an urban hayfield where the Instagram people come for photos against round bales of alfalfa. For me, the smell of hay is ever his hometown. Tonight, it is buried in snow.

From the pavement, in the daylight, the round bales capped with white look like breakfast cereal, shredded wheat. Nighttime dimness smooths their contours, and they are more like stones from cartoon Easter art—flannel board story pieces, sepulcher doors rolled onto the field and left here, nowhere near a tomb.

I can see each round door, can count them, even in the night. The atmosphere is frozen into trillions of tiny particles, crystals suspended overhead. They reflect the white of the snow, the yellow of the streetlight, and filter them through deep, dark blue. The glow is a cosmic green; not the slow fall of Northern Lights, but like it.

This passage through the hayfield is where I am most likely to meet a coyote, neither of us wanting the fairy-tale horror of it. The coyotes will know better how to miss me if I make the music louder. The song is by a woman my age from Toronto with a good dad and great boots. I wish I liked it more.

Past the gauntlet of the hayfields, I mount the steep hill up to the Holy Family Catholic Church. Its nativity display is seasonal tonight, but will last throughout the year, lit even when our eighteen hours of darkness flips to eighteen hours of daylight.

The parking lot sprawling around the church is oversized in anticipation of Easter and Christmas and teenage driving lessons. In its center, a man sits in a pickup truck. The engine is off, but the headlights and interior lights are on, his door cracked open, outlined in a deep yellow glow, venting his plague into the cold.

I will not give him more than a glance. He is the only human I have seen since I left the house, and I wonder, earnestly but casually, if this is when I die, how I die, with a rush of my great heat, steaming mice streaming from my body.

I swing my arms so my steps are quicker. The man may not see me through the glare of his dome lights on the glass. Or maybe he has seen me and is waiting, half-emerged, gathering strength to encroach.

My wondering takes a name, finds its pattern, performs its unending work. A prayer: *Father, don't let him see me.* Just in case.

The churchyard is lit with flood lights set in the ground, housed in sandstone blocks, the snow melted. The lights double and triple my shadow on the snowbanks—not invisible but magnified, multiplied. I lift my face to the church nativity: brass figures of stepfather, Son, and Holy Mother against a stone wall, halos lit red.

What I want to say about my hands, in everything that has gone before, is only this.

I stayed with the body of my father when he died. It happened in my mother's kitchen after the table was moved away, a hospital bed rolled into its place. It happened in the weeks after that. Hand coming out of its glove slowly with shouts of Hosanna when all we wanted was an amen.

The body was noisy, even after. I would not unhand him. While we waited for the funeral van, I held his arm in my bare hands, and I could not feel him, not as he was, not as dead. I stood in my own way. What I felt when I touched him with my hot hands was not his but mine: my pulse in my fingertips.

Do not say to me that all this time I have felt nothing but the distal beat of my own heart in my fingertips.

*

My long walk ends in safety, in peace. I come home to find him upstairs reading on the bed, but still dressed at midnight. We will not speak of my leaving. I will not speak of the footprints on the driveway, mine going one way, his another. For now, we will not speak of anything.

For an hour, I have been outside, alone and noisy in crystal green darkness, hands uncovered, in and out of sight, never safe, not unsaved. My cheeks are flushed, my legs stiff with cold and the river valley's hills.

He must know. I don't think two people could be happier than we have been, than we are tonight. Over the top of his book, I raise my fingers to the curve of his closed mouth, my touch beating, storming with cytokines and medicine, mice and the blood of my fathers, warm. The lamp at his elbow clicks. In the darkness, our halos will be red.

94

MRS. SEPPE

HEIDI NAYLOR

Mrs. Seppe, I can tell. You are just a wonderful lady. So kind, and really very sweet. Mrs. Seppe, I'm wishing I could meet you in person.

Oh, well. Thank you. But you don't really know me. I don't know how you can say ...

I can tell by the way you're talking. I can tell that you will make thoughtful choices with this money.

Mister, um ... Oh, I'm very sorry, I don't recall your name.

It's Joshua Jackson, ma'am. You can call me Mr. Jackson if you're more comfortable. I'm an officer with the Editor's Surplus Sweepstakes. You know, I've been doing this for years—I mean, I'm richly blessed to have this job—and I've found that some people are most comfortable with a more formal mode of address. And I get that. This is a big, big moment! Mrs. Seppe, what did you want to ask?

Well, I just want to say ... I want to tell you that I don't know what I could possibly do with all that money.

A lot of good, Mrs. Seppe. A *lot* of good!

You know, Mr. Jackson, I've been entering the Editor's Surplus Sweepstakes ... well, for as long as I can remember.

That sounds like it might be several years, ma'am, if I could be so bold. And I must say. For *years*, Mrs. Seppe? You're very persistent.

95

Oh yes. For many years! I've got a little trick up my sleeve. It's that I always send back special envelopes. Colored envelopes! Anytime I could find a pretty one in green or turquoise or pink. Did you know, Mr. Jackson, when you buy birthday cards, you can find the prettiest envelopes? But you can also find plain white ones at Target or Staples. So, I buy up a quantity of plain ones and then I switch out the envelopes that came with the cards, you see. Because really, people don't care about the envelope, just the card.

I'm not a letter writer so much, Mr. Jackson—that's become something of a lost art, wouldn't you say?—but I do like to send a nice card. And then I would keep the colored one for the sweep—

Mrs. Seppe, *this*. Connecting with people through the mail; brightening their day *through the United States Postal Service.* That giant bureaucracy. Few people do that in this day and age; few indeed. This is exactly how I know you are such a lovely person.

Well, thank you! It's very kind of you … And, well, I don't know, sir, I just like to stay in touch. What was I saying? I was … well …

Oh! Yes. I've fooled you, Mr. Jackson. The reason was not about connecting with people at all. No. The reason was that I could send my sweepstakes entries in the colored envelopes! I read somewhere that my entry should always stand out in some way. So, this was one of my little tricks.

Yes, that was a smart strategy.

It makes my entry easier to choose, isn't that right?

Obviously, it was a great strategy, Mrs. Seppe. Look at you now! That strategy helped you win!

I … I just can't believe I've won. I tell you; I've never won anything in my life.

You have won! You're our winner, Mrs. Seppe. We couldn't be any happier about it.

Oh, you know, Mr. Jackson. Something deep inside me knew this might happen one day. I'm kind of a dreamer. I always have been. I've wanted to win the Editor's Surplus ever since I can remember. I've dreamed about how my life would change.

Mrs. Seppe. Your. Life. Has. *Changed.* You've waited a long time. You've done everything right. You're exactly the person we love to present with this award.

Yes. [as though from far away] *I* have *waited a long time. I've … I've felt in my* soul *that this might happen. I've felt that I would be a winner, somehow, in the end, even though I never* did *actually win.*

But really … we've been awfully, very blessed in our life and our family. Oh, Mr. Jackson, honestly, we don't need this money.

No. Obviously you've managed things very well, ma'am. If you've got the time and the inclination to do for others, as I know you do, then you've managed your affairs very well.

But we could do … we could do some things I've always wanted to do. We could leave a real inheritance for our children. Mr. Jackson, I have seven children. They're all doing fine. But, in all honesty, some of our children have been more fortunate than others.

Seven! My goodness, ma'am. You're an American hero! And I know things don't turn out quite fair sometimes. Perhaps this money could ease your mind on that score.

Oh, my goodness. I just … I just … Mr. Jackson, how much money did you say I've won?

Mrs. Seppe, you've won thirteen million dollars. That's seven thousand per week for the rest of your life.

Oh, mister. Oh, mister. Oh my. Oh, Mr. Jackson.

It's a staggering amount. Take a moment to let it sink in.

Yes. Oh, I'm trembling. Oh, listen, just listen *to my voice … I'm shaking.*

Mrs. Seppe, are you sitting down? Are you alright?

Mrs. Seppe?

Yes. Yes, Mr. Jackson. Oh, I'm here. You know, my husband has always provided a good living. Don't please think he hasn't! He's the smart one. I am a careful spender; that's what I've always brought to the marriage since our children were born. I pride myself on that. I watch the coupons very carefully. I keep an extra freezer and a well-stocked pantry. I come from the salt of the earth. Humble, hard-working people who worried, Mr. Jackson, who understood that one day there might be trouble, or disaster. There would come those days where you'd have to add a little water to the soup. We're all about family, Mr. Jackson. We don't want any empty chairs in heaven.

And yet. Well. Even so, I have a daughter with a certain challenge, Mr. Jackson. She is, well, she is … simply … plagued with drug abuse. Illicit drugs. People might think it's shameful, but she's my daughter and you take the good with the bad. We love her. Of course, we do. There are times we don't know where she is living …

Mrs. Seppe, I'm very sorry to hear that.

She still pops in from time to time …

I mean, I'm glad that you still see h—

Yes, oh yes! That's what matters. As long as they're still breathing, Mr. Jackson, there's so much hope. We worked diligently to raise our children in the church. We are aware of a larger picture. And Satan is laboring just as diligently to thwart goodness, to replace it with evils like illicit drug abuse. Our daughter is a good person, deep in her heart, and maybe there's a way this money can help her regain her footing.

How gratifying that would be! Mrs. Seppe, I'd like to explain a little more about sending you the money.

Do you know that when our daughter was in her teens, she was the princess of—oh, what did my grandson call it—the … the side hustle. That's it! Oh, what a blessing when you can find the word!

Yes, Susaleigh used to babysit. Oh, people wanted her to tend their children because she was sweet. And fun. So much fun. A complete light!

She made beaded jewelry. And she would set out a little stand with our card table, the dearest little sign she made. Her pretties attached carefully to little manila cards. All of it so clean and bright. What a gem she was! What a little sprite.

Who could think of her tending children now?

Oh, but one time she made me a beautiful garnet bracelet. But then she ... well, she started in on this black corded jewelry, and then ... honestly, all her jewelry-making became clogged up. Darker. She made a necklace with thick leather and studs, like a ... like a dog collar. She just hammered in those big, pointed, ugly studs.

I tried to see that as clever. I knew that Susaleigh was really very clever.

But how could I ever get comfortable with her wearing a dog collar? I tell you, Mr. Jackson. I could not.

No? Well, but children are such a gift. I didn't have that blessing in life. I envy you, ma'am. And it's not for your winnings; no ma'am. It's the *meaning* that children bring.

But, Mrs. Seppe, money has meaning too. And about this money. As an officer here, I've been doing this a long time. There are some details we must attend to. We should be getting those details ironed out.

Oh. Yes, of course. Oh, I'm sorry. Please go ahead.

I'd like to send you an email with some clear, simple instructions. Plus, there are a few dates and other details on the email you'll need to see.

Oh. Yes. Oh, my goodness. An email. That's on the computer.

Yes. Mrs. Seppe, can you give me your email address?

Why yes, I can do that, Mr. Jackson.

But, oh. Oh, you see, I don't really do computers. I mean, I have an email, but it's really very old and I don't use it. I don't know how to find it on the screen. The email. That screen is such a jumble to me! I look at it and I'm completely nonplussed. Confused, is what I mean. You know, you touch a key and all those little blocks come tumbling, just diving across that screen. Those tiny little pictures. You can move your arrow above them, but which do you pick? My husband knows. I can't hold that in my head. It's all I can do to manage my medications. The kids' birthdays. [laughs] There are so many now.

I assure you I can always name the president of the United States. We're very patriotic.

My husband makes sure I can see the messages I'd be interested in. I hope you understand. I'll get him to print it out for me. Your emailed letter.

That's fine, Mrs. Seppe. Can you provide me the email address then?

Yes. Let's see. I think it's …

Yes? The email, Mrs. Seppe?

Oh, Mr. Jackson, my mind's a whirl. *The winning and everything. I don't know. It's been some time since I came up with that email address. I can remember when you would go to connect, and you'd hear that little dial and the squeak, the whirrrr … Many years since then! My address has my birthday in it, that's for sure. Or it might be my daughter's birthday. My daughter loves her birthday because it's got a pommodore in it.*

A what?

Oh, what's that word, when the backwards is the same as the forwards?

I'm afraid you've lost me, Mrs. Seppe.

It's like a mirror birthday. A pommel horse? Surely not! A … pommelo? Oh, Mr. Jackson, I don't know. But I think it's in my email!

I wonder, can your husband help you find it?

Yes. Oh, I'm sure he can! He's perfectly nimble *on the computer. But he's out just now. He's doing Meals on Wheels, Mr. Jackson. Oh, my husband loves to get involved, to stay busy. He likes to get out every day. He's a wonderful man, Mr. Jackson. I hit the jackpot with him.*

Out of all the daughters in my natal family—there are a lot of us! A family of sistren! That's a little church joke for you, Mr. Jackson, brethren and sistren—I got the best husband. I don't know what I did in the pre-existence to deserve him. Do you know he delivers to four different households, three days every week? *And then, too, he's a ministering brother for our church.*

I do some of the ministering too. It used to be a program with another name, but now we call it the ministering. They change the terms sometimes; it's hard to keep up. Like ministering angels. We are the Lord's hands, if we can be. His angels.

Mrs. Seppe, I've gotten lost again. The pre-existence?

Oh, now you've done it, Mr. Jackson. I'd love to tell you about the pre-existence. You see, before we were born, we lived with heavenly parents, and they presented a beautiful plan to—

A plan, yes! Don't you see? Can't you imagine that this money was likely part of that plan? *Nothing* is happenstance! Mrs. Seppe, with being a pre-minister and all, can I say that you and your husband are clearly an amazing couple! We're so thrilled that you've won this money. How can I get it to—

You know, with the size of our family, we've never had any extra. We've got plenty, and thank heaven we can travel a bit, visit our children, most of them, the ones with homes to live in, with actual addresses. We can visit them and have our fun. But I've always wondered what it would be like, Mr. Jackson, to really have some capital.

Ma'am, if you can't recall the email address, I have another option for you.

Oh good. That's great. What a relief! Because I don't think I can! Find it, I mean.

Yes. No problem. I can send my written message to your local Office Depot. Do you have an Office Depot nearby?

Yes, we do. It's in the Ryddington Complex.

Very good. … It's in the what?

The Ryddington Complex! My shopping center. I go there all the time. My husband says I go there to get "ryd" of all our money. Another joke

101

for you, Mr. Jackson! At Ryddington, there's a Trader Joe's and a Gross-Out Market. I mean a Grocery Outlet. The best deals there. And a moldy bread store.

A what?

A store that sells the moldy bread. Only it's not moldy, it's just the day-old bread. One of our daughters named it the moldy bread store. You know, she is just so funny. She's got such a quick wit. And she's ... well ... I'm sorry to get a little teary, Mr. Jackson. But it's just that she's the daughter with all the trouble.

Yes. I'm sorry. Perhaps a rehabilitation effort, Mrs. Seppe? Some sort of intervention.

Her name is Susaleigh. Isn't that the most beautiful name? It sounded to us like the Zuiderzee, a river in Holland where my husband served his mission. Susaleigh Seppe. Some music there in her name. He was a missionary for our church, many years ago. Before I even met him. Decades! How they fly by.

And we always planned to serve another mission. We've been meaning to get around to that, Mr. Jackson, and it still may happen. It just may happen! But I couldn't leave my daughter in such straits. Who knows when she might come round again? And us not here to welcome her. We named her for a river, and a river flows forever. My beautiful Susaleigh.

Mrs. Seppe—let's talk about—

Actually, Mr. Jackson, I'm not really sure it's a river. It may be part of the ocean. Or the lochs, like the loch where the little boy stuck his finger in to stop the flood. It's all the same area. And a lovely, lovely idea about the eternal river.

Surely ma'am, it is. And now—about that Office Depot.

Oh! Yes. Can you send the money to the Office Depot for me to pick up? The one in the Ryddington Center?

I've found it, ma'am. Ryddington Center Office Depot, Fawn

Grove, Connecticut. Yes, I can send it. You could drive there to pick up the instructions?

Mr. Jackson. Is that safe?

Well, I think so. Are you able to drive, Mrs. Seppe? Do you have a driver's license?

Surely, I can. Yes, of course, Mr. Jackson. I'm an old woman, but I'm perfectly capable.

Yes, Mrs. Seppe. It's just that you asked me if it was safe to go.

[sniffs] *I meant was it safe to send the money there. You can't be too careful!*

Oh yes, it's safe. The portal includes a secure link. Your message is sent with a cover sheet, and it's placed in a secure envelope. We are *all* about your security, Mrs. Seppe.

As for driving, I'm perfectly safe. I haven't had a ticket in years! Not since the time Susaleigh had a dance recital in Torrington and I forgot to pack her costume. I had her duffle with me, and I picked her up from school, and she looked to see that duffle empty. How her face crumpled. It just dissolved *into tears. We had to go back and get her costume, and she was very sweet about it, really. But, oh, to be on time we went flying along McMillan Highway and got stopped. And do you know, Mr. Jackson, that's when I knew I'd gotten old. For the first time, I was unable to talk the officer into letting me off with a warning.*

Yes. [chuckles] I suppose we all get to that point, Mrs. Seppe.

If we're lucky, Mr. Jackson. Only if we're lucky! I batted my eyes like the best of them, but he went ahead and gave me a ticket anyway! I had no charm left. No, none at all! I wasn't very lucky that day.

Mrs. Seppe, *today* you are lucky! And let me assure you that you are in fact *very* charming. I can easily wait on the phone, ma'am, while you drive—carefully, ma'am—to the Office Depot and retrieve the message. Listen carefully please. Just go to the customer service desk and provide your name and your identification—you do have a driver's license—and provide my name, Mr. Joshua Jackson, an officer of the Editor's Surplus. They'll have the email in a secure envelope for you.

Mr. Jackson, what if they read the email message? Isn't there a danger they could get the money?

No ma'am. For one thing, it's against the law for anyone to read your emails without some sort of warrant. It's illegal for them to look at it. Even a little. This is an accepted business practice, I assure you.

Yes.

And for another, the message is meant for you and requires a secure identification. Not only to pick it up, but to take the next step.

Oh dear. [trembling voice] *I'm beside myself. I don't know if I can find my keys.* [rummaging a little; drops the phone] *Mr. Jackson, are you still with me?*

Yes, of course, Mrs. Seppe.

I'm a headless chicken, Mr. Jackson. Just stepped right outside my mind. Still. I will do my best. I need to take a moment.

Of course, Mrs. Seppe. I'll be waiting.

Yes. Thank you for being so patient with me. I owe you my life, Mr. Jackson. I'll just be on my way. I have my keys now. Goodbye, Mr. Jackson. I mean, goodbye for now. Oh, do you know, I almost hung up the phone! Oh, my goodness. I'm just going to leave it dangling here. Or, not dangling, that's from corded days! I mean, days with those ringlet cords!

How my daughters used to stretch those cords out, talking to their boyfriends. But my Susaleigh … she didn't do that so much. She was a little more lonely, bless her heart. Her birthday was 0220, that's what it was! A palindrome. I remember now! And, anyway, no more cords! We've entered the twenty-first century! I'll just set the phone on the counter.

That's fine, Mrs. Seppe. I'll be waiting on the other end. You drive carefully now.

Mr. Jackson, would you mind, just in case I can't get back somehow. Oh, I'm in such a whirl, I just don't want to get into a fender-bender! Is there a number where I could reach you?

Of course, Mrs. Seppe. Take a moment to calm down. If we just move forward, we have seven days in which you can accept this money. Please don't worry. Let's do it this afternoon. But here's my number, and I want you to remember to stay calm.

Yes. The money's no good if I'm dead on the highway, is it, Mr. Jackson?

No indeed. I've been doing this a long time, Mrs. Seppe. I can assure you, staying calm is the best policy in this situation. Is there someone you might ask to drive you to the Ryddington Center?

No, no. I'm alright.

Let me give you my number. Do you have a pen and paper?

Yes, I do. I've got it right here. Please go ahead.

[gives her an 11-digit number]

Thank you, Mr. Jackson. I'm carefully setting the phone on the counter. I've got my purse and my identification. I'm practically driving off. It shouldn't be more than forty minutes. Thank you for your patience.

Mr. Jackson, are you there?

Of course, Mrs. Seppe. I'm here. How did it go?

I have the message. Oh, it's right here. My goodness. I'm holding the envelope. With the seal. From Office Depot. It certainly looks official.

Take your time, ma'am. We are not in a rush.

I'd like to show this to my husband.

Certainly, Mrs. Seppe. Should we go through it together first?

Yes. Okay, yes. Do you know, my hands are shaking! I can hardly get it out of the envelope.

Take your time, ma'am. It's a momentous day.

Oh. It's here. Oh, my goodness. Oh, it looks real, too. Oh, this is happening. I feel ... I feel dizzy.

Oh, yes. I'm reading through these instructions. I see that the money, should I choose to accept it, the money will be deposited right into my bank.

Yes ma'am. That's the way it works.

Mr. Jackson. I'm just a puddle. A muddle. Let me think.

Mr. Jackson, do you no longer come to the house with the flowers and the check?

Certainly, we can do that, Mrs. Seppe. It's our pleasure to do that. But we've found that some people don't want the publicity. You never know what sorts of charlatans and crooks might be brought out of the woodwork at such a spectacle there in your neighborhood, right out on the street.

Yes. Yes. The hustlers.

How funny it is, the things that enter your mind. I have always wondered, for instance, about Cal's mission. I mean, they call it a Dutch mission. And they call it Holland. And they also call it the Neverlands. The Netherlands, I mean. There are some side hustles for you. It is enough to monkey with the best minds, I'll tell you that.

Ma'am, you've lost me just a—

Oh, what I could do for my Susaleigh with this money. I could help her see there's a pathway forward. She could go back to college. She could ... she could have another chance.

Do you know, I'd like to help other illicit drug users with this money. That's really what I'd like to do, Mr. Jackson.

Mrs. Seppe, once again, in all my years of doing this, it's such a pleasure to talk with someone such as yourself. A giver, Mrs. Seppe. This is exactly what we hope for. We don't often see it! Many people think only of themselves.

But Mr. Jackson. I really feel that I need to go over this material with my husband.

Of course, ma'am. You should do that. Is he there? I'd be delighted to talk with him myself if you'd like to go that route.

He will be home this evening, Mr. Jackson. Are we in a rush?

We have seven days, Mrs. Seppe. If you'd like, I can phone you again tomorrow at your convenience and talk with you after you've had a chance to discuss the paperwork. Or I can talk with the two of you together. It's really up to you. I can assure you; we are above board. I couldn't do the work I do unless I saw how it benefits people such as yourself, people who want to share their good fortune and ... bless—yes, *bless*—the lives of others.

That's the kind of thing I want to hear, Mr. Jackson. And I can certainly wait a few more days. Blessing the lives of others. That's what I have always, always wanted to do. From the bottom of my heart.

Mrs. Seppe. It is clear to me that God wants you to have this money.

Well. It's kind of you to say that. But I don't know as you—as any of us—can say what God wants.

No ma'am. It's just that clearly you are the right person.

I ... I feel that I want to give this some thought.

Of course, ma'am.

I need some time, Mr. Jackson.

We have a *little* time, Mrs. Seppe.

Thank you ... How much time do we have?

We have seven days, Mrs. Seppe. But I'd like to go step by step, so we don't come down to the wire on this thing.

Yes. That sounds right.

Mrs. Seppe, why don't you talk this over with your husband tonight. Show him the materials we sent you; the ones you picked up at Office Depot.

Yes.

Then, if you two agree, I'll plan to phone you tomorrow at 10 a.m. Will your husband be there?

Yes. He should be here.

We can chat then, Mrs. Seppe. Does that sound alright?

Oh. Well. Will you really call?

On my honor as an officer, ma'am, I will certainly call you. And just to be sure, I've given you my number, you remember.

Yes. I have it here.

I'll talk with you tomorrow, Mrs. Seppe. You have a pleasant evening now. Goodbye.

Goodbye.

*

Hello?

Mrs. Seppe! This is Joshua Jackson from the Editor's Surplus Sweepstakes. It's good to hear your voice, ma'am.

Mr. Jackson!

Yes. We're going to finalize your winnings today.

Yes, Mr. Jackson. I was expecting your call.

Good. Mrs. Seppe, how was your night? Are you getting used to the idea of being a winner?

Oh. Why yes, I had a good n— Actually, Mr. Jackson, I didn't sleep a wink! I just ... I just am beside *myself. I can't believe this has happened.*

Congratulations, Mrs. Seppe. [laughs softly] I am just so delighted that it's *you*, ma'am. I love what I do, and I've been doing this a long time. But you take the cake, Mrs. Seppe. You are just the person we are delighted to award.

Oh, well, thank you, *Mr. Jackson. I talked with my husband. He did some research on the wide world web. He says it is not typical for you to call when this award is given.*

No ma'am. I'm sorry to contradict him, but it *is* typical. Or, I should say, it has become typical. In fact, it's been my privilege to make dozens of these calls over the years.

He says what you do is come to the door with a prize check. And a balloon. And flowers. Just as I mentioned yesterday.

Mrs. Seppe, I assure you this money will allow you to celebrate in any manner you choose. Balloons and flowers to the hilt!

It's not that, Mr. Jackson. Of course. No, it's the matter of our communication. It's the matter of providing you sensitive information over the phone, without meeting anyone in person.

You know, we did used to do that, just as your husband said. Come to the door. But expenses being what they are; and we discovered that many people just don't want the publicity. It's become more feasible for us to make the awards this way. I can assure you this award is real. And the website portal is secure. You'll notice a need to notarize all your information. You'll notice the legal disclaimers on the paperwork.

Mrs. Seppe, let me ask you this: would you like me to talk with your husband?

No, no, Mr. Jackson. Well, I might. But to be clear about it, my husband doesn't wish to get involved. He's made it obvious to me that this is my decision. This money ... this situation is one he's happy to let me handle. I can make the decision.

I see he places a lot of confidence in you.

I ... surely we trust one another, and we've learned to leave one another to it, if you see what I mean. He will honor my decision. That's the way we work it, Mr. Jackson, and I feel that ... well, last night when I couldn't sleep, I went to the scriptures.

Ma'am? I'm something of a Bible dabbler myself.

Oh, Mr. Jackson! How I love the Bible. You know, the Bible teaches us about money. The Lord says—I read this last night—actually made a list of scriptures about money (I'm a list maker, Mr. Jackson. You should see the fluttering pages on my refrigerator; they're perfectly wispy.)—it says, "Take heed and beware of covetousness: for a man's life consisteth not in the abundance of the things which he possesseth."
And then there's a story about a man whose soul is required of him the very night he plans on expanding his lands and crops.

Yes, Mrs. Seppe. The Bible has many lessons. I, myself, am partial to the story of the one-eyed Cyclops. It doesn't surprise *me* that you rely on the Bible. No, ma'am. And if there's a message from the Bible, it is that time is of the essence. I'd surely like to get on with the conveyance of this money to your hands.

The man says to himself, "Soul, thou hast much goods laid up for many years ... it is time to take thine ease and be merry."

Mrs. Seppe, perfect! Doesn't the Bible teach us that good things come to those who wait? Who work and wait, as you have done?

Well, yes, it does. Does it? I suppose it might say that somewhere.
But very next, Mr. Jackson, Heavenly Father tells the man he is a fool, that this *night shall thy soul be required of thee. And all his lands and riches are no good to him anymore.*

Mrs. Seppe. My dear. You are nothing like that man. Your soul is already very high quality. Why, think what you told me about wanting to do so much good with this money!

Yes. I would like to.

Rest assured about your soul. And now, let's go through the materials together. If you change your mind, of course, it will be necessary for us to choose another winner. You have the printout from Office Depot?

Yes. Why, yes, I have it here.

You can see that there are just a few simple forms, Mrs. Seppe. These forms tell us that you are who you say … who we believe you to be, with a witness—a notary. To be honest with you, I'm willing to forego the notary. I feel very certain of who you are, Mrs. Seppe. And then they provide the conveyance information and ask you to authorize us to provide you the winnings.

Yes. I'm looking at the forms right here. It says you need my account information … But of course, you would need that, wouldn't you, to know where to deposit the money.

Yes ma'am. I can assure you, it's very secure. I give you my word.

Integrity is so important, Mr. Jackson. Oh! Where, where is … right at my elbow … the rest of that scripture: "Sell that ye have, and give alms; provide yourselves bags which wax not old, a treasure in the heavens that faileth not, where no thief approacheth."

Yes, alms for the poor. Just as you said you'd like to do! But Mrs. Seppe? I feel you have stepped away somehow. I'd surely like to move forward.

Many good people have a lot of money, Mr. Jackson. Many.

It's true, Mrs. Seppe. That's the way of it. And the Lord rewards the good.

I have heard that. I have heard that when we obey, we will be made to

*prosper in the land. In fact, that scripture might be one of the items on
my list. Let me check here …*

Think of this money as a blessing. A gift based on the integrity of
your soul, Mrs. Seppe.

*I have wanted an opportunity like this all my life. I've always wanted
this. Think of all my sweepstakes entries! It's just like when my mother
used to save Green Stamps. She just knew they would come to fruition.
Still. After she passed on—once she graduated, as we say—and we
went through her things to settle her estate? There they were: boxes and
boxes of Green Stamps. Unused.*

A small tragedy, ma'am. How sad is that story.

*So many Green Stamps! And none of them redeemed, not one good for a
single thing.*

Yes. It's too bad. But that won't be you! You've earned this, Mrs.
Seppe. I feel it too. I said to myself last night, I am so grateful to
have been able to talk with such a goodhearted, salt-of-the-earth
lady as Mrs. Seppe. I'm so happy she's won! Think how very pleased
your mother is right now.

*I've … I've got to look at this scripture list again, Mr. Jackson. It took so
much of my time last night! I just felt it to be so important.*

Ma'am. Yes … Please take your time. I'm happy to listen.

*[reading] "But before ye seek for riches, seek ye for the kingdom of God.
And after ye have obtained a hope in Christ ye shall obtain riches, if ye
seek them; and ye will seek them for the intent to do good—to clothe the
naked, and to feed the hungry, and to liberate the captive, and adminis-
ter relief to the sick and the afflicted."*

That's … that's very good, Mrs. Seppe. Thank you for sharing that
with me. I'm sure—no—I *know*, as I've said, that you will use the
money well. We are so delighted!

Mr. Jackson. I just don't *know. You say that my soul is high quality. But*

112

I have to ask myself: Have I truly sought for the kingdom of God? That's the question. And I'm not sure. Why, just yesterday I got taken up—so taken up *with the thought of what this money could do. I could travel the world! I could replace my oven. I could get that beautiful Jenn-Air with the warming drawer, and all the dishes ready to eat at a moment's notice. I could set up funds for my grandchildren, for their schooling.*

They say money helps you forget. Do you know, when we bought life insurance for my husband so many years ago, the salesman told me how money can help you forget.

I have some troubles I would like very much to forget.

Yes ma'am. I believe we all do.

Of course, he was only trying to get us to buy as much insurance as possible.

Ma'am, with this money, you would be what we call self-insured.

Oh yes … Mr. Jackson, it makes me tired *to think about having charge of so much. Tired in a good way, I suppose!*

There are people to help you with the management, Mrs. Seppe. You could find a reputable financial advisor. And your husband. Though he respects your decisions, perhaps he would help you in the management.

Most people are reputable. I work hard to remember that. Not all, though. Not all. I often wonder. I have a lot of anger towards the young man who introduced Susaleigh to … to … oh.

And here's the biggest question for me. Have I truly obtained that hope in Christ? That's the question the Spirit seems to be asking me right now.

The spirit? You have a spirit with you right now? I'll tell you ma'am, I could do with some spirits right now!

[as from far away] I do believe in Christ. I believe, with my soul … but have I obtained this hope? Have I? How does one obtain … a hope in Christ?

It was just a little joke for you ma'am. Mrs. Seppe, we have gotten far afield. How can I—

It says, "Seek ye first *the kingdom of God." Have I done that? Have I really? After* all *that we've tried with our daughter. Have I sook ... have I sought ...*

[wearily] Surely, Mrs. Seppe, you are one of the finest people I've ever had the privilege of sending—

Oh, hell's bells, Mr. Jackson! Oh dear. I am sorry. That's something my mother used to say. And she was an angel on this Earth, but she did used to say that. I mean that I'm trying ... I'm trying, with all my high-quality soul, to think. *Give me a minute here.*

If you seek first the kingdom of God, then *you have a hope in Christ.*

Right. Ma'am. Thank you for reminding me.

And the next part is that when you have a hope in Christ, then if you obtain riches, you will use them to ...

Yes. What will you use them for, Mrs. Seppe? What did you tell me you would do?

I want to say I'd use them for good. But Mr. Jackson, it's all beyond me somehow. If I give Susaleigh money, what if she gets worse? *Oh, and you never could trust that girl with money. No, she is not to be trusted. The fact is, we did give her money. We helped her with money sometimes, many times! Many. It's what parents* do.

But each and every time, money just made it worse for her. She never did pay tuition with it. She never did get her car repaired or even her emissions checked. For Susaleigh, a little money just got her into a whole lot of darkness. A sleep. An ignorance, I hate to say. And a forgetting.

Mr. Jackson, I've realized something.

Yes. Look at the time. The time is just running away on a train, Mrs. Seppe. Is that what you've realized?

I've realized ... Oh, the time is *running. But what am I doing? Oh, Mr. Jackson. I wish I could call my daughter. The truth is that she never comes around. Never! I cannot find her and put my arms around her. I cannot wipe away her tears. I need—I hope—for Christ to do that.*

That's something money just can't buy, Mr. Jackson. That's something money can only make me forget, and that for just a little while. Like drugs make her forget. They take her someplace where she can't think of what's important. But then it comes crashing down around her. Jittery. Cold and itching, scratching, scrabbling, snarling; that awful torment. My beautiful daughter.

She can't stay in that place. No one can. Oh, forgive me for ever believing it could not happen to me, too, with this money. Take me to the same dark, tormented place.

My husband—bless his soul—bless him for leaving me this decision—he often says that he never wants to have so much money he couldn't stand to lose it. And … to think … how … we cannot stand to lose our daughter.

So, I must do … must … trust …

I can't forget my daughter, Mr. Jackson!

Mrs. Seppe, I wonder if—

You see … Seeking the kingdom of God means that we really are on our way to a more valuable sort of windfall. "Put aside the things of this world and seek for those of a better." It's written right here.

We can't be trusted with a bit on the side. And these winnings would be just that: a side hustle. Nothing but a wasted side hustle! Look at my life, Mr. Jackson. My wonderful husband. My children who make me proud. I have eight grandchildren—did I tell you that, Mr. Jackson?

Ma'am. I actually have no idea.

And I love Susaleigh not one whit less; not one jot less! Maybe even more. My beautiful daughter who's struggling. And I despair over her, Mr. Jackson. No hope. I'm not there. I must seek after something better. What if just this—exactly this hope is what will help her? I must obtain this hope in Christ.

Mrs. Seppe. Truly? If it's a matter of the forms, I can—

I'm unable to work with you in this matter. I appreciate your call so much. But I'm sure. I'm as sure as I've ever been. No. And definitely not. Thank you, Mr. Jackson.

Mrs. Seppe. Really? Take your time, ma'am. Here is an opportunity that won't return. People wait for years, decades, and they never … You told me yourself, you've waited all your life. I do not have the honor of calling everyone who is waiting.

I know. I know. I just … Oh, I just …

You have my number. We have up to seven days to certify this matter.

Mr. Jackson, thank you. But I won't be calling. I appreciate all you've offered me.

Mrs. Seppe, wait.

This is goodbye, Mr. Jackson. Thank you again.

Mrs. Seppe, think carefully now. This is once-in-a-lifetime. This is it. This changes lives.

…

Mrs. Seppe?

…

Mrs. Seppe?

THE CURSE

THERIC JEPSON

Nikos Gregopolis worked on merchant vessels. Although he had set foot in every port, island, and pier across Europe and up and down the east coast of the Americas by 1887, he did not care for any of these places. He went ashore mostly just to remember steady ground and why he lived on the sea. He might try some food or pay for a woman, but the full horizon was his homeland.

In Liverpool one Saturday night, he fell asleep drunk in a dark corner of a second-story space. He'd lost most of his money on cards, but what else was money for? He awoke to the sounds of shuffling boots and chairs being put into place. He looked through the legs of three or four tables onto a stained linen curtain. He tried to stand up, but his head ached and his balance was nil. On the sea the ship rises to meet you, but on land the floor is no help at all. He grabbed a table and pulled his torso atop it, then rested. People were speaking, but nothing was terribly clear. He couldn't remember what country he was in.

He dozed off, his head hanging from the table, and awoke again to the sound of hymns. Protestant hymns. In the north, then. Nikos got his feet under him and sidestepped gently along first one table edge then another until he reached the curtain. He paused to press knuckles into his eyes, breathe. Had he been breathing this whole time? It was hard to remember. What he needed was pure salt air. That would clear his head.

The song ended and one man spoke—sounded American— sounded like a prayer. Sure enough, the other voices responded

117

with an amen. Some more speech began and Nikos peered through a part in the curtain. Poor people dressed in their finest clothes. Women in full dresses. Men in coats over once-white shirts. All listening to the American. Bits of what he said came through to Nikos, but not a lot. Nikos had steamed under every flag, but he was more concerned with the language of sky and rope. He let the curtains fall closed and slumped on the nearest table. To occupy himself, he decided to count how many times the man said Jesus. He was in the mid-twenties when the number ceased to matter. Each time the man said Jesus, Nikos felt a piercing flame in his breast. He had difficulty breathing and he was … happy?

The experience terrified him. He burst through the curtain, hungover and stumbling, a dark lock of hair covering one eye. He found the stairs and barely kept his feet in the descent. Following the sound of creaking wood and seagulls, he walked out onto the *Arkansas*. He drank a quart of water then pissed off the fore. Then he went below and was rocked back to sleep.

Two days later, when his ship left port, that congregation was aboard. Mormons, apparently, bound for the Rocky Mountains. Nikos would first be attracted to a young English Saint named Bethelda Simmons, but he would first fall in love with the American gospel as taught by Elder Howell whose clear and steady voice made English sound holy.

When the *Arkansas* landed in Boston Nikos joined the Saints. They baptized him in the Neponset, put him on a train, and—upon arrival in Utah—married him to Miss Simmons. He never saw the sea or the inside of a whorehouse again, but he remained a hard drinker the rest of his life. Midway through his fifty-sixth year, his wife and sons buried him on a hill outside Tooele.

After years of negotiation with his brothers, son number two, John, took over the ranch. In his efforts to be a better man, he tore down the cider still and got involved in city government. His mother lived with him; his brothers wandered off. He saw them only at some harvests and the occasional holiday. Once they all appeared on the same New Year's weekend hoping for a handout and John tore into them with language that in other circumstances he would eschew.

John and his wife, Rezina, had three children: John, whose life seemed a repetition of his father's only with fewer calluses, finer clothes, and secular friends in Salt Lake society. Mary, who was sickly to a degree that seemed to demand no other attributes. And Gerald.

Gerald's father was busy training John how to be a John, so Gerald was free to do as he pleased. Many was the sunburn he picked up napping in a field during a long summer day. Many was the night he woke up shivering before a fire long since dark. Spring and summer, Gerald and his friends would ride horses into the mountains for days at a time. He would put in an appearance at harvest before going into Salt Lake for a bit of schooling during the winter.

At age twenty-two he was feeling finished with his piebald education when his father met him off campus at a favored cafe on North Temple.

"Look, Gerald," he said. "It's the 1950s. A man can't get his living off the land unless he has a great deal of it. And an education is only as useful as the career it is put in service of. But you do not seem to have much in the way of direction. Now, I am not only your father, I am your bishop. And to help you find the Lord's direction for your life, I'm calling you on a mission."

Gerald set down his coffee and added two more cubes of sugar. "A mission! Where to?"

His father rested his hand on the table, pressed the backs of his fingers against Gerald's mug, and pushed it to the edge of the table. "I don't know, Gerald. That would be for the Lord to decide."

Gerald popped a cube directly into his mouth. His brother had never served a mission. Between the war and the ranch, how could he? "All right. I'll do it. What's next?"

John smiled in his way that pushed the corners of his mouth downward. "Very good. I'll alert the Brethren, and they'll issue the call. You, meanwhile, need to pick up a new suit and—"

"You don't think John'll give me one of his?"

His father paused. "If you're that eager, we can get you measured today at the ZCMI. You'll also need to be ordained an elder, and you ought to receive your patriarchal blessing. I can take care of the former any Sunday, but you'll need to make arrangements with Brother Howard."

"Ol' Brother Howard, huh? He got a phone yet?"

"I don't believe so."

"Well, then. I reckon I'll just ride on out and see him after sac-rament this little ol' Sunday."

His father's eyes narrowed. Gerald decided to push on. "Yessir, you fixin' to ordain me this Sunday's well, or you gonna hold off till that call comes in from the Brethren?"

John's voice did not reflect the tightness of his face. "For now, Gerald, what say we just wait for the call to come in."

That Sunday, true to his word, as sacrament came to a close, Gerald hopped on his brindle mare and headed off across the valley to Aaron and Matilda Howard's home. Brother Howard had been a high-enough-placed administrator for the railroad to build for his growing family three gabled stories some decades past. Savvy in-vestments in the telegraph companies and during the past two wars had left his house still old-fashioned in Gerald's eye but opulent as a European prince's. Brother Howard himself wore a large white mustache and a gold watch chain as he welcomed Gerald.

"Very nice to see you, young Brother Gregopolis. Your father and I were just speaking of your prospects. I understand you have a very broad education."

"Um, thank you, sir."

"You needn't worry about my absence from church of late. My dear wife has been ill, and I do not care to leave her."

"Oh. Of course."

"But what brings you here today, Gerald?"

"I'm going on a mission, sir. My father sent me to receive my blessing."

"I see; I see. Are you just here because he sent you, or do you desire this blessing for yourself?"

Gerald laughed nervously. "Oh, yes, for myself. Sir."

Brother Howard nodded. "Mm. Very good then. In here."

He led Gerald into a small, velvet-walled parlor, a high-seated, low-backed chair standing in the middle of the room. A red plush stool sat just to the side of the central chair and, on top of the stool, a suitcase with some plastic machinery inside. Brother Howard gestured to Gerald to sit.

"My dear Matilda sits on that stool to transcribe—very skilled at shorthand you know, that's how we met—but she has not been well of late, as you know. That you see there now? The new Dictaphone. Very best available, I'm told. It will record your blessing and I will transcribe it myself. I'll put it in the mail by next week, I imagine."

His pause seemed to require a response so Gerald said, "Quite interesting, sir."

Brother Howard chuckled. "Yes, yes. But, Gerald, have you truly thought about what it means to receive your patriarchal blessing? This is a once-in-your-lifetime event, son. You are here to receive the word of the Lord—personal scripture. When I place my hands on your head, I will not speak until the Holy Ghost provides the words. If they do not come, you'll have to return. When it comes time to transcribe, I will not remember the words the Dictaphone plays back to me. You see, this is a private moment between you and the Father. Do you understand this?"

"Yes, sir."

"Very good. Let's begin."

Brother Howard walked behind Gerald, patted his shoulders, and stepped to his recorder. Gerald was surprised when Brother Howard placed the microphone in his hands.

"There you are. Just keep that button pressed and feel free to fold your arms as you normally would. Full name?"

"Gerald Timothy Gregopolis, sir."

"Gerald Timothy, Gerald Timothy."

A moment of silence, save for the click of Gerald's thumb pushing down followed by a light hum. Brother Howard's fingers pushed hard into the top of Gerald's head, knocking a strand of dark hair across his eyes, which he promptly closed.

"Gerald. Timothy. Gregopolis." A voice quite different from Brother Howard's filled the room. Loud. Stentorian. Impersonal in a godly sort of way.

Gerald struggled to not let his neck collapse under the pressure. Then Brother Howard's fingers suddenly relaxed and floated just above his scalp, in his hair. Tingles from the prior pressure and the cloudlike weight in his hair together left an impression of—

Angel dust.

Gerald didn't know what that meant. Bit creepy, really. When he became an elder, he would be sure at every blessing or ordination to make sure his fingers made a nice, firm, even pressure upon the recipient's head. If his hands were above someone else's, he'd push enough on their hands to be sure there was none of this in-the-hair touching, none of this fingertips-only thing. None of it. And if he were the mouthpiece, then—

"Amen."

"Amen?"

Brother Howard rested his hands on Gerald's shoulders. "Well, son, how was that? All stuff you expected to hear?"

"Um, hard to say, sir."

Brother Howard chuckled his low, measured chuckle. "I know what you mean. I know what you mean. Well." He slapped Gerald's upper arms. "Do tell your folks hello for me, won't you?"

"Sure."

"I'll get this typed up and mailed to you by week's end if it's not too long." He took the microphone and stooped over to look at the Dictaphone. "Oh, well! It's not too long at all. Quite short, in fact. That's not a bad thing, of course. Perhaps all it means is the Lord feels you're quite on the right path already. Who can say? Who can say?"

Gerald stood and shook Brother Howard's hand. He left the house, mounted his horse, and tried to remember one word outside his name and the amen.

"Welp," he told the horse. "I reckon that's why they write 'em down."

Two months later, Gerald, now Elder Gregopolis, sat in a room with twenty other newly called elders from Utah, Arizona, and California as they waited for President McKay to share some wisdom with them. Then they would hop on a train bound for San Francisco. From there, they would go to Australia, New Zealand, or—the California fellow—Japan. Gerald was off to New Zealand—a place he had thought was part of Australia until that morning.

President McKay entered the room in his famous white suit, smiled, shook everyone's hands, spoke briefly on the importance of bringing God's word to the ends of the Earth, and answered a few questions—he having seen all these nations earlier in life. The next morning, they boarded the train and soon Elder Gregopolis was crossing the Pacific Ocean. His grandfather had been a sailor, he knew. Grandmother had often spoken of it. His brother, John, had claimed to experience no seasickness during troop transport and that furthermore it was his Hellenic blood that had so sustained him. Elder Gregopolis was not so lucky. For a full ten days he moaned and rocked and vomited. He wondered how he continued to live with no nutrients in his body.

Then one morning he woke up well and ate a prolific breakfast. The rest of the voyage he alternated between eating and reading. He forced himself to read the scriptures but was much more impressed with Professor Talmage's *Jesus the Christ*. And every day he reread his patriarchal blessing, hoping it would reveal the contours of his upcoming mission.

> Gregory Timothy Gregopolis, having been ordained to the office of patriarch at the hands of Patriarch Hyrum G. Smith, I lay mine hands upon thine head and command thee to heed the words of the Holy Spirit, both as I speak them now and as they will speak to thou directly throughout thine life.
>
> Thou art of the house of Ephraim, Brother Gregopolis, and thus have a responsibility to carry the gospel to all the world. This thou shalt do, both at home and abroad.
>
> Thou wilt surely be called to serve the Lord as the president of an elders quorum. As thou servest thine brethren in this calling, thou wilt develop charity, yea, even the pure love of Christ, which charity will improve thine relationships with thine wife and thine children and thine brothers and thine sisters, both within the church and without, in the great world God our Father hath created and which He shall reveal unto thee.
>
> This blessing I leave thee, Brother Gerald, in the name of Jesus the very Christ, amen.

"The length isn't what matters," his father had said as they looked together over the mostly blank page Brother Howard had sent him. "This is a remarkable blessing."

"How so?"

"Well, for starters, this "elders quorum president" thing. That is remarkably specific. Clearly something to which you were foreor-dained before we came to this life. And it would seem to suggest that that calling will be just the first in a long list of honorable callings." He grabbed his son's shoulders and squeezed. And Gerald realized: his father now saw him as a fellow John.

Now, as he sat in his berth considering his blessing word by word, he squinted a bit and tried a prayer. *Heavenly Father. Thank you for this blessing. Thank you for my call to serve the people of New Zealand whom President McKay loves so much. Bless me that I'll be a good servant. Um.*

His mind drifted homeward to his father's ranch, to the good-bye jaunt he and his friends had taken. Dick's sister Esme floating in the Salt Lake, her white thighs sparkling like diamonds as the salt crystalized, and as they ate fried chicken and drank root beer from her father's cellar.

Esme. No longer Dick's little sister, but a woman, grown and ripe and ready—

Gerald stood, banging his head on the bunk above in his rush to the deck. As his father had said, he would never see the fulfillment of his blessing if he did not keep himself worthy. If Esme were unmarried upon his return, he could think of her then.

After eighteen months and forty baptisms in Christchurch, El-der Gregopolis was discouraged. They were teaching kindly Maori families who fed the missionaries with gusto and generosity. They tended to get baptized—and they might well be descended from Book of Mormon people, the children of Hagoth. But why weren't white New Zealanders open to the Restored Gospel? Not even those Greeks down by the docks?

Elder Gregopolis mulled over this, but Elder Anderson would only ever talk about the Lamanites as God's chosen, children of promise, heirs to prophecy, the last shall be first, and so on.

That month, President Ballif called on them personally. "The church is growing strong here in New Zealand," he began. "I have reason to believe we will see a temple before decade's end upon these shores. The number of worthy priesthood brethren is grow-ing by leaps and bounds, but many of them are still young in the gospel. Their worthiness and faith cannot be questioned but their experience is lacking. We're fiddling a bit with our organization, elders, and we've decided one of you should serve as an elders quorum president here in Christchurch. After some thinking and prayer, I've decided that Elder Gregopolis, as senior companion, should remain focused on missionary work while Elder Anderson takes on this new mantle. Remember, Elder Anderson, your task is to prepare your counselors to later take your place as …"

The words faded out. President Ballif kept speaking while Elder Gregopolis kept realizing, over and over, that he was not chosen. He had never thought he might serve as an elders quorum president while a missionary, so why *not* Elder Anderson? That selection was no comment on Gerald's own worthiness. He hadn't had a cup of coffee since leaving Utah; he had learned not to touch himself during his regular dreams of Esme; he had prayed for charity almost every day of his mission.

It was fine. The Lord wanted him to focus on missionary work. Some other time would be the season for being elders quorum president. Not now.

"Yes, President?"

"I said, can you support your companion in this new responsibility?"

"Yes, President. Of course. Of course, I can."

"Good. Well, I'll let you two get back to work." He pushed back his chair and thrust his meaty hand at them one at a time.

Upon his return home, Gerald's father—as his father and as his bishop—instructed him to get married as soon as possible and start on a career and family. Esme, Gerald learned, was now a lawyer's secretary in Ogden and still unmarried. She did have a boyfriend, but he did not mind her going out with an old friend for a simple dinner. Three months later he and Esme were married and settled in Salt Lake where Gerald found work on the sales force at Kennecott Copper, eventually running the industrial advertising division. The children came quickly, and before long they had seven of them. Esme's patriarchal blessing had promised she would "have children to fill [her] life and descendants to fill [her] eternities." Seven, she felt, was a good start. At church, Gerald served largely with the young men. Elders quorum presidencies were called and released; but Gerald was peaceful, certain his moment would come. When his father dropped hints as to his son's worthiness, Gerald would laugh and remind him that to the Lord time is one great round. Besides, Gerald was busy. He worked fifty, sixty hours a week and took his sons camping two weekends a month. He didn't have time to fret over the Lord's timing. And so, he felt at peace when the stake president called him in for a chat.

"Brother Gregopolis. So good to see you. Sit down; sit down."

President Oscarlin was a thin man, bald, spectacled—but strong in a way that radiated beyond his physical stature. His grip was tight, his gaze was fiery, and his voice was the calm that centers a hurricane.

"President. Good to see you too. How's Barbara?"

"Much better, thank you. Now, Gerald. You know Benny Allred, of course."

"Sure, yes, of course." Benny was his ward's elders quorum president. He'd been in the position for years and was due for a release.

"Keep this under your hat for now, Gerald, but Bishop Thomlinson's been called as a mission president, and I've received the Brethren's approval to call Brother Allred as his replacement. And Brother Allred has asked that you serve as his second counselor. Would you be willing to accept this opportunity to serve the good people of the Holladay Eleventh Ward?"

Gerald prided himself on his immediate acceptance of all proffered callings, but—"Of course, but—won't I have to be made a high priest for this calling?"

"That's right."

"I won't be an elder anymore."

President Oscarlin smiled. "You'll be done with the elders quorum for good."

Gerald frowned and stared at nothing. If he accepted this calling, he could never be an elders quorum president. But with God, all things are possible. Perhaps he should tell President Oscarlin of his blessing? But wouldn't that mean President Oscarlin had made a mistake? Misread revelation? But maybe the Lord expected Gerald to have enough faith in his blessing to speak up now, to stand up for it. But against his ecclesiastical leader—as good a man as Gerald had ever sustained?

And so, Gerald spoke the only words he knew how to speak. He accepted the calling.

He served as Bishop Allred's counselor for three years and then sat on the high council for ten. Then he was called as a counselor to the stake president for a short time before becoming a bishop. A high priests group leader. He served on the stake Sunday School presidency. His children grew up and moved away. They gave him grandchildren who gave him great-grandchildren. From the pastoral quiet of the high priests group, Gerald heard of new elders quorum presidents being called: Trevor Williamson, Jose Torentino, Allen Goode, Carl Beteran. He would leave after three hours of church and open the car door for Esme. Once home, they would sit in their respective chairs and speak when they had something to say. On her seventy-seventh birthday, Esme fell down the front steps of their home. Her brain filled with loose blood, and she died. The house was somehow louder without her. He could hear the refrigerator turn on and off. The fish tank humming and bubbling. Birds through the open kitchen window. His own footsteps walking past her shelves and shelves of books he had always been too busy to read.

At church, he stood in the back and welcomed people, giving programs to kids and cracking jokes with their parents. Brother Gregopolis, or President Gregopolis, or Bishop Gregopolis, was known for his old-fashioned brown suit, for slipping the occasional Three Musketeers bar to a deacon on Fast Sunday, for naming all fifty grandkids and seventeen—no eighteen—great-grandkids every time he stood for testimony meeting. Men in their thirties and forties aspired to his blend of sarcasm and faithfulness. Their wives who had known Esme spoke of how that loss still colored his eyes. He's a good man, they all agreed. One of the best.

His grandson Clarke, who was attending the U, brought his girlfriend over one Saturday afternoon in April during general conference. She was tall and thin and Black, though she had dyed her hair blonde, confusing Gerald's eye. Grampa Greggo was pleased to see them, he said. She made French toast while Clarke fixed Grandpa's internet connection so they could watch the next session of conference together. That morning, in the first session, Grandpa Gregopolis had been obliged to follow along on the radio as they sustained Russell Marion Nelson as prophet, seer, and revelator and president of the Church of Jesus Christ of Latter-day Saints. Now the picture was back and they three watched together. Every time Clarke glanced away to look at his girlfriend, a lock of dark hair fell into his eyes, which she would then push back. Gerald smiled and his mind wandered. The French toast was delicious, even though his taste was a bit fuzzy now in his eighty-fourth year. His grandson and this girl seemed happy enough together. He wondered if it would last.

He invited them to stay and for Clarke to join him at the ward building for the priesthood session—ice cream afterwards!—but they were young and busy with places to go. They held hands to her car and drove off. He watched them go. Waved as they turned a corner.

Gerald went back inside and took a brief nap. He watered the lawn, put on a tie, and walked to the ward building. The screen was pulled down from the chapel ceiling; the lights were off; the choir was singing—

Gerald dozed off, then startled awake when his left hearing aid screeched. As he pushed it back into his ear, President Nelson was saying, "Regardless of your individual circumstances, each of you is a member of a priesthood quorum with a divine mandate to learn and to teach, to love and to serve others.

"Tonight, we announce a significant restructuring of our Melchizedek Priesthood quorums to accomplish the work of the Lord more effectively. In each ward, the high priests and the elders will now be combined into one elders quorum."

The men in the chapel buzzed. They turned to each other and whispered. Some shocked, some delighted. All a bit startled and confused.

Gerald Timothy Gregopolis did not hear them. He did not need to. President Nelson continued to speak, smiling, on the screen, but there was no sound. Gerald watched the mouthpiece of the Lord and clasped his hands together. *Oh, God! I am ready!*

NARROW IS THE GATE

DANNY NELSON

No man or woman in this dispensation will ever enter into the celestial kingdom of God without the consent of Joseph Smith.
—Brigham Young

The alien ship was beautiful.

Ornately encrusted with organic shapes glowing with subdued mauve lighting, it looked like a series of pink cathedrals emerging from the clouds. The ship arrived over the Pacific Ocean near San Francisco and began a leisurely glide toward the shore. The Coast Guard hailed it. The Air Force hailed it. Californians fished dusty HAM radios from their attics and hailed it. The alien ship sailed on, mute and stately, clouds swirling around its buttresses.

An hour after the first sightings, the president of the United States flew to San Francisco, holding press conferences the whole way. Times were difficult and her once fresh face had accumulated the wear of years with each month in office. World politics were nearer a breaking point than usual and there was an election coming. In one press conference, she shook her head gravely when the topic of military action against the aliens was raised. Americans are calm, brave, and welcoming to visitors, she said. No one bothered to fact-check these claims.

By the time the president and her press junket landed in San Francisco, the ship had made landfall and was sailing serenely east over the scrubby deserts and mountain peaks. The president had a photo taken of herself listening to the city's overexcited mayor while wearing a serious frown and then boarded the plane again.

The ship sailed on. Satellites tracked its movement. The internet roiled with speculation. Conquest and annihilation. Scientific expedition. Diplomatic envoy. The ship would land in Denver. Las Vegas. Area 51. There was no hope left. This was the salvation of the world.

Fifteen hours later, the ship came to a stop above Salt Lake City.

Herbertson was prophet that year. He was short and soft-spoken; gray and grandfatherly. The church had enjoyed a contented period during his tenure. He did not thunder, as did his first counselor Holyoke, that the world had dragged the Saints' standards down. When he spoke, he relied heavily on the Book of John. He often ruminated, publicly and personally, that God is Love. Those Saints whose religion originated in the Old Testament found him weak, but his vague goodwill made him an excellent spokesperson for the modern church. He had the unflappable gentleness of a former middle school science teacher turned spiritual leader. His earnest modesty blunted the most pointed interview questions.

Unlike many prophets before him, Herbertson's appeal stretched beyond the Saints. The church may be a paranoid, controlling hotbed of outdated prejudice and petty cruelty, said those the church used to call gentiles, but at least it was run by Herbertson and not Holyoke. To the gentiles, when he remembered to speak to them, Herbertson replied that the God of the church was physically and materially incapable of being cruel to anyone. His sedate kindliness was such that few bothered to fact-check his claims.

It was a hazy evening in late spring when the aliens set down in Salt Lake City. The sky was smeared with white and grey, the air hot and dry. There was construction on North Temple, a narrow river of orange safety cones. A youth group was walking to the Family History Museum, their faces blank and cheerful. They pointed as the ship approached the spine of the Wasatch, its turrets and spires eddying the clouds as they boiled through. The ship slowed and came to rest fifty feet above the wide promenade between the temple and the tabernacle.

La Paz, the mayor, called the church offices. The call was not answered because the Church Office Building was emptying. A steady stream of men in blue and grey suits and women in knee-length skirts flowed up the hill to the Avenues. One of La Paz's aides had a niece who worked for one of the senior staffers at the church, so eventually the connection was made. The situation was a matter of city security, said La Paz, and the city would handle it with utmost respect for the church's property. The senior staffer who took the call was relieved. He had been promoted past his competence, and like many in his position, he was grateful to be told what to do. With genial force, he declared that the evacuation was officially sanctioned and organized his managers to make sure the masses of people proceeded calmly. At the last moment, someone remembered to call Herbertson and let him know the situation.

Herbertson took the call as he looked out the windows of his apartment, just across from Temple Square. A segment of the alien ship served as a pinkish backdrop to the familiar spires of the temple. He thanked the caller softly and hung up the phone, already planning what he would say if the public relations office asked him for a quote. "The truth of our religion speaks of a universal experience" and "we have faith in the security forces of our city" would be part of it. Or, rather, "the men and women of our city's security force."

Before the sun set, the aliens descended.

They came down on little hovering discs which seemed to wobble under them like hooked fish, but the aliens stayed still as statues. Drones buzzed them from every direction, frantically videoing, but the aliens were unperturbed by the bee-like activity. When they touched down, each seemed to genuflect, but it could have just been the impact of their landing. There were five of them, standing like conquerors in front of the temple wall, tall enough to easily see over it into the grounds.

The aliens were as beautiful as their ship. They had broad, thrown-back heads with three to four black, shining eyes. Their skin had the smooth vibrance of rainforest reptiles—olive green, mustard yellow, and ruddy purple. They wore flowing, colorful gowns of a material somewhere between cotton and feathers. On some, the gowns closed in the back under a hairy, sea-blue collar. They had short arms with many oddly jointed fingers and a retractable bone spur that seemed to function as a thumb. They walked with an eerie, swaying grace.

The city had cordoned off Temple Square and the surrounding streets, so the Square was empty. It was impossible to tell what the aliens thought of the abandoned grounds. They looked around them with inscrutable expressions, blinking and winking their black eyes. One reached up and touched a jointed finger to a tree leaf with what looked to some observers like reverence and to others like hunger. The setting desert sun shone dramatically on the colorful, organic curves of their heads.

The president was in Salt Lake by then. In the calculus of elections, Utah was too predictable to be interesting, and she hadn't campaigned there. She made cheerful noises to the press about the situation being a unique opportunity to see "this jewel of the West," but in truth, she would have traded significant political favors to move the meeting with these interstellar visitors anywhere else. Religion was divisive, and despite its origins, most Americans were not quick to claim the LDS Church.

Her staff set up a small camp just north of Temple Square near the Conference Center. The media took pictures of her speaking, the spiky trees of the Conference Center's rooftop gardens ringing her head like a crown. She said she would send a decorated general to speak to the aliens. A woman.

"Do you see this as a way to promote women's profiles in the military?" asked one member of the press. The president pointedly looked right through him as she called on the questioner behind him. Being rude to reporters was the only portion of her job the president truly enjoyed.

The general, Margoyles, marched into Temple Square flanked by two young, burly military men dressed in dark fatigues. She was bone thin and rigid, cutting through the cheery ambiance of the Square like a hot saber through a butter sculpture. She stopped a safe distance from the aliens and hailed them. One of the burly young men carried a computer meant to help with translation. The aliens were prepared, however. With great solemnity, they handed Margoyles a twisted box with several delicate coruscations. While holding it, which she did stiffly and uncomfortably, Margoyles could understand the aliens' speech. It was not the sort of understanding that translates words into other words. It was like dream-understanding, the strange certainty of knowing impossible things. Holding the translator, Margoyles's mind opened and fluttered like a papery flower, but it never showed on her face. She was an excellent soldier.

The people of Earth welcomed the aliens, said Margoyles. The aliens showed polite goodwill. The people of Earth were happy to meet the aliens as peaceful visitors, but they should know that the Earth was defended, said Margoyles. Of course, of course, replied the aliens, sending swirls of impatience through the device Margoyles held. If the aliens would reveal their purpose in visiting, perhaps the people of Earth could help, said Margoyles.

There was a disagreement among the aliens about their response. They each had two voices, a high reed and a low flute; they harmonized with themselves and each other as they spoke. They argued together for a moment in swift tonal snatches. At last, the one with blotches of yellow and mauve in lines along its elongated head responded.

Earth was very kind to offer help, it said through the box, which throbbed in Margoyles's hands. Fortunately, human help was not needed. No—not that. Margoyle sensed that their meaning was closer to *Earth's help would be ludicrously insufficient*. The aliens were not after anything material.

One of the aliens fished in its robes and pulled out a thin, metallic-looking square. Etched in lines of glowing blue was a picture of a man. He had a hooked nose, a high collar, and a strange, archaic bouffant of hair.

We must speak to the successor of Brother Joseph, buzzed the translator in Margoyles's hands. *Take us to the prophet.*

*

The drones recorded the picture on the metal square in crisp clarity. It was unmistakably the image of Joseph Smith, Jr., now long dead and—as far as anyone knew—as Earth-bound as any other religious figure from history. Frantically, the president declared a total media blackout. It didn't work. ALIENS SEEK LDS PROPHET blared the news scrolls, followed by ads, and then TEN THINGS YOU DIDN'T KNOW ABOUT MORMONISM—#5 WILL SHOCK YOU.

In truth, very few people who clicked through were shocked. For good or ill, public opinion about the church was set—congealed like over-refrigerated gelatin. Those who were already inclined to be incensed about the church found energy to be angry again, while those already inclined to approve smiled in serene satisfaction. Most were merely puzzled. The LDS Church, that minuscule branch of a decaying Christian tradition, seemed the most random and specific thing the aliens could have chosen as their entry point to all of human expression.

"It's like," said a popular comic to his late-night audience, "going to a buffet and asking to have a closed-door session with a green bean."

The apostles called an emergency session. Holyoke was the loudest voice in the room. It was a confirmation of the universality of the Restoration, he said. It would lead to a flowering of missionary work. What a testimony to the foundation of the church. An ensign—not just to the world, but to the universe. The church was justified—not that it sought justification, but just the same! No human soul could doubt the truth now.

In the heat of inspiration, Holyoke was impressive and beyond questioning. Under the soft lights of the meeting room, his bald forehead shone like a halo. The Brethren prayed together and, as was so often the case, a sweet sense of rightness and comfort prevailed in the room.

Herbertson, his stomach uncertain, visited the bathroom after the meeting. It had a picture of the First Vision. Looking at the familiar painting, Herbertson wondered. No matter how he tried, he couldn't insert aliens into his understanding of the scene.

*

The government brought Herbertson to speak to the aliens. They

had no choice. The aliens refused to communicate anything sub-
stantive without him.

Herbertson knew the layout of the temple complex more
intimately than his own apartment. He knew the order of the
yearly flowers that bloomed and then were rooted out to make way
for the next season's flora, knew the cheerful *Holas* and *Ni Haos*
from the smiling sister missionaries, knew the slightly medicated
smell of the standing pools and fountains. Swarmed by military
personnel, though, the temple grounds suddenly seemed strange
and overlarge. Herbertson himself felt shrunken and old, leaning
heavily on his cane while the two guards walked with careful steps
to match his pace.

The government had set up a white pavilion in the grass between the Lion House and the Church Office Building. Its spires
soared to the sky, a little sister to the granite temple to the west.
It hosted the aliens, shading their uncannily curved heads from
Utah's relentless sun. Electrical cords snaked everywhere along
the ground, feeding into boxy machines—translators and bio-
indicators, radar machines and a full field hospital kit. Someone
had set out a folding chair facing the aliens for Herbertson. The
aliens stood in a grand, multicolored group. As far as anyone had
seen, they didn't sit.

The chair was uncomfortable, but Herbertson was grateful for it.
Years of going from apartment to temple tunnels to private air-
plane made the heat of the day unfamiliar and unpleasant. And he
was old. His knees complained as he gripped them in hands mot-
tled with russet spots. Steadiness was one of Herbertson's virtues,
though, and he willed the irritation of the sweat away. He would
meet these emissaries of the stars with serene goodwill.

The aliens turned toward him with the unnerving collective
grace of a flock of birds as he sat. They raised their hands and
rattled at him. Herbertson smiled blandly. He had visited Ghana,
India, Peru. He knew how to arrange his face when he didn't understand the local customs.

Perhaps the aliens' culture deemed the translator box inappropriate for first meetings, for they did not offer it. Instead, they merely
spoke to Herbertson, first the one with yellow and ochre on its head,

then the one with deep-sea blue and turquoise. Their two-part voices dipped and swelled. At a certain point, they paused impressively.

Herbertson, sensing it was his turn, replied with a short speech he had prepared during his morning shower. The church of Earth was pleased to welcome the guests from the stars—fellow believers. What a joy it was to see that the good news of the gospel had touched more than this tiny planet, to know that God could transcend the narrow limitations of man's sight. There was much that each group of—he stumbled on the word souls, recovered—could teach each other. The unrelenting rules of gravity were like a tether keeping humanity's feet planted on Earth, but their faces were pointed to the stars, grateful to meet fellow travelers in God's vast creation.

The exchange was being taped by the government and Herbertson didn't notice the camera technician, whose lips quirked at his final sentence. Those who paid attention to these things would recognize the line as inimitably Herbertson's. He tended to start practical and crescendo into floridity. The pattern was more pronounced under stress. The blank stares of the aliens were oddly aggressive and discomfiting. Herbertson wished for a glass of ice water and a teleprompter but reined in his expectations. Brigham Young had stood on a stump and preached to a crowd boiling tar— he could sit on a folding chair and speak calmly with aliens.

The ritual seemed to be complete, if it was a ritual at all. The aliens rattled again, snapping their bone-spurs against their hands like castanets. Then the translator was handed to Herbertson, and for a second, he was overcome with nausea as the alien communiques soaked into his mind through his fingers. He gripped the translator too tightly and the messages swirled over him in see-sawing pulses of urgency.

We are pleased to meet Brother Joseph's successor, the aliens intimated between Herbertson's fingers. He felt their pleasure—their utter delight, alien and consuming and pure—and wondered at it. It made him think of snowball plants blooming, of popcorn popping on the apricot tree. He shook his head, and his glasses slid down his nose. Of course, he was pleased to see them as well, he thought back, hoping to use the same mechanism. To his unease, the thought traveled through his fingers into the machine like a physical thing, and with it trailed all sorts of other thoughts, like fish swimming in the wake of a shark—his pleasure, his unease, the discomfort of the flat planes of the chair against his buttocks.

The aliens accepted the confused response with dignified inclines of their heads. Perhaps they expected this muddled reply. Kindly, they sent, *It takes some time for purity of thought to be achieved. No doubt you have more elegant ways of sharing your [something] with your own kind.* That *something* was a concept near to *soul* but also, somehow, close to the concepts of *kidney* and *doormat.* Herbertson nodded patiently and realized the action was likely to be as inscrutable to them as the hand-rattling was to him, so he sent his willingness to keep listening through the machine. This thought went through more cleanly, though a regret from his teenage years bubbled up before it sent. The sweat was heavy on his forehead now.

The aliens conversed among themselves, their dual voices sounding like a flock of flamingos arguing with a herd of cows. Was there dissent in the group? Herbertson blinked. There didn't seem to be disagreement, exactly, but the aliens certainly had personalities. The yellow-tinted one piped up when no one had spoken to it for several breaths, and the turquoise one's voices sounded harried and businesslike. There was a larger alien in blue and black that rarely spoke, staring instead at Herbertson with unreadable eyes. The two whose heads were slashed with green spoke to each other with the easy back-and-forth of couples or siblings.

The aliens' conference stopped as abruptly as it had begun. The turquoise one turned again to Herbertson.

We abase ourselves, it sent through the translator. *It is our planet's never-ending honor to be in your presence.*

Herbertson gasped a little at the intensity of feeling that coursed through him with the alien's words. An emotion like exalted reverence radiated like a tiny sun from the machine on his lap. The aliens, pulsed the translator, *believed.* Such deep love, awe, and esteem poured from it that Herbertson blushed and tried to clean his glasses—an old trick from his teaching days to cover discomfort—nearly dropping the translator in the process. He resettled everything carefully but left his glasses askew on his nose, giving him a slightly drunk look.

At last, uncomfortable, Herbertson sent *I am honored to meet you as well.*

The aliens glanced at each other, their throats swelling and pulsing and—in the case of the two green-headed ones—flushing purple. It took a moment for Herbertson to recognize the flood of feelings, but then he saw clearly. The aliens were crying for joy, or rather, the alien equivalent of that human action.

Herbertson had been to Ghana, India, Peru. He knew how to turn the adulation of those who saw him as a savior back toward God. Without hesitation, he sent *The Lord loves you.* It was the cleanest thing he'd sent through the translator, and he meant it.

The aliens sent the feeling back to Herbertson five-fold. Herbertson felt his eyes grow wet. The translator between his hands buzzed with a transcendence of certainty and divine love.

Please, give me the message you have brought with you, sent Herbertson, still rapt.

The sending turned the moment sour. Spiky waves of uncertainty and confusion shot through the translator. The turquoise alien again stood as spokes-creature.

We have no message, it said—or was it, *It is impossible for us to have anything to tell you?*

Herbertson blinked, his own confusion swirling around the aliens'. *We have questions,* pulsed the translator in his lap. *We have so many questions.*

✳

The president felt that the military and the Mormons had the alien visitation handled. She wanted to be in Washington planning infrastructure, not stuck in a Salt Lake Marriott running attendance on these very foreign dignitaries. She had plans for a transcontinental network of supertrains.

Americans don't want supertrains, said her advisors. They want to know someone is taking control of the alien situation.

Irritated, the president followed their advice. She held press conferences, visited Hill Air Force Base, gave visiting lectures at the University of Utah. She even went to a BYU football game, though she sensed the entire stadium had voted for her rival in the last election. The marching band played "I Love You, California" in her honor, and she smiled and waved while the crowd cheered part-heartedly.

The president was not comfortable being confined to Utah. There were too many surprises, little backward eddies in the way the people behaved. She would settle into conversation with some Utahn, sailing forward on the small talk of politics, and then, suddenly, there it would be—some conversational artifact from another age, some impression or attitude untouched by the twenty-first century, bobbing up into the conversation as if it belonged. If she called attention to it, the Utahn's face would smooth over, wide, friendly, blank. They couldn't hear the anachronism in their own voices, couldn't process her discomfort. She spent longer than she should in phone conversations with her husband, enjoying the direct East Coast tones of his voice, his total lack of circumlocution.

So, it was not her favorite state. She strongly suspected it had never been any president's favorite state. But the president had three children, and not all of them were her favorite, either. That didn't mean she didn't care. She made an effort. She toured Temple Square, spoke to the protesters standing in their small clumps outside the walled grounds. She took easy hikes up the mountain, learned to know the smell of the Great Salt Lake tainting the air. She discovered, surprisingly, that there was excellent coffee to be had if one was willing to search for it. And she learned to love sipping that coffee while standing in front of one of the wall-length windows in the Marriott, watching the sun pulse pale yellows and pinks over the edge of the Wasatch early in the morning.

There are compensations for everything, she typed into the document where she kept notes for the inevitable book she would write following her presidency. The thought buoyed her through almost three meetings with representatives of the local legislature.

✳

Herbertson was, broadly speaking, looking forward to answering the aliens' queries. He was a great answerer of questions, and he had lived in the soft-edged universe of the church long enough that there were very few subjects he didn't have answers for. In his younger days he had spoken with the Pope, and during one of the rare occasions when the camera's gaze didn't force them to be friendly and noncommittal, the two gray-haired men had talked theology. Herbertson had initially been nervous to speak with the pontiff but had since felt he had won the conversation. It was, of course, difficult to tell when working through translators, but he trusted his instincts. He felt some of the same thrill of confident apprehension when he contemplated his interviews with the aliens.

The scores of attending military and scientific experts were less confident. It was time, they said, that the aliens made some concessions to the rest of the population of Earth. By this, they meant America and, more specifically, their own fields of expertise. Religious conversations were all well and good, but Earth had some very pressing questions about the aliens' visit. The scientists wanted to know *how*, the military wanted to know *why*, and the president's PR representatives wanted to know if there was an approved term for the species, because the word *alien* sounded a little nineteenth-century and was exciting the sort of people who scream on cable news shows.

If they could have insisted on having their questions answered, the experts would have done so. But the aliens didn't so much refuse to communicate with the scientists and generals as ignore them. If they managed to get a question mediated through Herbertson, the aliens would answer it to the best of their ability, but they had little patience for any matters outside their faith. At one point, pressed by the head of the scientific team, Herbertson had asked how the spaceships were fueled. The answer that swam through the translator was incomprehensible and terse—something about gathering a foam or mist that swirled around certain kinds of stars, then compressing and distilling it as fuel. The aliens said they didn't know the details, and the feeling pulsing through the translator was that they weren't at all interested in learning them. There were engineers who knew these things, but they hadn't been brought on this most important mission. Their ships worked; that was the main thing. If something went wrong, there was a station not too far from Earth's solar system that could solve mechanical problems.

The military and scientific leaders wanted to know a great deal more about *that*, but the aliens were already plying Herbertson with their own questions. The most the scientists and soldiers got after that was a short statement from the indigo alien who, with stately but clearly manufactured patience, pointed out that they had traveled a long way and that civility (a confusing concept in the translator, teetering between the ideas of *wind tunnel* and *box of souls*) dictated that they be able to complete their mission before gratifying everyone's idle curiosity.

The scientists and military experts withdrew, not entirely graciously. At least, they told each other, they were allowed to record the proceedings. And who knew, perhaps some snippet of the religious discussion would reveal something important about the alien's biology, technology, or whether (as the military experts believed) they were the advance scouts of an invading army.

Transcripts of the aliens' questions to Herbertson were therefore dutifully filed away in a smooth black safe, though the transcribers were uncertain about their usefulness. Herbertson did his best to describe the questions coursing through the translator, but was generally at a loss to comprehend, let alone put into English, the alien concepts flooding his brain. A typical sequence of questions punched into the transcription went like this:

The prophet said that hot drinks are to be avoided. Does the [unintelligible] *count as a hot drink, or does the fact that it* [unintelligible] *and sometimes* [unintelligible] *make it safe to drink, no matter its temperature?*

We are supposed to hold things in common, but [unintelligible] *cannot be split among* [unintelligible] *without negative effects to* [unintelligible]. *Is it right for us to decline to share* [unintelligible] *with other believers, or is this sinful?*

Many [unintelligible] *may be joined as* [unintelligible] *but does* [unintelligible] *or* [unintelligible] *counteract* [unintelligible] *or confirm it?*

This last question turned out to be about polygamy, and that was where the trouble began.

The aliens reported themselves to have three biological sexes—though the number was possibly four. There was debate on their planet as to which of the two or three "attendant" sexes should be a plural partner for the "presiding" sex.

As far as Herbertson, gripping the translator with sweaty fingers, could understand, some theorists in the alien culture claimed that one particular sex—was it those with green striping on their heads?—was the only acceptable one for polygamy, while others argued that the other attendant sex was the true polygamous one. Still others argued that any sex that wasn't a presiding sex was available for polygamy. No one in the aliens' culture seemed to question which sex was the presiding one.

The question was further complicated because the aliens couldn't clearly communicate their concept of marriage to Herbertson. It was somewhere along the lines of *legal contract of affection* and *life partnership* but it snarled together with other concepts such as *a severed root*, and *the flash of sunlight on a pane of glass, only eternal*, and *the ache of the bone of the back after sleep*. Even more confusingly, these barnacle-like meanings shifted around depending on which alien was speaking. So, for the turquoise alien, the *root* aspect was more pronounced and carried along the dizzying idea that *the fruit is the seed is the fruit is the seed*. The yellow alien also spoke of *butchery* when it spoke of marriage. For the dark alien, marriage was primarily *the war that has no enemies*. And hidden deep within the green-striped aliens' concept of *marriage*, so slight it was almost imperceptible, was *air escaping from a biological sphincter*, though whether that meant whistling, farting, or some process unavailable to humans Herbertson couldn't tell.

It took several hours of intense decoding for Herbertson to arrive at an understanding of the question, and he gave himself a few moments to consider it. The aliens peered at him as he sat sweating in the Utah heat, their black eyes expressionless. Inwardly, Herbertson prayed for guidance, but no immediate answer came.

I am sorry, but there is much that I still do not understand about your question, he sent through the translator.

The aliens looked at each other. *Perhaps you can use your own translator*, they sent through the device in Herbertson's hands. *A communication of Earthly design may provide you a more accurate picture.*

We sadly lack your powers of technology, Herbertson sent back with a rueful smile.

Flickers of uncertainty radiated between the tall alien forms and seeped into the translator. *But the translator is Brother Joseph's design,* it thrummed.

Herbertson sent back a blank wall of ignorance.

Something like panic surged beneath the aliens' communications. The flashing, black-eyed glances they gave each operated in concert with the feelings crawling into Herbertson's hands, giving him an almost native understanding of their facial expressions. At last, the dark alien pulled its personal translator from a knapsack slung about its shoulders. Pressing at its edges, the alien opened the translator, which came apart in two halves like a cracked egg. Embedded in its glowing blue machinery was a set of wire-rimmed spectacles, stones where the lenses should be.

＊

ALIENS USE MORMON MAGIC TRANSLATOR blared the headlines, followed with BUILDING A URIM AND THUMMIM—IS IT POSSIBLE? AN ENGINEER AND RELIGIOUS HISTORIAN WEIGH IN. More reputable and less popular news sites showed the president in an unguarded moment, pinching the bridge of her nose with a pained expression as she read the news.

The apostles called another emergency meeting. They had to find the original Urim and Thummim used by Joseph Smith. But it had been kept so safe—packed up with seer stones, dowsing rods, and other nineteenth-century bric-a-brac that had become embarrassing over the years—no one really knew where it had ended up.

After a frantic search, the artifact was located. They brought it to the apostles on a white cloth. It sat on the table, inert, the lamplight reflecting dully on the cut stones. Herbertson regarded it with trepidation. When he was a young apostle, he had thought of searching out the history of Joseph's Urim and Thummim, but it was the sort of project that gets shoved aside by other, more pressing matters. He wished now that he had made the study a priority.

Holyoke insisted that the Urim and Thummim be used—it was inconceivable that the aliens could make use of one of God's artifacts while they, his Earthly inheritors, could not. One by one the apostles tried on the Urim and Thummim, peering through the milky stone lenses, and one by one they reported no additional inspiration or influence. Finally, it was Herbertson's turn. He settled the glasses on his nose, feeling foolish and oddly transgressive. The spindly wires of the nose- and earpieces dug into the flesh of his face, and the stones were opaque and poorly cut, presenting his eyes with faceted, but blank, walls. He did not feel the familiar warmth of inspiration. Slowly, he took them off and forced himself to face the apostles' expectant faces.

Undaunted, Holyoke suggested they bring the Urim and Thummim to the next interview with the aliens, to demonstrate that the Earthly church was equal to theirs. Herbertson nodded noncommittally, but when the Brethren disbanded he quietly asked an aide to return the artifact to storage. He was a prophet of the modern church and had found from long experience that these items were much more comfortable when they were out of sight.

After nearly ten days, the president was fighting the feeling that she was going to spend the remainder of her presidency in Salt Lake. Rather than depress her, however, the feeling galvanized her. She was a remarkably resilient person, but inaction made her anxious.

She woke early one morning with the familiar, crushing "Utah" feeling hovering around her thoughts, and resolved as she curled her hair to accept the feeling and do something with it. For whatever reason, she was halted here—trapped like the smoggy air that lay some mornings like a blanket, straining at the lip of the mountain peaks, unable to disperse. The forces keeping her arrested couldn't be changed, so they were inconsequential. There must be something she could do, even in Utah. She sent one of her aides on an errand, pressing a folded square of notepaper into his hand. He returned three hours later laden with enormous maps of the state and sacks of markers and rulers. Overjoyed, the president canceled her afternoon meetings.

In the quiet of her Marriott room, she sorted through the maps and selected the largest: an almost archaic map that covered most of the floor when she unfolded it. The president kicked off her heels and stood astride the map for a few moments like the Colossus. She traced the delicate lines of streets and rivers with her eyes, noting the sprawling jumble of the Wasatch Front; the wide, empty deserts studded with minuscule towns; the southern-border growths of retirement havens. Having seen the whole, she focused on Salt Lake City. Though she didn't know their history, she appreciated the utopian grids lying cheek by jowl with the curves of prosperous western subdivisions, saw in her mind's eye the self-assured, self-righteous suburbs' drain on the city proper.

At last, she nodded in satisfaction. Utahns had been clever in the way they solved their city's transportation difficulties, but they had not been so clever that their designs weren't blatantly, laughably wrong. Here, at last, was something she could do.

The president sat cross-legged on the map and leaned over Salt Lake City. Drawing out a thick red marker from the sack, she put her tongue between her teeth and began to design a transportation infrastructure.

*

The aliens were willing to move on from the Urim and Thummim discussion, but they were less willing to drop the subject of polygamy. As far as Herbertson could ascertain, the debate about the proper configuration of the attendant sexes was the closest their culture had come to religious strife. From the glimpses he had of the historical roots of the question, the promise of a resolution to the polygamy problem was one of the ways the aliens had justified the expense and complexity of their interstellar journey. They would not leave Earth without some sort of definitive answer on the subject.

Other prophets in the church's history might have relied on spiritual promptings to arrive at a concrete answer and been perfectly comfortable giving an edict with no real understanding of the situation. But this was not Herbertson's style. He believed in detailed research, reflection, and serious contemplation—intermingled with prayer—before making any sort of prophetic pronouncement. He would not give the aliens a decree until he understood its implications and impact. And so, the discussions dragged on, both parties growing more and more befuddled.

At last, the indigo alien, who had been taking over more and more of the conversation, sent with characteristic impatience, *Perhaps you can tell us the Earthly church's approach to the problem of polygamy.*

This was a question Herbertson was prepared to answer, and he leapt for it. In fact, it was so well-worn in Herbertson's mind— honed after years of being asked by reporters, religious leaders, and the faithful alike—that he began sending the answer almost before he realized it. He told them of the Saints' expulsion to Utah, the years of political strife, the 1890 Manifesto, and then—with some habitual pride—the church's current strident policies against polygamy. He told them more than he meant to, fumbling a bit with the translator, of the success the church had in distancing itself from this embarrassing chapter of its history.

Suddenly he faltered as he recalled his audience.

The aliens stared at him, black eyes wide, horror and confusion crashing through the translator in Herbertson's hands.

You—countermanded—Brother Joseph's prophecy? came the first articulate question, *countermanded* flirting with *treason* and *blasphemy.* Herbertson, stung from an unfamiliar corner, replied too swiftly and too much by rote: *It was a political necessity at the time. Those who opposed the Saints would not let us live peacefully unless we adapted.* He was sweating heavily now, his fingers twitching nervously around the translator in his lap.

The aliens continued to stare at him, their contempt for the concept of *political necessity* welling up through the translator.

There must, thought Herbertson desperately at them, *have been those in your culture who resisted Joseph's prophecy?*

Again, horror and confusion bled through the translator.

At last, the indigo alien stepped forward in a swaying, mammoth movement. *Why would anyone resist the Prophet's words?* it sent. *What he spoke was the Truth.*

Truth in the translator was rocklike and impressive, as solid a fact as the certainty of gravity or the heat of the sun.

Not everyone can see the Truth for what it is, sent Herbertson uneasily.

The indigo alien blinked at him. *Then what good is the Truth?* it sent. There was fear and confusion in its words, but something else was growing beneath it, something hard, apprehensive, and accusatory.

Herbertson stared at the alien, his fingers hovering above the translator.

We are confused because two opposing Truths cannot exist simultaneously. Either Joseph's words are the self-evident Truth, or your adaptation is. In the translator, *adaptation* was neither a lovely nor congratulatory concept.

The church must adapt to survive, sent Herbertson. His communications were becoming messy and inconsistent again—his deep, unexamined feelings slipping out as he attempted to gain control of the conversation. *Surely, on your planet, adjustments had to be made—*

This thought went through the aliens like a sea-swell. They flashed glances at each other while shock, worry, and befuddlement burst like fireworks through the translator. At last, the indigo alien quelled the others with a single sweep of its arm.

This is our people, it sent. Herbertson gasped as a vision of the alien planet and its inhabitants burst into his mind. He could not make sense of the alien architecture, culture, and ecology that roared through his head. But he could manage the religion, for it was familiar in its nineteenth-century formation—its orders of administration, its fascination with the mythic past and the patterns of the universe. The aliens were not mindless drones in their faith. He saw flashes of genius and individuality—artists and architects, politicians and poets—but in one thing they agreed, and that was the divinity and accuracy of Joseph Smith's words. The uncountable billions of aliens that lived and worked and sang and died on that faraway world would be as likely to deny Joseph Smith as they would to declare that water and food were unnecessary. The aliens *believed*—uniformly, passionately, and securely.

Herbertson found himself clinging to the metal frame of his chair as the vision passed. *How is it possible*, he sent, *that all of you believe?*

How is it possible, sent the indigo alien, and Herbertson had the crawling feeling that it was looking at him the way a doctor might look at a pathogen under a microscope, *that all of you* do not *believe?*

*

The aliens called for the president. TAKE US TO YOUR LEADER, SAY ALIENS reported the news sites, though in fact what the aliens had sent was *We must speak to the foremost representative of your culture*, which the military and scientific representatives figured meant the same thing.

The president was unprepared for the interview. She had stumbled upon a casual club of women city planners in Salt Lake Valley and had gotten herself invited to their weekly bar night. Two glasses of red in, she had—with uncharacteristic bashfulness—told them of her sketched-out plans for the Wasatch Front's infrastructure. The evening had ended with the five women in her hotel room, speaking in excitable and too-loud tones about how *clever* her plan was, and how with a few modifications it could revolutionize the snarling traffic corridors, reduce the persistent smog, and even—after a few more glasses of wine—raise the profile of the state. The president suspected the city planners were buttering her up, but that was something she was used to.

So, it was a dangerously hungover president that met with the aliens, sitting carefully on Herbertson's former seat with her legs crossed—something she only did when her head and stomach were uncertain. She had no idea what she was going to say. All she could gather from her advisors was that something had broken between the aliens and the Mormons, and she was supposed to fix things so that the military and scientists could finally ask their burning questions. How she was supposed to do that was not touched upon.

"You'll be amazing," the aide had said instead as she propelled the president toward the tent. "Focus on collaboration. Ways we can be mutually beneficial. Our shared—um—whatever we share." Even hungover, the president made a mental note of the aide's exact phrasing. It would be an excellent anecdote for her book.

She had been under the impression that the aliens spoke democratically, so she was surprised when the alien with dark indigo and blue patterning stood forward while the others huddled together, stroking each other's backs with their strangely jointed arms.

Are they alright? the president sent through the translator, struggling to master it though she'd been talked through the process by scientists and Margolyes alike.

The indigo alien's communication was short and brusque. *They are—What? Lost? In mourning? Betrayed?* The president shook her head empathetically. Whatever the exact meaning might be, it was bad. *I am sorry*, she sent.

The alien made a movement with one of its fingers, and the translator beamed the concept of a resigned shrug.

I'm ready to speak as a representative of Earth, said the president. *Sorry, I should have started with that.*

The indigo alien stared at her, dark eyes flashing. At last, with a weird sort of articulation that the president interpreted as very considered communication, the indigo alien asked, *Why has your planet perverted the words of Brother Joseph?* Every concept coming through the translator rang with raw hurt.

Who? the president sent back.

The alien reacted as if it had been slapped. *Brother Joseph*, it repeated.

Through the haze of her aching head, the president remembered. *Oh, the Mormon founder. Yes.* She wracked her brain for any information. She had done her master's thesis on the Quaker influence on American politics. Perhaps there was something there. But—no, nothing beyond some footnotes that were mostly snide. She bit her lip and tried harder, her head reeling.

The indigo alien was aghast. *You don't know Brother Joseph?* it sent. In the translator, *know* was *understanding* and *love* and *reverence* and *gratitude.*

The president laughed.

The indigo alien stepped back. Shock, outrage, and offense bubbled up from the translator. If her last comment had been a slap, this was a body blow.

I'm sorry, sent the president swiftly. *I was unprepared for the question. I didn't mean to be disrespectful. It's just—*. She fumbled, trying to force herself to think diplomatically. *The church that Joseph Smith*

149

founded is—what word is best? Small? Inconsequential? Comically backward? A joke? Unsettlingly ludicrous?

A hissing sound caught her attention, and she glanced at the aliens, realizing too late that she had poured all her true feelings into the communication—shared how *tiny* the church was in her estimation, how the powerful, important people of the world would laugh up their sleeves at the thought of her trapped in the myopic, fanatic world of Mormonism.

I'm sorry, she said again, casting about for the right thing to say. *I am not good with this—communication.*

The aliens stared at her with black eyes, their throats pulsing.

✳

The aliens left Earth the next day, rising on their strange boards. Their ship lingered above Temple Square for a few hours and then, stately and slow, soared straight upward and out of sight. The images sent by the drones showed that not one of the aliens looked back down as they departed. Herbertson watched the ship rise from his apartment window, strangely hurt that the aliens had not bid him farewell.

There was a period following the aliens' arrival in which Mormonism was in vogue. A few well-known celebrities converted, and baptism numbers (as tracked on a graph in the Church Office Building) ticked upwards for several months. But the popularity was brief. The celebrities discovered, surprisingly late, about the restrictions on alcohol and coffee and either renounced their new-found faith or had their publicists quietly bury evidence of their baptism. Shortly after, conversion rates dipped back down to the slow decline common to all churches in the West.

The president returned to Washington, relief making her muscles shaky as she deplaned. She would set up a task force, she announced to the country, so that Earth (but more importantly, America) would be prepared for any future visitations. But for the task force to do its job properly, American infrastructure needed a dramatic overhaul. Most Americans stopped listening after the words "task force," but it turned out that the network of superfast trains the president had developed actually did improve their lives.

Herbertson sent the president a kind note in spidery handwriting when she was re-elected, which she meant to respond to but inevitably forgot.

Herbertson died later that year. His death echoed his life. Turning over in bed, he said, "Oh! Pardon me," loudly enough that it woke his wife. Then, he was gone. His funeral was well attended, and they wept for him as far away as Ghana, India, and Peru. At the next conference, Holyoke was sustained as the prophet. His first talk to the Saints was titled, "Continuing Revelation: A Blessing to All Mankind," and it was observed that he stressed *mankind* throughout his speech. He had become convinced that the aliens had been sent as a sort of trial for the church; a warning against clinging to the traditions of the past. The rest of the Brethren did not share their opinions about the aliens' visit, but they did voice their support for Holyoke's plan for an extended Manifesto that would, yet again, delineate the church's stance on important issues such as marriage and identity.

*

It was five years after Holyoke's sustaining that Elder Paulo Silva Araújo left his companion in their sweaty-walled apartment and wandered up the hill behind the row of tenements they lived in.

There was a stand of jungle at the crest of the hill, an island in the midst of Curitiba's sprawl. Feeling his companion's eyes on him through the oily windows of the apartment, Paulo set off for the seclusion of the trees. They'd had a fight—a stupid one, but one that left them shouting. Paulo couldn't stand another minute of staring at that pinched, white face.

He was asserting his power over the situation by breaking the rules, flagrantly and with a carefully contained casualness. Elder Crump would probably be on the phone with the mission president as soon as he disappeared into the gloom beneath the trees. Paulo bared his teeth at the stands of green as he passed them, resenting the eventual conversation, already imagining the mission president's smooth, conciliatory tones, the cheerful, patronizing way he would say, "The Lord wants you to have harmony in your companionship."

Paulo sat on a mossy rock, idly snapping twigs off nearby bushes and tossing them at the beetles and ants at work in the soil. Not for the first time, his thoughts wandered into something that was not quite a prayer: *God, but this is a colossal waste of my time.*

There was a sudden pillar of light around him, coming from directly overhead. Paulo looked upward, squinting into the sun-like brilliance. A figure was descending in the light: a giant, dark figure, with a thrown-back head that bore lines of indigo and blue patterning.

Paulo stood as the figure descended. It looked at him, its black, expressionless eyes flashing. Wordlessly, it handed Paulo a twisted box with delicate coruscations.

The figure spoke. *We have a task for you,* boomed the translator through Paulo's fingers. *What task* and *Why me?* bubbled uncleanly through Paulo's translator.

The figure gestured in what the translator communicated as a long sigh. *We are disappointed in the church, which has—was it lost?—the fullness of Brother Joseph's words. But we cannot leave our—kin?—on Earth to suffer in darkness.*

The indigo figure reached into a satchel hanging about its shoulders and pulled out a gleaming metal square on which were etched dense lines of an alien language, the script glowing with hidden light.

The figure's black eyes bored into Paulo's brown ones, and the translator throbbed with love and concern. *You will translate and bring the Truth of Joseph's words again to the Earth. A Restoration is needed.*

AFTER MIDNIGHT

PHYLLIS BARBER

One night, more than deep into the night, Laura sat at the dining table. Alone. Reflective. Suddenly, she sat forward. She'd just finished eating a bowl of late-night ice cream, which hadn't pleased her as much as it usually did. Ice cream = always satisfying. But not tonight. Even the candle she'd lit to create a romantic atmosphere didn't do anything except cast a shaky light on the walls. Then, out of the blue, like a flash of lightning, she was filled with foreboding.

I don't have much time left, she panicked. Her heart began to race.

Laura took the empty bowl to the sink and rinsed out the remains of salted caramel. She turned it over onto the towel where she aired dishes. She poured liquid soap and then water on her spoon and put it on the same towel. Straight next to round: the way a spoon should be set next to a bowl. Things needed to be put right before … She didn't want to think about it anymore.

But it was more than she could control. Against her better judgment, she asked herself the question that had disturbed the margins of her consciousness before, especially on the day Peter died. Time. How much is left? She stood motionless at the sink, feeling the ghost of the bowl's curve in her hands and thinking of Peter—her husband of forty years. He was gone. Last year. He'd run out of time, some had said. Out of gas. She smiled; she couldn't help it. But this was not the time to make light of anything. She placed her hands flat on the granite counter that surrounded the sink. The surface felt cool on this hot night, but she couldn't hide from the fact that a good part of her believed she'd reached her limit.

There *was* an end of time for her. She could feel it. Finite. Fixed. Finished. Like an egg timer filled with white sand streaming slowly through its tight waist, grain by grain. The years were spinning by faster and faster, and she hadn't consented. It was all coming to an end.

She turned from the sink to her bedroom. But maybe she had too much time on her hands; nothing to do for real anymore, no more committees to chair, no more important calls to make. She shrugged one shoulder before she blew out the candle, the one she'd lit to pretend there was someone waiting for her. Someone who'd be eager to hold her and kiss her cheek, maybe even her lips. Then she flipped the last light switch and negotiated the darkness, careful not to bump the walnut cabinet in the hallway.

The movie she'd just watched had been a waste of time. Too much TV, she told herself. It's numbing my mind. She rounded a corner to the bathroom, washed her face, brushed her teeth, and dressed in her nightgown. Then, she turned out the lights, tucked herself beneath the sheet, and squirmed to get comfortable in the dip she'd worn for herself in the mattress. The night was still hot. Humid even. The air felt like a wet blanket. She tried to find a cool spot on her pillow, stretching her arms over and under its softness. Then she turned on her side.

Her body felt stiff tonight—like a board. Why did she have to be by herself in this big bed? Where was Peter so she could reach over, pat him on the head, tell him a good-night joke, scratch his arm, or maybe even scooch close to him to let him know she was interested in something more? She could feel rigidity in her muscles that wouldn't let go. Even her thighs seemed tightly bound. She wished it was morning with the sun shining through the window, time to be up and busy with all the things needing to be done, which really weren't that many. But through the window, she could see the blackness of night, dark as dark because the moon had ducked behind a cloud. The inky black was too invasive for any reasonable thoughts of dawn. But she couldn't close her eyes.

If I go to sleep, she thought, I might not wake up.

Good grief. Where did that idea come from? It started pounding against the sides of her head as if it wanted out. You better not go to sleep, she thought again, then again and again. She turned over and buried her face in the pillow. She tugged her nightgown straight so it wouldn't pinch her shoulder too tightly. If I go to sleep ... her thoughts tumbled and turned. I can't. I can't go to sleep. I have to stay awake. Have. To. Stay. Awake.

The more she thought, the more the idea became like a balloon filling with hot air, getting bigger and longer. I don't want to die, she told herself. To cross over; to face the great unknown all by myself. What will happen when I pass? Her mind traveled and twisted. If what I hear at church is right, there will be a kingdom that will have me. But will I really go to a place where I can dance with Peter and sing hymns with those I've loved? Will we be a family—Peter, me, the two boys, my sweet daughter, Prudence? Or will I be a mere source of nutrients for the tree under which I'm buried?

She switched to her other side. And where will I go after I die? I know I'm not perfect, but ... Suddenly, her mind filled with a flood of images, all of them gates. The most prominent were the Pearly Gates, but they were locked and twice as tall as she was—a chain hanging from knob to knob. Everything was encrusted with pearls—embedded into each metal rung, dripping from the gold archway on threads of silver. Then a rusty, forbidding gate moved to the foreground, also locked. Whispery sounds filled her head, and she could hear shrill screams, a metallic moan, and then something like the sound of fingernails scratching a chalkboard. Is this the gate to hell, she wondered? Is this where I'm going?

Different gates towered over her, all of them locked. Gates like bombs dropping out of the sky; some as heavy as helicopters it seemed.

Perspiration dotted her forehead. She threw off the twisted sheets. She'd get dressed. She'd take a walk. She needed to move. Anything but stay in bed and tempt fate by going to sleep—which she couldn't do anyway. No more thinking about the possibility that she might be finishing her life.

As she slipped into her sweats and T-shirt and was tying her tennis shoes, she realized she wouldn't be able to see much walking in the dark, but, she finally decided, I'll think about the best frosting for Prudence's birthday cake. That's what I'll do. I'll decide where we can have her birthday party—my house or hers. I'll decide whether to take the Yoga for Sixty+ class at the gym. I'll find an open lawn and try a warrior pose to see if I'm still up for it. Nobody's awake. I'll be invisible.

She finished tying her shoes and decided it would be wise to take a water bottle. Who knew how long she might be, or whether she might get thirsty? She filled the bottle, screwed the lid on, made sure she had the key in her pocket, and locked the door behind her. But after she walked down her driveway and into the neighborhood, the moon escaped the clouds.

In that one sliver of a moment, she witnessed the highlighting of what seemed to be an inordinate number of white fences. And fences have gates. She couldn't help but panic. Not gates; not locked ones! No more tonight. Her mind became overactive, hyper, uncontrollable. Pearly gates. Gates of hell. Are they for real?

She tried to clear her mind. She needed to stay sane. No more thinking about this, she told herself. She took care to stand on a pristine slab of concrete, avoiding the unpredictable cracks on either end, not sure if they'd break *her* back—forget her mother who had passed long ago. She exhaled a deep breath, stepped off a larger-than-usual curb, and made her way across the empty street. I need to keep my wits, she told herself. But then, she laughed quietly, why shouldn't I be admitted to the supreme heavens above, to the place where I can be Queen of Something if the pearly gates have anything to say about it? She still had her sense of humor. Who's afraid of gates anyway?

Into the dark night, she walked past homes nestled in the foothills. The slanted sides of the valley where the houses slept cast even darker shadows across her path, and the moonlight was unpredictable as it parried with the clouds. The sticky soles of her rubber shoes squeaked on the sidewalk—an annoying companion normally—but tonight, in all this darkness, comforting.

Tall hollyhocks, colorless in the moonlight, stood sentry over the fences and framed the gates—the openings, the ways into, the ways out of. They could be doorways, entrances, entryways, exits, egresses, ingresses, openings, portals, barriers—but which were they? And were they locked? What would they open to? Backyards, side yards, gardens, fountains, trampolines, bedlam? Maybe some of them opened to paths that rose to the celestial world. Maybe she could walk her way into heaven and avoid death altogether. She'd become a light being. A shooting star, heading into the sky. Again, she laughed at her imagination.

Then, suddenly, a shadow appeared out of nowhere—a profile, an outline standing at a right angle to the sidewalk. It had four legs and antlers on its head. A deer? A buck even, traveling through the night, browsing the plants, eating the hostas—or maybe just examining the neighborhood like she was, while everyone was sleeping. She stopped walking and waited to see if the animal was aware of her presence. But the night was a good cover. The deer's stance seemed comfortable, incautious, almost irreverent. It didn't seem to care about the humans tucked away in their beds, unafraid of whatever animals might venture out of their hiding places. Laura felt envious. It seemed majestic. Bigger than life. A statue. A thing she would remember tomorrow—if, that is, there would be a tomorrow.

Then, as if someone stretched out a finger and nudged it, the deer bolted toward one of the fences. It was a beautiful thing to see, the way it ran, the way it lifted into the air, springing off its hooves, clearing the fence and gate. Just like that. An amazing moment: and Laura was there to see it. And then the deer was out of sight.

She stood still for a moment, feeling how tight the laces were on her right shoe. More than anything, she wanted to follow the deer. But she laughed to herself; she hadn't jumped a fence in years and wasn't about to try. Besides, she needed her z's. Otherwise, she'd be sorry, sluggish, tipsy. She was the kind who needed at least ten hours. She should go back to bed right now.

And if she found the gate and went through … it might lock on her. She'd be stuck in someone's backyard. She'd be illegal. There would be nowhere else to go once she'd opened the gate, once she stepped inside that private space. A place meant only for the homeowners. But there's a gate. A gate that opens and closes. That must mean something.

She loped across the grass toward the deer's fence, calculating how high it must have leaped. At least four feet. Very quietly, she lifted the latch. It opened. Careful to not make a sound that would alert the neighbors to a trespasser, she closed the gate behind her. She looked at the shrubbery to her left, then to her right. A slight breeze turned the leaves from side to side. But maybe it wasn't a breeze. Maybe it was the deer. She was sure the animal was here somewhere.

She stepped quietly through the side yard that opened onto the tilled rows of a vegetable garden—a full-blown tomato plant ready to yield. The backyard had a patio and lawn furniture; a barbecue with a cover over it; table and chairs, nice enough. And then there was a fountain, its gurgling water rushing down an artificial cliff. Then she saw it. At the back of a lilac bush with dried blossoms, two eyes—guarded, wary, shining more brightly when the moon escaped the clouds.

She stepped closer to the bush, held out her hand, and clicked her tongue as she would to a pet; but the eyes were telling her she'd come far enough. They stood that way for a frozen moment, Laura with her arm stretched out, the deer's eyes holding her in thrall—as if there were nothing else to see; both caught by the sight of the other. A few shallow breaths in Laura's throat. A riveting. A fascination. What would the deer tell her if it could speak? Did it know anything about time? Or the consequence of locked gates?

Then, the spell broke. The deer leaped out of the bush, almost knocking her over. She let out a small scream of surprise, then watched it graze the barbecue as it ran, making a brutally loud clang. Finally, it jumped over the fence in the exact same place it had jumped to enter. Then it disappeared.

Laura was so surprised, she couldn't move. She felt paralyzed in this foreign backyard with its barrels of green herbs, flowers, fountain, and ripening tomato plant. Mental pictures of the gates began to mock her again, especially the gates of hell. A porchlight came on, and the backyard flooded with light. "Who's that?" yelled a voice. "Who's out there?" The profile shadowed its eyes with a hand and was pulling up what appeared to be pajama bottoms. "Somebody's out there. Who is it?"

Laura didn't think she'd better answer; nobody would ever understand why she was here. She sank to her knees in the shadows of the same bush the deer had been hiding in. She was an invader.

A prowler. She'd never been one of those before. She could show up on the police blotter. What if the neighbor had a gun? What if he sent her to her final resting place without sleeping after all? She stayed as still as she knew how. Her underarms poured with wet fear; shivers ran up and down her spine; she could hear her heart thumping and wondered if the man could as well.

"Looks okay out here, Molly. Don't be afraid. I'll leave the lights on."

The back door opened, the screen door pulled closed, and the man in pajama bottoms disappeared. Laura dropped her head to the ground, her nose pressed against the grass. She couldn't believe she'd been spared. Anything could have happened. She could have been arrested. Shot. She submitted to Mother Earth, trembling, holding onto the grass blades as if they were lifelines. The beautiful grass that grew in all the lawns. The smell of the grass. Water in the earth. Thousands of miles to the China she'd once thought she could dig to.

As soon as she was able, she placed her palms flat on the ground, pushed herself to a standing position, and pressed her hands into the prayer position she used in her yoga class. She felt like saying alleluia to whatever and whomever had left her intact and out of jail. She closed her eyes in silent invocation, then inched her way out of the yard, keeping to the shadows. Gradually she side-stepped her way toward the front yard, working her way past the vegetable garden and tomato plant (with, now she could see, three ripening tomatoes). And there it was—the beloved gate. White in the moonlight. Almost shimmering. She lifted the latch, and the gate opened. Hallelujah! It opened. It let her both in and out. She closed it as quietly as she could, her ever-present heart beating with anxiety … or joy—whichever it was. She ducked beneath tree branches and tip-toed to the sidewalk, to the street. A way. A path. Freedom. The night. Escape.

She ran as if she were second place in a marathon, straining to pass the runner ahead as they approached the finish line. She felt freer than she'd ever felt, running without caring. She'd get back home as fast as she could and cocoon herself in the sheets. She wasn't worried about sleeping or squeaky shoes. Everything would be okay. She was out of harm's way. Something about the eyes of the deer. Something about their steadiness, their steadfastness, their commitment to staying alive. Something reassuring, especially now that she was free of that backyard.

A pair of headlights lit up the street. Laura ducked behind a leafy shrub, not wanting to be seen at this unholy hour—feeling like Eve and her fig leaf hiding from God. She laughed, almost delirious, as the lone car careened down the street, zigzagging slightly. She hoped it wouldn't cross paths with the deer. As the car went by, she heard the beat of rap music on its radio. She felt like boogying in the bushes. In her tennies, T-shirt, and sweats. She took a swig from the water bottle. What a night! Time and no time and endless time. She looked up. The clouds seemed determined to cover the moon again. Good luck, clouds!

1A: LITERARY PALS;
OR HOW NOT TO DOUBLE DOWN

RYAN MCILVAIN

Today: a typical text exchange with my crossword-loving family after I finished a difficult Thursday puzzle and submitted my time to the three others in our running competition—

My mother-in-law, NINA, taking first place with 18:46, a day after her second course of the Pfizer cure: "Full vaccine brain tonight."

Followed by GIL at 20:55, my father-in-law and a man of few words, at least over text:

With newcomer/virtuoso SAMANTHA, my sister-in-law, taking third at 22:16: "Even with vaccine brains you smoked me."

Finally, hours later, there's ME at 41:16, draped, as usual, in what Samantha once called Ryan's Special Medal. I'd complained that I rarely ever get on the podium and maybe the problem is the podium itself. Why only three places, three medals? Why not gold, silver, bronze, and nickel, say? Samantha's clever and very cutting rejoinder—

"Phew! This much work for just the first half of the week! Worried about the second half."

ME: "Need to gamble more to really excel at this puzzle [referring to the puzzle's theme, answer, and clue (*Doubledown* [32D: Blackjack bet ... or a hint to applying the five circled regions in this puzzle]). Also, *hanging indent*? I've been around bibliographies for a while now, but that's a new one. Of course, it wouldn't have been such a problem if I could just commit those damn Musketeers' names to memory [referring to Athos (1A: Literary pal of Porthos)]."

It's my inevitable strategy: I reach for chattiness to cover my awkwardness, or, in this case, to span the widening chasm between me and my comrades in the crossworld. The family tolerates me, lets me tag along, the runt (in-law) of the litter. Which is generous of them. Occasionally, I do sneak onto the podium and relegate one of them to the embarrassing Ryan position ...

*

I've been puttering around with the *Times* crossword puzzle, off and on, since undergrad, ever since I watched a pair of my whiz-kid friends mow through a Monday at the BYU Creamery on Ninth. It was the puzzle that the campus paper, *The Daily Universe*, ran on Mondays, possibly the only puzzle it paid to run. (A question of fact I could probably investigate and confirm but, truth be told, I lack the emotional wherewithal this morning to wade back too deeply into that campus and that paper and that world, all of which I used to be an active part of. We liked to tease our paper—I'll re-call that much. *The Daily Uni-farce*, we called it. And we teased the university's tagline, too, rather Mormonly—that is to say chaismi-cally—such that *The world is our campus* became *The campus is our world*.) In any case, I envied my crossword-puzzling friends their quick, easy-ranging wit; a pair of too-smart-for-the-humans types.

Dai and Hannah had the smarts and the grades and the test scores coming out of high school to attend much fancier univer-sities than the Mormon Harvard (more of our self-deprecating humor). It's just that their devout parents wouldn't hear of them matriculating anywhere else, at least not for undergrad. I recall that Dai and Hannah, mutual friends of mine, briefly became more than friends with each other. I hung around the outskirts of their relationship, ferrying messages occasionally, laughing at in-jokes I didn't quite understand. Once, Dai confided in me, in that teasing way of ours that had become a kind of religion within the religion, a hedge about the law—"Hannah's getting bored of my company in the evenings: 'How can you just bake and watch

movies every—single—night?'" Dai laughed at himself: brilliant
but domesticated Dai, who'd taught me about the Pillsbury Bake-
Off, whose feverish brownie and cupcake making, or fondant cake
baking, tended to peak at midterms and finals.

I see I'm wading in after all—and maybe the water feels cooler
on my shins than I'd expected; or maybe it's that Hannah and Dai
make good vicarious guides here. Here goes; up to my waist now—

*

At last Dai and Hannah's romance disappeared lightly, or
anyway it appeared that way from the outside: a gentle, soundless,
soap-bubble popping. Hannah stepped away from our circle a little;
a bit of a breather. By the time she came back, I understood that
she was helping her friend to come out of the closet all the way—a
very BYU story, actually. And this one ends better than most.

Twenty years on, Hannah is camped on the edges of the
Mormon worldview/Church in her own, *sui generis* way, working in tech up in Northern California, married with a kid whose
Buddha-like rotundity contrasted in a kind of running joke with
the marathoner who held him in the early Facebook photos.
Dai and his husband, Ely, live in Columbus now, and maintain a
studied-casual distance, I understand, from orthodox Mormonism
and Orthodox Judaism, respectively.

A hell of a wedding, Dai and Ely's—outdoors in a public park
in Syracuse, New York, under the shocking orange-yellow foliage
of an October Saturday. Dai was doing a master's in religious studies in town, and one of his fellows from the college, an ordained
minister in the ecumenical tradition, said beautiful things that stay
with me less as discrete bits of language than as a mood, an open-
ness. The words and the mounting hills beyond the park moved the
eye inevitably skyward, I recall.

It was a morning wedding so that Ely's parents could attend
temple in the afternoon. That night, at the reception at a local art
gallery—

Let me interrupt myself to say how I loved, and still love, this
Mormon frugality, genuinely—how it enforces all the right behav-
iors and priorities. You should see how glarey and shadow-pitted we

look in all the photos, under those small-museum track lights. Fine. Perfect, actually, since every shot became a kind of candid shot, and a spirit of candor and love and relaxation suffused the whole evening … I got a chance to catch up with Hannah that night, and Daine and Amanda and Robert and other friends from my BYU days. Too-smart-for-the-humans-and-yet-socially-graceful Hannah had dropped out of a linguistics Ph.D. at UC Berkeley to take a job at Facebook, where she quickly climbed the ranks.

"Aren't you going to miss the dilatory grad school life?" I'd asked her at the time, myself a dilatory grad student in the Bay Area.

Hannah's insight, acute and typical: "Oh, we say we're all lazy and working catch as catch can, but we're really working all the time, eighty hours a week; more. We're never *not* working, really, and all so we can enter a scarcity-economy academic job market in which a colleague's success is zero sum: their success means your failure; their slice of the pie is the slice you'd been gunning for … In Tech it's not like that. There's more space, more opportunity. I can celebrate with my colleagues when something good happens for them …"

I envied Hannah her new industry again as she caught me up on things at the reception. And sometimes (zooming back to the present)—maybe not *often* but more than rarely—I envy Hannah's decision still, having staked my own tent in the Hobbesian academic world that she correctly described.

What else happened that night? I managed to corner Dai—literally, as I remember it. Over by the black-and-white photographs and the pile of coats, I came on with the earnestness he always loved/hated in me—

"You're going to ask if I'm still in the church," he said. "Right? You want that whole long conversation."

"It is a long one …"

"I'll give you a hint," Dai said. "I'm the Sunday school president."

He said his new husband had no interest in going with him to church, ever—and fair enough. But Dai was in it to win it in his own way, at least until they called him out and forced his hand or excommunicated him, whichever came first. That ball would remain in their court. ("Only who's 'they'?")

"They" was the bishop of Dai's Syracuse-area ward, apparently. He didn't know about the engagement or the wedding. "He's not really checked in too much," Dai explained.

Zooming to the present again, I'm not sure if Dai's relationship with the church is still active in some way, in his own way. (I think of Bellow's famous opening to *Augie March*: "I have taught myself, free-style, and will make the record in my own way: first to knock, first admitted; sometimes an innocent knock, sometimes a not so innocent.") In any case, I'm sure a continued membership in the church for Dai would mean a more interesting church—maybe a more interesting Dai, who knows? It was always impossible to pinpoint Dai's precise metaphysical coordinates at any given moment, perhaps because they were changing moment to moment. Nor have I tried to pin him down recently, in the middle of a plague year, just to write down these memories.

I remember speaking to Dai's mother, Helen, immediately after the wedding ceremony. I'd said the usual truisms: a beautiful service, etc. (I happened to mean them.) Helen looked off a little and said something between "Hmmm" and "Huh." I had reason to wonder how many of Dai and Ely's religious family members had their feelings on ice just then.

Later at the reception, in lighter spirits, Helen asked me what Wallace Stegner I'd read. I'd recently finished a Stegner Fellowship in creative writing at Stanford, but I hadn't read too much of the man, actually. Maybe half of his book on the Mormon handcart pioneers, some of them my ancestors. Plus, his strange, lyrical novel *The Spectator Bird*.

"You haven't read *Angle of Repose*?" Helen said. "You haven't read *Crossing to Safety*?"

"I know; I know," nodding my head in time, playing the hangdog.

"You'll take the money in his name, but you won't read him? I see how it is …"

I saw exactly where Dai's questing intelligence had come from; his default teasing humor; his slipperiness and beauty.

*

Only I was supposed to be talking about crossword puzzles—
how to fit things into the right squares, how to force your brain
to work as the puzzle wants it to. It's a useful exercise—nutritive,
often fun—but occasionally the pieces just won't fit. Your brain,
or whatever it is that makes you you, just won't square. And that's
okay, too. One of the things I'm learning from the NYTXW is
how to fail—not on the difficult Thursday I began with, but on the
Saturday after, for example.

I'd suffered on that Thursday, again on the Friday, clocking
two-plus hours between the two puzzles. The Friday solve had been
particularly Pyrrhic, as the saying goes. ("Pyrrhic," after the Greek
king Pyrrhus, who said after a costly battle, "Another victory like
that and we're undone.")

Sometimes it is better, I think, to count your losses, mourn
them, and retreat in your own way. By the time I got to the Saturday puzzle I had no stamina left and knew it: DNF (did not finish)
at the 30-minute mark.

I'd regroup for the Sunday.

THE MATHEMATICS OF GOD

JACK HARRELL

They introduced themselves as Kaja and Stanislaw Bondar, a brother and sister from Ukraine. Stanislaw worked at one of the oil refineries in North Salt Lake, a couple of miles from here, and Kaja was taking classes at the community college—"Boring classes," she often said. "Stuff I'll never use." They paid cash for the deposit and first month's rent, and twenty minutes later, an old American car with four doors and a big trunk appeared in the driveway. They unloaded a few boxes and suitcases. After that they walked or took Ubers wherever they went. Until the final incident, that is, when they departed in a big black SUV driven by a man in a suit and dark sunglasses.

Under ordinary circumstances, yes, I would have done a background check. I live in the basement apartment and work from home doing cybersecurity. I rented the upstairs to them—two bedrooms, a living room, kitchen, and bath. It would have been easy to check them out. But there's a reason I didn't. You see, I believe the Book of Mormon to be the word of God and the best possible means for bringing souls to "the waters of Judah." On that first meeting, I received a clear impression that I should introduce Kaja to baptism and the Book of Mormon. So, I trusted in the Spirit, knowing that if I did my part, the Lord would do his and bring to pass his strange act.

My house was built in the 1960s when this part of Rose Park was developed as a blue-collar alternative to Salt Lake City's east side. My apartment door is around the side, past the driveway and down a small flight of stairs. When Stanislaw was at work, Kaja would come around with Ukrainian dishes—potato pancakes, dumplings, borscht—and ask what I was working on. She liked all the computers I had running in my living room and on the kitchen counters, some screens as large as TV sets.

One afternoon I was at my big whiteboard, working on a math equation. This was just a few days after I'd given her a copy of the Book of Mormon in Ukrainian. I had the door open when she came—that many computers can really heat a room up. "Look, Preston," she said from the doorway, "I have *paska.*" She held up a beautiful round loaf of bread with a golden braided top. It smelled delicious. "It's Easter bread," she said. "You're going to love it." She put the bread on the kitchen counter and started looking for a knife.

By this time I knew I was in over my head—an attractive Eastern European woman in yoga pants and flip-flops bringing food to my door whenever she had the whim. I had to be like Nephi and follow the Spirit, not knowing beforehand the things I should do. She found the bread knife and motioned toward the whiteboard, crowded with symbols and numbers. "What is all that?" she asked.

I saw a dropped-integration error and quickly corrected it. "It's a subset of a problem I'm working on."

"It looks too complicated," she said.

"Right now, I'm creating problems," I admitted. "But you have to do that to find solutions. The best math just uncovers what's already there. I think that's why Galileo called mathematics the language of God."

"Is this problem for the cybersecurity?" she asked.

"No, this isn't for work. It's one of the Millennium Prize problems. I've been at it for weeks—for years, really. It's a problem called *P versus NP.*"

"Pee and not pee?" she said. "That sounds funny. You have butter?"

"On the counter." I put the cap on my marker and set it in the tray. "Did you read those passages I marked? In the Book of Mormon?"

"Passages?" She handed me a piece of *paska* slathered in butter.

"The verses I marked. The ones on baptism and the Gift of the Holy Ghost?"

She picked at her bread. "Some of them. Was the book really made of gold?"

"The Golden Plates? Yes! It had to be preserved for generations."

I hadn't eaten all day, and the bread was delicious. "When you were reading," I asked, "did you feel the Holy Ghost? Did the Spirit speak to you?"

She went to the whiteboard and stood there a moment, looking at the numbers and symbols. "Tell me about the Pee and Not Pee," she said, "and I'll tell you about the Mormon Book."

I began to explain, as best I could, that certain polynomial problems, P, are the kind of problems a computer can solve in just a few hours. But other problems, NP problems, even if they're easy to verify, are much more difficult to solve. "It's like a combination lock," I said. "If someone tells you the combination, you can check it in a few seconds. But if you're just guessing, it might take days or years to figure out."

She tore off a piece of bread. "Like a bike lock or something?"

"If you take an NP problem with maybe a hundred inputs, and an algorithm proportional to 2^N—that might take a computer a hundred quintillion years to solve. Which is longer than the age of the universe."

"Quintillion?" she said. "That's a funny word."

"Are you sure you want to hear this?"

She waved her hand. "Yes, professor, continue. It's so interesting."

I wrote $P = NP$ on the board, and next to that $P \neq NP$. "If P and NP are equal," I said, "that means there are no real mysteries. Every problem, every puzzle, is just a matter of finding the right formula. If God is a mathematician, as Galileo says, that's how he does it. Someone wants to make the perfect Easter bread, they apply the formula, and anybody could do it the first time. Having a happy family, knowing which church to join—just plug in the numbers and your solution is there."

"But living is not like that," Kaja said.

"There's a science institute in New Hampshire—they're offering a million dollars to anyone who can solve this."

"A million dollars? For the P and the NP?"

"If I win, I think I'll be like Perelman and not even pick up the prize."

"You would be very sexy guy, Preston, with a million. You could wear a cowboy hat and drive a big truck. Live in a house on the mountains and look down on the Mormon temples."

"I don't care about the money," I said. "I just want to be part of the Great Conversation, you know? Bring God and science together into one great whole—the way they once were. Anyway," I said, "it's your turn. What did you think of the Book of Mormon?"

She went to my desk and started poking around the papers there. "The book says about baptisms of fire. You have that in your church?"

"That comes later," I answered. "First you have to enter in at the strait gate."

"Where is this gate?" she asked.

"Baptism is the gate," I said, "like going through a doorway. To a new place."

She picked up one of my notebooks and started turning through the pages. "The diving in the water," she said. "Why does it have to be that?"

"It could be anything, right? You could sign something or take a test—but not everyone knows how to write. There could be feats of endurance, like going into the desert for forty days. You could swear an oath. Anything, really."

She turned the pages of the notebook. "Why the dipping in the water?"

"Death and resurrection," I said. "It's symbolic. You go down in the grave and come up a new creature. You leave your old self in the grave."

"Ugh!" she said. "Why are old religions always about death?"

"Because we're all going to die, and we've all been born. Everyone is on the same journey, the same path."

"Come on, Preston!" She swatted me with the notebook. "You are always working; always doing the maths. Then you want to talk about the Mormon books. When are you going to take me out to have some lunch?"

"I could do that," I said. "If you want. But this is important, Kaja. I can buy you lunch anytime. But the Word of God feeds you forever."

She turned up her nose. "Sounds like a fishy story." Then she opened the notebook and held out a page for me to see. "What are all these codes? Are they the codes for the cybersecurity?"

"Some of them," I said. "I write down certain things on paper, so they don't get hacked."

"Ha!" she said. "Stanislaw is hacker." She watched me, gauging my response. "I'm not supposed to tell. He hacked Russian energy minister once."

"Doesn't he work at an oil refinery?"

"Sure! But he does computers there, like you. Totally boring! He stays after work at the sports bar with the guys. I say, 'Take me with you!' But he says guys have wives and would be jealous. So, I come here with you and talk about maths and Books of Mormons? Ugh!" she said, dropping my notebook on the desk. "Just as boring!"

She went to the kitchen, cut a couple of slices of Easter bread, and put them on a napkin. "Next time you take me to lunch, okay?" she said. "Or maybe I cook you lunch before Stanislaw comes home from sports bar."

"That's fine," I said. "But I want you to listen for the Spirit, the Holy Ghost, when you're reading the Book of Mormon. And I want you to pray about it."

She turned in the doorway and frowned. "Stanislaw says the Book of Mormon is like stories for children. For people who believe in ghosts, not in real things."

"No," I said, "It is real, I promise."

She patted my cheek. "You're cute guy, Preston. When you win the million dollars, take me for a ride in your American truck." Then she was out the door and up the stairs.

I could have been discouraged at that point, but I didn't plan on giving up—not after the witness I'd received. It had happened that first day, when they came to look at the house. Stanislaw had just given me the cash for the rent and deposit when I saw something, a deep yellow aura, gathering around Kaja's whole form. Some people hear music in the sounds of ordinary things. Others feel the spirit of a rock or an animal. For me it's numbers. Each number has a character, an essence, and I can feel it when I'm reasonably in tune. That afternoon, the yellow aura around Kaja was at a wavelength

171

near 6 X 10⁻⁷, bringing to mind Moroni 6:1–7, which begins, "And now I speak concerning baptism." The witness couldn't have been clearer. I only wish my thoughts had been as clear on the day I gave Kaja a Book of Mormon.

I probably had too much on my mind that day—this can be a problem for me. I'd been working on P versus NP for days, several computers crunching the numbers. Of course, I was doing a dozen systems checks for work—banking transactions, financial networks—noodling around behind the firewalls of several major institutions and government agencies. I'd also recently completed a projection of phenolic substances produced by the number of dead in the final Nephite battles, as well as an algorithm to predict the effects on the soil in the region. (I'm confident those findings could be used, by the way, to determine the true location of the Book of Mormon lands.) I had a copy of the Book of Mormon in Ukrainian, and, after a bit of internet research, had highlighted passages for Kaja to read—verses on baptism (*khreshchennya*), faith (*vira*), and atonement (*spokuta*). So that morning, after fervent prayer, I went up and knocked on her door.

She was in the living room at the time, doing yoga, her back to the screen door. There was some kind of Indian music playing, and she didn't hear my knock. She moved through her poses—bending, rising, reaching arms to the sky. I knocked again, but she still didn't seem to hear. At that moment, I'll admit, I was no better than the priests of King Noah gathering to watch the daughters of the Lamanites dance. Then, suddenly, I realized that Stanislaw was right behind me. He brushed me aside to go in. "Are you needing something?" he asked. Stanislaw is a big guy, and rather intimidating. Speaking over the music, he said, "Kaja, downstairs guy is here. He is watching you do the yoga."

I don't remember much after that. I was very embarrassed. I handed Kaja the Book of Mormon and she read the title aloud: "*Knyha Mormona.* That's so nice of you, Preston!" Stanislaw waved both hands over his head and said, "No! That book we don't need!" The two of them started arguing in Ukrainian. Stanislaw pointed at me and said something that sounded insulting.

The next thing I knew, Stanislaw had me out on the front porch, looking down at me with two heavy hands on my shoulders. "My sister is very beautiful woman," he said. "You need to be careful."

After all that, after the borscht and the dumplings and the Easter bread, I thought it best to involve Stanislaw in any effort to bring Kaja to the waters of Judah. So I went to work trying to convince him to come down with Kaja to discuss the gospel and science. I had something to show him, I said, a digital model that would impress him. It took several days, but I finally got them both there, sitting on the couch in front of the biggest screen I had.

"Are we here for the million dollars?" Kaja asked.

"What millions?" Stanislaw asked.

Kaja took the notebook from my desk. "It's right in here," she said, handing Stanislaw the notebook. "This is where he keeps his secrets."

"No, that's not it," I said. I sat on the couch between them, a keyboard in my lap, and said, "Now, watch this." I tapped on a few keys and pulled up an expression of pi to the tenth decimal point. "I've been thinking about what the Book of Mormon says about baptism: how it's the gate, the entry point, the first covenant we make with God."

Stanislaw was looking at the notebook, turning the pages, not paying attention.

"Then comes the baptism with fire?" Kaja asked.

I asked Stanislaw for the notebook and put it aside. "And then I was thinking about pi, the way that it's paradoxical. Because a circle is infinite, but the diameter of a circle has a clear beginning and end. Pi expresses both of those truths at the same time."

"Those are your security codes?" Stanislaw asked. "In that notebook?"

"Yes," I said. "So don't try to hack them." I struck another key. "When you add the Fibonacci numbers, you start getting into fractals, self-similar patterns in an expanding symmetry, like Zion: a population of complete beings with no poor among them—an order that's totally scalable, by the way."

"What are you talking about?" Stanislaw asked.

"Here, you'll see," I said. I jumped up and grabbed virtual reality headsets for each of us. "Put these on," I said. They put on the headsets, and I activated the server. I had already created an avatar for each of us. A sleek cheetah for Kaja, a Russian bear for Stanislaw, and a stoic bison for me.

"So, I wondered what it would look like if the whole human family passed through the finite gate of baptism, on an infinite journey with no beginning and no end."

"For a smart man you're very stupid," Stanislaw said.

"Stanislaw, you're a dog," Kaja said. "You promised to be nice."

Ignoring them both, I continued. "I combined a few algorithms with my P and NP calculations. This is what came out."

I hit Ctrl + Alt + F7, and an image of expanding yellow and green fractals emerged all around us—symmetrical seashell shapes unfolding and expanding, each lovely form growing out of the one before.

"It's so pretty!" Kaja said. I turned to see her cheetah head looking all around in wonder. "Look at it, Stanislaw," she said.

"This is wasting time," he said. He pulled off the headset. He stood and put his hands in the air. "Every time, Mormons give you nice pictures. Things will all be so good. Just go to the baptism. Every time."

Kaja took off her headset and so did I. "When did you hear the Mormons?" Kaja asked.

"When I was teenager in Ukraine. Mormons come with the nice words and American teeth. This guy just adds VR. That's all."

Kaja stood and got in Stanislaw's face. I stood and tried to calm her. "Stanislaw," she said, "your words stink like you're a pig or something."

That's when he exploded. He started walking in circles, waving his arms, and shouting at her in Ukrainian. Then he pointed at me and spoke English. "Ask him, Kaja! Ask him if all the blessings come. Just get baptized, right Preston?"

But before I could speak, she shouted something at him in Ukrainian, something that silenced him. I don't know what it was, but the room went cold. They stared at each other for a long, silent moment. Then she went out the door. Stanislaw turned to me gravely and said, "We go now." And then he was gone too. That was my last chance, I thought. I'd put together a whole presentation, thinking I'd take it one step at a time and follow the Spirit. But

now it was over. At least an hour had passed before I realized my
notebook was missing.

I couldn't sleep that night. It wasn't the notebook—those
codes could be changed. But I wrestled with God, reasoning and
pleading. Hadn't I received a revelation about Kaja? Hadn't I tried
to share the gospel and be kind? I tossed and turned, my soul
harrowed up, wracked with all my sins. To think I could convert
anyone—or dare solve P versus NP! I was a weak vessel in the
Lord's hands. Yet I knew in whom I had trusted.

When I finally fell asleep, I dreamed that I stood surrounded
by computer screens, above and below and on all sides, with more
and more fanning out in all directions into infinity. The screens
displayed my every question, my every hope and doubt and mistake—not in images or words, but in numbers and formulas. In
the mathematics of God. The laws of math, I realized, had to come
from God, because no man could break them.

The screens before me scrolled through billions of bytes of
information, until, in an instant, they all turned to the brightest
white, and the screen in front of me displayed a single formula. The
light was so bright I could barely read it.

$$F = G \frac{m^1 m^2}{r^2} + \alpha \propto \omega \vdash \forall \exists \infty$$

The image was so bright and piercing that, when I awoke, I
recalled it perfectly: Newton's formulation of gravity, plus alpha
proportional to omega, yielding that for all things there exists
infinity. I dressed and went to the living room where I wrote down
the formula and began testing it. It felt more suggestive than
certain. To be honest, I couldn't tell if it was revelation or nonsense.
I must have been at it for an hour, working various proofs, when I
heard a noise outside my door. Kaja was there.

She stepped inside and said, "We have to go. Stanislaw will have
another job now."

"What?" I said. "You're leaving?"

"He has been up all night with your notebook. He connected a
New York bank to an account in your Pentagon. Then he got more

companies and U.S. government departments. So now he is very glad, and he says we go to Houston for a while."

"Do you have to go with him?" I asked.

"He has papers—on him and me. I have to go too."

Of course, I knew then that my career was over.

Then I realized she was holding the Book of Mormon I'd given her. She put it on the counter. "Stanislaw said to give this back. We don't need it, he says."

"You should keep it. Hide it or something."

"If you want to baptize me now," she said, "you can do it. I don't mind."

"I can't," I said. "Not now. It has to be done the right way."

"How about the bathtub or something?" She went to the sink and turned on the water. "Sprinkle me from here. Then I'll read the Book of Mormon and get the baptisms of fire, is that right?"

That's when Stanislaw appeared in the doorway. "Is that what you want, Preston?" he said. "To sprinkle her and give her to God?"

"Ha! Stanislaw," Kaja said. "Preston is going to take me to the temple. He's going to show me the Golden Plates. Aren't you, Preston?"

Stanislaw laughed. "Stupid woman! The angel took the Plates. There are no Golden Plates, are there Preston?"

Kaja turned to me, concern in her eyes. "Is that true?" she asked.

"It's true," I said. "The angel has the Plates."

"Joseph Smith gave them away," Stanislaw said, "to the angel." Then he turned to me and said, "That's what the whole problem is. Your God gives everything away. He says, 'Without money and without price.' So, she gets baptized now, or she doesn't, and with your God, it's no big deal!"

He moved toward Kaja then, looking at her. "So, you get baptized some other time, with some other guy just like him. In Ukraine I see it over and over." He leaned toward her, his voice rising. "The missionaries come to baptize. Then they go away and others come." Shouting now, he said, "There's no stopping to it!"

She withdrew from him and came to me. My arms went around her instinctively.

"Just stop it!" she said to Stanislaw. "You're barking like you always do."

But Stanislaw only smiled. "Look at you now," he said to me. "Now you are holding my wife. Is that what you wanted all along?"

"Your wife?" I said. But I didn't let her go.

"I'm sorry, Preston." She pulled away and I let her. "He made me pretend. He thinks everybody is out to get him all the time."

"You see," Stanislaw said to me. "Your God gives away everything. So you have to give away everything. You get baptized, and it's like you're dead. You have nothing. Then you come out of the baptism, and you're born again—like a baby with nothing. Except what the missionaries tell you to do. You do what they say after that. God gives the sunshine to everybody, even hackers like me who steal codes. And God makes America for everybody. Come to America; or America comes to your country. Freedom is for everybody! If they are in the jails, they will be free too. Just be baptized. Your God is like a homeless bum with nothing. 'Blessed are the poor.' He doesn't even care. Tell me I'm right!" he said.

"Are you done?" Kaja asked. "Leave him alone!"

"Say it!" he demanded.

I tried, but something held my tongue.

"I'll tell you something else, Preston," he said. "Those were good things in that notebook. I will make a lot of money from those."

I opened my mouth, and nothing came. But I knew—it was only then becoming clear—that Stanislaw was right. I had dreamed the very same thing. God held all things together, like gravity, and yet he was the author of eternal expansion—an infinity of fullness. P and NP both: eternally fixed yet ever moving.

"You are just like your God," Stanislaw said, "always giving things away."

"That's enough," Kaja said to him. "Let's go."

And then my tongue was loosed. "Wait!" I said in a loud voice. All was silent, and for a moment they stood dumb before me.

"You'll meet a sister," I said to Kaja.

Her face showed wonder. But she didn't speak.

"You'll ask about the Book of Mormon, and she'll start to cry. She prays, even now, for the chance to share what she knows."

That was all I was given to say.

The silence lifted, and Stanislaw spoke. "God will give it all away," he said. Then, turning to Kaja, he said, "Until then, you will come with me."

She pulled away from him, picked up the Book of Mormon, and went out the door.

That's all I know. I've told you everything.

Ten minutes later, a black SUV pulled into the driveway. A man wearing a suit and dark sunglasses helped them load their things into the back. Then they drove off.

I don't know anything about the Russians. I don't know anything about the government agencies that got hacked. I didn't know he was hacking the refinery's computers. He must have taken the notebook. I searched the house and couldn't find it.

You can take my computers, my hard drives, and cloud accounts. I'll give you access to everything. Arrest me if you want. I won't fight it. Let me get you that paper with the formula on it, the one from my dream. Maybe it will help you.

God did his strange work. He does his own math. That's everything I know.

LANA TURNER HAS COLLAPSED!

DAVID G. PACE

> *... suddenly I see a headline*
> *LANA TURNER HAS COLLAPSED!*
> *[...]*
> *I have been to lots of parties*
> *and acted perfectly disgraceful*
> *but I never actually collapsed*
> *oh Lana Turner we love you get up*
> —Frank O'Hara (1964)

"How was the temple?" asked Gloria. Her husband, Don, had just spent the late afternoon dressed in white and saving the dead.

"The way I remember it, for the most part," he said. "More computerized." She looked at him blankly. "The recommend, you know." He reached for his wallet and pulled out a thin white paper folded in half and housed in clear plastic, about the size of a credit card. Gloria leaned in, studying the paper with the church's cumbersomely long name stacked on top of itself, the name of her husband, the ecclesiastical signatures scrawled at the bottom. Don smelled of sweat and cologne—that new generation of cologne she'd gotten him for his birthday, hoping to add a little spice to their life after twenty-one years together.

"I don't get it," she said, moving toward the refrigerator and pulling an apron off its hook in a single gesture—the apron with the silk-screened torso bulging under a watermelon-patterned string bikini. A joke for her birthday. "A little larceny," Don had

179

said to her the day she unwrapped it, nose scrunched. "A little larceny for our little life," he'd said. And she'd collapsed it into her lap with a smirk, shaking her head.

"Little life" was code for their life of routine. A truncated life of casseroles and green beans, Friday night dinners at The Old Spaghetti Factory, and childlessness.

She walked back to Don, pulling the apron over her head, tying it behind her back. She snatched the recommend out of his hand. "What's this strip on the back?" she asked.

"When you enter the temple, they slide it through a reader," he said, leaning in. "It records that you're there." She dropped it on the table in front of him. He picked the card back up and studied it as if he might find something hidden he had missed earlier. "My name is magnetically encrypted on this strip, and when you run it through, you know, it links to a database." She politely waited for him to finish but was already formulating her response.

"And if you're not part of the system, two very nice men from the mafia turn you right around and show you the door?" She turned back to the stove, stirring hard macaroni into boiling water. She looked at him over her shoulder and grinned.

"Now why would you say such a thing?" he asked. He was prepared for this.

"Say what?"

"Gloria," he said, in his new vernacular of pleading. (They *were* talking about religion.) "You should come with me. Let's go together. Today I went through a session for a man named Joseph Forsythe, born in 1832. Maybe he was a relative of mine. Or someone famous. Who knows?"

She trained her sights on her husband just as she did on artwork and prints at work, on the endless family portraits with grandchildren popping out of them like seedlings. What she saw was a man in his late 40s, his white shirt crumpled, his tie askew. He was thickening, yes, but still topped with that tangled moor of black hair; still the man with whom she slept. Then she looked at him like she had thought of looking at Michael at the frame shop, fifteen years her junior, whose swimmer's body he could barely contain under his T-shirt. She imagined she was someone—not herself—who better fit into the cartoon bikini she wore on her apron and who wasn't shy of guiding a swimmer's body into the dark back room where they kept the moldings. Framing with purpose. Was it the vision of Michael, his broad back and worn jeans, that now made her husband look like a boy himself behind his glasses, even with his five-o'clock shadow?

How she wished she could have given her husband a child. Given herself a child. She didn't want to save the dead like Don was trying to do, a bizarre practice that Mormons, replete with passwords and secret handshakes, had been doing since the mid-1800s. She wanted to save the living. To save themselves.

That night, Don dreamt he was walking down the street. It was the 1930s and all the men wore hats pulled down so that he could barely see their faces. The streets were muted gray like those Depression-era paintings he and Gloria had seen the week before at the museum—hobos in boxcars, a dejected man sitting on the curb, gray flannel legs moving briskly past behind him. In Don's dream the tide of men in hats flooded the street, and Don strained to look into each face. Perhaps, he thought, I'm looking for Joseph Forsythe. Attach the name to a face. The face of a man who is in search of something that will rescue him. Then one of the men looked up and stopped in front of him. He was smoking a cigarette. His face opened into a crooked grin, a pencil mustache crackling above his lips. The rugged look, the dark hair. The eyes. It was not Joseph Forsythe. It was Clark Gable.

The next day, Gloria was eyeing a photo print the size of a desk blotter, the woman across from her old enough to be her mother. "Sister Baker," to use the respectful term with a fellow Latter-day Saint.

"We don't want anything to take away from the portrait," Sister Baker said. She cocked her head at the print that was, to her, upside-down on the counter. "The photographer insists that it be very simple, maybe a black metal frame?" Gloria knew she was being asked to provide a different opinion. The woman didn't want anything like a black metal frame, and probably not anything "simple." Gloria scanned the composition, a grouping of over a dozen people, Sister Baker and her smiling husband at the center, one hand of each clasped tightly and resting in the woman's lap. The family was impossibly good-looking. All dark hair and gleaming white teeth. Like the Osmonds.

"Well," said Gloria. "As a designer, I would try putting on more than one mat." She turned to collect corners in various shades of gray: an off-white one; something warmer. Returning, she noticed that the woman was looking at the displays of framed pictures on the far wall. Gloria placed three mats on the upper right-hand corner of the print, each with a one-eighth-inch reveal, then turned it so that it was right-side up for her client.

"What about something like this?" Gloria heard from across the room. Sister Baker was pointing at what Gloria referred to privately as the Manic Titanic, five mats of varied reveals and a five-inch wide, bright-white shellacked frame, dwarfing the picture of a smiling, Nordic-haired family. The frame alone would set someone back six hundred dollars.

"I like this one," said the woman, cocking her head. "It speaks to …"

Your ostentatiousness? thought Gloria, pursing her lips.

"It's very glamorous," Gloria said out loud after a beat. The woman was trying to read Gloria, who was very good not only at design, but at telling a story to her clients that would make them walk out of the shop believing that not only did they get a deal but that they had an artistic gene that would rival Michelangelo's. ("That's why everybody's framing around here looks like the flippin' Vatican's," she had often complained to Don.)

While she took the woman's name and wrote up the work order, Gloria closed the deal. "You have such a lovely family, Sister Baker. All of them are simply gorgeous. Like their parents." She looked up over her glasses and smiled. The woman smiled back politely, still trying to figure her host out.

"You don't think this will overwhelm the picture?" the woman asked, peering at the gargantuan assemblage. Gloria looked thoughtfully at the arrangement—the sample corner, the mats—all under the full spectrum light she had positioned over the project. "Well, it might be a little bright, Chloe," she said, this time opting for the woman's first name—more intimate. She came around to the other side of the counter and gestured across the expanse of smiles and the dark, brooding garden behind them. Gloria could tell by her expression that Sister Baker was not really "there." One of the grand-children, perhaps fifteen, and one of the sons—Don's age?—carried a certain gravity behind the smile that spoke of something profoundly unfinished, even disturbed. "The frame complements the composi-tion, I think. The white frame, the gloss. It makes everyone's teeth really pop." The woman adjusted her glasses, leaning into the portrait then leaning back. Gloria waited, looking into her client's face. Sister Baker smiled and nodded. "You're right," she said. "Thank you!"

"No ..." said Gloria, continuing the script. "Thank *YOU*!"

*

Gloria sat drinking her coffee and thumbing through a mag-azine. She was early, taking a long lunch break so that she could talk to Trudy who was just finishing up with her eleven o'clock. Sister Bodell sat in the chrome and padded hair-drying chair. She looked like a prune with a giant bonnet on her head, the traditional style and set that, it being 1995, seemed more than outdated to Gloria. Grotesque, she thought. Just like her own name: antique and grotesque. Like something out of the *Dick van Dyke Show*. In spite of this, the old woman was smiling away, quite pleased to be under the caring, skilled hands of her trusted beautician, who kept checking on her, smiling conspiratorially. Who am I to judge Sister Bodell? Gloria thought. This could be the highlight of her week.

Trudy extracted Sister Bodell from the hair dryer and helped her back into the swivel chair where she dropped like a sack of sand. She turned her client around to face the mirror, and after working a brush expertly through her hair, sprayed the woman's bouf, now dyed a gentle blue. "A regular Lana Turner," said Trudy finally, her hands resting lightly on the woman's shoulders. The two of them smiled into the mirror. It was the very picture—even a framed picture, thought Gloria—of sisterly affection and the commerce of beauty.

While Trudy took a phone call, Gloria walked Sister Bodell to the door. "Trudy has made you look like a movie star," she said as she helped the old woman on with her coat. She asked how her children were doing, her grandchildren. They now numbered thirty-two, she learned.

"Oh, my. You are lovely to help me. Bless you!" Sister Bodell said.

"And it's pretty darn sexy, if you ask me," Gloria continued. She couldn't resist spiking her language a little. Sister Bodell leaned hard against Gloria as she lowered herself down the steps to the walk, but then she didn't let go. Suddenly, her tone changed, as if someone had flipped a switch. "You know, Gloria, the only regret I have since my husband died is that I didn't suck on his penis the way he always wanted me to." Gloria coughed. "I loved that man," continued Sister Bodell. "But when I asked the bishop about whether it was allowed, he gave me one of those priesthood lectures. Said that I should not be behaving in bed like a pole dancer." She gripped Gloria's arm harder. "What does dancing have to do with it? The dope was almost young enough to be my grandson. Imagine that. And telling me that I couldn't suck on my own husband's penis?" She let go finally, hiked her purse up over her shoulder, and moved toward her car. Then she turned, and in a stage whisper said, "Give him what he wants, sister. Don't wait until you're living with regret like me." Gloria watched the LTD lurch away from the curb.

"You're the only one in here who drinks coffee," said Trudy when Gloria returned to the shop—and her mug. "It makes every-one uncomfortable, you know."

"And it's lousy coffee," Gloria quipped.

"Like I say. You're the only one. And if the bishop finds out, he'll be calling you in." Trudy shook Sister Bodell's hair clippings from the plastic covering and readjusted a large aluminum hair pin on the rolled-up cuff of her sleeve.

"Only among the Mormons could drinking coffee turn into a social statement," said Gloria, collapsing into the chair next to the sink. "I need something more up-to-date, Trudy," Gloria sighed, her back to the sink. She looked at herself in the mirror opposite, turning her head from side to side. "Don's gone back to the temple, and he wants me to go with him."

Trudy tipped Gloria's head back. "Mid-life thing going on? Couldn't he just buy a fast car?" Gloria closed her eyes and took a deep breath. The water gurgled and sprayed. Negative ions elevated her mood. Twenty, thirty years from now she would be Sister Bodell getting her wash and blow-dry once a week and walking out of the Wildflower Salon smiling beneath her helmet hair. That was as good as it was going to get for her.

Trudy sat Gloria back up and wrapped a towel around her shoulders, dabbing at the strands. "Let's get you ready for your close-up," she said. Gloria smiled at the reference to her namesake, Gloria Swanson, in *Sunset Boulevard*. The age of glamour and Hollywood royalty. A simpler time, it seemed to her. Black-and-white photos of women in shirtwaists gazing back at the world in a way women had never gazed before. Poised. Arch. Confident. A construction, but still appealing. Gloria was hungry for that. Five years ago, she had asked herself, since there would be no children, why did she and Don still "dress the part"? The lumpen, thrown-together couple with four, five, six, even seven kids in the back seats of a Suburban? She and Don were a traditional-looking couple that wasn't traditional. A husband and wife who could not fulfill the covenant they'd made when married in the temple to "multiply and replenish the earth."

"Trudy," said Gloria, again facing the mirror, "why are Don and I trying so hard to look like everyone else when there's no room for a childless couple in the celestial picture?"

"At least you have someone to go to the House of the Lord with," Trudy said. Her fingers threaded through Gloria's hair; it looked strangely ragged now—wild. "My sister Stella told me the other day that she went to the temple for someone named Amelia Earhart. Now ... what are the chances that she did that sacred work there for *the* Amelia Earhart?"

Gloria thought for a second. "Pretty good, I would say. How many Amelia Earharts do you know of?"

"Exactly."

"You can do that?

"Do what?"

"Go through the temple for a famous person?"

"As long as they're dead. Everyone needs saving, you know."

Gloria thought about this for a while.

"I've heard that Marilyn Monroe has had her work done at least ten times," Trudy continued.

"No!"

"You heard right, sister. Ten different people have gone through the temple believing that they were the Blonde Bombshell."

"The *proxy* for the Blonde Bombshell," Gloria corrected.

"Yeah. Whatever."

That night, Gloria stood in front of the bathroom mirror waiting for Don to come home. The meatloaf sizzled in the oven; the side of frozen peas steamed atop the stove; the half-gallon of Snelgrove's sat in the freezer; and she wasn't happy with her hair. Trudy had cut it short, with long bangs reminiscent of the 60s that swept over from left to right over one of her eyes, and she was feeling self-conscious. She combed it, fluffed at it, held herself in contempt, tilted her head from side to side to see how it looked from this angle and that. She sighed, put the comb down, picked up the brush, looked at her reflection again, sniffed, slammed the brush into a drawer, and slammed the drawer shut.

She turned. There was Don. "Nice hair," he said tentatively. "*You* like it?" She pushed past him, toward the kitchen, embarrassed now for real, still touching her hair. "Dinner's about ready. We just need to make the salad."

At the kitchen sink, Don moved behind her and looked at them both, his head floating above hers in the window's reflection. His hair was tousled from the day, sideburns nearly to the lobe of his ear, pursuant to the current style. And Gloria? She looked like Lulu from *To Sir with Love*: right out of London's East End but without the miniskirt. It turned him on; but no one would have known. Being aroused, even by his wife, was a mere synaptic blink that tingled in his scalp then dropped south where it dissipated in a twenty-year sea of responsibility and resignation. It had been a long time since the tingle had settled in his testicles, a problematic region for a man like him anyway—especially one who had just returned to the temple without his wife.

Still, there was this vision of them as a couple in the window—and the hope could spread, couldn't it—through his chest and end-of-the-day shoulders that Gloria had gripped in days past when she rode on top of him during sex—a position that seemed especially thrilling at the time.

In the earlier days. Especially when they were still trying to get pregnant. Yes. That. Glorious Gloria, the love of his …

"I've gone back to doing our genealogy," she said suddenly, tearing at the lettuce in the sink. "Did you know that you're related to some famous people?"

Don was rising back out of his balls and into his head. "Like who?"

"Like Clint Eastwood."

"Dirty Harry?"

"Through his mother's side. Third cousins, once removed."

"Never could figure out what that meant," he said. "Once removed instead of just second cousins. And please don't explain it to me again. I can never remember the difference."

Years earlier Gloria had taken a nosedive into the family group sheets, the pioneer journals, the old Books of Remembrance. It was shortly after they'd returned from the doctor who had told her that there was something wrong with her eggs—or their behavior, anyway. The way they failed to make it down the correct tube and attach to the correct layer. The next weekend she had headed to Gunnison and raided her Aunt LaRue's den of old papers, sepia-toned photos, birth certificates—all painfully pasted together into a kind of crude family album. Gloria had sifted through the den and returned with five boxes of stuff, becoming the *de facto* family genealogist. Soon she was called by the bishop to be the family history specialist in the ward before she abruptly asked to be released a year later and stopped going to church altogether. "Genealogy is too time-consuming," she had told Don. "Everyone who's into it is a fuddy-duddy, just like my aunt. It doesn't fit me. Besides, who wants to read about the lives of dead people? Better to live your own life while you can."

Don had acquiesced, but he resented it when the bishop called a meeting with him and the rest of the bishopric to determine how they could *re-activate* Gloria in the church. "Why don't you ask *her?*" he had said to the three men sitting there in their suits. "*She's* the one who made up her mind not to come anymore." They sat looking at him as if he had just told them to bugger off, which, in retrospect, he had. It gave him a little surge somewhere behind his sternum.

Eventually, he drifted away from church himself, siding with his wife's decision. There were no family obligations, no children to escort to the temple. None of his nieces and nephews, or Gloria's, for that matter, expected the strange couple who'd never had any children to show up at their weddings. That is, until he had suddenly appeared before the appropriate ecclesiastical gatekeepers to ask for a temple recommend. Don was back.

"Dirty Harry?" he asked again. "That's kind of cool!"

Earlier that day at work, Gloria had been in the back room of the frame shop and found a stash of dust-covered *Life* magazines. On top was the October 1941 issue with Clark Gable in his thin mustache and black lacquered hair imposing himself on … her heart seemed to stop … Lana Turner.

Lana Turner. How could she have forgotten the platinum blond, the flawless complexion? Good heavens, those legs! And who could forget she was originally from Idaho! She stared at the cover for several minutes. When she returned to work, she was fingering her hair. When she looked up into the plate glass window, the shop lights reflected off it in such a way that she saw herself looking at the face of her long-dead mother. Gloria remembered the way her mother's hair "flipped" like Turner's. It occurred to her that her mother, like many in her generation, had modeled her look after the Hollywood stars. Her mother was the Lana of Sanpete County. How could she have missed that? Why had she never put two and two together?

She recalled watching The Big Money Movie with her mother on Channel 5 where she first saw Turner in *Ziegfeld Girl* and then *Imitation of Life*, the first film she'd starred in after her daughter had fatally stabbed the film star's lover, Johnny Sompanato. There was turmoil in those smoky eyes. And that flipped hair in *The Postman Always Rings Twice*, Gloria's favorite.

Lana had died just months earlier, she remembered, the star's last appearance a horrible cameo on *Falcon Crest*. More of a scandal, in Gloria's estimation, than any stabbing. Her mother, the Lana of Sanpete County, was not a woman of scandal. In fact, Gloria

188

remembered her mother trekking off to the temple in Manti, her little suitcase of sacred clothing in hand, where she would change into the white garb, the white shoes, the bridal veil, to save the dead by doing proxy church ordinances.

A longing rose up in Gloria. A sweet remembrance of her mother who was suddenly no longer her mother, but Lana with the legs. Lana in white. Lana with the smoky eyes. Oh, how she adored her mother! Even still, years and years later. Perhaps if Gloria had had her own children, perhaps then she would have had somewhere else besides the memory of her mother to place her affection, to posit her dreams. Instead, she seemed captive to the peripheral sight of her own Lana: Lana in the kitchen, her shirtwaist swishing at her knees. Lana in white.

Gloria had tucked the magazine into her tote bag that day. Gloria's hair was blonde, not platinum blonde like Lana's. Whose was, really? But she saw herself—and, more importantly, her mother—in that saucy flip, and hungered for more of it, for the lustful eyes of John Garfield, the itchy-footed traveler, moving over her in the kitchen of the ill-fated Twin Oaks diner outside Los Angeles. Clark Gable? He'd do in a pinch.

Despite the disastrous Lulu bangs, she made love to Don that night the first time in nearly a year. She had forgotten how strong he could be, holding her in his arms, how the tendons in his arms alternately surfaced then disappeared as he rocked and moaned above her. How tender he was as she looked into his face when he came. The way his eyes rolled back in his head. The way he sighed and smiled and even blushed at his passion when it was all over.

"I want to do the temple work for Lana Turner," said Gloria as they lay in the twisted sheet, her arm up over her head. He rose up; looked at her. "The starlet? The sweater girl?"

"She died last summer." She rolled over on her side, looking at him, a hand propping up her head. She fingered the stubble of his chin and smiled. "Lana needs saving as much as anyone, right?"

"Do you think Clark Gable has had his work done?" he asked, the idea rising in him like a bubble. "Maybe I should go through the temple for *him*!"

Gloria gave him a faux frown, then laughed. "I was hoping you'd say John Garfield. But Rhett Butler will do." Then she reached under the sheet. Don was hard again. She threw off the covers and giggled.

"What?" he said, turning red. "I *love* you!" She gripped him tightly. He moaned. She lowered her mouth to his penis but stopped an inch away from his ecstasy and looked up, sincerely—as if she were holding the mobile microphone in fast and testimony meeting.

"And I just want to say. . ." Gloria said with emotion into the head of his penis, "that I know the church is true, and that Joseph Smith was a prophet and that the Book of Mormon is true, and …" She fell backwards in laughter, shaking so hard she had to hold her breasts so that they wouldn't jiggle. When she looked up, however, Don was ashen-faced … and limp.

She stopped laughing. Don gave her a tight, consoling smile. "I'm sorry," she said.

*

The bishop was very happy to see Gloria. "Sister Stark, thank you for coming in. It pleases the Lord to see his children—"

"—Return to the fold? Well, here I am." She thought that the way she pursed her lips, almost a pout, was the way Lana would have done it. "Actually, Don has really set the example. He's found a lot of meaning by returning to the temple. I've noticed a change." She was saying all the right things. Both she and the bishop knew it. But it occurred to Gloria, sitting there in the bare office with the picture of the prophet and the twelve apostles—badly in need of a good mat—that she really was telling the truth. Don, in fact, *was* a new man. The last time he returned from the temple he had told her in detail how doing the work for Clint Eastwood's father had made him feel, well, like Clint Eastwood. That he sat taller in his chair at his desk. Found himself smiling in a ragged way, with squinting eyes. That Joyce, at work, had even commented admiringly on his swagger. Another time, he said that while giving the signs and tokens at the temple veil as proxy for Steve McQueen, he felt a surge of adrenalin and a sense of his future expanding before him through—yes—the eternities.

"Are you sure you weren't just re-living the car chase scene in

Bullitt?" Gloria had ventured. She immediately regretted it. Don was serious. The whole next week he had a smoothness to the way he moved that was right out of *The Thomas Crowne Affair*, and she found herself one night wondering how she would look with the long, black hair of McQueen's wife Ali MacGraw.

The bishop smiled warmly at Gloria. He began asking the worthiness questions—about her fidelity to her husband, her faith in Joseph Smith and the Restoration, her support of the modern-day prophet and the general authorities. Her adherence to the Word of Wisdom. As she confidently answered each of the questions, some of the old faith seemed to return. The connection she had to her mother. The abiding hope from when she was a girl graduating from Manti High that the gospel really was true. She had a testimony, didn't she? Her path was clearly marked, brilliantly lit by the detailed programs of the church she had followed ... well, religiously. The promise of eternal marriage to a worthy man. She *did* have a testimony! The gospel *was* true! And even though the program had not worked out so well for Don and her, there was the assurance that all would be made well in the hereafter. That she would have increase through spirit children who would populate "worlds without end" through eternity.

Armed with her newly minted temple recommend, Gloria prepared to return to the House of the Lord. For three months she had attended church regularly with Don, paid her tithing, stopped drinking coffee. But most importantly, she had grown her hair out. And finally, the week of her return, she had Trudy bleach and style it.

"Ready for my close up, Mr. DeMille," Gloria chimed. The smock Trudy had just pinned around Gloria's neck rose then fell with a giant, nervous sigh. Trudy gave her a knowing look. "How does it feel to finally be doing the right thing?" she asked. She separated Gloria's hair into quadrants with plastic clips, claws bared. She had assured Gloria that the blonde hair she had inherited from her mother only needed a modest treatment to transform it into a blinding sheen. As Trudy worked over her, Gloria's excitement turned to anxiety. What if she was doing all this for the wrong reason? Was she leading Don down the road to apostasy? She saw again her mother's face mirrored, and she realized that when her mother was her age, Gloria was a junior in high school. Did her mother dream like she did of being someone else? Even if it was just for two hours at the movies, or an afternoon of television over her ironing? The smell of peroxide began to sicken Gloria. Her scalp tingled hotly.

But Gloria's anxiety turned a corner when Trudy began styling her hair, its natural body beginning to roll and rise. She loved how her hair seemed to locate its own nuance in form, color, and light. Her anxiety turned towards Lana, or who she thought might be Lana, watching from the spirit world. Could Gloria be a worthy embodiment of Lana Turner? Would she do Lana proud? The anniversary of the celebrity's death was just two days away. She had already submitted Lana's name to the temple registrar the week before in preparation for her proxy ordinances: first baptism and then the initiatory. And now it was the holy endowment—the crowning ordinance—starring none other than Gloria.

Was she ready?

It was June 29, 1996, one year to the day that Lana Turner had expired in her Beverly Hills mansion from an unfortunate recurrence of throat cancer. And Gloria *was* ready. She took Don's hand as they walked from the parking lot to Temple Square and then through the Endowment House where they handed over their cards. The man at the counter, with spearmint breath and a practiced smile, ran their cards with great seriousness. For a moment Gloria wondered if the sentinel angels who were standing invisibly by would spitefully scramble the digital impulse that traveled to and from the sacred database of worthy Latter-day Saints. But the light blinked green. All systems go. She looked at Don, who had grown a mustache the past several weeks and just that morning had sliced away at it with his straight edge until it was pencil-lead thin. Standing there in her white dress, beige pumps, and spectacularly blonde hair, Gloria loved her husband in his black suit and tie. Loved him more than she had ever loved anything.

In the women's dressing room, she stood in her private stall, pulling the white gown over her undergarments and wishing she could wear the smart shirtwaist that swung off her hips and down to her knees: the better to honor the memory of the woman who had captured the hearts and imaginations of an entire generation of both schoolgirls *and* their mothers. (When was the last time *that* had happened?) To usher into eternity the woman who seduced and spurned the whole lot of them—not only Clark Gable but a real actor in John Garfield.

"My goal," Lana reportedly said late in life, "was to have one husband and seven children, but it turned out to be the other way around." Yes, it would be better to forgive the extravagance of a Hollywood star while dressed in the uniform she was immortalized in. But the temple *was* the temple. Modesty and tradition demanded that in this final passage of her earthly sojourn, Lana Turner's proxy be dressed as all female proxies are—as a bride.

Then Gloria saw it. For the briefest moment. A flash of platinum blonde hair, dolloped and waved, set and flipped—in the cubicle across from her. She stood stunned, watching, waiting for the woman to turn, to present herself. And then she saw another Lana Turner walking away from her toward the curtained portal where patrons are given their new name. Just the back of the woman, her hair jouncing. Gloria opened the door to her cubicle and was nearly run over by another Lana Turner headed toward the toilets, pulling at her bra strap.

"Oh, excuse me, sister!" said the Lana. Then she looked at Gloria and her face fell. She moved quickly away, not gliding on legs the color and clarity of ivory, but ambling on fat legs, rocking side to side. Gloria stood in her stocking feet, straining to see the faces of the other Lanas. The smoky eyes she imagined below a corona of white so glorious, so perfectly unreal—above that strong but perfectly contoured chin, the neck, the bustline … oh, dear Lord! the legs. But all the Lanas were moving away from her, busy in eternity's endless tasks, looking for the man of their dreams, the warm studio lights, the adoring eye of the camera.

Gloria returned to her cubicle and sank to the bench, her knees knocking below the temple-appropriate, satin-white dress she had married Don in so many years ago. The dress that still somehow fit her. She dropped her head to her hands and felt the old, auguring sting. The mother she loved. The mother she would never be.

She gathered up her things and fled.

A COURTSHIP

CHARITY SHUMWAY

A January night, 1976. Ken sits behind the counter at a 7-11 in Provo, Utah. He has been skiing all day—cutting classes again—and he has his physics textbook out, attempting between customers to get through some of the material he missed. He is a mechanical engineering major at Brigham Young University, and even though he is good at it, if he keeps skipping classes this way ...

As usual, his boss, Mr. Lund, is in the back office looking at hunting magazines. A car pulls up to the store, lights shining through the glass, wheels skidding a little through the slush, and moments later Ken's cousin Jim pushes through the door, a blast of cold and the smell of exhaust following him in. No one would guess the relation from their looks. While Jim is dark-haired and burly—the belly that will eclipse his belt in later life already begun—Ken is fair and sleek, a cowlick giving his hair an almost girlish wave that somehow amplifies his general air of athletic readiness—a look that, like Jim's, will endure.

"I've got tickets for the game tonight," Jim says. "Courtside. Karen got them. You want to come?"

Ken closes his textbook, a pencil marking his page. "I wish I could."

"Courtside," Jim says, leaning on the counter. His look is half dare and half entreaty.

Something about being in trouble as-is, knowing he may never catch up with physics and that he has already lost this day, pricks Ken just so—does one irresponsible deed deserve another? He has felt this recklessness before. He smirks, a watch-this expression.

"Hey, Mr. Lund," he yells back toward the office. "I quit!" There
is the sound of a chair scraping against the floor. Ken doesn't wait
for him. His nerves surge, a pulse of surprise and fear at what he
has just done, but he lifts his coat casually from the hook behind
him, as if he's in no hurry at all. Jim gives him a wowed smile,
and together they walk out of the store. Ken never collects his last
paycheck, and brazen though he may have been that day, doesn't go
back to the 7-11 for years, until he is sure Mr. Lund doesn't work
there anymore.

He is twenty-one.

That same night, Laura is in her apartment wearing yellow
rubber gloves and scrubbing the burned edges of tomato sauce out
of a casserole dish. She and her two older brothers, also students
at BYU, have made an arrangement. They'll provide the grocery
money if she cooks dinner every night. Her roommate, Karen, has
gotten in on the deal too, switching sides at will, sometimes on the
cooking side, sometimes on the adding-money side. Laura never
switches sides.

Karen missed dinner tonight, and by now Laura has gotten so
good at portioning that there remains one roll, one piece of lasa-
gna, and a single helping of beans. She wraps them up and puts
them in the fridge. After that, she puts on her nightgown and goes
to bed early, pulling her quilt—one she tied with her mother last
year—tight against her chin. She has chemistry homework, but
whenever she thinks of chemistry she wants to cry. She cries a little
now, in fact; turns her head and pulls the covers over her face. Even
though it's her fourth year, Laura has no major. She has to pass
chemistry for the one major she has actually considered, food science; but she failed it her freshman year, and in the years since has
taken folk dancing, kayaking, religion—everything but chemistry.
Over Christmas her father gave her a talking to: she had to retake
chemistry. After an hour of lying very still in the dark, craving the
forgetfulness of sleep, she is no closer to it. Her pointed dread has
only increased.

At last, Karen comes home, walks into their bedroom, flips on
the light.

"Oh, sorry," she says. But she leaves the light on as she pulls her pajamas from the bureau and takes off her shirt. Karen isn't modest like Laura, who changes in the bathroom, and Karen's body both fascinates and disgusts Laura. Where Laura is slim ("flat as a board," her similarly built mother always says) Karen is garishly voluptuous. Not fat, but ample, and she does nothing to hide it—sweaters that cling, skirts that cinch and squeeze.

"You know Jim Gardner, right?" Karen says. Facing Laura, she takes off her bra. Laura looks up at the ceiling.

"Yeah."

"Well, I went to a basketball game with him tonight. He's okay, but he brought his cousin Ken. Woo wee!" She pretends to fan herself. From the corner of her eye Laura can see Karen's pendulous breasts swaying as she gestures. At last Karen pulls on her pajama top.

Laura relaxes her neck. "So, you like his cousin now?" She tries to hide the edge in her voice with a little laugh. This is nothing new. Karen is the type of girl Laura marvels at and slightly resents: a flirt, popular with boys, not because she is "easy"—she's a nice Mormon girl—but because, just as Karen is unashamed of her body, she is also unashamed of all that goes on between men and women—the jokes, the looks, the dancing, the kissing. In the years they have been rooming together Karen has been living her mother's advice: brush your hair one-hundred times every night and date at least one-hundred boys before you get married. Laura, however, has been trying to live her own mother's advice: in all thy ways acknowledge Him, and He shall direct thy paths.

Karen takes off her pants and, seeing the flash of her rounded thigh, Laura turns over to face the wall.

"So, what if I *do* like his cousin now?" Karen says.

"Goodnight," Laura says.

Another minute of shuffling, and at last Karen turns off the light.

Laura is twenty.

A few days later she has just failed a chemistry exam. She won't receive the grade for another week, but she can feel it. She closes the door to her bedroom, collapses against it—not crying, her feelings too empty for that. Finally, after ten minutes or thirty, she can't tell, she picks herself up and heads to the kitchen to get dinner ready. She is grateful for the nightly ritual, the regular need. She prays silently as she takes food from the fridge. "Please help me not to fail," she thinks, meaning the course at first; but the more she repeats the plea, the larger it feels, a plea not to fail at everything.

Everyone arrives at seven, as usual. Except Karen.

"Let's just start," Laura's brother Jeremy says, looking to her. Laura agrees, glad that the decision is hers to make. Jeremy blesses the food, then round the table the chicken and vegetables go. Seconds later, Karen comes through the door. She throws her coat on the chair, drops her bags on the floor, and says, "Hey, I brought someone," gesturing to Ken, following behind her.

Ken has been in this apartment complex before; lots of girls live here. Things look normal: the white cinder block walls, the slip-covered couch. But the table is different—an actual tablecloth, an actual dinner. The air is heavy with the warm smell of food. And around the table, a family meal. He is momentarily taken aback. He responds to his discomfort by standing a little straighter and half-smiling, a look that people perceive as either self-assured or smug, not knowing what it really is: barely disguised vulnerability. The two men at the table give him respectful nods. A small, pretty girl with long, dark hair and a stiff, straight posture—more traits that will last and last—stands up to get a place setting.

"My roommate, Laura," Karen says. "Her brother Jeremy; her brother Dave."

"So, you're Jim Gardner's cousin?" the girl says.

Ken nods and looks back at Karen. She has talked about him. Karen returns his gaze, her eyebrows arching, the corners of her lips turning up carefully, calculatedly. Ken knows that after dinner he'll ask Karen to go on a walk. She'll agree. She'll kiss him, perhaps even neck.

"Ask Ken how he ended up coming to the basketball game the other night," Karen prompts. Ken takes a seat and tells his story, embroidering details—Mr. Lund, wheezing over his magazine in the back room; Jim frenziedly running through the door ...

And so, it begins. Whenever he comes over for dinner, which is often, Laura gives Ken her portion. She is always dieting anyway (though she never says so aloud), and she is half-grateful as she watches him eat up the calories she might have otherwise consumed. For Ken's part, he seems hardly to notice where the food comes from. He offers several times to contribute to the cost, and when Laura says no, she wouldn't think of letting him, he leaves it at that. Although it has been years since someone cooked for him, he slips back into that easy mode. Of course, there is a nice meal on the table. His job is to enjoy it and say thanks, which he always does.

When Ken praises her meals night after night, Laura imagines she's blushing, but in fact, she grows pale, pleasure and embarrassment pulling her feelings into a tight whir in her chest. Soon enough, her daily planning for dinner loses its calm. Will Ken be there? Will he admire her work? These chanting thoughts easily and completely become her new ritual. When he is absent, her feelings plummet, dinner depleted of comfort, displaced by a chasm of disappointment she can't seem to shake, sometimes not until the next day. But when he is there, Laura lingers over his every word about the rolls or the potatoes because in them she begins to hear other things, warmer intonations. Love, if that's what you call it, has always been spoken this way in her world. Between her parents, among herself and her brothers, even with friends: service given, service accepted and acknowledged.

One night after dinner her brother Dave stays to wash the dishes with Laura. "What does Karen see in that guy?" he says. "He's so full of himself."

Laura swallows hard and hands him a dish to dry. "The same thing she sees in every guy," she says with a sneer, thinking she's responding in kind to Dave's remark. But Dave doesn't smile, and she instantly regrets her meanness. She holds another plate out for him to dry, but he doesn't take it. He sighs and looks at her face intently—there is something surprised and defeated in his expression, his eyes softened, sad even. When he finally reaches for the plate, she is sure Dave meant the question not for Karen but for her. And she begins to wonder, in the grandest sense of the word—awe laced with fear—what exactly she does see in Ken.

Soon, Karen has a new crush, Paul, who never comes to dinner but whom she relentlessly pursues, learning his class schedule, "bumping into him" whenever possible. Meanwhile, Ken keeps coming to dinner. At the table one night, her brothers listening, he says to Laura, "We should go out sometime." Simple as that; a breezy assurance in his voice. It is no act: Ken is well versed in asking girls on dates. He can see that Laura conspicuously ignores him at dinner. He knows the signs. Her silence is her communication. So, he says the magic words.

Laura is mortified to have this private romantic exchange enacted so publicly. She can only think in single syllables. "Sure," she says with a tight-lipped smile. After too long a silence, Jeremy brings up BYU's latest basketball game, and conversation among the men resumes. Laura says nothing for the rest of the meal, hardly eating, embarrassed even to chew since she now feels all eyes on her. But she is not unpleased, only unhappy that their date has been noised abroad. She remembers Dave's look so clearly, and now she will have to report on the date or have it become an uncomfortably avoided topic. Perhaps the news will even reach her parents. But still, a date.

That weekend, Ken and Laura go to the movies. Throughout the film she is aware of his shoulder, so close to hers, only half-pleasantly. And then, as they are leaving their aisle after the show he reaches out and puts his hand on the small of her back, the lightest of touches. She jumps, startled, and as he pulls his hand away her eyes flit down against her will, as if his hand is an offending object. But his touch wasn't undesirable, only alarming, and she bursts into an apology. "Oh, I'm sorry. I didn't mean to jump. I guess I'm just ..." her voice dwindles. She feels suddenly as if she's sweating. Still, she is relieved. How long would he have left his hand there? How could she have walked with him there, feeling the movement of her muscles?

When he opens the car door for her, he again touches her back in that same low spot, and this time she doesn't stiffen. The moment passes, and soon he is beside her, driving her home. They talk about classes briefly and then Ken tells her about his favorite skiing spots and that she must come with him one of these days. She nods, smiles; absorbs and hoards every word of it.

At her door, he leans in and kisses her. It is her first kiss. It is not sweet. It is frightening and foreign. Ken opens his mouth against hers, enters her mouth with his tongue, the entire feeling more athletic than she would have liked. But she is glad he has kissed her. Ken Gardner. He has chosen her to kiss. When she is in bed with only her desk lamp for light, she writes in her journal, in handwriting so small she hopes it will be illegible to anyone but her: "I think I am in love."

That same night, Ken drives home with the radio silent. He is smiling, so deep a smile it is almost laughter. When he returns to his apartment, he tells Jim that he is unrivaled as a dater: "You should have seen it. From the stiffest girl you've ever seen to practically making out with me on her doorstep." But later, as they relax into the couch and fade into the television, Ken says, "She's a nice girl, you know. Sweet. Most girls aren't sweet all the way; but with her, you can tell." And this, he knows, is as much the source of his blooming smile as her timid kiss. What he does not tell Jim, or even himself quite yet, is that for the entire night he felt larger than himself, the way he could see her watching him, her small prompts—asking him to explain, to tell more, to talk. His surety is borne up by her attention, the sweetness directed at him. It is the same pleased, even giddy, feeling buoying him up as he falls asleep. He goes to dinner at her house the next night, and the night after that.

They go out again: a Saturday night dinner. Over Mexican, Laura learns Ken went on his mission to Guatemala—ordinary enough for a boy at BYU; but then he tells her he went to high school in Turkey, his father working there as a civil engineer. She reaches across the table and grabs his arm, almost before she knows what she is doing. "Me too!" she blurts. "Not Turkey; that's not what I mean. But we lived abroad too. Germany. Outside Munich. My dad was in the Army." She has already withdrawn her hand, but the excitement that overtook her hasn't dissipated. She sits back in her chair, smiling. "What's your favorite memory of living overseas?" she asks.

He tells her a story he has told before: climbing over the walls of the American compound; hopping on the back of a motorcycle; riding over bumpy roads to the hills above Ankara to sit around a fire; eating kabobs; looking at the city lights with a crew of other kids from the International School, all of them flush with the liberation of their clandestine rendezvous. She laughs and smiles exactly where he hopes she will; she leans forward, eager, it seems, for every detail. "You would have loved it," he finally says. The fact that she wouldn't have loved it at all, that danger—both physical and moral—crush all fun for her, flickers for only half a second in his mind.

Laura hardly realizes she wouldn't have loved it either, hardly considers the smothering worry she would have felt. "Sounds amazing!" she says, her excitement genuine.

Ken doesn't ask Laura for her favorite youthful memory. He goes on telling stories about Turkey. But she remembers it anyway: Weekly picnics on the lawn outside the church between sacrament meeting and Sunday school. Her family and other ward members—people from all over the world—lounging in the sun; her father the bishop of the ward, her mother the provider of the feast. The pleasure of her family presiding over the gathering; the bells of all the churches nearby; the comfort of knowing the same gospel had drawn everyone there. She imagines Ken as the bishop, herself as the sandwich-maker. She feels such warmth, and then a prick of embarrassment at the reach of the idea. But she doesn't push the image away as she might have before; she lingers on it, wonders if this is what people mean when they say, "You just know."

When she again kisses him at the door and lets herself in, she is blushing, warm all over. She imagines him feeling the same as he walks home. In fact, he feels nothing of her warm blush, only slight amusement and irritation. A pretty girl; a sweet girl—he still likes her a great deal—but he is young and wants a little more fun. He makes a decision to ask her out regularly, but never on weekends.

"You won't make out with him. That's why," Karen tells Laura in their bedroom one night. "That's what Saturdays are all about. He's going out with other girls then."

Laura doesn't cry, but she feels hollow. She should refuse to see him ever again. She resolves to say she's busy when he calls. Trying to convince herself of this, though, is half her unhappiness. She knows she will go out with him under almost any terms. Long after Karen's breath shifts to the soft exhalations of sleep, Laura lies awake, overtaken with critical searching, a desperation to find and root out her inadequacy.

In the middle of the semester, Ken, his rent money spent on new skis, moves to a cheaper apartment. It is closer to Laura's, and as a result they are now in the same ward. Despite Ken's Saturday-night dates with who-knows-who, he sits next to Laura at church. One week, he tries to put his arm around her, but she moves away, stinging with embarrassment at his attempted public possession of her, ashamed even to be sitting with him regularly—ashamed of the whole awful mess that is dating, flirting, caring. He is baffled. He will try again the next week. Once more, she will move away, but a little less quickly, and that is all that matters.

Although he is indeed spending his Saturdays with other girls, Ken likes Laura; likes her more and more. One of the reasons, in fact, is her prudery. A week after he moves into her ward, they're eating lunch on campus—burgers and fries from the Cougar Eat, his treat—when he motions to a boy with a buzz cut across the way.

"See that guy?" he says. "He's a real dingleberry."

"What's that?" she asks.

"You've never heard that term?" His lips curl, a half-smile. He likes introducing her to the world. Her innocence and embarrassment charm him—the way her forehead wrinkles, the quickness of her protective laugh. "Dingleberries," he says slowly, enjoying the words, "are the pieces of manure that get stuck in a cow's tail and then swish around every time it moves."

She makes a shocked face, just as he knew she would, and he laughs. She tries to laugh too, but the truth is Laura feels each of Ken's dirty instructional moments—dingleberries, hickeys, NCMO (non-committal make out)—like a little bruising blow. She knows this feeling from Karen, who, despite her virginity, talks about sex regularly—things she's heard from her married sister, her mother; stories about ripping, stretching ... horrors, really. Karen, too, thrills to erase Laura's innocence, or so it seems to Laura. But what Laura doesn't acknowledge is that her relationship with Karen continues because she also finds satisfaction in it—the reassurance that she is more innocent, purer, better, and accordingly more desirable to the right person. She smiles, hoping Ken will reach his hand across the table and take hers. He does, and she feels a tiny swelling of power.

The months go on. They continue seeing each other, continue

THE PATH AND THE GATE

kissing at Laura's door. When the semester draws to a close, Ken calls Laura to tell her he aced physics. "It's all you, Baby!" he says, and means it. He can't bring himself to skip class when he knows he'll have to report to Laura on their next date. And in the evenings, after their dates, he has begun staying up late, doing all his homework.

Her stomach seizes at the word "Baby," a jolt of delight and fear at its sexiness. He has never called her anything but Laura before, but she likes it. It is safe enough. She says, "I knew you would!"

Laura fails chemistry. She doesn't tell Ken. She will have to take a fifth year. An ache of failure and frustration assaults her whenever she thinks of it. Two days after getting her grade, she at last closes the door to her bedroom and calls her father, suggesting to him that she stay for the summer and retake the course. He agrees.

The real reason Laura wants to stay is because Ken will be in Provo for the summer. Thanks to his mission, even though he's older than she, he has only finished his second year of school. But still, he's in a hurry—he'll be taking classes all summer. She wants to be near his confidence and drive.

On the night before Karen is set to leave for the summer, a group gathers in Laura's apartment. She has baked cinnamon rolls and brownies, arranged prettily on plates. Amidst Karen's boxes and suitcases, everyone eats and talks, Laura's brother Dave plucking at his guitar, Karen sitting on some new boy's lap. Over Dave's playing, Ken is telling a story, his arm around Laura, the first time she's ever let him put his arm around her in public. In the story, Ken is in high school, sneaking his father's car to drive across Ankara and meet a French girl from school at a coffee house. But before he can get there, he is caught and punished. The girl never forgives him for standing her up, but there are amusing details upon amusing details. Laura has heard the story before, and she watches her brother, hoping he will laugh at the right moments, but Dave doesn't look up from his guitar. Eventually, she stops watching him and listens only to Ken.

Ken can feel Laura curled in next to him, her admiring warmth. Does he love her? She is exactly what he wants in that moment. Yes; love. When his story is done and people are talking in small groups again, he says to Laura, running his hand over her hair, loud enough for her brother to hear, "Someday when we have kids, we'll have to take them to Turkey." She would be a good wife. He can see that. So, he says it.

For Laura's part, the words elicit a jump in her heart that doesn't fully settle till it's held fast by sleep.

But as the weeks go by, the more Ken says things like "when we are married ..." and "when we have kids ..." the more Laura feels strong-armed. Shouldn't he ask her? Shouldn't he shyly, nervously petition her hand? And how can she—who still does not go out with Ken on Saturday nights, who knows her defining attribute is her spiritual goodness—even consider him? Yes, he is here at BYU; yes, he went on a mission; yes, he goes to church; but he is not like her. Where there is reverence at her core, something else is at his. She can't say what. Her brothers have never acknowledged him as her boyfriend, if that's what he is. She sees there is no natural affinity there. Still, she feels a burst that must be happiness whenever she sees him.

As for Ken, he becomes more and more earnest when he talks about their future. He wants to succeed in life, whatever that means, and he imagines that with her always expecting so much of him, he will. Her wifeliness is so appealing. Timid, pretty Laura—he wants her very much. He tells his parents during their weekly phone conversation that he is in love. When Jim asks, he says he's not sure he wants to share an apartment that fall. "I might have other plans," Ken says, waggling his eyebrows.

And then, at last, Ken leads Laura on a hike up Provo Canyon one Saturday afternoon, mosquitoes biting at their skin, weeds cutting at their ankles. Halfway up the mountain they stop to rest, the two of them leaning against a boulder, looking down at the valley. He takes her hand and—no shake in his voice, he is certain she'll say yes—pronounces the words: "Will you marry me?"

At this first real question, Laura feels an emptiness she could not have predicted, a fearful void. And in the absence of delight, what drives her answer is the fact that she has not protested the "whens" and "somedays" for so long now that saying no would be more than just saying no *now*; it would be backing out where she has already given consent. And so, after a long moment, she nods, tears up, kisses him, lets him place the ring on her finger, and waits for the flood of joy. They don't climb the rest of the mountain. They walk back down the trail side by side, occasionally tripping because the trail is too narrow for them both, until Ken finally walks behind, his hand reaching out again and again for that low spot on Laura's back that once so surprised her.

For days thereafter, a mix of deep uncertainty and misty pleasure clouds Laura's every thought and feeling. She drops her summer chemistry class. She is free from the shame of school for the first time in years. She will not return to college in the fall. She will stay home and set up house for her new husband. She begins to look for apartments. She stops by the fabric store to look at material for drapes.

Two months later, after Laura has withstood the pleadings of her brothers to reconsider Ken, after she has refused her father's pleadings to finish school—get a degree, even if it's in general studies—she and Ken are married.

Laura sews her own puffy-sleeved wedding dress; makes her own wedding cake in the shape of the Salt Lake Temple; smiles for pictures in the living room of her parents' home. In the pictures, Ken in his tan suit is so young and so eager. Laura, loose curls around her face, is so young and so still. Her stiff pose doesn't change from one photo to the next.

✻

Years later, Laura and Ken's teenage children ask, "Why did you get married in the first place?" and "Weren't you ever happy? Not even at first?" Sometimes they ask in tears. Sometimes they ask angrily, never yelling—no one in the Gardner family ever yells except as a joke—but with an undeniable sharpness. This is a question they direct only at Laura, never at Ken. The resistance, it seems to them, should have been hers.

With either question, either tone, Laura rarely talks about their courtship. Instead, she cites, but never fully explains, a moment on their honeymoon. "The morning after our wedding, I just cried and cried," she says.

That, Laura seems to believe, explains it all. And maybe it does.

Imagine a slightly musty hotel room at a lodge in Logan, Utah. Low taupe carpet, orange and yellow floral curtains and bedding. Ken has gone out to grab food. Laura sits on the floor. She doesn't hang her head; she just looks out the window at the fall leaves, unwiped tears running down her face.

Before he left, just-turned-twenty-two Ken would have kissed Laura voraciously. He would have touched her hair, smiled, said he'd be right back, then walked quickly out the door, barely registering her slightly flat affect, thinking that his wife, his lovely young wife, was waiting for him, and that in a few minutes he'd be back with their lunch, they'd eat, and then they'd return to each other.

By the time he came back, she would have dried her tears and returned to bed, and she would have smiled up at him, because what could she say? And he would have accepted that smile, because why would he search her for sorrow?

Perhaps Laura had an inkling of their fundamental incompatibility even then. Or maybe it was not a stunning foreknowledge, only the confusion that a girl who has spent her whole life shunning the thought of sex, protecting herself from all but the safest mentions of it, finally feels when her innocence is gone. A girl who has worn undershirts and slips and changed in bathrooms and closets so that even her mother and roommates have never seen her body. A girl who has then found herself married, alone, abandoned to a man who feels none of her shyness, none of her shame.

There were so many differences, so many ruptures of warning, but sex must have been their first great divide: his appetite and her abdication, the model for every advance and surrender to come in all their years of marriage. Just that. Very simple. She pretended it didn't matter. He never thought it did in the first place.

BARRY DUDSON: THE GOD JOURNALS

RYAN SHOEMAKER

As man now is, God once was; As God now is, man may be.
—*Lorenzo Snow*

And the same sociality that exists among us here will exist among us there.
—*Doctrine and Covenants 130:2*

Yes! After nine God years I have finally completed degree at Celestial Kingdom University. Very emotional as I sat in lustrous white robes with other CKU graduates under crystal chandeliers and gilded dome of Holy of Holies Auditorium, absorbing inspiring words of commencement speaker admonishing us to go forth and ascend our heavenly thrones, to create worlds and spirit offspring, to rule and reign in righteousness forever.

And after ceremony, still emotional as I held diploma, rereading elegant calligraphy declaring: *Celestial Kingdom University has conferred on Barry Dudson the rank of God and has granted this diploma as evidence thereof.* So emotional because road to godhood, for me, so long! Had to retake most of math and science classes. In mortality, never good at math and science. Had resolved in retirement to overcome lifelong math/science ineptitude by taking classes at local community college but died of massive coronary in Burger King parking lot one year before retirement. Well, had to wait for post-Earth life to reach goal, but finally did!

From this day forward, as official CKU graduate, have decided to keep detailed journal, a heavenly record, to document life as new god and soon-to-be proud father of many, many spirit children who will live on worlds I create. With journal, hope to provide anyone interested, maybe future generations, maybe soon-to-be gods and goddesses, a sense of my journey to godhood, and, as a god, all the decisions to make and matters to decide. Will call today God Day 1.

God Day 2

Hello, future generations! Forgot in last entry to mention super smart eternal companion Vivica, who, by the way, finished CKU degree with honors in three God years. Amazing! All through my ups and downs at CKU, Viv so surprisingly patient, so supportive as we lived in student housing, even as her parents, siblings, and friends moved on to occupy heavenly mansions in their everlasting kingdoms while I retook classes.

Amazed at how different Viv and I are as gods, so unlike petty, mortal selves. Like as newlyweds in Earth life, how Viv so critical when I forgot to drain dirty dishwater from sink or didn't form perfect "hospital corners" when making bed. And how I, sullen and resentful, would wait for her to run errands, then use her electric toothbrush to scrub skuzzy brown crust from around edges of kitchen sink. Now as partners in celestial journey, as god and goddess soon to create worlds and spirit offspring without end, so glad we've overcome mortal squabbles.

Now, as official CKU graduate, must wait for kingdom assignment. So excited to begin life as all-powerful god!!!

God Day 4

Well, have already missed one day of journal writing. Even gods sometimes forget things.

Thought I would share one delightful surprise of godhood: perfected body! Chiseled biceps, washboard abs, thick mane of blond hair. In life, was very large bald man, what doctors called obese. Strange to look down now and see feet and genitals.

Will admit: was compulsive overeater in Earth life. Wasn't just big bones and faulty thyroid that parents and grandparents, also enormous, blamed. Long history of Dudson family struggle with weight going back to great-great-great grandfather Erastus "Pork

Chop" Dudson, first member of Mormon Church in family who famously stopped walking one mile after beginning journey to Utah, then waited thirteen years for Central Pacific to build rail line with first-class dining car to Salt Lake City. All those generations! How many Dudsons were chubbiest kid at school? How many teased to no end about fleshy jowls and saggy breasts?

As a child, was so depressed about flabby body. Coped by eating through boxes of Ho-Hos and Little Debbie Nutty Buddy Bars secretly purchased with birthday money and hidden in bedroom closet. By high school, wore special spandex undershirts to contain jiggly breasts and protruding belly. As young adult just out of college and living alone, once bought large dog muzzle from local pet store to wear around studio apartment in desperate and absurd attempt to stop snacking. Had such warped view of food, like thinking everything at Trader Joe's was healthy, then feeling justified scarfing down three boxes of chocolate almond butter tarts because package said portion of profits would go to restore 200,000 acres of rainforest.

And then by mid-fifties, knees and back shot, blood pressure through roof. Could only fit slacks and shirts custom ordered from Handsome and Hefty, company out of Tulsa that also made tents and tarps. Deluded self with lifetime of justifications. So many excuses! And then dying of massive coronary in Burger King parking lot, smear of barbeque sauce still on chin from three Rodeo King hamburgers.

Hated mortal self. So happy to be done with bloated, unwieldy body.

God Day 5

Just read over previous entry. Such a downer! Must apologize. Don't want to be dark cloud because now, as buff, all-powerful god, with awesome goddess wife, everything so great!

Will share something positive, another delightful surprise of godhood: Viv's sexy, perfected body. Grrrrrrrrr! Curvy and buxom, skin like ivory. Can't stop ogling her. And she's just as surprised by perfected body: always standing in front of mirror, staring at self with disbelief, caressing taut, flawless thighs once pocked with cellulite and bursts of purple veins. Even crooked nose from college cooking accident involving cast-iron frying pan now perfect.

But enough sexy thoughts about Viv. So much work to do. Spirits to create! Matter to organize!

God Day 6

Exciting day! Received kingdom assignment from Department of Celestial Housing and Galactic Development (DCHGD). Viv and I now proud owners of galaxy MACS0647-JD; really nice piece of space with some breathtaking star cluster and spiral galaxy views, and—because universe always expanding—plenty of room to fill with worlds for spirit children.

God Day 13

Oops, has been a while since last entry. Very good excuse, though. Spent very productive week creating spirit offspring with Viv.

In mortal life, could never quite picture heavenly parents creating spirits. Never really discussed in Sunday school. As teenager, imagined (and hoped) for steamy lovemaking on bed of billowing clouds with heavenly wife who might vaguely resemble Scarlett Johansson. Somewhat disappointed by spirit-creation process. Really more of Viv and I telepathically collecting star dust by raising hands to heavens and intoning sacred words with commanding, godly voices. No steamy lovemaking atop clouds required.

But then so awesome to see spirit children grow! Process like watching tadpoles mature, first foot and then arm, and then another foot and arm, and soon crawling, taking first steps, falling, speaking gibberish.

Good to see smile on Viv's perfect face—so happy, so content as heavenly mother to many, many spirits. Can't help just putting arm around her and soaking up pure joy of watching spirit children grow.

God Day 14

Have confession, future generations: am really nervous about being first-time father. Was never father on Earth because mortal body couldn't produce essential protein for viable sperm. Planned to adopt children but spent ten years on waiting list before giving up. Adoption agency finally said teenage moms probably not interested in large couples.

In first years of marriage, broke heart to find Viv's internet search histories for baby clothes, the long stares at toddling children at McDonald's, the crying in locked bathroom with shower running.

But all painful memories of infertility now gone as I watch spirit children—my children—maturing, asking questions about Earth life. How to respond? How to prepare them for life's harsh realities? Beginning to wonder if suffering really necessary? Don't parents want a better life for children, better than life they had? Nothing wrong with that, right?

Well, no time to write more. Must think about mortal bodies for spirit children.

<u>God Day 15</u>

After much thought, have decided not to burden children with obesity. Obesity will not exist in world Viv and I create!

In fact, have decided to do away with all sickness, disease, handicaps, delays, and deformities. None! Will make all children beautiful, athletic specimens. Will test and try them instead with trappings of beauty: vanity, pride, narcissism, shallowness, etc. No bad breath, jock itch, hemorrhoids, flatulence, diarrhea, profuse sweating. All embarrassing maladies of Earth life gone! Never will they experience gastrointestinal assault from eating pound of old cold cuts, speeding home at eighty miles an hour, then pulling off road to explosively relieve self in stranger's side yard while passing mail carrier pretends not to notice fat man squatting in bushes. In fact, no defecation or urination! Will create biological process by which waste leaves body through skin pores as aromatic vapor smelling like freshly baked cinnamon rolls.

Viv really excited about modifications. "But what about female complaints?" she asked, rocking armload of spirit children. "Bleeding an entire week every month! How's that fair?" Totally agree. So, as per Viv's recommendations: no vaginal birth, no menstruation, no sit-down peeing, no fuzzy upper lips and chins, no hairy legs, and upper body strength equal to men's.

This I declare!

God Day 16

Lately, can't let go of one nagging thought. Is this: how is God not crushed by sadness of omniscience? Like staring into a child's eyes and seeing chain of poor decisions that would lead to unhappiness and eventual damnation.

Couldn't help thinking about this all day with great sadness, but after much pondering, have come to conclusion: As God, will switch off omniscient powers. Can't bear to see which of spirit children will not return to heavenly home. Absolutely crushing. Can't do it!

God Day 17

Spirit children maturing so quickly! Almost ready for mortal existence. Time to create Earth.

Said to Viv with deep, authoritative voice while gazing down at space's great formless void: "Shall we go down to organize and form the heavens and the Earth?" Wouldn't think of creating world without her. But Viv just looked up from gaggle of spirit children at feet and said with sad voice that knows this moment with spirit children won't last forever: "Barry, you go. I just want a little more time with them." Had to turn away to hide great godly tears. Want endless happiness for Viv. Want her to look down on smiling children. If children are happy, then Viv is happy. Have sudden thought: why not just give children beautiful Earth, beautiful sun-filled days with soft breezes, sandy beaches, and swaying palm trees? Don't parents want the best for their children?

God Day 43

Wow, creation not easy. Very complicated. Kept having to reference class notes from CKU. Handwriting so bad! Barely legible! But am proud that after twenty-six days of dividing light from darkness, water from dry land, planting grass, herbs, fruit trees, making all fish in sea, fowl in air, every creeping thing that creepeth upon the face of the earth, have finished.

Made some minor modifications during creation process. Well, maybe major modifications—like tweaking Earth's axis so sun always plentiful.

Also, got a little carried away creating flowers, but kind of figured: "I'm God. I can do what I want." Have always loved flowers since taking floral arrangement class in high school. Always thought: how cool if all flowers glowed, like actually emitting light. Imagined self at night, skipping through fields of glowing tulips and carnations. Never told fantasy to anyone. Actually a little embarrassing now that I think about it. So, as all-powerful god, have made modifications to chemical composition of all flowers, infusing petals with powerful element called Virilium, undiscovered on Earth, to give them bright indigo glow at night.

Hard to believe that I, Barry Dudson, very large man on Earth who struggled even clipping toenails and replacing windshield wiper blades, have created a planet.

Can't wait for children to see and experience grand world!

God Day 44

Now must consider medium to express message of salvation so children find spiritual path back to heavenly home.

In life, was great lover of music. Sang in high school jazz choir. Was backing vocalist for local doo-wop band of very large men called The Chubby Checkers. Very popular at weddings, retirement parties, convalescent homes, and one bar mitzvah.

All this to say that I've decided to make music the medium through which to speak to mortal children. Prophets proclaiming message of salvation won't be skinny, bearded men wandering in from desert, but virtuoso crooners in mock turtlenecks and red sharkskin suits, belting out catchy words of salvation to adoring crowds—Frank Sinatra and Tony Bennett in their primes. And Savior of world, Christ-figure to save all humanity? Will be greatest singer to ever live! Will be Singing Savior!

God Day 45

Have decided that first-born spirit child, Chip, will be Singing Savior. Not brightest of spirit children, but very sweet, very sensitive. Took Chip aside to extend great honor.

Said: "Well, Chip, as my Firstborn I'd like you to be the Singing Savior, king of kings, and lord of lords, declaring in song the gospel of salvation to all my children. The prophets will sing of you. Many will look for the day of your birth."

Kind of piqued Chip's interest.

"A king?" Chip said. "Like, I get a sword and a golden throne?"

Chunked little guy in upper arm. Thought: So cute, so innocent.

Said: "Son, I'm loving your excitement, but no sword, no golden throne. In fact, you'll be a pacifist, born in lowly circumstances. Most will despise your simple message of love, but you'll have a few loyal followers—though most of them will turn on you. Oh, and those who despise you: there's a really good chance they'll eventually kill you in the most prolonged and painful way they can invent. And I forgot: before you're tortured to death, you need to take upon yourself the sins of all who've lived and will live, even those who'll kill you, and you'll sweat great drops of blood and writhe in agony."

Wow, kind of didn't realize awfulness of job until I actually had to describe it. Maybe was too blunt. As first-time father, still learning how to effectively speak with children. Probably didn't explain whole Singing Savior thing that well.

Said: "Son, what do you think? You up for it? What an honor, right?"

Chip just kind of looked up at me, not saying anything, then cried for two hours.

God Day 46

With Chip unwilling to be Singing Savior, and really not even speaking to me anymore, have offered holy calling to next spirit child, Addison. Not interested. And then to next, Bobbie. And then to Dylan, Harper, Jordan, Pat, Reese, and Taylor. All declined. Just asked 3,289th child, Toby. Again declined.

Maybe word got around about difficult role of Singing Savior. Now, all children avoiding me, always too busy when I come around, always rushing off to some place. "Sorry, Dad, no time to talk."

Freaking out just a little. Must have Savior figure to lead children back to heavenly home, to atone for sins. Will stay calm and table problem. Still have few thousand human years to find Singing Savior.

God Day 47

Okay, future generations, big day has arrived! Time to send spirit children down to beautiful Earth I created, to try and test them, to refine them in the great crucible of mortality, all in the hope they'll return to us and eventually ascend to their own heavenly thrones.

Viv just an emotional mess: bottom lip trembling, tears soaking her heavenly robes. Well, must admit that I'm barely keeping it together myself. Like good father, hoping for the best. Hoping spirit children follow strait and narrow path, and return to heavenly home.

God Day 48

Future generations, how to describe godly joy of watching children grow and mature?

Only a hundred Earth years in and everything going so well, way better than expected. Way better than crappy Earth life I remember, with all the political turmoil, wars, diseases, poverty, and famines playing out every night in gory detail on the evening news.

Amazed nothing like that exists among children! In fact, quite the opposite: like children are living in a state of heightened civilization, no war and greed, just an equitable social order promoting cultural creation! No chaos and insecurity to stifle their indomitable will to learn and understand their marvelous world. They spend blissful days in pursuit of science and arts, serving one another with kindness, welcoming singing prophets and embracing their catchy message of love. Can't help patting self on back—in very humble, god-like way—for creating such bounteous, temperate Earth where all is beautiful, with plenty to eat and drink.

Have to remember to keep ego in check when listening to children's prayers: "Dear God, thank you for the glowing flowers." "Dear God, thank you for the singing prophets and their toe-tapping message." "Dear God, thank you for the soft breezes and the plentiful sunshine."

So much enjoyment now in just staring down at productive children. And then to hold spirit children awaiting bodies and say, "Look at it down there, all your brothers and sisters living in peace and harmony. Soon you'll be down there, too."

All wonderful until Viv, arms and lap brimming with spirit children, says with slightly perplexed look on perfect face, "Strange that none of our children have come home. I mean, I know it's not a pleasant thought, Barry, but people die. They get sick, they have accidents, they grow old."

Felt jaw drop open. Have been so caught up with Earth children's accomplishments, that haven't considered this. Quickly allay Viv's concerns by touting Earth's pure air and clean water, the pesticide-free cornucopia of fruits and vegetables and grains, the prosperous social order. And what does it all mean? I tell her. High life expectancy, outrageously high life expectancy, biblical life expectancy! Say this knowing something doesn't feel quite right. Say this knowing I might have made huge mistake!

God Day 49

Yes, on closer look at Earth children, now see that I've made huge mistake! Problem is this: Earth children, with superior intellect, have developed very complicated process to extract Virilium from glowing flowers, and have used it to create powerful serum administered to fetus in utero that eliminates cellular degeneration and mutation. Even repairs damaged cells. No more heart disease. No more cancer. Not even common cold! And accidents? Traumatic brain injury, cracked skull, compound fracture? Not an issue. One shot of Virilium and ten minutes later, not a scratch. Almost can't believe it. Children have eliminated death! I mean, as Earth father, would have been so proud, would have clapped hands and wept as children received Nobel Prize. But death kind of big deal, kind of essential for eternal progression. What does this mean? The reality is mind-blowing—even for a god. No spirits returning to loving arms of heavenly parents, no final judgment highlighting and touting children's Earthly accomplishments, no resurrection, no warm embrace as I say, "Well done, sweet child, welcome to godhood." Can't bring myself to tell Viv. Can't bear to see fisted hand on hip and cutting stink-eye (posture Viv often used in Earth life and now, as goddess, a posture she's perfected). What to do? Don't know. Will wait until absolutely essential to tell Viv—approach I often took in Earth life.

God Day 50

Continue to tout to Viv pristine, unpolluted, nonviolent world as reason for children's freakish longevity. Randomly, have begun to reference long-lived prophets of Bible to allay her concerns. For example, might clap hands in joyful display and say, "Viv, we got a bunch of Methuselahs down there!" Say this while experiencing terrible guilt.

Children living to be 1,000+ years old! Not normal! And with deathless world, know that population will soon increase until all livable space gone. Soon, whole debacle of deathless world will really be obvious to Viv!

And in all this, just have to keep sending spirit children down to inhabit available bodies.

God Day 51

Quite obvious now that beautiful world is filling up with children.

Went to very edge of universe and sat atop magnificent, star-embedded nebula to contemplate predicament. Thought of pirate card game Viv and I used to play with Earth friends. Whole point was to destroy other players with scurvy, explosive dysentery, typhoons, and ravenous cannibals.

Gosh, feel so bad hoping for catastrophic event to decimate Earth children.

God Day 55

Today, after more than 3,000 Earth years with no children returning to heavenly home, have finally confessed to Viv that children will never return, that children, in fact, will forever live a mortal existence. Had to tell her since Earth children, having filled world, stopped having children. Are now content just to enjoy healthy life on beautiful planet. No bodies to send spirits to. And with no reproduction, whole process of eternal progression grinds to halt. Spirit children just hanging out, bored, nagging us about their turn on Earth.

After explaining all to Viv, the Virilium and the serum, tried to soften poor decision by articulating good intentions of giving children beautiful world and lives way better than ours. Viv threw me scalding stink-eye, done with perfection. But luckily Viv, as perfected, celestial being, no longer throwing cookware and hairbrushes. Not fast man in Earth life because of size, so took many spatulas and ladles to head and back.

"Good intentions?" Viv said. "I assumed you'd learned something about good intentions on Earth."

Ouch! Low blow; but deserved. A reference to major financial mistake in Earth life, all done with very good intentions because man at church, perhaps not very honest, convinced me to sink most of retirement in a herd of alpacas. Said alpaca sweaters would be next fashion craze. Invested with grand vision of Viv and me traveling world in oversize first-class seating, motoring through St. Peter's Basilica and Piccadilly Circus in custom-made Jazzy scooters. Never got clear answer about what happened to alpacas but did hear that their teeth fell out before they died.

Could see disappointment on Viv's beautiful, perfected face, that familiar expression from our Earth life. "Way to go, Barry. How you gonna fix this mess?"

God Day 56

Spent most of day in dark funk, staring down at Earth.

Keep mulling over one option: Could give distant meteor a little nudge. Could shake sun just enough so solar eruption burns Earth to charcoal crisp. Kind of ungodly thought. How could a father, without provocation, destroy his sweet children?

But earlier did consult *The Code of Gods and Goddesses, Volume 1* just to make sure, and, yes, destroying children not a good idea. Article 3 states: "*In cases of general wickedness and unrighteousness, plagues, including but not limited to blood-tinged water, deafening frogs, fiery hail, lice, and locusts, may be used to rectify behavior. Only in cases of universal wickedness and unrighteousness, after god or goddess has repeatedly attempted to rectify errant children, is the use of global destruction warranted.*"

Gazing down, what do I see? Paradise, a utopia, no rich or poor, no hunger or disease. No errant children.

God Day 58

Funk continues. Can't bear to look down at Earth children.
Spent last couple days in bed, then this morning, surprised to
receive Inter-Celestial Communiqué from Brother Birch, god of
neighboring galaxy. It said:

> Dear Brother Dudson,
>
> I hope this communiqué finds you well.
>
> This is a slightly awkward matter to broach, but yesterday I discov-
> ered that a number of your children are occupying a planet I'd already
> prepped for my own children. With millions of light years separating
> our galaxies, you can imagine my shock at finding them there, espe-
> cially since I've never heard of mortals leaving their galaxy for another.
> I can only assume you placed them there—perhaps just an honest error.
>
> I can see they're a good bunch of kids, happy and hardworking,
> quite industrious, not those lazy, degenerate types Father cleansed with
> the flood. I'm sure you're proud.
>
> Let me know how to proceed.
>
> Your celestial brother,
>
> Brother Birch

I couldn't believe it! Quickly beamed down to Earth. Not a soul,
no one, completely empty! Not even a straggler or two. Couldn't
understand what happened! How could children leave Earth and
travel vast distances of space? Beamed to global research centers
and laboratories children had created. Found plans and brilliant
schematics for intricate rocket ships, fueled by Virilium, with ability
to propel spacecraft to light speed. In space observatories found star
maps of wormhole networks gods use to travel through universe.

So proud! So sad! How should I feel, future generations? How?
How?

God Day 59

Have screwed up this whole godhood thing. Wanted to do things
differently. Wanted to bring more happiness into dark universe.
Wanted to make *God* synonymous with all things wonderful. Wanted
God to be present for all, not just some distant authority figure.

Will admit that during time on Earth, God scared me with His
great silence. Always felt His silence around me as I lay in bed at

night, the day's stinging humiliation circuiting through my mind. Thought of God as enormous spider staring down from web littered with dry husks of dead insects. Silent. Distant. Scary. Obeyed Him my whole life, maybe out of fear.

Was still resentful, even after death—maybe more resentful. With death, could see my whole mortal life, every moment from time as blot of goo in mother's uterus to last crushing beat of my heart in Burger King parking lot. And all the tragic in-between: a fat child with his hand in a peanut butter jar, a fat teenager eating a stick of butter, a fat adult stuck in an elevator. So much humiliation, so many moments of weakness, so much self-abuse. A lifetime of it. But tried every day to stay positive, tried to put one foot in front of the other while lumbering through gauntlet of taunts and oinks and atomic wedgies. Who wouldn't feel bad for that self-loathing fat man?

On Earth, always prayed, always asked the deep questions that bothered me. Would ask, "God, why are you so mean? All those people who died in the flood. Even the children. The slaughter of the Canaanites, the execution of those poor Israelites for just looking at a golden calf. Why? Did it really happen? Was it just creative license? A bunch of bored medieval monks craving some adventure? Please tell me it was just that. And me? Why are you silent when I cry out at night, when I want you to take away the hurt and the embarrassment? Why don't you stop it?" But never an answer.

While at CKU, finally did send God a letter telling Him everything. Have never told Viv this. Hoped God would finally reveal the secret of human suffering, and why His great silence.

His response: "Dear Barry, I appreciate your letter. I know this won't satisfy you, but I can't answer your questions. The Universe won't let me. I know you're angry. I know you felt alone. All I can say is that the journey continues, far beyond here, and someday you'll find the answers. With understanding and affection, God."

And I didn't understand, not at Celestial Kingdom University, not as Viv and I created spirit children, not as I summoned a world into existence. Through all that, held tightly to that kernel of resentment for God, always thinking: "I'll be the cool God, the hugging God, the shoulder-to-cry-on God, the lean-on-me God."

And now, staring down at an empty Earth, maybe I understand a little more. Maybe the cool God, the hugging God, just ends up as the God of a deserted world.

God Day 60

This afternoon, went looking for Chip, firstborn child. Finally, found him hiding behind the couch.

"Listen here, Chip," I said. "You're gonna be the Singing Savior." And then came the tears and the thumb sucking and the pleading. "Yes, it will be uncomfortable," I said, "and painful and lonely. People will despise you and spit on you and call you the worst names imaginable. But you'll keep at it, despite all the rottenness around you, until you make the greatest sacrifice anyone can make. You can do it, Chip. I know you can."

Had a second part to the speech, comforting words, affirming words, words to inspire and uplift, but there was no need. Suddenly, the tears and the wailing stopped. Chip stood up, a fierce glint in his eyes. He wiped at his dripping nose and said, "Okay, Dad. I'll do it."

So proud!

God Day 61

This morning, with Viv at my side, gathered spirit children for very serious talk.

Said:

Dearest children, tomorrow your mother and I will go down to create a new world, a world that will be subject to decay and disorder. In fact, order and peace will be the exception. And what will determine your standing in that world? For the most part, nothing more than a genetic toss of the dice.

Most of you will live average lives—average looks, average grades, average jobs that will pay just enough for you to get away a couple weeks a year. You'll pass your lives in bland suburban homes with a couple of kids, and then you'll grow old and die, and it will be said at your funeral that you lived a good life, and then you'll be forgotten.

Some of you, a lucky few, will emerge into the world at the top of the socioeconomic ladder, with facial symmetry like the gods, sculpted cheekbones, and full, pouty lips. And when you glide into a room, people will turn and stare, and when you speak, they'll hang on your every word. You'll be persuasive and elegant, instantly likeable and trust-worthy. History will remember you as stalwarts of business, politics, and medicine, forever honored and studied.

And now you, my fat children, my unattractive children—yes, my favorites. How you'll suffer through life, with pants that never fit right, with damp armpits, with lungs constantly gasping for breath. You will pass through a gauntlet of hateful stares and daily put-downs, openly and privately ridiculed, an easy target for bullies. But don't despair, my children. From the shadowed corners where you'll seek shelter from life's ridicule, I want you to look up at the night sky where I'll place a constellation for you: an enormous man and woman whose faces say it all. A million endured offenses, a life with little affection, both in the tight embrace of a loving god as fat as they are, who bends to them and whispers: "My beloved plus-size children, I know perfectly what you endure, for I have endured it, too."

With my words still ringing in the ether, I closed my eyes and remembered my Earthly body, the great amorphous bulk of it, the unwieldy gravitational tug on all that flesh. From deep within, I summoned godly powers of physical transformation. Could feel perfect, sculpted body morph into doughy mass: cheeks sagging, giggle of fleshy pouch under chin, droopy tickle of hairy belly against upper thighs, fingers swelling into pink sausages.

Opened eyes and gazed at Viv, who smiled at me with perfect understanding, cheeks wet with tears. I marveled at her transfor-mation, at her rotund cheeks, the crooked nose I remembered from Earth, the swell of her colossal breasts straining the white linen of her heavenly robe, and the broad shelf of her backside. How I'd missed all of it!

Smiling back at Viv, I flipped on my omniscient powers. Could instantly see arc of our lives stretching forever into eternities. Then looked out at vast multitude of spirit children and saw perfectly a trillion trajectories, some returning to Viv and me, and others never. But could feel it in deepest part of godly heart, the most profound love for them. For each of them. Understood, perhaps for first time, the beauty of all things, perfect and imperfect.

GHOSTS

MICHAEL FILLERUP

The Janitrol furnace that had kept them warm for nineteen winters gave up the ghost late Friday afternoon, minutes after the last repair and parts shop had closed for the three-day weekend. Trapped in a veritable icebox, during a long, sleepless night, Dale was forced to re-examine the wisdom of installing an attractive, eye-pleasing fireplace of malpaís rock (his preference) instead of a utilitarian woodstove (hers). Thanks to his bullheadedness, aesthetics had overruled pragmatics, and he now found himself alone and without heat on Christmas Eve.

Last night the cold had grown so intense he was tempted to call the bishop for help, but his pride had overpowered his suffering. Besides, that would have been a bridge back.

What pride? he muttered to himself.

But he knew.

So had she.

Dale hooked a finger between two horizontal slats, drawing the lower one down a fraction, peered outside, and grimaced: stars, zillions of them, shining like frozen tears. Clear skies meant another cold one. He could barely hear the mixed-and-matched voices of carolers rolling down the street like a slow ocean swell: Shirley Stedman's annual Christmas Eve block party. Dale had already closed the blinds and doused the outside lights to discourage any holiday do-gooders from paying him a charity visit. But for good measure he quickly hit the family room light, leaving the house in inhospitable darkness. He waited by the front door until the chorus of "We Wish You a Merry Christmas" crescendoed and faded, then flicked the light back on, pulled the thermal blanket around his neck and shoulders, and settled back on the leather sofa, close to the tiny space heater he had disinterred from his basement. Ten seconds hadn't passed before he heard a loud rapping at the front door.

Dale knew he couldn't ignore the visitor because he'd just turned on the light. He tried waiting him out, but the knocker persisted until Dale reluctantly opened the door.

"Brother Watson! Mele Kalikimaka!"

A tall, gangly, Quixote-looking figure was ensconced on his doorstep.

"Excuse me?"

"Merry Christmas!"

Dale flipped on the outside light for a better look. It was Wayne Hampton, wearing faded blue jeans with frayed cuffs and a flaming red-and-orange aloha shirt. He was holding a coconut in one hand and a pineapple in the other. A white puff exploded from his lips with each breath. Just beyond the Sahara of snow in his rolling front yard, Dale noticed several cars—Toyota Camrys, Honda Accords—parked in front of the Desmond's home. Bundled up against the weather, couples bearing wrapped and ribboned gifts were marching up the long, sloping driveway lit by luminarias.

*

Dale had never liked Hampton. He didn't dislike him exactly, but he had never warmed up to the man. His looks were as odd as his mannerisms, with that stringy blond mustache and goatee dripping from his chin like Spanish moss, and a nose long enough to hang your hat on. He had an annoying habit of wheezing between words, as if breathing through a box like Darth Vader. Even more irritating was the way he would size you up with those bulbous blue eyes and overconfident grin that, in Dale's opinion, was totally unwarranted; or the giant Adam's apple that jerked around as if a bird were trapped in his throat; or the junky Rambler station wagon with the spare tire lashed to the roof rack; or the antique washers, dryers, and refrigerators rusting in his front yard, which also happened to be the lone eyesore in the neighborhood. What right did he have to parade around with such beaming optimism? A new move-in to the ward, Wayne wasn't privy to Dale's recent history, which may have partly explained his unwitting obtrusiveness. Several times he had tried to make a home teaching visit, but Dale had averted each attempt.

"Thanks," Dale murmured, reluctantly accepting the two exotic edibles. "Well, Merry Christmas!" Smiling falsely, he started to close the door, but Wayne had edged into the entry like a cunning salesman. He noticed that the interior icebox effect was turning each man's breath into a little cloud of cumulus. He reminded himself to breathe sparingly and discreetly lest he arouse Wayne's suspicion.

"Like I said, Mele Kalikimaka!" Wayne blew on his reddened knuckles. "Mind if I come in for a minute?"

You already have, Dale thought. But it would be rude to say no, especially tonight. Dale wondered, sourly, if this might be the answer to his earlier plea for help. If so, he wanted to repent and for God to renege. *Lord,* he mused sarcastically, *I'll take my chances with the elements. Make this guy evaporate, pronto!*

"Sure," Dale conceded.

Wayne stepped into the entryway, rubbing his bare hands briskly. "Boy, it's cold in here, too! Colder than out there, almost!"

"I left a window open earlier," Dale lied. "To get some fresh air."

Wayne's bushy eyebrows contorted as he took silent inventory: no tree, no twinkling lights, no colored bulbs, no advent calendar, no smiling papier-mâché reindeer pulling a fat little papier-mâché Santa across the window seat, and no miniature salt-dough wise men peering down at the baby Jesus in a Popsicle-stick manger. All of that disappeared when she did. Wayne motioned towards the bed sheet Dale had thumbtacked to the walls, creating a sagging curtain between the kitchen and the family room, a desperate (but surprisingly effective) attempt to contain the modest warmth generated by the space heater.

"New curtains?" he quipped.

Dale's smile came slowly, as if a razor blade were being drawn carefully across his face.

227

Wayne dropped to one denimed knee and placed his hand over the metal floor vent. "It's like ice! You sure your furnace is working?"

"Yeah, I think so. It was, anyway."

"Well, let's have us a look!"

"That's okay, really. You don't—"

But Wayne was already striding down the hallway in his big clumsy snow boots, through the laundry room, and into the adjoining garage, with the intuitive foreknowledge of a cat burglar.

Wayne removed the louvered metal cover and genuflected before the silver furnace. He twisted a brass clasp, shutting off the fuel line, then switched it back. "Got a match?"

*

Dale trudged inside and returned with a small box of wooden matches. Irritated at first, now Dale was flat-out angry. He'd spent all day in this sub-zero Antarctica he called his garage trying to breathe some fire into this damn machine. His nearest brush with luck had occurred shortly after dark when, inexplicably, the furnace had issued three short, hard gasps before sputtering out for good. Dale had dropped to his knees on the concrete floor. He'd felt like bawling but instead offered a short, heartfelt plea for help. Seconds later his hands had begun shaking like a diviner's, not from the fires of the Spirit but the cumulative wrath of the drop-dead cold. The arctic tremors had spread quickly throughout his body until he was convulsing like an epileptic. He'd staggered through the back door, down the hall, and into the bathroom where he'd twisted on the faucet and plunged his phantom fingers under the hot water, tossing handfuls onto his face and throat, heedless of the volumes streaming down the front of his winter coat.

When he'd finally paused to look, he'd flinched from the stranger staring back at him in the bathroom mirror: bulging brown Pekinese eyes; thin, stiff bangs flattened by his ski cap; zinc-oxide lips; bushy, twisted brows. Most alarming was the mouth, a deeply grooved frown that arched down to the tip of his chin. After thawing out in a hot bath, he'd layered himself in coat, sweater, thermal underwear, and ski cap, and then curled up on the sofa chair with a thermal blanket. And now, when he finally had a chance to get somewhat warm for the night, this church busybody was dragging him back out into the cold again for who knows how many more hours of freezing futility. Who did this knothead think he was, Merlin the Magician?

Dale handed him the box of matches, noting the red warning label on the panel: EXTREME DANGER! DO NOT ATTEMPT TO IGNITE THE PILOT WITH A MATCH OR OTHER OPEN FLAME!

"Well," Wayne said, "we've got gas. Now let's see—"

He struck a match and stretched it towards the two parallel rows of metal tubes near the igniter.

"Hey, you're not supposed to—" There was a loud bolt, followed by a spooky whoosh as small blue flames bloomed along the metal tubes.

"Yep, we've got flame! Now let's see if we've got ignition."

Dale had to confess that the sudden appearance of fire, the promise of heat, momentarily filled him with a rush of warmth that had been absent in his home this holiday season, even *with* the furnace working. But his hopes were crushed when, inexplicably, Wayne switched off the gas, instantly killing the flame. Dale lunged for the offending hand. "What are you doing!"

"Let's have a look at that igniter."

He really didn't have a clue, did he? The rumors were true. Hampton wasn't playing with a full deck.

"Got a screwdriver?" Wayne asked, oblivious. "A flathead?"

Mumbling crossly, Dale ferreted through an old toolbox until he produced three flatheads of different sizes. Wayne rubbed his chin pensively before selecting the middle one. Dale looked over Wayne's bony shoulder as, arms and elbows jerking and quirking, he performed minor surgery on the machine.

"Aren't you freezing in that shirt?" Dale asked.

"Nah!"

"I've got a coat if you'd—"

"Got it!" he said, withdrawing his head from the exposed belly of the machine. He held the part up to the lightbulb overhead, examining it like a scientist: a small square of metal with two short porcelain tubes set parallel to each other and a stiff wire curving inward from each tube, like calipers. "Yep, this is the old model, all right. A real dinosaur. Let me see what I can drum up."

*

In a surprising feat of athleticism, Wayne snapped from his kneeling position to his feet, like those Cossack dancers in *The Nutcracker*. "Be right back! Don't go away!"

Wayne pressed the remote bar, and the garage door rattled open slowly and noisily. "You got some WD-40? You ought to grease those runners! Well, stay warm!"

The streetlights had cast a golden glaze on the snowy expanse, rendering the look of a desolate outer-space city. In the frigid semi-darkness of the garage, Dale watched the rangy figure trot off into the magical night, a little miffed, a little annoyed, a little amused, but mostly overwhelmed by an old sadness and nagging guilt.

*

His father had once said they were oddly, even tragically matched, like a pair of star-crossed lovers in a Greek myth: inextricably bound yet doomed to imminent disaster. In some ways Dale had spent most of his life trying to prove his father wrong. In other ways he seemed determined to fulfill the prophecy.

He first saw her late one afternoon as he was rushing out of the library en route to his 5:00 p.m. class. As the daily recording of the national anthem began blaring across the bucolic Brigham Young University campus, twenty-thousand-plus clean-cut, bright-eyed students stood at robot-like attention; she alone had refused to stop. From the library steps, Dale watched curiously as the young iconoclast in paisley skirt, sandals, and macrame shawl slalomed around the obedient bystanders crowding the walkway. One of them, a towering, blue-eyed Aryan, hollered at her in righteous indignation, "Hey! Stop for the anthem!"

She never broke stride, never looked back. "I will when Nixon does!" she hollered over her shoulder.

*

It was 1972. Watergate was nothing more than a swank hotel in downtown Washington.

To further ruffle the feathers of the self-anointed Patriot Police,

230

she committed another unpardonable by veering off the concrete path and marching defiantly across the middle of the lawn, a collective gasp trailing behind her.

The instant the music stopped, Dale lit out after her: up a flight of stairs, across an expansive parking lot crammed with economy cars and station wagons, and up a residential street lined with elm trees whose naked branches pierced the twilight sky like giant pitchforks. She turned left on one street and right on another, gradually ascending into a little universe of box homes that cluttered the foothills of the mighty Wasatch. A slight winter chill still lingered in the April air, but bits of spring green and gold had begun to bleed through the massive white wall that sheltered the little university town from the rest of the planet.

Dale believed in spiritual promptings, to a point. Since returning from his mission to Argentina almost two years ago, he had dated dozens of marriage-minded mannequins, and in every case the Spirit had ordered him to bail out—sometimes in a front-seat whisper, other times with a clarion call. He didn't know if the Spirit or lame curiosity had directed him to follow this unusual young woman to her residence; nor, at the moment, did he really care.

She turned into a short, narrow driveway leading to a small brick home where two tricycles and a host of Fisher-Price toys were scattered across a dormant lawn. He cleared his throat: "So what's wrong with Nixon?"

She turned. He was expecting something, or someone, quite different: cast-iron jaw, sledgehammer chin, maybe a little hair bristling her upper lip, tougher eyes, a scar on the cheek perhaps, or a tattoo—a knife, a flower, a hammer and sickle. A peace sign. Something.

Lightly freckled, her face looked soft, gentle, Madonna-like. An angel's.

But her tongue cut like a razor: "He's a crook! They'll put him behind bars! Mark my words!"

"Is—is this—is this your house?" Dale found himself stuttering, and he never stuttered.

"I rent a room in the dungeon."

"The dungeon?"

"The basement. It's cheap. Twenty a month for a bed, a bath-room, a hotplate, and a refrigerator. What more do you need?"

Dale nodded. Sure. Right. What more?

Dale knew he didn't believe in love at first sight, but she must have. How else could someone like her have fallen so wholly and in-stantly for someone like him? They were the Owl and the Pussycat.

"I'm Dale," he said.

She smiled. "Hello, Dale. I'm Verna. How long have you been back?"

✳

On August 9, 1974, Richard M. Nixon resigned from the pres-idency in disgrace. Two months later Dale and Verna were sealed for time and all eternity in the Salt Lake Temple.

Verna liked to think it was a storybook romance, but Dale's parents, multi-generation members of the Mormon aristocracy in Mesa, Arizona, had opposed the union. Yes, she was intelligent, ambitious, hard-working, all the more admirable for having pulled herself up by her bootstraps, defying genetics and genealogy to put herself through school, but ... *This is life*, his father, the silver-haired surgeon had argued, *not the movies*. She had no lineage, or at best a broken one, and a dubious past. She was still wet from her baptism, for pity's sake. There was more, much more, to consider in a marriage. She's not just going to be your wife but the mother of your children and our grandchildren.

All his life, Dale, the firstborn of seven, had obediently jumped through the requisite hoops: Eagle Scout, seminary, mission, and now temple marriage.

"So, what's wrong with that?" he said.

"You're making your bed; you're going to have to sleep in it."

"As long as she's in it, I'm okay with that."

His father was shocked. So was Dale.

"Don't, Dale. I know what you're thinking, but the novelty will wear off and you'll regret it. She's like nailing jelly to the wall."

"I like jelly," Dale said, emboldened. "Jam, too."

"What's that girl done to you? You've never talked like this before."

Dale smiled and shrugged. "I guess I've never been in love before."

"You think this is funny? Don't expect me to bail you out when this all goes off the rails! We've got six more kids to put through college. Do you hear what I'm saying?"

"Loud and clear, Dad."

Hordes of Dale's aunts, uncles, cousins, and shirt-tail relatives attended the sealing ceremony. On Verna's side, a half-brother hobbled into the reception wearing mangy brown hair to his shoulders and a thrift-store suit.

After graduating that spring, they drove across the country in Dale's old Ford Pinto, resurrecting it once with bailing wire and again with the laying on of hands, to attend law school in Baltimore, conveniently distant from relatives of either tribe.

They celebrated their first Christmas in a tiny apartment with a bedroom so small they had to shuffle sideways to get around the queen mattress on the floor. Too broke to buy a Christmas tree, Verna constructed a hearth out of cardboard boxes, painting the bricks red, the mortar gray—golden flames wavering in the grate. At a yard sale, she bought a string of twenty Chinese lights for a dollar and strung them around the perimeter. Christmas Eve they shared a simple dinner, half of it from cans. Alternating verses, they read the scriptural account of the Nativity and sang a few carols. Dale was accustomed to a vast Christmas Eve gathering of family and friends, complete with baked ham, candied yams, and eggnog flowing like a river—an all-night festival of conversation and song. But their evening was still young, barely 8:00 p.m., and they had already exhausted their itinerary. All that remained was their modest gift exchange.

She opened hers first—a pocketbook of Shakespeare's sonnets—and thanked him profusely. Her gift to him was a soft bundle about the size of a small pillow, swaddled in butcher paper she had decorated with Crayola markers: a solitary star shining above the domed silhouette of Bethlehem. Unwrapping it, he looked at her oddly and forced a smile. It was a heavy wool scarf, the ugliest plaid affair he had ever seen. "Thanks," he said. "This is—it's really cool."

They tried so hard to be happy as they sat at the little kitchen table with the warped Formica veneer. But the bright-eyed baby face that had greeted her that first day in the foothills of Provo sagged with sadness.

"What's the matter?" she asked, leaning across the table and stroking his forearm. "It's Christmas!"

"I'm fine," he said, but his smile was an anchor waiting to be dropped.

"You look so sad."

"I'm fine."

"You miss your family, don't you?"

"No."

"Yes, you do. I would if I …"

"If you what?" he asked a little more sharply than he'd intended.

"If I had a nice family like yours."

"Look, I don't miss them, okay?" He waited a moment for his anger or frustration or whatever was eating him to subside. "And I'm sorry for barking at you like that."

"You don't bark. Dogs bark."

"Oh, I don't? Then what do I do?"

"You kind of scowl—maybe like an alley cat when you take his food away."

"An alley cat, hunh?"

"Yeah. An alley cat."

Then he turned the tables on her. "I'm sorry, Verna."

"Sorry about what?"

"This. I didn't mean for it to be like this."

"Like what?"

"This!" he shouted, and she winced as his arm swung out and around, indicating the entire apartment—the cramped kitchen, the paint-peeling walls, the cheap plastic dishes, the tiny ground-level windows buried under snow.

He would carry his remembrance of her expression to the grave. Although he didn't fully appreciate it at the time—wouldn't until it was too late, really—he realized at that moment that she absolutely adored him. It wasn't the puppy-dog admiration that had trailed him through his letterman days in high school, but something altogether different. He wondered, at that moment, if he could ever possibly love her as deeply as she appeared to love him.

He waited for her to say the obvious: "Hey, cheer up! We have a home, food, a nice soft bed. The snow's falling but it's warm. I have you." But she had other plans.

"Aren't you going to try it on?" she asked.

"Sure," he said, slowly unfolding the pathetic piece of cloth. Hidden inside he found a collection of objects: toothbrush, toothpaste, a bar of soap, a hand towel, three packages of trail mix.

"Are we going camping?" he asked sourly. "This looks like a survival kit."

"It *is* a survival kit!" she said. Popping up, she reached across the table and grabbed his arm. "Let's go!"

He gazed around the tiny apartment incredulously. "Go where?"

"Come on!" she said, tossing him his down jacket. "And don't forget your survival kit!"

As she led him up the dark stairwell to the ground floor, he pressed her for details: Where are we headed? What's going on?

She remained elusive. "It's important," she replied, "for families to establish Christmas traditions."

"I agree. Now would you mind telling me about ours?"

She smiled. "Trust me," she said, and they stepped out into the frigid night.

The snow had stopped falling, but the wind had stiffened, tugging curtly at their winter coats. As they plodded through the ankle-deep snow, she instructed him to read the note taped to the tube of toothpaste. Reluctantly, he did: *Please deliver to someone less fortunate before the clock strikes twelve on Christmas Eve. If you fail, you'll turn into a mistletoe and spend the rest of forever hanging from a rafter watching happy young couples kissing passionately in broad daylight. Good luck and God bless.*

He stared at her, uncertain whether to laugh or cry. What on earth had he gotten himself into? They were so totally, absolutely different. Maybe his father had been right. Nailing jelly to the wall.

She blew him a kiss. "Smile," she said. "It's painless."

✳

They hadn't gone half a block before they found an old man in a threadbare windbreaker curled up asleep on a metal grate, trying to salvage some subterranean heat. Dale quickly surveyed the igneous moonscape that was the man's face, his prickly-pear chin and gaping mouth. A green ski cap covered his head; his stubby fingers poked through his mittens like bloated worms. Dale knelt down, gently lifted the man's head, and placed the bundle underneath it. Rising, he gazed down the street where a handful of colored lights were blinking on the grim storefronts, barred and locked up for the night. For a moment he thought he could hear carolers belting out a hearty Christmas tune, but the distant screaming of a siren chased away that holiday illusion. Dale removed his down jacket and placed it tenderly over the old man.

As they hustled back to their apartment, Verna hooked her arm around his waist and leaned her head against his shoulder. "I love you," she whispered.

He hastened his pace: humbled, embarrassed, something.

"Next year," she panted, trying to keep pace with him, "you get to make the kit and I get to do the honors."

*

Such was the birth of their Christmas Eve ritual. Each year they alternated roles, one person creating the kit, the other delivering it. During their law school days, when they lived downtown, it was quite easy to find a needy soul. But as Dale's practice flourished and they moved higher and higher up the hill, their search for worthy recipients became more like an annual odyssey. Their survival kits grew bigger and more elaborate as well until they found themselves purchasing Alpine backpacks from R.E.I. and stuffing them with dome tents, mess kits, sub-zero sleeping bags, and a week's supply of food. But they were always faithful to their tradition, even when they returned late from a Christmas Eve party—or the year he contracted a nasty virus that chained him to his bed for a week. Even the year he broke her heart.

*

Last year was the first time in thirty they had missed their Christmas Eve ritual. He'd sat up all night in the sofa chair waiting for her, hoping and praying that God in his infinite mercy would part the veil and allow her to pass through for a few moments to offer a bit of comfort to a lonely man staggering through middle age. In retrospect, he'd longed to see her not so much to perform their annual ritual but to apologize, to tell her the many things he couldn't because it had happened so fast. An hour would have been heaven, but all he really needed was four seconds. Four words. "Thank you. I'm sorry." Make it seven. "I love you." Eight. "Always."

*

In retrospect, it had been a silly, naive, childish hope—a Christmas wish far beyond the permissible pale. Death would have been the next best alternative; death and reunion. But taking his own life now would have jeopardized theirs together in the hereafter: there was that much religion left in him ... or fear. So, while he didn't actively seek out death, he'd taken no precautions to avoid it. Late one night as he was meandering down the cul-de-sac, a black pickup truck had swept around the corner of a merging side street, tires screaming, engine roaring, headlights coming at him like a pair of Nolan Ryan fast balls. Instead of diving for safety, Dale had sauntered towards the speeding fireballs, unflinching, wearing a smile that had unnerved the driver even more than the impromptu game of chicken. The driver had managed to swerve around him, hollering a string of obscenities in his wake, but at that point Dale had realized deliverance was a distant country, and many miles remained in his journey. Lonely miles.

*

He was awakened by a loud, yet intimate, rapping at the front door. Groggily, he cast aside the thermal blanket, rising from the sofa like a drunk in a rowboat, and trudged across the family room. Pushing open the French doors, Dale confronted an invisible wall of ice. The oak bannisters, the Tewa pottery occupying the antique nightstand, the walnut coat rack, the chandelier, the framed portrait of the prophet—everything in the entryway looked cold, sterile, cryogenically bound. A thin layer of ice framed the vertical window beside the door. He placed his finger tentatively in the lower right-hand corner and scratched, confirming his fears: the plague had crept inside. It began squeezing his bare scalp and mercilessly pinching his ears and the tip of his nose. Each breath blossomed ash-white before his eyes. There was a cold, creepy presence, as if the Ghost of Christmas Future had moved in for the night.

Dale yanked open the heavy oak door.

"Come in! Come in! You must be freezing!"

Wayne's mouth arched into a clown-like smile. "Not too bad." He was still wearing his aloha shirt, his bare arms pebbled with goose bumps, the blond hairs levitating from the chill. He was holding a cigar box overflowing with assorted metal parts, wires, tubes—a mini junkyard.

Wayne stepped eagerly into the frigid entry, his free hand buried deeply in the pocket of his faded blue jeans.

"What time is it?" Dale glanced at his wristwatch. "Eleven-thirty—hey, you didn't walk all that way, did you?"

Wayne shrugged. "It wasn't that far."

Dale silently chastised himself for being so self-absorbed and inhospitable. Verna would have been disappointed in him—not angry or ashamed, disappointed. She would never have turned someone out the night before Christmas, or any other night. She was always bringing strangers home, rescuing them from the camps and shelters and freeway on-ramps—the *will work for food* folks. One night she brought a mangy couple she'd seen hobbling across the railroad tracks. Their clothes were ragged, and they reeked of urine. Dale greeted them guardedly in their majestic entry, then pulled Verna aside. "What are you doing? Are you nuts?"

"They need a bath."

"I can smell that!"

"And a place to sleep."

"Sleep? We can't—they can't—"

"How can we say no?"

"We don't know anything about these people!"

"So, let's get to know them."

She smiled at him, fluttered her eyelashes, not mockingly but flirtatiously, and whispered, "Inasmuch as ye have done it unto the least of these—"

"Come—come in here," Dale said, directing Wayne into the family room and seating him next to the space heater. He placed the thermal blanket over his shoulders. "You want some hot cocoa?" Dale was already moving towards the kitchen counter.

"Yes. Yes, that would be nice." Wayne's lips looked pale, dangerously blue.

Dale pulled open a cupboard and rummaged around until he located the box of Carnation hot chocolate. He tore open two small packages, emptied each into a mug, filled the mugs with water, and placed them in the microwave. He punched several buttons on the control panel. The machine purred softly as he scanned the refrigerator for snacks: cheese, carrot sticks, lettuce, cranberry juice, a half loaf of twelve-grain bread. Verna's vegetarian tendencies had gradually prevailed over the years.

"Are you hungry?" he asked. "Will you eat a grilled-cheese sandwich?"

"That would be great!"

Wayne seemed genuinely pleased, which eased some of Dale's guilt. He was not ready to admit that perhaps it made him feel good as well.

Dale cut several strips of Wisconsin cheddar, slathered Shedd's Spread on four slices of twelve-grain, and placed the sandwiches in a frying pan, checking them periodically. The microwave bleeped. He quickly removed the two mugs, stirring the chocolate froth bubbling darkly on top until it formed a rich, smooth blend. He offered the bigger mug to Wayne, whose face was beginning to appear less paralyzed and more its saggy old self.

"Thanks," he said, sipping loudly. "This is great! Wonderful!"

Dale retrieved the two grilled-cheese sandwiches, and the two men sat side by side on the sofa and ate.

"You should have asked me for a ride," Dale said.

Wayne took a slow sip and smiled. "You should have offered."

"True."

Wayne wolfed down his sandwich and began licking his greasy fingertips.

"Let me get you a napkin," Dale said, rising. "Want another? There's plenty?"

"No, no! I'm fine."

When Dale returned, Wayne was sitting on the carpet, leaning back against the sofa, his legs crossed yoga style, crowding the penurious warmth of the space heater. Dale sat beside him on the floor.

"So, what made you come here tonight?" Dale asked. "And don't say you were prompted by the Spirit. I used to be a bishop. I know the script."

"And all the tricks too, I'll bet."

"All of them. So, tell me, the bishop put you up to it, didn't he? Or old Brother Wyman. He's always trying to light a fire under the high priests."

Dale was bantering, trying to thaw the ice that he himself had hardened. Wayne peered thoughtfully into his mug, as if he were reading tea leaves. "I guess I just didn't want to be alone tonight." He looked up, but this time his face cracked like plaster from his effort to smile. "I wanted some company. I thought you might want some too."

Dale nodded cautiously. It was one thing to share food and shelter; it was something else to assume associations.

"Yeah," Wayne said, "I lost my Cheryl five years ago."

My Cheryl? It sounded so intimate, so endearing, so—human? Odd, or perhaps indicative, that he had never regarded Wayne in a married state, or any other state. He tried to picture Wayne and his wife. A watery image from *American Gothic* formed in his mind.

"It's hard," Wayne said. "Isn't it?"

Hard? Which part? Before or after? Giving or receiving or taking away? Dale recalled fights that seemed so picayune now, sandbox quarrels over infertility, adoption, vacations, his second marriage to racquetball, hers to whatever cause was en vogue at the time: save the rainforest, save the spotted owl, walk for hunger. Things that should have been mere asterisks to an otherwise beautifully told tale had been blown grotesquely out of proportion in his memory. His grief, he realized, was grounded less in loss than in regret: little things he had and hadn't said or done; wishing he'd graciously taped over this or that part of their life story.

In retrospect, he had secretly hoped that over the years she would grow out of her idiosyncrasies. But while he had climbed the ladder socially and professionally, she had moved laterally, if at all. At forty-five she still wore funky broad-brimmed hats to church, and long paisley skirts to her ankles. "The Hippie Lady" the church kids called her behind her back. When they moved into their dream house—a gabled Victorian manor that, more accurately, was *his* dream house—it annoyed him that she didn't seem to fully appreciate his hard-earned bounty. When she joked about "great and spacious buildings" and too many rooms to clean, he took it personally.

The day after he was called to serve as bishop, he took her out to lunch for a heart-to-heart. He was looking handsome and professional in his three-piece suit, like a junior general authority. While she had the Thai salad, he ordered ahi Hawaiian-style, and they sat in an intimate little booth overlooking the canyon, talking casually. Towards the end of the meal, he mentioned his new calling.

"Oh, you'll be wonderful!" she said. "I just know it! You always are!"

Twenty-seven years and she still adored him. Somehow, she had managed to overlook his moodiness and after-cracker fits, his insistence that the dishes be stacked just so.

Setting an example was so important now, especially for the youth, he said. Not just for him, but for her, the new mother of the ward. Avoiding even the appearance of evil.

"So, who's evil?" she asked, batting her eyes seductively. She still wore no makeup except for a touch of blue under her eyes. It was beginning to show now, her cosmetic indifference, all those years loitering in the sun without protection. Little webs were engraved on her cheeks and grooves spread from the corners of her eyes like spokes from a wheel. Still, she hooked her foot around his, tugging it gently, teasingly.

"No one's evil," he said. "That's not what I meant. I think you need to be—look, will you knock it off for a minute? Can't you be serious for once? I think you need to be, oh, a little more fashion-conscious, that's all."

She was silent for what had seemed like a short lifetime.

"Verna?"

"You really want me to do this, don't you? I mean, it means a lot to you, doesn't it?"

"Yes. Yes, it does." And then he said the one thing that she could never forgive. "My church career ..."

"Okay," she said, dabbing the corners of her lips with her napkin. "Okay, I can do that."

She asked for the check, although he paid the bill. They kissed and parted company. He drove back to the office in his Lexus while she zoomed off to the mall in her little Subaru where, in her words, recorded in her journal: *I strolled into Dillard's like a rich bitch and bought out the store: dress suits, heels, three-piece drop-dead showcase stuff.*

He was forty-nine that summer; she was forty-eight. They would share three more years together.

He was trying to recall how it had gone that October morning: who had cast the first stone? Was it him, mumbling something about her half-brother's devil-may-care, ship-without-a-rudder existence; how he was brave and adventurous with the macho stuff of the world, but in the spiritual wilderness of commitment and sacrifice, he was a total washout? Or had she started it, sensing his annoyance, beating him to the draw: "Of course you don't want to! It's spur-of-the-moment, unplanned, unscheduled, unapproved by sixteen committees and four show-of-hands!"

It went back and forth like that, childishly, thoughtlessly, and then cruelly: "And most of all, it just might be fun, heaven forbid! Just because you're afraid of your own shadow doesn't mean you have to lock the rest of the world in a box!"

Contrary to her accusations, Dale's fear of flying wasn't entirely irrational. Shortly after his eighth birthday, his Uncle Lenny and favorite cousin, Chris, were flying down to attend Dale's baptism when their Cessna suddenly dipped and spun, and what had at first appeared to be a simple sky trick ended up being a tragic pillar of smoke and fire in a sahuaro-studded Arizona desert. Dale and his father had watched from the runway where they had arrived right on schedule for the landing.

"You're not going up in that Tinkertoy plane with your half-cocked half-brother. End of discussion!"

But she had mentally drawn a line in the sand. No more knuckling under—she'd even used that phrase: "And I suppose you expect me to knuckle under again?"

*

Afterwards came a dark period of second guessing: if he hadn't been so insistent, dictatorial, pig-headed, maybe she would have relented. Or if he'd agreed to join her. Maybe she was just testing him to see. If he'd gone with her, things would have run smoothly. No gasping engine, no twirling free fall, no smoke and fire. At worst, they would have died together. But why did she have to ride the damn plane to begin with? Why didn't he just grab her by the arm and say NO! NO, YOU WILL NOT GO! Why didn't he back off for once? If he'd just let her see the worry in his eyes. If he'd told her about his cousin Chris and Uncle Lenny. No, he had to have it his way, always his. He was the priesthood holder; he was the boss. But it wasn't even that. No one could have lorded it over her by virtue of the priesthood, or any other hood, unless she allowed them to. And why had she allowed him to all those years?

As a bishop he used to wonder how some of his most staunch Latter-day Saints could lose their faith so quickly. Now he knew. The words of comfort and logic he used to shower on others (adversity is part of life … the refiner's fire … if God answered all our prayers all the time … mortality is the twinkling of an eye, and then we'll be united eternally …) suddenly rang hollow. At best, God seemed coolly indifferent; at worst, sadistically ironic.

"Well, you know what they say?" Wayne was hunkered by the sofa now, cradling the cigar box of junk.

"What's that?" Dale asked. He was still sitting on the floor cross-legged, close to the space heater.

"It's always hardest on the one who stays behind." Wayne hopped to his feet and began marching down the hall.

"Hey, where are you going?"

"Work to do!"

*

Three hours later, the two men were kneeling side by side in the freezing garage, not in joint prayer but in a desperate effort to

243

work a miracle in the cold belly of the furnace. The cigar box was almost empty, the misfired parts forming an altar to futility on the concrete floor. Dale's hands were tucked under his armpits; he was rocking slowly back and forth, trying to generate some warmth, as Wayne jerry-rigged yet another old igniter with a pair of needle-nose pliers. Both men were wearing down jackets and ski caps that Dale had salvaged from the basement. Although they were in no grave danger yet, the bitter cold had lowered their defenses, and like doomed men in a Himalayan blizzard, they began sharing confidences. At one point, Dale asked Wayne about his wife. "Do you ever get over it?"

Wayne withdrew his head from inside the furnace and smiled sadly. "Nope."

"That's encouraging."

"It does get better, though. The first year was awful. At first, I'd look around and see her everywhere: as a twenty-year-old in faded blue jeans strolling to the post office, at thirty-five checking out the vegetables at Safeway. One day at the mall I saw her from behind. Twenty-four or twenty-five, streaked blond hair past her waist and cheerleader curves. I picked up the pace, began weaving through the Saturday crowd. When I finally caught up to her, she was standing in line at the Sears charge card place. I reached out and put my hand on her shoulder and gave it a little squeeze, in a certain way, like I used to do. She looked back with a split-second smile, as if she were expecting me, but in that moment my Cheryl disappeared, and I was looking at a total stranger. All I remember now is her mouth, this big giant pit with red around it and the awful sound coming out, like a broken siren. And then a thousand rent-a-cops, pot-bellied old guys in uniforms, reaching for their guns like it was their first time ever. And the woman's still screaming like a siren and I'm standing smack there in the middle while the rest of the store's crowding around to watch. And there's a dozen folks from church or work or the neighborhood—folks you really know, you know. And next thing they're putting cuffs on me, and I'm standing there with my eyes closed—wishing, praying that everyone else has theirs closed too, hoping they can't see me because I can't see them. But it was never the same after that. The bishop, when I explained it, he said he understood, things like that happen, no harm done, really, but I really ought to be more careful from now on—you know how people are about things like that nowadays. I said yes, yes of course, I'll do that, Bishop, I will. But it wasn't another week before I was released as Blazer Scout leader and made secretary to the high priests. You just get so lonely sometimes, you know what I mean?"

Dale nodded. "So, have you got any plans tonight?"

Wayne reburied his head in the machine. "Fixing your furnace, I guess. Give me that flathead, will you?"

Dale handed him the tool. "Why don't you spend the night here?"

Wayne's elbows jerked and pulled as he inserted the jerry-rigged igniter. "Okay, give me some gas."

Dale twisted the brass clasp.

"Power?"

Dale inserted the plug into the outlet and turned the pilot knob to ON. Dale's heart soared as he heard three quick clicks, like ticking teeth. A thread of laser-blue began writhing as if it were being tortured. Then nothing.

Dale's shoulders collapsed. "Damn!"

Wayne calmly removed the igniter and, with the pliers, twisted one of the wires inward a fraction of an inch. "Amazing what a teeny tiny little adjustment can do."

As he reinstalled the igniter, Dale watched from behind.

"You never give up, do you?"

"Nope."

"Do you think you'll ever remarry?"

"Nope. Do you?"

"I don't know. Maybe. Do you think that's wrong?"

"Nope."

"You just don't want to remarry? You said you were lonely."

"I try to keep busy."

"You know something? I think my wife would have really liked you."

Wincing, Wayne tightened the last screw. "Why do you think that?"

"I don't know. She just would. And believe me, that's a compliment."

"I believe you. Gimme some gas."

Dale turned the fuel valve and twisted the pilot knob. He heard the ticking teeth; the blue thread wriggled like a worm on fire.

"Come on," Wayne muttered, tapping the screwdriver against the metal frame. "Come on."

The furnace issued a deep, consumptive breath. There was a moment's silence, and the cold belly belched blue flames. It was a modest show of pyrotechnics, but to Dale it seemed like sheer wizardry—as if Prometheus had just pulled off a cross-cultural whammy, stealing fire from the Norse gods. He gazed fondly at the gawky Christmas Eve intruder who had become a miracle worker.

"You did it," he whispered.

As blue flames bloomed along the metal tubes, Dale listened for the first warm breath to puff through the interior vents. And for a moment he thought he heard a jubilant shout from within, as if a dear old friend had been magically raised from the dead.

CALF CREEK FALLS

LARRY MENLOVE

It was late in the evening, and Gloria knew it would be dark before
she got back to the truck. It would be dark before she even left the
falls, but she had a small headlamp in her shoulder pack, and the
moon would be up a little later. She just had to make the hike. This
night of all nights.

She didn't like the crowds in the daytime, so here she was,
mindful of the two cars still in the parking lot—a Chevy with
Minnesota plates and a Subaru with Ski Utah! plates—and the
shadows darkening against the high sandstone wall to the west. A
raven, perched on the roof ridge of the restroom, turned its long
beak and black eye to her, cawing as she walked to the trailhead.
She looked back; the raven had glided through the warm air to her
truck and landed on the camper shell to investigate.

The sand trail was soft and red and well-trod with cupped tracks.
She could smell the creek and hear the laughter of people in the
distant campground. She walked quickly. It was August. The heat of
the day still bore down, but the cliff wall put her in shade; only the
highest walls to the east up on Hogback Ridge held any sunlight.

What did she want? Yes, there was the calm beauty of the waterfall, but more than anything Gloria wanted to get away from the
house, the dog, the family. Him. She needed water all over her body.

Two boys born, and the last such a struggle. Many years gone
by. But not so many. In the realm of life, it was a blink, really. He'd

named them: Dominick and Virgil. She'd had different names in mind, though she'd never even spoken them out loud, not once suggested them to Dalen. She held the names inside her; a secret that was hers. Even as Dalen was giving them their names in the blessing at the front of the church with those other men in a circle gently bouncing Dominick, then two years later, Virgil, she gave them hers as well. A silent prayer of her own. A mother's blessing from the fifth row back in the side pew. All those faithful Mormons, eyes closed, heads bowed, but she watched with open eyes and chin straight. Those righteous men in the circle. Those men twice holding her baby boys. Him.

She came across a couple on their way back along the trail. It was on the little switchback portion where if you didn't know to look, you'd miss the pictographs on the opposite canyon wall. She stepped to the side and stood to let them go by.

"Gettin' a late start, aren't ya?" said the man with a calm and gentle accent. So, the Chevy Minnesota tourists would be gone.

"Maybe. We'll see."

"Still a couple of miles left. Hope you have a light."

She just smiled.

The young woman glanced up at her in passing, thumbs lodged in the shoulder straps of her Camelbak, hair wet, shorts wet, sand on her bare toes in her river sandals. The scent of sweat and creek water. Of renewed youth.

She watched them walk down the trail, the girl in step behind the man, easy strides on her long legs, calves brown and strong. When they rounded a bend and disappeared behind willows she turned and studied the pictograph art across the canyon. Three ancient mute figures holding hands. She always felt they were staring at her, invoking some wise message from the past. An epistle that she waited to be delivered in sign. A bird chirp; a chipmunk's tail flashing far out on a branch. The voice of a mournful breeze licking the sandstone canyon walls.

To be a wife. A mother. To bear children. Wasn't that what she was here for? Here on Earth? Why did this place pull her away with such force: alone it seemed, more often than not. If Dalen had noticed, or the boys, they had not said anything to discourage her periodic announcements, like tonight, "I'm going to walk out to the falls."

"Oh?" Dalen. "Want any company?"

"No." A pause as she slathered butter onto a roll. "I need some me time."

"Take a light."

Simple as that.

She journeyed further into the canyon, almost at a jog, pushing herself until she felt a stitch in her side and then stopping to rub at the sinewy muscles of her abdomen. Virgil was the last to have occupied the thin walls of her inland sea. He'd been a troubling dweller, causing morning sickness with no regard to morning, noon, or night; indigestion, backache, swollen ankles, hateful feelings, and no end to unpredictable leakage from every orifice of her body. He rolled and kicked and punched until he had grown so tightly against his flooded plain that he resorted to hiccupping nonstop until he was born—on a hot August evening not unlike the one Gloria was hiking in now, toward cool, pure soul cleansing.

How time had shaped the canyon. Eons of rain, wind, and river—always the river. Calf Creek. So named for the industry early Mormon settlers had used the natural box canyon for, to raise calves into cattle. These pioneers had simply fenced in the narrow gap between the walls. The oasis provided all a cow and her calf could need. Shelter, food, water, shade. Over and over again for generations.

The time had come for Virgil's baptism. Eight years old. This upcoming Saturday afternoon he would walk into the warm depth of the baptismal font in Escalante with his father. Dalen would raise his right arm to the square and baptize him in the name of the Father, the Son, and the Holy Ghost. Amen.

And this was fine with her. It was. An act of ritual, and wholly necessary in the teachings of the church she believed in. But there was something about the baptism that was disrupting the balance at home with Dalen. It was all very complicated. She thought it had much to do with her unwillingness to have more children. She was only thirty-four, well within bearing years, but she had made it very clear to Dalen after Virgil's birth that she was done, and she had maintained her own birth control with the help of sweet Dr. Hensley—Kimberly, she'd insisted she be called—a young OBGYN in Torrey, who had fitted Gloria with an IUD that secreted a pleasing cocktail of hormones into her body that had brought about the best years of her menstruating life. So, no. No more.

Dalen, mostly out of spite, she sensed, had gone out when Virgil was two and found a dog and named him Vagabond. But no one, not even Gloria, protested. It was a mutt of a dog through and through, and one year in, it developed a cancer in its left eye that required removal of the entire eyeball. Enucleation. What a word. Lid sewn down with eyelashes intact. Vagabond did well with just his right eye. He adjusted and was an important part of the family. Just six months ago the dog developed a glaucoma in its one remaining eye. Last week that eye had been removed, enucleated, and its eyelid sewn shut over the socket.

They brought home a dog with no eyes.

The birds in the canyon were starting up their evening calls. Their chirping echoed, and Gloria stepped deeper into the canyon. She looked up at the granary on the east wall. It blended in so well with the natural rock that, even in plain sight, it was mostly unseen by those who looked for it. She remembered the first time Dominick saw it. Truly saw it. The joy of seeing what before wasn't there, like an optical illusion becoming real. He had shouted in surprise. Virgil, still a toddler in a pack that Dalen carried. Gloria with Vagabond on a leash, jumping with excitement and pressing his sandy paws against Dominick's chest, knocking him over into the sand of the trail. They had all laughed.

"It's right there," her son had said to her, pointing at the granary. "It's where people kept their food. Was it a kitchen, Mommy?"

Just this morning they'd had to clean up after the dog. Disoriented and blind, he had stopped in the middle of the kitchen floor while they were eating breakfast. Vagabond stopped and turned his sightless face to the family and sniffed. No doubt he could smell the eggs, the bacon. He strained at the eyelid, so recently sewn, puss still weeping from the slit that would soon grow over.

250

"Hey, Bond," Dominick said, pointing a wedge of toast with fresh, hot butter dripping over his fingers at the dog. "What ya doin'?"

"The poor thing," Gloria said.

"He'll be fine." Dalen slid scrambled egg, European style, onto the overturned tines of his fork with his knife, picked up a slice of bacon and pointed it at the dog. "He's lost one eye before, Hun. He's a dog. They don't need to see. Their senses, you know: smell, taste. He'll be fine."

Gloria looked from Vagabond to her husband, watched his jaw work the food in his mouth. Chewing so daintily. Did he learn how to chew like that on his LDS mission to Germany, she wondered? She looked back at Vagabond. His nostrils were flaring. She could hear the snuffing, loud and anxious, but underlined with a calm, evolving acceptance that this would be the way of life now.

"I know." Dalen put down his knife and fork with care on the edge of his plate. He glanced at Gloria and leaned over his knees and looked deeply at the dog. The dog lifted its snout toward him. "We'll rename him. A new christening."

"What's that mean?"

"Like a saint, Virg."

Virgil shrugged his shoulders, stuffed a handful of egg into his mouth.

"Saul."

"Saul?" Gloria said.

"Paul."

Gloria said, "Paul?"

"Saul, who was a Pharisee, made blind on the road to Damascus." He sat up straight, turned from the dog, and addressed his family: "His name is Saul."

"Who's Saul?" Dominick this time.

"Vagabond is."

"Huh?" Gloria. "Use your fork, Virgil."

"Saul will see the light."

The dog dropped its snout and gathered his haunches in a way they all knew. His hind paw nails skittered on the tile of the kitchen floor as he bore down.

"Vagabond! No!"

"No!"

"Who's Saul?"

"St. Paul." Dalen rose up and went to the pantry and got a plastic shopping bag. He put it over his hand, kneeled on the kitchen floor next to the tidy pile of shit, and scooped it up. Inverting the bag, he looked at the dog, shivering and cowed against the refrigerator, his snout down. "St. Paul, you will believe, and your vision will be restored in three days." He scratched the dog's forehead over the empty sockets and added, "Maybe."

Gloria had gone for the paper towels and the soapy-water spray bottle and cleaned the spot on the floor while Dalen reminded the boys about the Bible story of Paul, or Saul, on the road to Damascus.

"His name is Vagabond, though."

"No. He's St. Paul now. We can call him Pauly if you like. St. Pauly will see."

Gloria tore one more sheet from the roll, swiped at the spot on the floor, and took the bag of shit from her husband with the other soiled towels outside to the garbage can beside the garage door, throwing it all away.

Across the road in the dried weeds a killdeer was calling with its high, shrill shriek, darting in and out of sight, pausing when visible, bobbing on its long skinny legs as though to dare Gloria to hear. To see. To draw her away from her young.

✴

Gloria could feel the air in the canyon cooling. She was getting close. As she rounded the last bend under the box elder trees, their leaves heavy from the water drawn up in this desert sanctuary, she came across the Subaru couple with the Utah plates walking out. Almost bumped into them in the darkening shadows. A middle-aged man and woman dressed for church.

"Oh, god!" The woman in a green long-falling skirt, sneakers. "Sorry."

"Oh no." The man, shirttails pulled, collar loose, sneakers. "You're fine. We just weren't expecting anyone. The sun's going down."

Gloria nodded. "I have a flashlight. I'll be fine. Where are you folks from?"

What was this? Here, just fifty yards from her solace, she was being chatty.

"Salt Lake."

"Bountiful area." The man.

"How about you?" Again, the man, with a sweep of his arm. "You must be local."

"Yes. In Boulder."

"You live in paradise." The woman.

Gloria nodded. "It does have its special places." She lifted her chin, noted how the light was gloaming the canyon walls with summer dusk. She looked back down at the couple. "Have you been to a wedding or something?"

Two laughs.

"Yes."

"Friends of ours. Out on the Burr Trail a ways." The man. "Deer Creek? You must know it."

"Sure do. We hike out there a lot."

"Oh. There's a trail then?"

"Real nice one."

"We just crossed the road from the campground. The mayor married them."

"Boulder Mayor?"

"Yup. Nice old guy. Brought his wife. Couldn't get too far out along the creek with her."

"She wore heels." The woman.

"And kind of old."

"I love Sharlene."

"Oh, you know her?"

Gloria nodded.

The hell was she doing? She should have been floating in her pool by now, face up waiting for the stars, listening to the collapse of the falls underwater.

"We're supposed to be having dinner at the restaurant there. What's it called, Hell's Spine or something? Some people were starting to annoy us."

"Annoy?" The woman. "Pissing us off is more like it."

"I get it."

253

And Gloria wanted to send this woman's husband down the trail and take her hand and share her solace with her, but she couldn't. The man said something about the night coming on, and she knew they would never make the trailhead before dark, so she offered her headlamp. The woman said no, and Gloria said yes; the man said no, and she insisted.

"I can do it with my eyes closed."

They thanked her, and she described her truck so they could leave the headlamp for her.

"And shoo away the raven if he's there." She chuckled. "He eats my wipers."

The couple headed down the trail, and Gloria turned toward the last minute of her journey.

"Oh, god!" The woman again.

Gloria stopped and turned around. The couple had rounded a bend and was out of sight.

"Oh, I'm sorry." Another man's voice.

"Oh, really, no, it's OK. We just weren't expecting anyone else to come around the corner like that. Again."

Gloria listened and back-stepped up the trail.

"It's getting dark. Do you have a light to find your way back?"

"I do. Thank you."

"You live around here, too?"

"Sort of."

"Shit," Gloria hurried along the flat trail towards the falls. She worked her way back along the west wall into the willows and box elders that grew thick here near the catch basin for the falls. The light was very dim. She sat on a sand hill obscured in the shadows but with a view of where folks typically stood at the trail's terminus.

The man behind her came into view. He walked slowly, looking around, as though he knew she was here. He was young, mid-twenties, handsome. No. Beautiful. She did not recognize him, but she recognized something in the way he looked around. And when he said in a voice she barely heard, "Is anyone here?" she knew.

Swallows darted through the air, heralding the end of day and start of night with chattering calls; phantom bats began to flutter in the corners of her eyes, and she could not look away. She moved

to a better vantage point and watched the young man take off
his clothes. He stood watching the water flow over the rocks and
into the pool. His back was broad and carved to his waist, his bare
buttocks white with striations of muscle and tan at the beltline and
mid-thigh.

Had Dalen ever looked like this one? Surely, he had. Years go
by. Memories fade. But do they? Surely, they must be shaded with
the day-to-day of life, the graying of hair and thinning of flesh. The
promise of eternity muted.

The man stepped into the water under the falls and quietly
submerged.

Gloria crept forward, emboldened by the fading light amplified
in the canyon.

He came out of the dark water facing her. He rubbed at his face
and eyes as he stood up, water flowing off him, the surface of the
pool rippling around his legs.

She could not look away.

And hadn't it always been like this? She watched. Everything.
It was as though her life spooled out on a reel of others' lives. Her
mother and father, siblings. Husband. Sons. Dog.

A strange, handsome young man naked in her oasis of solitude.

Her heart leapt, urging her to stand up and join him, a vessel
moving through her life to intersect here. Why couldn't it all make
sense in that way? Lives crossing, baptisms, names, sand on the floor
of a canyon on this Earth cupped with endless tracks of wandering.

She had not wandered. Every step was deliberate to this place.
And now she had to wait hunkered behind thin willows as the man
dropped back into the water. Out and in, floating and howling into
the night.

She waited until he rose up for the last time and toweled off
on the shore, invisible now, just sound. The satisfied sighs of desert
pleasure.

*

And after the man finally left, did she need the Spirit to guide
her? She didn't think so. The darkness was full. She left her folded
clothes and pack on a rock right there before the falls and slid

naked into the water. She toed the sand and rocks over to the deep trench along the east wall where the flow was yet warm, swirling back onto itself. There, she held her breath, dove under the surface, and then floated face up.

Eyes open.

Desert sandstone water covering her ears, tickling at the gentle wrinkles where her eyes met her cheeks. She floated, spinning slow in the eddy, arms outstretched, legs hanging in the freely given suspension of stream and gravity.

Eyes open.

She fought to stay in the moment; she here alone. She would never go back over the trail, the dire drive over the Hogback, back to home. Back to her family. It was fine. All of it. Most of it. They were all more or less on a forward path that needed little attention. The boys. She said the names she gave them now, out loud to the night, to the stars. To the waterfall. For herself. For who she was.

But St. Pauly would need her now in his darkness. With his new name. And she would need him.

The Dog Star was there. Sirius above her in the black heavens surrounded by a billion of its brothers. And sisters. Some bright. Some just a hint of existence coming in and out of view from the canyon wall, the skirt of the falls, as she rotated freely on the eternal axis of Calf Creek.

THE FUNERAL

HOLLY WELKER

I didn't mind funerals when I was little, because they were the only time my sisters and I got to see all our cousins at once, even our second cousins. Someone was always planning a family reunion, but grownups always found excuses for those, work or something; for funerals, though, I guess they all felt guilty. People in our family die old, eighty-nine or ninety-seven, ages like that, of things like broken hips or just not waking up. They get older and older and smaller and dried out and brittle, like everything else that lives in the Arizona desert. And then we bury them in the old cemetery on a hill outside of town, a hill just as brown and dried out as the people in it, and without any grass—the green kind, at least, but with lots of rocks and jack rabbits and even a few scorpions and rattlesnakes.

The services were always held in the old, kind of gothic, sandstone chapel on Church Street. The youngest kids would fidget and cry, not because they really knew and missed Great-great-aunt Louisa or whoever, but because it was strange and scary to be in church when it wasn't Sunday. My mother led the Relief Society Chorus—that was its official name, but everyone called it the "Singing Mothers"—and they always did a special number and then sang "God Be With You Till We Meet Again" for the closing hymn. After that everyone went to the cemetery for the burial. Then we all went to our house, us and all our cousins from out of town. All the neighbors who weren't close relatives would send food, and we'd have a big party with ham and roast beef and four kinds of cake and the best fruit salad that was really dessert made

257

with Cool Whip and cherry pie filling and pineapple and pecans. My big sister, Margaret, heard one of our uncles call the meal "food for the dead" and we all thought that was so funny. We'd take the plates our aunts filled up for us and go in the backyard and play on the swings, and never even think that the person who died hadn't always been old.

A long time ago, I know babies would sometimes die before they were even a year old, but besides them, I only knew of two relatives who died young: my grandmother and my aunt Dorothy. My grandmother got mad at my grandfather one Sunday and went to a movie instead of church. Walking home afterward she got run over in front of the bank by a drunk driver. All I really ever knew about her besides that was that she was twenty-eight when she died, that when he was three my dad locked the bathroom door from the outside while she was taking a bath so she had to climb through the window wearing nothing but a towel, and that she taught school in the same building where I went to the first through the eighth grade.

Aunt Dorothy, though, I was sort of named for her. She was only six months old when my grandmother died, and when I was born, Dad named me Gwendolyn Dorothy Lewis. I didn't like it very much. Aunt Dorothy was crazy. Everyone in a small town knows when someone else is crazy. Dad said she always had bad dreams, but when she was almost done with college, she started insisting that demons were trying to get into her face. She wore scarves and sunglasses whenever she went outside to keep them out. But after a while she said they were in her, and then she used to cut her face with a pair of hair scissors to get them out. She talked about weird things every single testimony meeting, and she scared a lot of little kids, but she wasn't dangerous to anybody but herself. She lived with my great-grandfather and took care of him. He was ninety-five and ornery and very proud of the fact that he was the oldest native in the valley and could remember the Indian wars. We would visit him and he would give us round peppermint candies while Aunt Dorothy complained about the family next door who spoke only Spanish and who she said had been persecuting her since before she was born. But Great-grandpa got along very well with Aunt Dorothy. Even though she was crazy, she was a very good cook, and she held his hand when he went out every day for his walk to the post office and back.

Aunt Dorothy had been a good student when she was young, and my big sister, Margaret, was in Honor Society and stuff like that too. I'm the second daughter. I wasn't a bad student, but I decided I wanted to do something different. I ran cross country and the mile in track. And that's another reason I didn't mind funerals. The graveyard was right next to the city ballpark and track. The road through it was soft and you never met any cars, so we ran there all the time, and we never saw anything strange. Not once.

They took Aunt Dorothy to the hospital for appendicitis the day Mike Kimball asked me to the Prom. It was a Friday and we were at a track meet. I came in second in the mile, just like he'd done in the boys' race. It's hard to think about what he means to me. I have a memory from when I was pretty little, like four or five, of walking home from Primary with Margaret and deciding to play this game with Mike where we threw sticks off one side of the footbridge over the canal and then ran to the other side to see whose stick would get there first. We thought we invented this game, but somebody told me it's called Pooh Sticks and is in the *Winnie-the-Pooh* books. Mike's a year older than I am and I used to wish he was my brother or my cousin until I got old enough to have crushes, and then I was glad he wasn't. After my race that day, he came up and told me I'd done good. We talked about something unimportant for a while, and then he said very quickly and kind of flat, "So do you want to go to the Prom?"

Mom was home from work and cooking dinner when I walked in the kitchen door. I told her I needed a new dress. "So, Mike finally got around to asking you," she said.

"Yeah," I said. "So, do you think you'll have time to make me a dress or not?"

She stirred the spaghetti sauce awhile. "How about if we buy one? Aunt Dorothy has appendicitis so we're all going to be kind of busy around here for at least a month."

"Really? Guess those demons finally got to her after all," I said.

"That's disgusting, Gwennie." My little sister Janet was setting

259

the table. We made faces at each other. But it really didn't seem important. I found a dress the next day, long and blue, with lace sleeves and cut low in the back, so it wasn't just like a Sunday dress. I thought it was so pretty on me. It made my eyes look really blue.

But then about ten days later—I guess it was Tuesday night—I was doing my geometry homework and my great-grandfather called. He was crying and wanted to talk to my father. Dad had to drive Aunt Dorothy back to the hospital. Janet and I went to bed before he got home. Early in the morning, Mom woke us up and said, "There was a blood clot from the surgery. Aunt Dorothy had a stroke and died about two o'clock this morning. The funeral is Saturday."

I didn't think about it. All day I wouldn't think about it. But then at track practice when we were running through the grave-yard, I thought, Aunt Dorothy will be here soon. I knew my relatives were all buried in the west part of the cemetery, but I had never bothered to figure out how to find it when there weren't peo-ple around. I didn't really want to know now. I found out anyway the next day when the backhoe came to dig the grave.

The Prom was Friday night. Mike picked me up and we went to dinner with some of his friends and their dates. I was having a good time at the dance but Mike got tired of sweating in a suit so we left early and went driving around. On almost any of the foothills, you can drive up and see all the lights in the valley. There aren't a lot of lights, and cotton and alfalfa fields are stuck right in the middle of everything, but it's still pretty.

We were sitting there and he had his arm around me. "What are you doing tomorrow?" he asked.

"Going to my aunt's funeral," I said.

"Oh, that's right. Crazy Aunt Dorothy." He probably thought he embarrassed me because then he said, "She was pretty nice, though, wasn't she?"

"Yeah, yeah, she was. She liked me a lot since I'm named for her. I'm trying not to think about her. Feeling kind of guilty, to tell the truth."

"Yeah, I guess that's why you've been acting a little strange to-night. Not your usual self."

I hadn't known I was acting strange. I even thought I was doing a good job of having fun. "I'm sorry," I said. "I guess it just seems weird that someone should die when she's only thirty-five or something."

"Why should you feel guilty, though? It's not your fault."

I shrugged and looked out the passenger window a moment. "Maybe because I resented her a little.... I mean, she's *crazy*. Sister Sanders even told Mom it was a blessing, the way Aunt Dorothy did things to her face; who knows how much worse it could get? It's horrible, but I felt that way a little, too. Then I remembered: Great-grandpa really, really needs her. We don't know who'll take care of him now."

He stroked my hair. It felt nice. I wanted to think about that, not Aunt Dorothy. "Well, you know, maybe she is happier now, Gwennie. And people die all the time even when other people still need them."

I sat up straighter so his hand fell away from my hair. "Not in my family they don't. People die old, so old *they* need people, or so young I never knew them."

"But all the time in the newspaper ..."

"That's the newspaper," I interrupted. "I don't know those people. It's not me. It's not my family."

"Gwennie," he said, in a patient voice like he really was my brother, "don't you remember all the lessons about the Saints crossing the plains? Death isn't fair. It happens to the good and the bad and the young and the old." He sounded like a Sunday school lesson himself. It made me sick.

"I never thought of it like that, though," I said, even though it made me feel worse to admit out loud how stupid I had been. "I never thought of death as something that happens to ... I just never thought of it. I would go to all those funerals and I would never think of it."

He tried to intertwine his fingers with mine. "I'm sorry, Gwennie. It's OK."

But I was already upset. I pulled my hand away and balled it into a fist. I almost wanted to hit him, even though he was trying to make me feel better. "I just—I just never thought of it as something that could matter. I never thought of it as something that could change anything. I never thought I could die until I was so old it didn't matter whether or not I kept living."

I felt like I might cry, so I went along with it when Mike changed the subject to baseball or something. When he took me home he kissed me good-night, just a little kiss, and told me to have fun at the funeral. I said I'd try.

Margaret came home from college for the funeral. Dad gave the eulogy and Mom led the singing. Then we went to the cemetery. It was such a beautiful day, the end of April and only about eighty degrees. The sky was completely clear and there were little white wildflowers and orange poppies all over the foothills. We stood facing the mountains as they lowered the casket and threw dirt on it.

Not all our cousins were at the dinner afterward. Their parents came, but the ones in college were studying for finals. One had already made arrangements to visit her fiancé's parents, and three were on missions. The rest of us sat in the backyard and watched the grade-school kids play on the swings and eat cake. We didn't talk about Aunt Dorothy.

Monday, Mike and I went running in the cemetery after warm-ups. I turned down the road where my family's graves were and stopped without saying anything when we got to them. Five generations of my family were there, from my great-great-great-grandfather, who started the town farming cotton, to Aunt Dorothy. The roses in wreaths around her headstone had opened; when the breeze picked up we could smell them.

"Are you going to be buried here when you die?" he asked me.

I shrugged. "I don't know. I guess. If I don't move somewhere else."

"My family's over there." He pointed toward the mountain. "I'll probably be buried with them too, even if I move somewhere. My grandpa bought so many plots, it'll take a lot of people to fill them all. So, no matter what, I might as well be shipped back here." He smiled, like it might be a joke, but I knew he meant it, too.

I picked one of the roses out of the arrangement. The petals fell on the fresh earth drying loose and crumbly because it was so dry. The ground would stay that way until monsoon season in late July.

I looked at the name on one of the oldest headstones. His name was James Monroe Peel; he was born September 16, 1822, and died

July 31, 1891, more than seventy years before I was even born. Next to him was his wife, Agnes Dreghorn; she was born April 28, 1827, and died January 19, 1902. I had no idea where they were born, but I knew it wasn't here. They probably thought of me even less than I'd thought of them, and always in some general way. Their unborn offspring. My dead ancestors. At least I knew their names.

"Let's go look at your family," I said to Mike.

He touched my hair and smiled. "Later," he said. "After practice. I really need to get a good run in today." He started to go but I caught his arm.

"Please," I said. "Can we do it now?"

He stopped. "Sure, if you want to." And we walked over, holding hands.

WE'RE GOING TO NEED A SECOND BAPTISM

RYAN HABERMEYER

Last row on the left nearest the door. That was the pew. Same one Early Sheasby occupied all his life. Seventy-four years, if anybody was counting. Never missed a Sunday. His mother gave birth to him at four o'clock in the a.m. and the whole family was lined up in the pew not a minute past noon without a wrinkle in their clothes. Last row on the left nearest the door. Early Sheasby had his first erection in that pew, may Missy Pulsipher rest in peace. His wife sat next to him each Sunday. She'd been dead nine years but the moment he sat down he could smell her perfume and knew she had left the other spirits and crossed the veil of forgetfulness that separates our kind from theirs to be with him. It was nine years ago she died at nine o'clock in the A.M. but Early was in the pew not a minute past noon. Everybody knew where the Sheasbys sat. His father, Olaf Sheasby, whose grandfather crossed the plains with Brother Brigham and helped build this chapel, walked through the doors the first Sunday and sat in their pew and announced, *This is the place.* The Sheasbys had been there ever since.

The woman sitting in his pew with the three kids could not have known any of this. She was a visitor. Or heathen, depending on your persuasion. Early could see she was dressed saintly for the Lord's Supper, that is, if truck-driver fashion is holiness to the Lord. She even had a nose jewel. All this was forgivable. What was not forgivable was ignoring the Holy Ghost whispering to her soul to get the hell out of the pew reserved for Early Sheasby.

Early stood at the end of the pew sucking his tongue.

265

"Oh? Have we taken your spot?" the nose-jewel woman said.

"No, ma'am," Early smiled. "There is no reserved seating in heaven and none here."

What else could he do? He sat in another pew.

And so, it was a terrible Sabbath. He tried to sniff out his wife but she must have been confused by this absence and thus attended services somewhere beyond the veil. By the time the sacrament tray came to him there were only crumbs and stale crusts left. The water tasted like something from a toilet. The acoustics on this side of the chapel were terrible, and Early couldn't hear the hymns much less sing them. His back went stiff. A dribble of piss leaked out. It was. as if his soul were slipping away.

So, who would blame him if his foot slipped? Yes, it was an accident. He had been telling the bishop for years it was bedlam in the parking lot after services—a real Sodom and Gomorrah. Do you think the bishop listened to him? Hell no. The man is an idiot, Early told anyone who would listen. Earned a doctorate in poetry for God's sake. When the world needs doctors for poetry, Early was fond of prophesying in the church bathroom, you know the apocalypse is just a few blocks away.

Early could not explain how his foot slipped off the brake. Not like he was *trying* to trample the poor girl. The Sheasbys were not violent by nature. But there it was. Accident in the parking lot. Mormon Road Rage, the newspaper said the next day. Well, fetch, Early thought, if the nose-jewel woman had just sat somewhere else it would have been a holy Sabbath.

✳

It was a broken leg. Heard it snap like a tree branch under the tire. Early stood nearby as the bishop put his hands on the girl's head, presumably to heal her, but Early knew better. Since when does the Lord listen to poetry? God is a potter, not a wordsmith. The blessing may have eased the pain but the bone was stubborn and required medical intervention.

What really cured the child was the pharmaceuticals. The girl was in the third heaven when Early visited her at the hospital later that day.

He kept his eyes on the floor as he apologized to the nose-jewel mother. She was gracious, which surprised him because with the tattoos painted up and down her arms like the devil's playground and the bandana covering her hair, he could have sworn she was a gang person.

"Accidents happen," she said, half smiling.

Early knew she had that much right. The first law of heaven is accidents happen. Were it not so God could not slam a window on your fingers to point out, *Hey, I opened a door on the other side of the room. And that room is full of syphilis. And the house is on fire.* He is a God of small accidents, indeed.

"Amen," Early whispered.

Early didn't tell the nose-jewel mother any of this—like she would even understand—just smiled and half-heartedly proposed that if needed he could be of assistance. Early knew better than most the second law of heaven for Mormons: deepest sincerity with insincere words.

"You can baptize me," the girl said, enthused by his offer.

It was an awkward moment. Early thought the request was the result of a hallucination. He turned to the mother who looked sheepish.

Me? Why me? he wondered. He tried to look old and senile.

"My dad's away," the girl said.

From the corner of his eye, Early saw the mother stare at the floor, embarrassed or saddened he could not tell. He almost reached out and put his arm around her, worried she might faint.

"You're the oldest person I've ever seen," the girl said. She was speaking very loudly, but she seemed to think she was talking in a whisper. "Like, really old," she continued. "I bet you got your priest-hood from ... whoa ... *Methuselah*."

Her eyes got wide and she gazed dreamily around the room, still mouthing *Methuselah*. For a second Early thought she might try to summon the dead prophet from the grave.

"Manners," the nose-jewel mother hissed between her teeth.

"I *am* old," Early said. But even he knew that was like saying a fart is odorous. Suddenly, the Sabbath did not feel like a total waste. Early had learned something: he did not like children, but he did like children supplied with oxycodone.

"Old-ass priesthood," the girl said, moving her hands like some oriental kung-fu shows Early liked to watch on Saturday nights.

So, it was settled. In eight to ten weeks, or whenever God healed the bone, Early would use his old-ass priesthood to give the kid a glorified bath and save her soul.

"Thanks for the cast," the girl said before Early left. "It's cool."

"Glad to help," Early smiled.

*

Early Sheasby never had children. Practiced quite a bit with the missus, but the mail got mixed up at the post office. He always thought it would be nice to have a child who looked like him. A back-up. Just in case. He didn't remember much about his own baptism and had never baptized anybody. It looked simple enough. But looks can be deceiving. The last thing you want to do is half-ass a baptism with old-ass priesthood.

It was difficult finding a volunteer to practice the baptism on. The neighborhood kids all thought Early was some weirdo, and mothers seemed generally suspicious of an old man asking to borrow their children for a little splashing around. He thought about using an animal proxy, because kids are not so different from critters, but the neighbor's dog refused to get in the river. Early went to the fire department but they said the mannequin they used for CPR training was unsuitable for aquatic situations.

Early's wife would have known what to do. Fifty-four years she fed his mind what it needed to know. Now his brain was starving.

He walked in circles downtown until he was in a daze. It was only when he stopped looking at his own feet that he saw the window lit up like a Christmas tree. Dolls. Lots and lots of dolls. Of course! The mannequin in the window display was naked save for a green fig leaf on her crotch. Eve, mother of us all.

Normally, Early would never step foot inside an establishment called Good Vibrations, but he knew the Lord works in mysterious ways. Inside, the owner said his name was Joshua. Early took that as a sign he would be delivered into the Promised Land.

Joshua gave Early a tour. Toys, he called them. Hmph. Some toys. Fur pelts, leather masks with zippers, vibrating wands that required straps, and an ungodly assortment of gels and lotions and scented candles.

"No, no, no!" Early said. "Show me the dolls!"

"I see," Joshua smirked. "A man of refined tastes."

It was quite a selection. Brunettes, blondes, red heads. Like heaven's laboratory. Don't like one head, swap it with another, Joshua said. Early rubbed the hair between his fingers. They moved on to the ethnic section. Japanese, Russians, even Africans. Dolls made from vinyl, latex, and silicone. Some inflatable, others so life-like Early was surprised when they didn't talk back to him. Some ran on batteries and screamed *Yee-Haw!* when pinched in the right place. Early tried but none of them said *Yee-Haw!* for him. They all had names. Molly. Candy. Ginger. Ophelia.

"What will the primary use be?" Joshua asked after a brief sales-pitch. "Anal? Oral? Traditional?"

"Baptismal," Early said.

Joshua put his lips together like a blowfish. "That's new. Like a fetish?"

"No," Early said, "I don't speak Japanese."

Eventually, Joshua recommended Fatty Patty. She had been dis-counted to $487.62 which, Joshua persuaded Early, was something of a miracle.

That night they shared their first supper. Pork medallions with marinated beans. Hundred-year-old family recipe courtesy of Patricia Sheasby who crossed the plains with Brother Brigham and shared his bed with fifty-three other women. Nana Sheasby, meet Fatty Patty. There are no coincidences in life, Early knew. Jesus is at the wheel.

The recipe seemed like a good opportunity to explain to Fatty Patty the family history, even if he felt a little silly talking to a doll. The silence was always suffocating this late at night, but the doll's presence made it both more and less difficult. Early told her about Anabelle Sheasby, who set fire to the family farm, and Jeremiah

Sheasby, who was a bodyguard for Brigham Young, but he felt like he was getting nowhere with her, this strange doll that seemed both alive and not alive at the same time.

Afterwards, they watched television. It made him a little nervous just to have her sitting there, eyes unblinking, and he would be lying if he didn't admit her open mouth made him feel a little stupid, as if some secret were leaving her lips and he couldn't hear it.

They started a game of chess but Fatty Patty didn't seem interested. Early tried reading her instruction manual but it was all in Chinese. They studied the diagrams together.

Early phoned the nose-jewel mother.

Yes, the girl would still be baptized, she told him. Looking forward to it, actually. Was anything the matter? No, nothing at all, Early insisted. A few weeks until the cast comes off, the nose-jewel mother reminded. Early could hear the uneasy smile in her voice.

He hung up the phone.

Fatty Patty sat with Early in a darkened room, their fingertips just barely apart.

*

The South Jordan pond was no stranger to baptisms. Early's great-grandfather wrote in his journal how it shimmered like a sheet of celestial glass when the pioneers walked into the valley. They stopped using it shortly before Early was born because the trout, disobedient celestial conspirators, would attack the poor souls being baptized.

Around dawn, Fatty Patty and Early stood on the soft sand a good hour just watching the water. Some joggers passed. Early waved. They disappeared around the bend.

Sighing, Early went down in the water with the doll tucked under his arm.

After seventy-four years, Early was well aware of that moment when the sun edges over the mountain peaks and light spills down the slope and across the valley, turning the the twists and turns of farmland a burnt orange. Early never missed it. It was just so goddamn beautiful, enough to make a man forget about baptizing a doll and the cruel injustice of cold water lapping at his testicles.

Early raised his arm and called on the powers of heaven to wash clean this poor soul from the sins of her generation. A bird screeched. The wind rustled leaves off trees. Fatty Patty went under with ease and came up with hardly a splash. It was quiet. Early waited. Was it over already? What was he waiting for? He had expected something different, something more. A change; a feeling. Something. She smelled the same, albeit a little fishy. Maybe God hadn't accepted this offering.

On the third try her left nipple fell off. He couldn't get it to reattach. Perhaps, Early mused on the long walk home, love dolls are touched more easily by the Holy Spirit, or maybe they have no need for baptism, or they exist outside the designs of salvation.

Things grew weird between them now that Fatty Patty had received her baptism. It was a fake baptism, no doubt, but still. Something was different. Before, the doll could be sitting next to him on the couch but feel halfway across the universe. Now it was like she was sitting on his chest, both giving him breath and taking it away.

On the Sabbath, Early removed Fatty Patty's Catholic school-girl uniform and covered her in one of his wife's old dresses. He made sandwiches and some sharp lemonade. They sat next to each other on the couch, the sandwiches in Early's lap and the photo album in Patty's. Early could almost hear her speaking to him.

Who is that?

Me. Early Sheasby.

That's a funny name. Fatty Patty had a raspy voice, the way his grandmother sounded after raiding her supply of laundry vodka.

You're one to talk, Early chuckled.

Fatty Patty wanted to know why on earth Early had such a ridiculous name.

Mother said I was never on time to anything in my life, Early told her. Watch out, she used to say whenever he would leave the house, the day you have may be your last.

They found a picture of his mother standing at the kitchen sink with a handful of vegetables, back before her smile was swept away by things she never dared to speak of.

Do you miss her? Fatty Patty seemed to ask.

Early had never been good with words and he was surprised that this doll could speak without words—by the power of the Holy Spirit? It felt like a welling in the throat. Yes, he said without words, how often I have wanted to see my mother standing at the sink.

Fatty Patty was quiet. Then she said, Your dead are never far from you.

Early didn't know how she knew that, or how she said it without the words, or why when she said it without the words it was as if a ghost tap-danced over his heart.

He put her in the closet. He looked out the window. He went upstairs. Then he hurried back into the room, almost tripping on the rug. He pressed his ear against the closet door to hear if the doll was breathing, but all he could hear were words without sounds.

*

Early placed Fatty Patty at the backyard window each morning where she could enjoy the sun without worrying the neighbors. He clipped the rose bush and put the flowers in a vase near her, hoping it would please her to see such things.

After some mild gardening he sat in the armchair next to the window. He poured her untouched cup her tea down the drain and refilled it. He gazed through the window, anxious to see what she had been looking at these past few hours. When he pictured himself through the window—wrinkles, flab, and whiskers—disappointment seized him by the throat.

Over the next few weeks, and Early was not a man prone to imaginations, he glanced at her through the window and somehow, inexplicably, caught her watching him. Later, when he was in bed reading scripture he noticed her eavesdropping from across the room. Not always. Sometimes he perceived a kind of knowing in her eyes. Early was no idiot. He knew it was a doll and God never put in her the breath of life, but just as he had often been surprised by the cat

272

staring quizzically at him when he emerged from the shower, so did Fatty Patty pierce Early's conscience with her counterfeit gaze.

The more they shared each other's company, the more she intruded on his solitude. Once, by accident, Early slipped on the kitchen linoleum and was lucky when Fatty Patty—with all her spongy cushioning—broke his fall. They lay there in silence, her fat nipples hardened against his chin. Her touch especially surprised him. Despite dancing with her once or twice with the curtains drawn, only now did he notice how her rubbery skin so utterly lacked warmth. Alien yet incantatory. He had not been touched like this in many years. He almost kissed her. It scared him.

That night, Early dreamt of his dead wife. In previous dreams she was always out of focus, a blurry shape whose voice sounded as if it were on the other end of radio static.

But tonight, Early could see her as clear as she had been before she was sick. She stood on one side of a river calling his name. Long streams of curly hair fell over her face. She never let it down when she was alive. Maybe it was a malicious spirit pretending to be his wife. Early was barefoot, mud squishing between his toes. She motioned for him to cross but the river was swirling with blood and filth. She told him not to worry, that if he crossed he would be cleansed if only he had faith.

Early awoke, sweaty and sticky. Fatty Patty was under the blankets, a childish innocence greased on her face. How she had gotten from the guest bedroom into his own was a mystery.

Frightened by this nightmare, Early threw her out the window. The doll tumbled across the lawn, disappearing into a neighbor's yard.

It was a few days before Early spied Fatty Patty dangling from a neighbor's leafless tree. The cold air bit the insides of his nose as he saw how cruelly the storm had mishandled her. A long tear shaped like a crescent moon just under her ribcage smiled at him. It was sad to see her so pathetic. Early tucked her under his arm, her latex dripping with morning dew.

The instruction manual offered few diagrams on how to repair damaged material. Luckily, Early had some leftover glue from his bicycle patch kit and managed to fix her just in time to go to dinner with the nose-jewel family.

Before Early could even knock on the door, one of the children swung it open with a shriek. As they swarmed him, the girl hobbled onto the porch.

"Whoa," she blurted, hand stroking Fatty Patty's curvaceous hip, "who's the babe?"

The mother's cheeks flushed pink, like after you've skinned a piglet.

"How nice!" she said without a hint of phoniness, "You brought company."

Maybe the mother was just pretending, Early thought. He could spot an impostor from across the room. But then she asked about Fatty Patty's dress. "You can't find clothes like that anymore. Such an amazing color," she admired. "And it even matches her eyes. You've got fine taste, Early Sheasby."

Early was not one to argue with the truth. Neither did he put up a fuss when dessert arrived with an extra scoop of ice cream in Fatty Patty's bowl.

Later, the girl asked Early to sign her cast. "Sign her name too," she said, nodding at the doll.

Everyone watched as Early's hand trembled.

They listened to music while the girl showed Early pictures of her father who got blown up not far from where Jesus walked on water.

"Bombed so high he got carried away into heaven," the girl said.

Early looked at the nose-jewel mother whose face looked far away.

On the walk home, Early squeezed Fatty Patty's hand, worried she too might suddenly get carried away.

*

When Early saw the family the following Sunday they were the only ones who shook his hand. He moved Fatty Patty to the end of the pew and invited the children and their mother to sit with them. Others in the congregation either pretended he did not exist or scowled. Behold the man, Early imagined them whispering. Behold, the Judas Iscariot of Sugar House.

After the services, Early waited outside the bishop's office. A man with his wife and two boys sat across from him, trying not to stare.

"Your wife looks weird," one of the boys said.

The father asked Early if that was appropriate in the house of the Lord and his wife made a noise like a mouse fart. Early told them to mind their own damn business.

*

The bishop did not offer Fatty Patty a chair. He shuffled around the room to open and then close the door before leaving it slightly cracked. He sat in his chair, twisting a pen in his fingers.

"I don't see any reason why you can't baptize sister Merrill's daughter. You're a good man, Early Sheasby."

And with that the bishop stood up like the meeting could adjourn. He breathed heavily when Early didn't stand to leave. Then he buttoned his suit coat and sat down again.

"How else can I be of service to you, brother Sheasby?"

"I'm entertaining the possibility of another marriage," Early said.

The bishop shifted in his cushioned chair from one butt cheek to the other. He kept doing this, as if he were suffering from a celestial hemorrhoid.

"I'm sorry, brother Sheasby," he smiled, "but I don't follow."

Early spoke slowly in words even a poet-bishop could understand. "The Lord took my wife and so I've found another companion. We would like to be married. To avoid the appearance of sin."

"You can't marry a doll, Early," the bishop said, doodling on a piece of paper and not looking him in the eye. "No matter how nicely you dress her up."

"Why not?"

"Because ..." his voice trailed off. "Well. Because. Yes. You just *can't.*"

He coughed up a half-hearted laugh and picked at a hangnail until his finger bled.

Early straightened in his chair.

"Is it in the handbook?" he asked. "The Church Handbook of Instruction," he stated officially. "What do the Brethren say about this matter?"

The bishop cleared his throat. His lips parted, but the words got caught there in a kind of groan. He blinked twice.

"She's not alive, Early. There's nothing inside her. No soul. You can't love that. You sure as hell can't marry it."

"She's real to me."

"She—listen, *it*—has no soul. Just latex. She doesn't need to be saved. You understand, Early?"

Early was quiet. He picked at his own hangnail until it was bloody.

"I've never seen my own soul," Early said, "but I know it's there."

What felt like a lifetime ago, before the sickness took his wife away, Early had sat in this same chair with a different bishop and talked about the sin of love. Later, his wife had asked if he still loved her. "I told you I did," he said, hurridly thumbing through the newspaper. "That was fifty-two years ago," she said. "Well," Early said, "if anything changes, I'll let you know."

Maybe he had loved his wife all those years. But recently, he'd decided he was no longer sure what love was. Maybe it was reaching out in the middle of the night and feeling the familiar soft shape of a hip beside him in the bed, or sitting down for morning Postum and having an entire conversation without words. Maybe it was remembering the dead and believing you had a future together. Whatever love was, it stretched within him just out of reach.

"Early," the bishop mumbled, massaging his jaw as if suddenly afflicted with a toothache. "Things have been difficult for you. We all have trials. But there are real things and then there are fantasies. Don't go through life confusing the one with the other."

No. She's there when I wake up in the morning. We've laughed. We've prayed. When I need someone to unscramble the thoughts in my head, she listens. She speaks to me without the words. She's as real as anyone I've ever met.

That's what Early wanted to say. But he knew a man who studies poetry six days a week and then forgets it all on Sunday wouldn't understand.

*

It was not until the night before the baptism that Early got nervous. When he was seven, he was almost baptized. Like most baptisms, it was a kind of kidnapping. Early was walking home from school one day in October: the time of year when frogs filled the country roads like a plague of Egypt. He was chasing them down by the river when he met Amos Gibbs. Everyone knew Amos, half-idiot son of Mordecai Gibbs, chief chicken inspector at the processing plant.

"Frog hunting, huh?" he said.

"Yep," Early said.

Amos Gibbs shuffled his feet in the leaves. "Wanna see Frogman?"

Early wasn't an idiot. He collected comic books. Of course, he followed Amos Gibbs.

There were a few other kids on the riverbank waiting to see Frogman. They were in their underwear. Early recognized some of the boys from school. One by one, Amos invited the children down into the water where he initiated them into the Church of Frogman. Even now, Early could not attend a baptism without feeling a lump in his throat the same as he had that day. Every baptism he'd seen since had made him want to get clean.

Early was being initiated underwater when two fishermen came around the bend. They took one look at Early in his muddy undies being baptized by naked Amos and threw down the tackle box.

"Goddamn it, Amos!" one of the men shouted. "We've been through this. You're no preacher!"

"Get behind me, Satan! Do not persecute the Church of Frogman!" Amos yelled.

The fisherman persecuted alright. While his friend left to phone the police, the man whipped Amos like a chocolate pudding. Early never forgot Amos's cuts and bruises as he came out of the water … and the thing between his legs that looked like a broken tadpole. Worst baptism he'd ever been to.

Early remembered asking the fishermen helping him find his clothes: Did the baptism count? Am I clean?

The man put his hand on the back of Early's neck.

"Oh, son," he said, "you're going to need a second baptism."

*

Very few came to see the girl get baptized. Early did not find this particularly surprising, just sad. Here the girl was, entering into the kingdom of God, a girl who wanted to be washed clean, and nobody could come unglued from their lives long enough to watch it happen?

After the hymn, Early and the girl walked down the steps into the font.

"Feels like Jell-O," the girl giggled.

Early recited the appropriate prayer. Hesitating only a moment, he lowered the girl completely under the water.

Early did not fully understand what happened next, not even many years later.

The center of his chest warmed, like somebody had wedged a fiery grain of sand in there where it slowly exploded. The second baptism, Early thought. Baptism by fire.

Maybe it lasted an hour. Maybe only a few seconds. Early did not remember. When he came to his senses, the girl was still underwater. Only it was no longer the girl. It was Fatty Patty. Except it wasn't quite her either. Her hair floated like bioluminescent jellyfish tentacles, filling the pool with a golden light. Her skin looked softer. There was no mistaking it. She was now flesh and bone.

Early knew what he knew. It was a vision. A miracle. And he knew God knew it, and he would not deny it.

And in that same breath, Early knew that once he pulled her up, once she left these strange baptismal waters, the vision would be taken and Fatty Patty would lose this tabernacle of flesh, reverting to nothing more than latex.

Unwilling to abandon his vision, Early held her under.

She jerked, gently at first, then with limbs flailing like an insect about to be pinned. There were voices above them, low at first; then shouts. The nose-jewel mother yelling. Men scrambling to grab him. Early ignored them. He looked at his Fatty Patty, brought to life by the Holy Spirit of Promise. Her smile twisting, her mouth opening, but the screams being swallowed up by water. She wanted out. Maybe she was already tired of being human.

Years later, before he stopped telling people the story, Early said he kept her submerged as long as he did as an act of charity. To make sure all her sins were washed away. So they could both be clean.

SISTER CARVALHO'S EXCELLENT RELIEF SOCIETY LESSON

STEVEN L. PECK

Pleasant Grove has always been a home to the downtrodden, to the stranger, to the broken. Here is one story.

He: Mbaye Diop. Living in Touba, he had grown up learning stories about the life of Aamadu Bamba Mbàkke, that great Senegalese Sufi cleric who formed the Mouride Brotherhood. Mbaye's father, a bookbinder, had been a prominent local leader known for the beauty and craftsmanship of his Korans. At age eight the boy's father pulled him aside and told him he had had a dream in which he would grow up to be a great mujaddid like Aamadu Bamba and enjoined him to a life of holiness; he gave him a postcard with a picture of the holy man that Mbaye carried with him wherever he went. From his father, he learned Arabic and the art of making leather and gold-leaf quartos and at age seventeen he left to study the Koran at Sankore Timbuktu University, a great honor. He was a good student, and at the end of his first year he had memorized the Koran as expected and was known for his seriousness and commitment, but with an edge of humor that his professors and classmates enjoyed. However, Allah's will had stranger paths. His father died of a heart attack and his mother had no means to support his continuance at the university. They moved to the coastal city of M'bour where his mother took work as a maid in a French-owned hotel while he started work at a souvenir shop that sold T-shirts and knickknacks to the tourist trade. He carried

279

the postcard of Aamadu Bamba still. Then bad things happened. His boss accused him of theft—of what he never found out. He went to Dakar and fell into darkness and anger. He joined the Army; this would have been in 1994 about the time of the terror in Rwanda. He was dispatched there as part of a UN peacekeeping force and he watched with horror the atrocity as it unfolded in depraved genocide. He helped pile the bodies for burning. Sub-ḥana'llāh. The bad dreams started then. He carried the postcard of Aamadu Bamba still. A few years after, he was on patrol in the Casamance region to put down the MFDC rebels. His APC took a direct mortar round, and two of his best friends were killed. His leg was broken, he was temporarily deafened, and a wicked gash in his forehead was leaking blood into his eyes. A rebel was running towards him and in a panic he drew his pistol and shot him. It was a boy of nine or ten coming to offer help, or so he supposed, he never knew why the boy was coming, just that he killed him. In the hospital, he took out his postcard and tore it up. His dreams sought to kill him, and he often thought he was going mad. He made his way to New York. There he met Yona Lindenstrauss.

She: Yona Lindenstrauss grew up in Tel Aviv. Her parents were both physicians, secular, second-generation Israelis—liberal and generous. She had attended the best schools. She loved computer games. When she entered the Israel Defense Force at eighteen to serve her mandatory two-year stint, she became a programmer in a missile defense unit. Two things structured her decision to leave Israel. First, one of her best friends growing up was Hanan Almajdoubah, the daughter of a Palestinian doctor who worked with her parents at the hospital. After high school, Hanan studied journalism for two years and had gone to do an internship with *Al Jazeera*. She was killed in an Israeli attack while covering the Intifada in Gaza. It made no sense. Hanan. She was just Hanan. Second, because Yona was bored, she decided to drive up with her friend Rachel, who had to go up to the Northern Command to give some training on new technology for field missile detection. Ironically, a rocket found them while Rachel was setting up her PowerPoint presentation. Yona lost her foot, her four front teeth, a piece of her maxillary, and Rachel. It made no sense. Rachel. She was just Rachel. While she was convalescing, she read Martin Buber's *I and Thou* and *Time and the Other* by Emmanuel Levinas and she felt called back to Judaism. Not to God. After Gaza and the Northern Command, there could be no God. She talked her father into letting her attend the Institute of Jewish Thought and Heritage at the University at Buffalo in New York State. She would not return to Israel. After two semesters, she transferred to Columbia's philosophy department. She suffered nearly crushing PTSD and at a group for survivors she met Mbaye. He was working as a binder of fine books, and his Korans were gaining a reputation for their excellence and beauty.

An old story of magic and impossibilities—they fell in love. Married. And whatever winds blew them together blew them to Pleasant Grove, Utah. He opened a bindery and continued with this work making the most beautiful Korans west of Dakar and selling them on the internet. She taught philosophy at Utah Valley University. They bought a small house east of the junior high school with a white picket fence, a small lawn with lilacs on every corner and tulips in the spring. They attended the Mormon church, not because they believed it, but because they loved their new community and found it the best way to be part of it. It is here the story begins.

Them: It happened just by coincidence that Bishop Baxter of the Pleasant Grove Fifth Ward received the records for the Carvalho family, who had temporarily moved into a rental at 350 North 300 East at the same time that Mbaye and Yona had moved into the house at 300 North 350 East. Realizing the couple were foreigners, the ward clerk assumed the church records had confused the north and the east, welcomed Mbaye and Yona as the new move-ins, and updated the records accordingly. In this way, Mbaye became a former bishop, and his wife became Sister Carvalho. The real Carvalho couple attended church faithfully for two months without records until the house they were building in Lindon was finished and they disappeared from the ward. For their part, the newly created Mbaye and Yona "Carvalho Family" enjoyed the ward immensely. It gave them a chance to practice their English (at home they used French) and to better know the amazing culture in which they found themselves embedded.

Bishop Baxter was thrilled to have a minority couple in his ward. In fact, he had always dreamed of having minorities in his ward; having a mixed-race couple made him feel particularly modern and forward-thinking. He had been one of those who welcomed the revelation on the priesthood and had taken the time to read the 1960's classic *Mormonism & the Negro* by John Stewart even before the revelation giving the all-male priesthood to people of African descent in 1978, demonstrating his interest in racial matters before it was popular. He was determined to treat them just like everyone else and called Brother Carvalho to be second counselor in the Sunday school and his wife to be the third-Sunday teacher in the Relief Society, which he knew would shock some of the members, but he thought that it was time to shock people a little for their own good and teach them that God was no respecter of persons.

A returned missionary in the ward hinted the Carvalhos might be from Brazil where he served his mission, because he knew several people there with the same last name—this despite his failure to get them to speak Portuguese—however the rumor stuck that it was so and became true by the authority of what everyone believed. One good brother had the temerity to ask about their ancestry, but when Sister Carvalhos answered New York he gave up. Of course, he knew that could not be right because their English, especially Brother Cavalho's, was difficult to make out. Nevertheless, they were welcomed into the ward by most. They especially liked Sister Carvalho's lessons. She taught them songs in Hebrew, of all things—how she knew the language of the scriptures so well was anyone's guess, but she did and the songs were lively and fun.

Mbaye and Yona found Pleasant Grove a strange culture. This is what Yona wrote in her diary:

> They enjoy a kind of performance of military fervor, and yet despite such displays of nationalism, few have actually served in the military themselves or can speak to its reality. It feels strange, especially when the threats they face are distant and indirect. They love to wave flags and shoot fireworks and highly value displays of patriotism but despise their president and talk much of acts of insurrection—all the while

creating mythic figures of their founders who are more like gods than humans. What they know of world affairs seems limited and often wrong—believing things that confirm what they already think and hold in suspicion things that don't, regardless of the evidence.

They often appear simplistic and naïve. They are rarely actually threatened yet seem to be filled with great fear despite living in the safest place I've ever known. There is constant talk of the great evil of the day, but I have trouble getting them to articulate what it is exactly that they are afraid of, and they talk vaguely about the family being under attack and evil being abroad. They remind Mbaye of the Muslims in his village with rules about drinking and tobacco and fears of demons. He points out that they are richer than kings here—about like the people of Tel Aviv, I'd say, but from Mbaye's perspective no doubt it is true. Even so, they find much to complain about despite how few people die except by old age or cancer.

Despite these strange peculiarities, they are mostly kind and willing to help each other. They care for those in their circle with tenderness and concern. And like all people, they love TV and computer games. And I must say when all is said and done, I like them much and am comfortable here. The "ward" as they call it is making us feel connected in important ways. It's like a little kibbutz in the middle of the city.

And they did like it here, however, they both still suffered terrible dreams. The past had followed them across the oceans and mountains. When one would wake in terror, sweating and screaming, the other would hold them and bring the comfort of a warm body of someone who loved them. Once they woke up at the same time in panic and fear and they looked at the state of dread and shock on the other's face which mirrored their own and they broke into laughter—who should comfort whom? A lovely irony.

Bishop Baxter was also happy that a former bishop had moved into his ward and found Bishop Carvalho a rich source of wisdom. He would bounce those troubles he could speak of off the foreigner and often enough the man would impart some bit of insight that would stay with the bishop for days and prove useful in the worries he was facing. Once when he complained that the stake did not seem to be listening to his concerns, the wise brother said, quoting a scriptural poem of sorts: "The sun runs on its course, And for the moon, We have appointed phases, Each floats in its own orbit.

Neither of them can overtake the other, nor can the night outstrip the day." It helped Bishop Baxter realize that perhaps the stake had concerns the bishop was not aware of and that he ought to not let his own ward-worries try to overtake the stake-worries. Like the moon and the sun. What scripture was Bishop Carvalho reciting? Must be the Old Testament.

One day the bishop appeared at the Carvalho's house agitated and upset. There was a crisis in the ward and he came to see if Bishop Carvalho had ever experienced its like. Mbaye had tried to correct him about his serving as a Mormon bishop but had given up and thought since he had spent a year in clerical training in Timbuktu maybe that counted.

The bishop explained as best he could. A rift was developing in the ward. The first counselor in the Relief Society sold Sunshine Naturals "essential oils" in a multilevel marketing business. The second counselor sold Eternally Fresh Essentials and Oils, a similar company. At first, they had carved out their own territories in the ward and kept a cordial distance between their church duties and their growing business ventures. But the ward was approaching an almost even split in the women's downlines. And for the remaining uncommitted skeptics or holdouts, the competition had turned ugly. Half of the sisters were not speaking to the other half based on which oils they used. The bishop had been late in noticing the problem and it had gotten fairly serious.

Visiting teaching was down, and hot spots of discord were bubbling to the boiling point. For example, Brother Calhoun found out that one of those he home taught had a sick child at home. Nothing serious, but when his wife found out, she sent him over with some Sunshine Naturals, On Guard—Protective Blend, to help the poor child. However, when Sister Clyde, of the Eternally Fresh persuasion, saw what was in his hand she froze in anger said, I won't have that in my house! Confused, Brother Calhoun laughed and said, No worries, no worries, and put it in his pocket. She apologized for her reaction, but he knew enough not to pull it out again.

In another confrontation, one of the sisters tried to give Brother Jenson some oils for his recurring headaches. When Brother Giles, the high priest group leader found out, he was outraged. He warned the high priests against falling prey to the tricks of false teachings. He had worked with Brother Jenson before and pointed out that the problem was that his lumbar tended to fall out of alignment, and without proper adjustment his headaches would get worse. He suggested they listen to a licensed chiropractor, who had two degrees in science, rather than the quackery going around the Relief Society. The bishop had received multiple complaints against Brother Giles' diatribes against essential oils.

As the bishop explained what was happening, the look on Yona's face went from disbelief to confusion to raw anger. The bishop became fairly uncomfortable as an animated conversation started between the Carvalhos in a foreign tongue. Sister Carvalho was almost yelling and was obviously disgusted and angry. Brother Carvalho was clearly sympathetic to what she was saying but seemed more surprised than angry. She at last calmed down and asked a number of clarifying questions about the oils, their use, and intermediately stopped to explain things to Mbaye, who just shook his head and said, "Way. Way. Way." Obviously a Brazilian word.

She thanked the bishop and said she would deal with the problem during her lesson on Sunday. He was surprised, because he'd just come to get some advice from Bishop Carvalho, but the way Sister Carvalho had reacted and then said "I'll handle it Sunday" was so authoritative and certain, he felt a comfortable feeling that she was right. A great air of satisfaction and spirit settled over him. He did not doubt her. He knew he'd been inspired to visit them.

It was a lesson the sisters would never forget. Yona limped in late with the flowery canvas bag she'd been given by the Relief Society president in which to carry her lessons. It was a gift when she'd been called to teach and she treasured it. She noticed that the first and second counselors were sitting as far apart as possible. They had an opening prayer and song and then turned the time over to Sister Carvalho. She was wearing pants as she always did, which none of the sisters dared to notice, as she was Brazilian, and likely played by different rules. Yona asked if the two counselors would join her and then guided them to opposite sides of the table. She removed the centerpiece and the tablecloth; the latter she carefully folded and laid on the piano. She then had the two sisters move the table off to the side of the room. The sisters in the room were all smiling. This looked to be a fun lesson. Then Yona took out a three-foot length of white rope and tied the left hands of her two helpers together. Everyone was smiling. This is what was great about having foreigners in the ward—the object lessons had not all been done before!

Yona then told the rest of the sisters to fold up their chairs and put them against the walls. They obeyed swiftly and efficiently. Then things took a decidedly darker turn. She said, All of you who use Sunshine Naturals, move to the left side of the room. If you use Eternally Fresh, move to the right. If you don't use either or both, stand against the back wall. There were audible protests, some looked confused, some moved to their appointed place with an air of superiority, but some just stood there refusing to be manipulated in a lame and clearly inappropriate exercise. She barked at them in her most forceful and intimidating Israel Defense Force basic training voice, MOVE. They jumped and started to move to their positions. The Relief Society president stepped forward and said, Sister Carvalho, I know you are new to Utah but I'm afraid this is not really appropriate. So I think it would be best if we all …

You. Shut up. Sister Carvalho said. The poor Relief Society president's mouth was moving but only strange squeaks were coming out. By now nearly every face reflected fear and a couple of sisters made a move for the closed door. DON'T YOU DARE TOUCH THAT DOOR AND ALL OF YOU PUT AWAY THOSE CELL PHONES. The would-be escapers backed away from the door. By now some of the sisters were visibly upset and almost all were looking confused.

It got worse. Sister Carvalho grabbed the rope and moved, really pulled aggressively and rather forcefully, the two counselors to the center of the semi-circle now formed by the shaken sisters. She then pulled two daggers out of her floral bag and placed them into the hands of the two sisters, one of whom was crying hysterically. She then said, We will settle this which-oil-is-better question once and for all. I came from a world where blood runs in the streets because hatred has created hatreds upon hatreds that have lasted centuries. I came from a place of horror to a small pocket of peace and safety and you *and she pointed at the sisters on both sides of the room* are trying to make it a place of terror and blood. I will not have it. So, you two fight it out to the death. The woman who survives gets to sell her oil to everyone. GO.

The two sisters tied together dropped their knives and hugged each other in fear, saying over and over, Please. No. We don't do this. Please. What are you doing? You can't make us do this. We won't do this. Please! They whimpered and cried.

Sister Carvalho let them go on for a minute, then took out another knife and cut them apart—not in a threatening way; it was obvious from the beginning what she was intending with the blade.

Then she spoke again and said, Set your chairs back up and listen. I have something to say.

The women did, with a sense of restrained terror and tepid relief. When they were sitting again, frozen into an attention rare in a church setting, Yona began telling them about growing up in Tel Aviv and the threat of terrorist attacks, the times her family had hidden in shelters wearing gas masks during the first Gulf War. She told them about her friend Hanan and the love they had for one another. She talked about their dreams and boyfriends. Then she told of her senseless death. And as she talked she wept openly and in agony. At one point, she could not speak and the Relief Society president came and hugged her and held her while her shoulders shook and she sobbed. Then she told about her time in the Israel Defense Force and the rocket that killed her other friend Rachel. The tragic story continued as she moved the table back to its original position with the help of a couple of nearby sisters and placed the knives dropped by the counselors where the centerpiece had been.

As she continued her story, she pulled off her pants and sat on the table in her panties and detached and pulled off her prosthetic leg to the shock and dismay of the sisters who were for the most part audibly mourning and weeping—only the most stoic had a dry eye. She then slowly took off the liner exposing her leg terminating somewhat above where her foot would have been. Her stump, which she held straight in front of her from her seated position on the table, was blotched red and covered with a white vicious scar that encircled the terminus of her leg. Then she pulled out her dental appliance and exposed her missing teeth and the gap created

287

when her maxillary bone was broken open below her nose and laid it beside her prosthetic leg.

She said, These kinds of wounds are where hatred leads. This is what war and anger and separation produce. This is what you reap when you sow enmity. Over scented oils? Is it worth it? I lost my friends. I lost my foot. I lost my ability to sleep. My dreams are terrible. And some of you want to tear this wonderful place apart over oil? It really would be better to have one of you kill the other than let this fester and corrupt you. Do you know how lucky you are? Do you know how blessed? Do you even understand what I'm saying? My husband ... *her voice broke* ... My husband helped load trucks with bodies in Rwanda. Neighbors just like you. Neighbors who helped watch each other's kids. Who borrowed sugar. Who helped each other when one was sick. Just like you. Can you hear me? They let hate in and you know what they did? Do you know? They let hate in and then took a machete and hacked their neighbors to pieces. Do you understand? They were just like you. And. They. Hacked. Their. Neighbors. To. Pieces. And they had less reason than this.

She pulled out two bottles of lavender, one Sunshine Naturals, one Eternally Fresh, unstopped them and sprinkled them on the women like a blessing. The room filled with the sound of weeping and the thick overwhelming smell of lavender.

Look around, she continued. Look around, do you see your neighbor's face? Look at it. Look hard. That's the face of God. Do you understand? That's it. Right there. If there is any God at all, that's what it looks like. Do you see it? Do you see him? Her? Look hard because you won't see God in any other form. It's your neighbor's face. That's it.

With this, she started violently weeping again. The two counselors moved forward and picked her up balancing on her one foot and embraced her. Then the two women who had been at war embraced each other and held each other for a long time, shaking in tears and repentance.

The person giving the closing prayer could not speak. And none of the sisters got up to leave. No one ever spoke of the lesson as Yona had requested when a semblance of normalcy had been restored in the room. Then a wonderful feeling came over the assembled sisters. Yona called it the aura of human transcendence. The sisters said it was the Comforter—the Holy Ghost. Months later, rumors would say that Yona was glowing at the end of her lesson, her face lit with a holy light.

The bishop was most pleased when the two counselors came to confess their recent sins to him. He knew Sister Carvalho must have given a really, really fine lesson that day.

CONTRIBUTORS

Phyllis Barber is the award-winning author of ten books, the latest being *The Precarious Walk,* a collection of essays. She has received awards for both fiction and nonfiction (her memoir *How I Got Cultured* receiving the AWP Prize for Creative Nonfiction) and has been cited as Notable in *The Best American Essays* and *The Best American Travel Writing*. She is the mother of four sons, lives in Park City, Utah, and was inducted into the Nevada Writers' Hall of Fame in 2005. She received the "Outstanding Contribution to Mormon Letters Award" in 2016, given by the Smith-Pettit Foundation and the Association of Mormon Letters.

Alison Brimley holds an MFA in creative writing from Brigham Young University. Her work has appeared in *Dialogue: A Journal of Mormon Thought*, *Sunstone*, and *Western Humanities Review*. She is currently working on a novel of Mormon historical fiction. She lives in Sandy, Utah, with her husband and two daughters.

Michael Fillerup is the award-winning author of numerous short stories, two short-story collections (*Visions and Other Stories* and *The Year They Gave Women the Priesthood and Other Stories*), and two novels (*Beyond the River* and *Go in Beauty*). He is the co-author (with Jim David) of the novel *Just a Teacher* (2020). He has also written children's books and published several articles on indigenous language preservation. The founder and former director of Puente de Hozho Tri-lingual Magnet School, he lives in northern Arizona with his wife, Rebecca, who doubles as his best friend, confidant, ruthless editor, and full-time muse. Learn more at www.michaelfillerup.com.

Eric Freeze is a Canadian writer of five books: *Dominant Traits* (stories, 2012); *Hemingway on a Bike* (essays, 2014); *Invisible Men* (stories, 2016); *French Dive: Living More with Less in the South of France* (memoir, 2020); and *Story Mode: Teaching Writing for Video Games* (textbook, forthcoming 2024). He has published essays, stories, and translations in numerous periodicals including *The Southern Review*, *Boston Review*, *Harvard Review*, and *Prism International*. He is a tenured professor of creative writing at Wabash College in Indiana. He is married to academic and birth educator Rixa Freeze and is the father of four bilingual, soccer-crazed children. He lives half the year in the U.S. and the other half in Nice, France.

Ryan Habermeyer is the author of the short story collections *Salt Folk* (Cornerstone, 2024) and *The Science of Lost Futures* (BoA, 2018). His stories and essays have appeared in *Conjunctions*, *Alaska Quarterly Review*, *Copper Nickel*, *Massachusetts Review*, *DIAGRAM*, *Cincinnati Review*, *Cimarron Review*, and others. He is Associate Professor of Creative Writing at Salisbury University. Find him at ryanhabermeyer.com.

Jack Harrell is the author of two novels and a collection of essays. His book *A Sense of Order and Other Stories* won the Short Fiction Award from the Association for Mormon Letters. He teaches writing at Brigham Young University–Idaho.

Annette Haws, a native of a small town in northern Utah, examines the tribulations and foibles of characters playing their parts on a small stage. She is the author of three novels, *Maggie's Place*, *The Accidental Marriage*, and *Waiting for the Light to Change*. "Planting Iris" is her fourth published short story. She's been nominated for numerous awards and has won three, Best of State, League of Utah Writers Award for Best Published Fiction, and a Whitney Award.

Theric Jepson is a former president of the Association for Mormon Letters, the current editor of *Irreantum*, and the author of such things as *Byuck*, *Just Julie's Fine*, and *The Prophetess of Mars*. He has zero descendants who have read any of that stuff, making for a total of four descendants. Find him online by looking for thmazing and clicking anything that comes up.

Ryan McIlvain is the author of the novels *Elders* and *The Radicals*. His other writing has appeared in print and online in *The Paris Review*, *The Rumpus*, *Tin House*, *Post Road*, *The Believer*, *The Daily Beast*, *The Los Angeles Review of Books*, and other venues. A recipient of the Stegner Fellowship at Stanford, he now lives and works in Florida, where he is at work on his third novel.

Larry Menlove writes from Utah. His work has been published in many venues including *Weber*, *Sunstone*, *Dialogue: A Journal of Mormon Thought*, *Drunken Boat*, and *saltfront*. He has won first place in the Utah Original Writing Competition in both the short story and non-fiction categories as well honorable mentions in novel and short story collection.

William Morris is the author of the story collections *The Darkest Abyss: Strange Mormon Stories* and *Dark Watch and other Mormon-American Stories*. He co-edited the anthology *Monsters & Mormons* and edited *States of Deseret* (both from Peculiar Pages). He lives in Minnesota with his wife and daughter. His Mormon fiction and criticism can be found at motleyvision.org.

Heidi Naylor's short story collection, *Revolver*, was published by BCC Press in 2018. She writes and teaches in Idaho. Find her at heidinaylor.net.

Danny Nelson writes speculative fiction focused on personal and community identities. Previous Mormon-related work has appeared in *Press Forward, Saints*; *Dove Song*; and *The Fob Bible*. He lives in Salt Lake City with his husband and two intelligence-challenged dogs.

David G. Pace is the Salt Lake City-based author of the novel *Dream House on Golan Drive* and of stories and essays in multiple anthologies and literary journals. The story included here is part of a collection of shorts titled *American Trinity and Other Stories from the Mormon Corridor*, which won second place in the Utah Original Writing Competition.

Steven L. Peck is an ecology professor at Brigham Young University. He has published five literary novels: *A Short Stay in Hell*; *The Scholar* *of Moab*; *Gilda Trillim, Shepherdess of Rats*; *King Leere, Goatherd of the La Sals*; and *Heike's Void*, as well as two short fiction collections and a poetry collection. For the body of his literary work, he received the 2021 Smith–Pettit Foundation Award for Outstanding Contribution to Mormon Letters.

Todd Robert Petersen grew up Portland, Oregon but now lives in Cedar City, Utah. He teaches creative writing and film studies at Southern Utah University. Petersen is the author of four books: *Long After Dark*, *Rift*, *It Needs to Look Like We Tried*, and *Picnic in the Ruins*.

Joe Plicka's poems, stories, and essays can be found online in *Brevity*, *Ekstasis Magazine*, *Braided Way*, *Booth*, *Hobart*, and others. He was featured in the anthology *Fire in the Pasture: 21st Century Mormon Poets*. He lives and teaches in Hawaii with his family, an auskydoodle, and a red-vented bulbul.

Jennifer Quist is an award-winning novelist in Alberta, Canada. Besides her novels *Love Letters of the Angels of Death*, *Sistering*, and *The Apocalypse of Morgan Turner*, she also writes short fiction, journalism, criticism, and translations. She edits the fiction section of *Dialogue: A Journal of Mormon Thought*.

Ryan Shoemaker's debut story collection, *Beyond the Lights*, is available through No Record Press. T.C. Boyle called it a collection that "moves effortlessly from brilliant comedic pieces to stories of deep emotional resonance." Ryan's forthcoming story collection, *The Righteous Road: Stories*, will be available in 2024 through BCC Press. His short fiction has appeared in *Gulf Stream*, *Santa Monica Review*, *Booth*, *New Ohio Review*, and *Juked*, among others. Find him at RyanShoemaker.net.

Charity Shumway is the author of two novels, *Bountiful* (BCC Press, 2020), which won the Association for Mormon Letters Novel Award, and *Ten Girls to Watch* (Washington Square Press, 2012). She earned an MFA in creative writing from Oregon State

University and a BA in English from Harvard College. She and her family live in the Hudson Valley.

Mattathias Singh's ancestors crossed continents and oceans before his grandparents' journeys brought them to Provo in the 1950s. His family has been described as "Jewish on one side, Sikh on the other, and Mormon in the middle." All three traditions have nurtured his love of stories and his hope that sharing them will help us all learn to love one another as we ought.

Holly Welker is a fourth-generation native Arizonan with deep Mormon roots, including ancestors who arrived in the Salt Lake Valley with Brigham Young in 1847. She is the editor of *Baring Witness: 36 Mormon Women Talk Candidly about Love, Sex, and Marriage* (University of Illinois Press, 2016) and *Revising Eternity: 27 Latter-day Saint Men Reflect on Modern Relationships* (UIP, 2022). Her poetry and prose have appeared in dozens of publications, including *Best American Essays*, *The Iowa Review*, *Slate*, and the *New York Times*.

Tim Wirkus (they/them) is the author of the novels *The Infinite Future* (Penguin Press, 2018) and *City of Brick and Shadow* (Tyrus Books, 2014), which was a finalist for the Shamus Award and the winner of the Association for Mormon Letters Novel Award. Their novella, *Sandy Downs*, won the 2013 *Quarterly West* novella contest. They hold a PhD in creative writing and literature from the University of Southern California.